Overboard

ALSO BY SARA PARETSKY

Overboard

A V.I. Warshawski Novel

Sara Paretsky

HARPER LARGE PRINT
An Imprint of HarperCollinsPublishers

OVERBOARD. Copyright © 2022 by Sara Paretsky. All rights reserved. Printed in the United States of America. No part of this book may be used or reproduced in any manner whatsoever without written permission except in the case of brief quotations embodied in critical articles and reviews. For information, address HarperCollins Publishers, 195 Broadway, New York, NY 10007.

HarperCollins books may be purchased for educational, business, or sales promotional use. For information, please e-mail the Special Markets Department at SPsales@harpercollins.com.

FIRST HARPER LARGE PRINT EDITION

ISBN: 978-0-06-324180-0

Library of Congress Cataloging-in-Publication Data is available upon request.

22 23 24 25 26 LSC 10 9 8 7 6 5 4 3 2 1

For the company of readers and writers,
who kept me and each other going during the
hard times of the pandemic

"And what is hell? Can you tell me that?"
"It is a cold and bitter pit where demons from hospitals and insurance companies torture people who need medical care."
"And should you like to fall into that pit, and to be tortured there forever?"
"No, sir."
"What must you do to avoid it?"
I deliberated a moment; my answer, when it did come, was objectionable: "I must keep in good health."

—*JANE EYRE*, EDITED FOR THE
TWENTY-FIRST CENTURY

Overboard

1
The Girl in the Rocks

It was Mitch who found the girl. I'd stopped at a cemetery on the Chicago–Evanston border to let him and Peppy stretch their legs, and he took off. I ran after him, but I'd left the dogs in the car too long: Mitch was out to prove I wasn't the boss of him. Cars swerved, honked, brakes squealed as he bolted across Sheridan Road and disappeared down a boulder-covered hill to the lake.

Somehow I hung on to Peppy's leash as she chased him. We crossed the road without being hit, but almost toppled a cyclist on the other side.

I peered anxiously down the rocky hillside, trying to see Mitch, but he'd vanished. He still had his leash on, at risk for a broken leg or worse if it caught on an outcropping. There were too many crevices in the rocks and concrete blocks the city had dropped there. I called to him, strained to hear a bark or a cry, but the lake was crashing into the rocks in front of me; cars on Sheridan kept up a steady roar behind me.

Peppy was still straining to follow Mitch. I unhooked her leash so she'd find him for me. She began sliding and clawing her way down the wet rocks and stopped at a spot about twenty feet below me.

A strong spring wind was slamming waves onto the shore, sending spray high enough to wet my legs as I backed down, crablike, holding on to the rocks to keep from sliding into the froth.

When I finally reached Peppy, she was barking at Mitch's hindquarters. His head and shoulders were wedged between two boulders. I shoved her out of my way and pulled Mitch out. I managed to muscle in front of him and stick my own head into the narrow opening. He was whining, even snapping at my ankles in his desperation to get back in.

I shone my phone's flashlight inside the opening. I'd been expecting some dead, rotting animal, but it was a girl. Young, wearing a thin T-shirt that revealed small breasts. I slid forward, put my fingers on her neck, felt a faint pulse.

I backed out. Mitch instantly ran in again, Peppy slithering in next to him. I tried calling 911 but couldn't get a signal down there. It would be impossible for me to force the dogs up the rocks, not when they had a mission and I was in slip-sliding shoes. I left them and worked my way back up to the edge of the road and called 911.

A squad car appeared almost instantly. The driver got out and demanded an ID.

"A girl is stuck in the rocks down there. She needs help—I can't manage—"

"I got a complaint about a lady and her dogs. You can't let them run around off-leash. Let's see some ID."

"Please! Look! There's a girl trapped down there. I came up to call for help. She needs an emergency crew with ropes and a stretcher!"

He pressed his lips together, called into his lapel phone that he was investigating a possible emergency. He came to the barrier between the road and the rocks, gripping my arm, but he looked down and saw Mitch's tail. Peppy was smaller; she must have squirmed in front of him.

"That your dog?"

"The girl is barely alive," I said, frantic. "Please! You can see for yourself if you climb down."

He looked sourly at the rocks but was saved by his phone. He exchanged a few sentences, then turned to me. "Someone called in a complaint from the high-rise there." He jerked his head at a building on the other side of the road. "Said a woman was taking her dogs down the rocks here. I guess that was you. Can you call the dogs, get them to come up?"

"They won't leave the girl and I'm not strong enough to carry them up these boulders."

He looked over the side again, communed again with his lapel phone. "We're locating a rescue team, but if this is a false alarm, it's a class four felony."

"It's not a false alarm," I said through thin lips. "How long until they get here?"

"Fifteen, twenty minutes. You go down and leash up those dogs. You cannot let them run wild in the park."

I maneuvered my way back down the rocks. I attached the dogs' leashes to their harnesses and managed to hook the ends around a crack in a neighboring rock so that I could check on the girl. There was a faint fluttering in her neck pulses.

Her face still had some of the softness of childhood. I thought she had fresh welts on her cheeks, but they were so grimy, I wasn't sure. I was wearing a new jacket, red basket weave, not cheap, but I draped it across her front, tucking the sleeves behind her shoulders.

"It's okay, baby," I crooned. "Help is on the way. Hang on. We'll keep you warm and get you safe."

I took some pictures. When the flash went off in

her face, her eyes fluttered open. "*Nagyi?*" she asked, and then repeated, "*Nagyi,*" with a little sigh—relief, it sounded like—and closed her eyes again.

My phone's light showed holes in her jeans, the edges scorched. They were caused by fire, not scissors. Pus was oozing from her wounds. An extreme form of self-mutilation, or a hideous form of torture. Either way, she needed medical attention.

Mitch and Peppy were pawing at my legs, desperate to return to the girl. I scooted out of the opening and let them go in. Perhaps not hygienic, but they would keep her warmer than I could.

It was almost half an hour before the rescue team appeared. They dropped ropes and jumped down to meet us. They pulled the dogs out, handed the leashes to me. Keeping them away from the rescuers took my last bit of strength.

"She has burns on her legs," I warned the rescue team. "Maybe on her face, too."

The team moved quickly. They set up a rope sledge and slid the girl out, wrapped her in blankets, and strapped her shoulders and hips in place.

"She's still alive, isn't she?" I asked.

"Barely." The speaker didn't look up from the stretcher. "Good thing you and your pooches came when you did." She and her partner tugged on their ropes to let the team above know they were climbing back up.

The dogs were frantic as the crew took the girl away. They barked and strained at their leashes, desperate to get to the girl. I went on my hands and knees, still clutching the leashes—Mitch and Peppy could easily jump the barrier between rocks and road and fling themselves into traffic in an effort to reach the girl. I held them until I heard the siren above me signal that the ambulance was taking off.

When we emerged at the top, my legs were shaking and the skin of my palms was rubbed raw. I leaned against a tree to catch my breath. Now that the rescue had succeeded, I felt the cold. My clothes were damp from the spray, and I was wishing I'd grabbed my jacket before the EMTs wrapped the girl in their blankets.

The cop who'd arrived first was still there, directing traffic around a series of TV vans. Of course. Newsrooms monitor police frequencies and show up, eager for gore.

Beth Blacksin was there from Global Entertainment. "Vic! When I looked over the edge, I was sure that was you down there with your dogs. What happened? What can you tell us about the girl they brought up? Is it true she was in a cave? We tried to get our GlobalCam in play, but it crashed into the rocks."

"GlobalCam?" I echoed.

"Our camera drone. Costs a fortune. They're going to try to find it."

"What, the CPD's rescue team will rappel down for you?"

"No, we have some divers."

"On the payroll just to rescue errant drones?" I asked.

"Oh, Vic, you're so literal-minded. We have a couple of guys in production who scuba dive for fun. They'll take care of it. I hope—I didn't exactly have permission to authorize the launch, but it would have made great footage."

I bit back another snarky retort. I was wet to the bone, my clothes were covered in dirt and whatever slime grew on the rocks, the heel had come loose from my right shoe, and my car was at least a mile away. I would play nice in exchange for a lift in the Global news van.

Beth agreed, if I gave her an exclusive. We spoke with the wind whipping our hair into our faces and the camera getting nice footage of the waves and the spray. Also of the dogs, who were whining loudly.

"Most Chicagoans know V.I. Warshawski as the go-to detective when life or the law have trapped them between a hard place and a rock. Today she found someone trapped literally in a hard place in the rocks. V.I., we watched the Chicago Police search and rescue team bring a teenage girl up on a stretcher. We understand they got her out, probably in the nick of time, thanks to you. Tell us how you came upon her—no sane person would climb these rocks for fun."

I stepped her through Mitch and Peppy's heroic work, omitting the fact that Mitch was a hero because I'd lost control of him.

"And you know this girl?"

"I never saw her before," I said. "The rescue team said she's alive, barely. I'm sure her parents must be scared sick. Did you get a picture of her face to put out on your site?"

The cameraman gave a thumbs-up for that. Beth had him take more footage of Mitch and Peppy, some B-roll of the lake and the rocks, and then the heroic dogs were bundled into the van—which had GLOBAL MOBAL etched on the side—and the crew drove us into Evanston to my car.

I didn't tell Beth about the burn holes in the girl's jeans or the strange word she'd said. I didn't say I hadn't seen signs of food or water. Nor did I add my biggest question: Had the girl been seeking refuge, or had she crawled down the rocks to die?

2
No Good Deed
Goes Unpunished

I'd spent the last watches of the night in my car out-side a tiny synagogue in West Rogers Park. Today was a special service connected with Passover, and the handful of elderly people who still belonged to Shaamar Hashomayim were worried about their safety. They'd come to me through Lotty Herschel—some of the people who worshipped there were patients of hers. Every now and then, someone defaced the synagogue, and on major holidays, synagogues around the world were at heightened risk.

Shaamar Hashomayim's neighbors made it seem especially vulnerable. There was a vacant lot on one side, with enough of the remains of a foundation for vandals to hide in. I was more worried about the derelict house on the synagogue's west side. I was pretty sure someone was cooking meth or cutting fentanyl in there. I'd brought the dogs. We toured the area several times, but all they flushed were rats, the big kind, made robust by the garbage Chicagoans kindly drop for them on our streets and parks.

A few of the old men in the community had kept coming together to worship, even through the worst of the pandemic. There were so few of them, they'd been able to stay well apart, even in the building's small spaces. Now that they'd been vaccinated, a full complement showed up this morning—eighteen instead of the six or seven who'd attended during the winter.

At nine-thirty, with plenty of traffic on the street, I figured it was okay to leave. I had a noon appointment downtown with a potentially lucrative new client, but I wanted to stop at Ilona Pariente's apartment to assure her that her husband was safe.

Mrs. Pariente was the patient of Lotty's who'd gotten me involved with the synagogue. She didn't go to the services: it was an Orthodox temple, which meant the women had to climb stairs to their private gallery, and Mrs. Pariente's legs didn't serve her well these days. It was hard enough for her to get to the street from the third floor of the shabby building where she and her husband lived. I often brought her groceries, to save her the climb.

She served me coffee, brewed in the strong Italian style my mother used to make. We spoke in Italian, a pleasure for us both. Besides her coffee, speaking Italian made me feel close to my mother. Donna Ilona was from Rome, but she knew Pitigliano, Gabriella's hometown.

"You will pick Emilio up at the end of the day?"

I assured her I would be outside the synagogue at six P.M.

"And you will eat with us?"

I assured her I would but made my excuses instead of drinking a second cup. I needed to run the dogs before my meeting. After six hours in the car, with short breaks to patrol, the dogs were antsy. The park nearest the synagogue was filled with toddlers. I drove to the lakefront, where a gigantic cemetery, bigger than the city parks, separates Chicago from Evanston. Its eastern boundary is Sheridan Road. Lake Michigan lies just beyond. I parked at the western entrance. That was when I lost the dogs.

My decision to run them in the cemetery meant we saved a girl's life, so I guess it was a good thing. It cost me a new client. When I called late in the afternoon to explain why I'd missed the meeting, they didn't want to reschedule. I also lost an expensive piece of my wardrobe, the jacket I'd wrapped the girl in. I suppressed a peevish twinge. I could always buy another jacket, assuming I paid off some of my more pressing bills, but how often did I get to save a teenager's life?

By the time the Global van got the dogs and me to my car and I drove home, it was well past noon. Mr. Contreras, the elderly neighbor who shares the dogs with me, and who monitors my life, had already seen us on the news.

"That was something, you going down them rocks like that. You seen that girl go over the side?"

"It was all Mitch," I assured him.

He was delighted with the tale of Mitch's heroics and promptly thawed a steak to serve in his honor. I went up to change from my torn and soiled clothes and watched the footage on my laptop. Global had given us a whole three minutes—an eternity on TV—and included a still of the rescued girl, with a plea for anyone who recognized her to come forward.

Her face in the close-up was covered in dirt, the skin raw in places. Unless someone knew her well and knew she was missing, she'd be hard to identify.

The Global clip ended with a statement from Beth Israel's chief medical officer, interviewed at a Covid-sensitive location outside the hospital where the ambulance had brought the girl. He merely reiterated that she was unconscious and they couldn't identify her, and that if anyone recognized her, they should contact the police or the Beth Israel Department of Medicine.

Beth Israel was also the hospital where my friend Lotty Herschel had her surgical privileges; her partner, Max Loewenthal, was the executive director. One of them should be able to tell me how the girl was doing, or whether the admitting team had found any identification on her.

My escapade, along with my nighttime watchwoman work, had worn me out. I thought I would lie down for twenty minutes, but it was after five before I woke again.

I scrambled into my clothes and scurried back to Shaamar Hashomayim to collect Mr. Pariente. He and the other men lingered on the sidewalk for a time, gossiping, giving each other Pesach blessings. They all wore masks, as did I. People were still nervous, despite our recent vaccinations. By this point in the pandemic, we all knew people whom the disease had claimed.

The Parientes lived a scant half mile from the synagogue, but the sky was getting dark: a frail old man walking home alone in the evening was an inviting target for the creeps who prey on the old. When we reached his building, he climbed the three flights slowly, breathing heavily, but refused the support of my arm.

We ate at the kitchen table. Donna Ilona and I tried our best to make the meal festive: we drank sweet wine, ate fish baked with olives and tomatoes, my spinach with raisins, and finished with mascarpone with honey, almonds, and berries. But a heaviness hung over us, borne of the dwindling population at the synagogue, the weight of the pandemic, the Parientes' increasing fragility.

In addition to my own shopping, Lotty or her clinic manager also sometimes bought them groceries. Lotty, or her advanced practice nurse Jewel Kim, made house calls, but the worry over their future was inescapable.

"We won't move," Mr. Pariente said. "I have made that clear, and so has Ilona. We will die here, where we lived for all these years. You know what happens in nursing homes. Even if they don't infect you with Covid, they leave you to die of loneliness and bedsores."

The literal translation from the Italian: sores from the position of the lying of the body, as if the body were laid out for burial.

Donna Ilona nodded in agreement. "Estella Calabro, her husband died. They belonged to the synagogue, and when he died her son persuaded her to move into one of those assisted living centers. Assisted dying, they should be called. They made her give up her apartment. She owned it, a condo in one of those nice buildings up the street from us here. We are just renters, but her husband owned a fur company. For many years they lived well. Then Estella's health broke down. She had to give them the deed to her home to continue to receive care. But in reality, she received no care and she died, right before the Covid struck."

"That's enough, Ilona," Emilio said. "Don't dwell on sad news on a holiday of liberation."

He turned on the small television that sat on the kitchen counter, tuned to Global's cable news. About five minutes into their dreary political frothing, my escapade came on.

"Victoria! That is you!" Donna Ilona cried. "Look at her, Emilio! You are a mountain goat, scampering up and down those rocks."

The atmosphere in the kitchen lightened. I washed the dishes and relived the event for them as I had for Mr. Contreras and left them in brighter spirits: if I could rescue a child from the lake, I was surely powerful enough to protect Temple Shaamar Hashomayim.

As I was leaving, Emilio put his hands on my head and said, as he always did, "All blessings, *carissima*." I, too, had a lighter spirit as I drove home.

I woke in the morning to excited text messages from

Peter Sansen. He also had seen the story, and phoned as I was dressing, lavish in his praise.

Peter was an archaeologist who'd been with a team exploring Phoenician remains on the Spanish coast when the virus struck. As the pandemic waned in Europe and waxed in the States, we'd agreed he was safer staying in Spain. But then, after a harsh winter of illness and insurrection, America became less vulnerable, Europe more so. We were caught, like many people, between conflicting quarantine regulations and travel restrictions.

Peter had thought about coming home for a visit, but he'd spent too much of the past twelve months in lockdown. As restrictions on his excavation site were lifted, he decided to stay in Spain.

Peter wanted more details on my search-and-rescue mission. "This makes me nostalgic for the first time we met," he said. "I held you upside down from a window while you did a Spider-Woman routine on the wall. I hate to think you can crawl around without my support—makes me feel superfluous. Don't climb too far out on a ledge when I'm not there to hold your feet."

"I'm feeling pretty much the same, three thousand miles away," I said. "Don't climb down in a hole so deep you can't get back out."

We hung up with the miming of kisses and hugs, promises to talk again in two days, but the conversation was only half satisfying. When you can't see or touch each other, just stare at an image on a screen, it's hard to maintain a sense of intimacy.

"I am happy with where my life is today, in this moment," I announced out loud. "It's true I'm stiff and bruised, and three thousand miles from my lover, but I am doing good in the world and that's way more important than physical or emotional health."

Peppy, who'd spent the night with me, gave what sounded like a derisive snort and went back to sleep.

I did a full workout—stretches, weights, squats, sweating away discontent along with my stiffness. Before heading to my office, I called Max Loewenthal's PA at Beth Israel.

Cynthia Dijkstra was delighted to hear from me. "Everyone in the office saw you, Vic! That was amazing, the way you rescued that girl."

I channeled the old Marlboro man—*shucks, ma'am, just doing my job*—and asked if they'd come up with an ID. Cynthia said the ER team hadn't found anything in her pockets, and the girl herself hadn't spoken.

"She was in a state of shock when she came in, unresponsive, it says on her chart. She needs rehydrating and is suffering from burns on her legs and thighs, but they didn't find any head injuries, nothing to explain why she's mute except maybe shock. Did she say anything when you were with her?"

"One word," I said. "She briefly gained consciousness when my camera flash went off. She said something that sounded like '*Nagyi*.' I took it to be a name, as if she thought I was someone she knew."

Cynthia and I guessed on the spelling. She said she'd pass it on to the attending and add it to the bulletin they were giving the police.

"Do they have an idea how old she is?"

Cynthia read through more of the chart. "They think she's mid-teens, probably fifteen."

"Why did they bring her to you?" I asked. "There's a hospital in Evanston just a few blocks from where I found her."

"That is why Beth Israel constantly teeters on the brink of ruin," Cynthia said. "The Evanston hospital, and two Chicago hospitals closer to the accident, had their emergency rooms on bypass just to avoid this kind of problem. If we wanted to work that way, we could have kept the ambulance shuttling the poor girl around the city until she died in transit, which would have ended the problem. Max won't let Beth Israel operate like that—hurray for him, and hurray for him being able to sweet-talk our high-end donors into keeping us going."

"It's that British accent," I said. Max had learned English as a teenaged refugee in London. "People think he sounds like Richard Burton and they can't resist writing checks."

Cynthia laughed and we hung up. I figured the dogs and I had both had enough exercise yesterday. I didn't need to run them this morning. I drove down to my office, where my lease mate, the sculptor Tessa Reynolds, was also arriving for the day. She specializes in giant metal pieces for business installations, as well as commissions for sculpture parks.

Tessa is a Black woman. One of the few good outcomes of all the turmoil of the past year was the spotlight focused on Black artists. Tessa had an international reputation but wasn't much known in the States. Since she couldn't travel to the Pacific Rim, where her work was most in demand, her new recognition at home was keeping her busy.

She, too, had seen my fifteen seconds of fame, and asked for news of the girl.

I gave her the update I'd had from Cynthia. "I feel responsible for her because I rescued her," I said. "But there's nothing I can do, except hope she has a family that cares about her."

"You're not convinced?"

"Her legs were burned. There are a dozen possibilities. Maybe the rest of her family was destroyed in a fire and she's in shock—it would explain why no one's come forward to claim her. But—a kid with burns on her legs and maybe her face—there's no Hallmark backstory."

Tessa nodded soberly. Her mother was a lawyer who covered family law. She'd heard most of the horrors that people inflict on children. "She could be a runaway, you know, hundreds of miles from anyone who'd be missing her."

She put out a hand to clasp my shoulder but pulled it back. One of Covid's many residues: When would it be safe for us to touch each other again?

3

Feeling the Burn

I was behind on a project for my most important client, involving a drug ring in his Peoria plant. I began work on an action plan for him, then started on some other assignments, but I felt sluggish. I had a picture in my head of a donkey tied to a mill, endlessly walking in a circle, grinding up corn or something. Was that me, doing the same repetitive task over and over for the same clients?

My usual coping strategy is exercise, but I felt too beat-up for a long run. Singing, my second choice. I'd go home and work on my vocal exercises. I hadn't done that for months.

I swapped out my backup drives and was shutting off my lights, switching on alarms, when the street doorbell rang. I checked the camera feed on my monitor. Cops. Specifically, a sergeant I knew, Lenora Pizzello, and a uniformed officer as support, in case I said something so actionable that she needed proof. I put on my mask and buzzed them in.

"Sergeant! This is incredibly exciting. You've never visited me before. And your friend is—?"

"Officer Howard. Rudy Howard."

"Come in, Officer, Sergeant, let me get you coffee, tea, gin—whatever you drink at this time of day."

"This isn't a social call, Warshawski. We're here to take your statement."

I'd been about to lead them up the hall to my office, but I stopped, the street door still half open.

"I don't know what you think I can state, Sergeant, but I have no idea what this is about. You'd better back up half a mile and tell me your business."

"The Jane Doe you found in the rocks yesterday. You left the scene before anyone could talk to you."

"How wrong you are. I spoke at length with Beth Blacksin, and people all over the country heard me. Even people in Spain, and I expect Australia and Japan were tuned in as well."

Pizzello turned to Howard. "This is why they sent you with me. So you can see how to restrain yourself with a member of the public who prides herself on being a royal pain in the ass. Warshawski, we need some details to help us try to locate a family."

"Really, Sergeant, ass-paining aside, I don't know as much as the doctors at Beth Israel who've been treating her. I saw her for all of two minutes, and she was unconscious for almost the entire time."

Pizzello looked over my shoulder at the hallway. "Is there a chair in this building somewhere? It's hard for Officer Howard to take notes standing up."

I gave an ostentatious sigh, but led them up the hall to my office. Tessa Reynolds was packing up for the day. She raised quizzical brows at the sight of the police. "Whatever you did, I'm on your side, Vic. Text me if you need my mother to bail you out."

I gave her a thumbs-up, but Pizzello was sour. "Officer Howard left the academy six weeks ago. He's already getting an education in how much fun it is to serve and protect the public."

There were a lot of possible responses, but I didn't make any of them. Everyone was strained to the breaking point these days—no benefit to my pulling harder on the ropes.

When we were in my office, Pizzello wanted a thorough description of the cave where I'd found the girl.

"It wasn't a cave, just an opening between two of the bigger slabs down there," I said. "You know these lakefront barriers. They dump concrete blocks from demolition sites down among the boulders the lake has washed ashore. This girl was in between two of the concrete blocks, which had settled so that there was a gap about two feet wide. She'd backed herself in there before she lost consciousness."

"Could someone have put her there?" Pizzello asked.

"It's not impossible, but it doesn't seem likely. A strong person could have done it, easily, except for the location—those rocks are slippery, and if you wanted to make sure you weren't going to crash into the boulders in the water, you'd need ropes, belaying pins, maybe even a partner. People are watching the space from the nearby apartments. I was almost ticketed before the rescue team arrived because someone reported me and the dogs. You'd have to do it in the dark, which would require SEAL-team skills."

"So someone with SEAL-team skills could have approached from the water."

I stared at her. "What's this about, Sergeant? Do you think she was leading a smuggling ring? An enterprising cartel sails up the Mississippi and the Illinois River and then, instead of offloading at some easy river point, goes into the lake, drops the cargo and a teenaged diver with burns on her legs—"

"All right," Pizzello snapped. "You've made your point. What did you see inside the cave—the opening?"

"Slime. Dirt. She hadn't lit a fire. However she managed to get into that cleft in the rocks, she arrived with those burns."

"No thumb drives, cell phone, anything like that?"

"Pizzello, what is going on here? What do you know about this young woman that you're hiding? She's clearly got a high profile in the CPD if you think she had electronics that need to be recovered."

Pizzello shifted uncomfortably in her seat, pushing her hair back behind her ears. It was a nervous gesture she often made, but now her fine hair had tangled in the ear loops of her mask and she had to take off her glasses to undo it all. Finally, she muttered that she was checking, that was all.

Rudy Howard, who'd been taking notes, stared straight ahead, as if he was someplace else, or at least wished he were.

"We put her picture out on a national Amber Alert. Hopefully we'll hear something. And you, Warshawski"—her voice gathered strength—"if anyone brings you news, tell me about it."

"You will be one of the first people I notify," I promised. "Of course, Mitch deserves to be told first."

"Mitch?" She sat up, alert.

"My dog. He's the one who found her."

If she hadn't been wearing a mask, she might have spat at me. As it was, she got to her feet, her back so stiff you could have laid her sideways and used her as an ironing board.

"One last thing, Warshawski." She paused in the doorway. "You said she was unconscious for *almost* the entire time. What did she do for the nanosecond she was awake?"

I grinned behind my mask, not that she could see. "Good catch. She uttered a single word which I heard as '*Nagyi*.' From the way she spoke, it sounded like the name of someone she knew. And someone she trusted—seeing my face made her feel comforted, not threatened."

"That makes her unique in the six counties."

"Ah, Sergeant, you only meet the evildoers I round up for you to arrest. I regularly bring comfort to my nearest and dearest."

"Is she one of your nearest and dearest? Did you recognize her just as she seemed to recognize you?"

"Leave it alone, Pizzello. You can't trick me into an indiscretion, because there's nothing for me to be indiscreet about. I'd never seen her before. I assume her face splashed across the Net and the news didn't bring family members running, or someone would have leaked that by now."

Officer Howard coughed, ready to rescue Pizzello from the corner she'd backed herself into. "I wondered if she could be a runaway, ma'am, if that's why no one in Chicago identified her."

Pizzello nodded. "It's possible. And it could take time for people around the country to start thinking a teen in Chicago might be their own missing child. Later, Warshawski."

I walked down the hall with her to make sure she really left the building. Meeting her had taken the time I'd imagined spending on vocal exercises. I hadn't taken the dogs out this morning, so I needed to walk them tonight. Even so, I sat at my desk and brought my computer back to life.

Something about the girl in the rocks had triggered an alert with the Chicago police. I opened the file of photos I'd taken inside the rocks yesterday afternoon.

Many police departments, including Chicago's, subscribe to facial recognition software. Companies troll social media and harvest our photographs, without our knowledge, and compile databases that law enforcement uses to identify people they find threatening, usually protestors or immigrants.

I hadn't shared my own pictures with Beth Blacksin

at Global, but her crew, and all the other media outlets in town, had photographed the girl as she was lifted from the rocks into an ambulance.

It was hard to guess her age or ethnicity from the photos. Behind the grime and dried blood, her skin was dark, her hair thick and curly. She could have been African American, or Latinx, or from any Levantine country.

If she were the survivor of an unusual crime, there should be a record somewhere. This year had seen so much violence, nationally and locally, that no one could keep up with all of it. And a teenager who was a victim of domestic abuse didn't have a lot of options for reporting it.

Still, the burns on the girl's legs made me look for fires in the last week or two where a family was missing a daughter. Thinking of Officer Howard's suggestion that the girl was a runaway, I looked for stories in a hundred-mile radius around the city. A number of apartment buildings and homes had burned down, but no one seemed to be looking for my Jane Doe. I gave up on it and drove home to my dogs.

4
Hate Mail

The next morning, Mrs. Pariente called while I was in a virtual meeting with a client. I saw the call come in but let it roll to voicemail. She called again ten minutes later, and then Lotty Herschel phoned.

As soon as the meeting ended I called them back, Mrs. Pariente first. "Donna Ilona—what's happened?"

"The *scola*—windows—like Rome!"

She was so distressed that it took five minutes to get the story. Emilio had walked to the synagogue at eight, to join with the other men in their daily prayers. When he got there, he found graffiti painted across the door and the windows broken.

Donna Ilona had been a little girl in Rome when Mussolini's race manifesto led to street violence against Jews and Jewish shops. She still remembered the broken glass outside her grandparents' shoe shop, the smell of fear rising from her parents and aunts and uncles. It was hard for her to be coherent.

I canceled my next meeting and drove up to Shaamar Hashomayim. Emilio Pariente and three other badly shaken men were sitting on a bench near the curb. Emilio struggled to his feet when he saw me. He didn't speak, just pointed at the synagogue. It was a small box of a building, constructed from the Lake Calumet clay that ages to a soft rose. Now it was defiled with ugly messages and symbols. The round window above the double doors had been shattered.

I spoke gently to the men: Had they called the police? No. While the men watched anxiously, I phoned in the report. I got the name of the synagogue's insurance agent from one of the men in the group and phoned the agency as well.

When two blue-and-whites flashed up the street, most of the men retreated into the shadows. Like Ilona and Emilio, many members of Shaamar Hashomayim had terrifying memories of law enforcement from their European childhoods. One of the oldest men stayed with me. He introduced himself as Istvan Reito. He was a lawyer, he said, mostly retired now, but he tried to look after Shaamar Hashomayim's minor legal matters.

Three officers emerged, just a driver from the first car, two men from the second. The tagalong officer was Rudy Howard, who'd been shadowing Sergeant Pizzello yesterday afternoon. Today he was learning how to respond to citizen complaints.

Reito reported what the men knew, which was nothing beyond the damage to the building. They'd been too shocked to go inside. Don Emilio produced a key, and everyone trooped in.

Even in their misery, the men were concerned about having a woman inside the sanctuary. I stayed in the vestibule while the officers—fortunately all male—checked out the premises. While they were inside, I started picking up fragments from the broken window. And came upon a bullet. I called to the senior officer on the scene, who put the bullet in an evidence bag, shaking a weary head.

"It's possible we'll find the punks, find the weapon this came out of—but you know we're up to our keesters in murder and armed whatnot. I hate to say it, but—" He let the words hang. They wouldn't be putting resources into a building defacing, even when it was a house of worship. I didn't argue, just said I'd keep my eyes open, let him know if I heard anything.

"You a daughter?" one of the officers asked. He'd heard me speaking Italian with Emilio.

"An old friend of the family. They've had a few episodes in the past, but shooting out a window—that's escalating the violence in a scary way. You'll report this as a hate crime, right?"

"That's the state's attorney's call, not mine," the officer said.

"But you'll present it as a hate crime, right?"

He scratched his nose. "Yeah, I guess. It wasn't a love crime, that's for sure."

"Have there been other episodes in the area?" I asked.

The two senior officers talked it over: a Korean furniture store and a Japanese restaurant had both been attacked a few weeks ago. They were a couple of blocks away, and the messages had been about Covid, telling them to get out of America while they still could walk out.

"A death threat? I hope the police are taking it seriously. We don't want another Squirrel Hill or Charleston in Chicago. Which is why it would be prudent to pay serious attention to this crime."

The senior officer scowled. "You talk to my watch commander about funding our overtime, and we'll work all night on it."

"You'll mention it to Sergeant Pizzello, of course,"

I said to the rookie, but he already knew better than to engage with an annoying PI; he moved behind the senior man.

When the police left, I offered to drive the synagogue members home, but they wanted to walk. They locked the double doors, tried the handle, and went slowly down the street, leaning on each other for support.

I took a few dozen photographs of the damage, because I wanted to get the windows boarded up right away. The insurance claims adjustor would take care of cleanup and replacing the windows.

I walked to the Parientes' in case Emilio had physical difficulties along the way. Even after lingering to take pictures, I caught up with him a block from his front door. I waited while he made his goodbyes to his friends and climbed slowly up the stairs with him.

Inside, we found Donna Ilona weeping with misery. She'd never renewed the synagogue's insurance policy, she cried.

"It expired when the pandemic was so bad, and I forgot to pay attention to it. How could I have been so careless and stupid?"

I calmed her as best I could, promised that between Lotty and me, we'd get the building cleaned and repaired.

Lotty called while I was still there. When she realized what was going on, she promised that Mrs. Coltrain, her clinic manager, would get the synagogue reinsured. Like me, she promised to provide what help they needed to restore the building.

When she finished talking to Donna Ilona, Lotty spoke to me again, inviting—or was it ordering?—me to come to dinner at her home that evening.

After that, I chained myself to the cornmill and walked in circles, grinding out reports on potential job candidates for two of my regular clients. I ran the dogs, changed into a knit top and dressy trousers, and walked the two miles from my home to Lotty's.

The doorman greeted me cheerily. "How's it going, Ms. Warshawski?"

"You know how it is, Mr. Garretson. A good day is when only a small disaster happens—cockroaches in the basement instead of rats in the kitchen."

He laughed obligingly, called up to Lotty, summoned the elevator for me. "There's sanitizer in the car. Use some before you touch the buttons, Ms. Warshawski."

I used a little sanitizer, wishing I could pour it into my turbulent brain, or maybe douse the outside world with it.

A welcome change brought by the vaccine allowed

Max and me to sit at the same table with Lotty. During the worst of the pandemic, if I visited Lotty at all, I stood on the balcony outside her living room. We would bellow at each other through our masks while I froze in the winter air.

Lotty doesn't drink, except for the occasional medicinal brandy, but Max has an impressive wine cellar. He'd brought a Brunello, an Italian red that I love but can't often afford.

Lotty was worried about the way the attack on the synagogue affected the Parientes. She urged me to try to track down the vandals.

"Lotty, that's an impossible job. Probably impossible for the cops, definitely for me."

"You often take on jobs the police can't or won't handle," Lotty objected.

"I'll ask some questions, of course, in case someone on the street can ID them, and I'll put up surveillance cameras in case they strike again, but I don't have the resources or the time to give to that kind of project."

"I understand you did more unpaid labor when you provided us with a mystery guest at Beth Israel," Max said quickly, before Lotty could argue further with me.

"A mystery guest and a very non-mysterious memo from our chief financial officer," Lotty said, "reminding us that the hospital is deep in the red and we can't afford to be the welfare dumping ground of Cook County."

Max winced. "He didn't put it quite like that, Lottchen."

"I get a memo from Ludwig Kavanaugh every month on the ratio of insured to uninsured patients I see. Why did you allow the board to hire someone so determined to undermine patient care?"

"Lotty, please. You know that we're bleeding money. If we can't turn the finances around we either have to close or join a network that will have much more punitive policies toward our patients. Kavanaugh helped streamline finances at St. Helena's Hospital. Anyway, he knows that you bring prestige to the hospital, which means you bring paying patients. He's one of your fans, not an enemy."

"Have you learned anything more about the girl I brought in?" I asked, before Lotty could resume battle. I'd sat through these conflicts before, and they always ended with Lotty accusing Max of putting profit before patients. Max would get up, bow with an exaggerated formality, and leave me alone with a fuming Lotty.

"She's not our only Jane Doe," Max said, "but the other is a homeless woman with advanced liver disease, so not interesting to the media. Tell me about your Jane Doe."

"There's something about her that's exciting law enforcement," I said. "I'm wondering if the cops have an ID for her." I told Max and Lotty about the visit from Sergeant Pizzello. "Have the police been around the ICU?"

He pulled out his phone and sent a text. In another minute, someone called him back. He took the phone into the kitchen for a private conversation.

"She's regained consciousness," he said when he came back into the room. "They've moved her out of intensive care, since she's able to keep fluids down on her own, and the burns on her legs aren't as severe as they first feared. She's eating a bit, but she hasn't been speaking. They've tried Spanish and Arabic on her, trying to guess her nationality, since she hasn't been responding to English."

I repeated the word the girl had spoken when she saw me. "I thought it might be a name."

Max put his wineglass down. "*Nagyi*? Like that? I suppose it could be a name, but my mother's mother was from Nové Zámky when it was Hungarian. My mother spoke German, like most people in that part of the world before the war, but my grandmother liked me to call her *Nagyi*. Hungarian for 'granny.'"

"I can't believe she's a Hungarian refugee," Lotty said. "Even if you could get into the U.S., no one is coming here from Central Europe these days. They go to Germany if they're looking for a better life."

"Maybe hers is the one Hungarian family who didn't get the memo about Germany," Max teased her. "Anyway, it's impossible to know. I don't speak the language myself, just the few words that brought my grandmother pleasure, but we must have someone in the hospital who speaks Hungarian. I'll get a notice out to the staff in the morning. However, it could be someone's name in an African or Central Asian language—we don't know anything about the girl, after all."

"Did the person you were talking to just now say whether the police had been around?" I asked.

"You mean, were they there in an unusual way? We always have a unit in the ER, you know. In this case, since the girl's a juvenile, they're trying to help find family or a guardian. And so far, we haven't had any success."

"What will happen to her if she's healed but she doesn't speak and you can't find her family?" I asked.

"We call Children and Family Services and they make a placement. They may put her in a therapeutic setting where she can recover the memory and language her trauma has taken from her, but we're a hospital. We can't care for her once she's able to live without medical support. And that shouldn't take more than another day, two at the most, given that she's already eating on her own."

Lotty had recovered her equilibrium enough to move the conversation into neutral waters. She and Max had started attending virtual performances from an experimental theater in Berlin. They were enjoying the productions more than they had anticipated, as well as the chance to hear German spoken.

As I was leaving, I thought of Max's other Jane Doe, the critically ill homeless woman. "What will become of her?"

Max grimaced. "Nothing very good. She'll have to go into a nursing home, and the quality of care—doesn't bear thinking about. But, again—we're limited in how long we can keep her. All the regulations over who pays the bills, and what they cover—we don't have a lot of say in it. Some say, and we're exercising that—"

"Don't let Ludwig Kavanaugh hear you say that," Lotty said sharply, "or you may be looking for a job."

Max took her hand and kissed it. "That wouldn't be the worst thing, at my age, to be forced into retirement. I'm not a surgeon, I don't need the hospital to make me feel useful. Or important."

I made a beeline for the elevator before Lotty replied. The two of them never used to fight, but lately that'd been a too-frequent part of evenings with them. Covid and the destructive political situation were wearing down everyone, even Max and Lotty.

5
On the Lam

In the morning, I had an anxious call from Mrs. Pariente, frightened at the thought of her husband over at the synagogue. "What if these monsters return and do more damage? Can you not watch over our *scola* in the night, the way you do on the important holidays?"

"Donna Ilona, I wish I could, but I can't." The anguish in her voice was gut-wrenching. "I'll install some security cameras; if anyone attacks the building, an alarm will wake me up and I can get the police there."

She was silent for a moment and then replied with dignity that she understood, she wanted me to understand that she appreciated all I did for her and Emilio.

I went back to work. Before Mrs. Pariente called, I'd heard from my bookkeeper, reminding me of the balance I owed my lawyer, which hovered around six figures these days, and my outstanding debt to the forensic lab I use, which ran a close second.

Investigators are sort of essential workers. I'd kept going during the lockdown, but the economic contraction meant my clients hadn't outsourced as many queries as they used to. I couldn't afford not to meet my deadlines. I returned to designing a subtle way of solving the drug problem at my bread-and-butter client's factory, but I couldn't get Mrs. Pariente's anguish out of my mind.

At least I could take care of the cameras now. I'd program them to send messages to my phone. I was at the Rapelec outlet on Milwaukee when Cynthia Dijkstra, Max's PA, phoned.

"Vic, you know the girl you rescued from the lake? She's disappeared."

"Disappeared?" I felt a jolt of fear.

"She was in her bed at the seven A.M. shift change, but when the burn unit nurse went in to replace the dressings, she wasn't there. That was at nine. The nurse went back twice, thinking maybe she was in the toilet, but she's gone."

It was eleven-thirty now. My Jane Doe had been missing for over two hours. "Did she have any visitors? Maybe someone came for her before the burn unit nurse got there."

"You know what it's like on the floors here during the day—we're understaffed, but at the same time there's a lot of traffic. Visitors aren't supposed to be allowed onto patient floors, so it's possible someone came for her. But they'd need to get her room number. The information desk can't remember every patient someone asked for, of course, but Jane Doe stands out in everyone's mind.

"The ward head says a cop went to see her, along with one of our janitors. Max thought maybe the girl was Hungarian, and I found this guy, he's close to retirement, but he came here from Hungary as a kid. Anyway, the cop tried to talk to her, and Jan Kadar, the janitor, says he translated the cop's questions as best he could, but the girl didn't respond in either language. And I don't think she ever spoke to anyone on the ward. Vic, you know she's weak. If she took off on her own, she can't have gone far. We reported her disappearance to the police, of course, but—you know what she looks like—could you?"

"I'll scout the area," I said, "but your best bet is the CPD. If they put out a missing persons bulletin, they'll be most likely to find her."

"Having you involved would make me feel better."

Right, that was me. I tracked missing persons between one and two, moved on to vandals before three, and solved routine murders by suppertime. Whenever Wonder Woman saw me coming she folded up her cape and retreated to Themyscira.

I finished buying my cameras, then used Rapelec's business center to print out a few dozen copies of the clearest of my photos of the Jane Doe. I stopped at home to collect Mitch from Mr. Contreras. The girl was so slight and frail that I might not see her if she'd collapsed in an alleyway, but Mitch would know her by smell.

Mr. Contreras badly wanted to join the search. A day on foot, hunting in dumpsters and alleyways, was not good exercise for a man in his nineties, even one as fit as my neighbor. I left him in a morose mood. He likes to be useful and felt I was putting him into a dumpster of his own.

At the hospital, Cynthia Dijkstra summoned the Hungarian speaker to Max's office. This made him nervous: he was sure there was a reprimand on the way. Cynthia introduced us.

"Honest, Cynthia, I didn't say nothin' to spook the girl." Whatever language he'd spoken growing up, Kadar's English accent and grammar were textbook Chicago.

"No one's accusing you of anything, Jan, but we've

hired Ms. Warshawski to look for her. Anything you can tell us might help us find her."

I'd been hired? That was pleasing—I'd thought this was going to be pro bono, a thank-you for all the free care Beth Israel had given me over the years.

"The timeline seems quick," I said to Cynthia. "You put out a bulletin for a Hungarian speaker and—what? half an hour later?—a cop takes Mr. Kadar up to see her? Did you put them together?"

She shook her head. "Who asked for you, Jan?"

"Not one of the regulars who hang out in the break room." He cast a sidelong glance at Cynthia: janitors and cops were hanging out in the break room instead of manning their posts, but she didn't react. "I got a page, asking me to come to the ER desk. You know, Cynthia, the cops have their little office behind there, and a guy said, was I the Hungarian speaker, could I go up with him to Jane Doe's room."

"You don't remember his name?" I asked.

"Like I said, I didn't know him, I didn't think I needed to pay special attention. I'd already told my boss to give my name to Cynthia when we saw the bulletin."

"So the two of you went up to her room together. Was she awake?"

"She was in the bed with it cranked up partway.

The TV was on, but I don't think she was watching. So the cop goes up and shakes her shoulder. Not hard, just trying to get her attention. First he talks to her in English, and she keeps looking at the ceiling. Then he asks me to translate. I don't speak that good, you know, I understand better than I talk, but it's simple: what's her name, where did she get those burns, does she have any documents or phones or computer stuff where someone could trace where she lives. And she just stares at the ceiling."

"Was her hearing tested?" I asked Cynthia.

Cynthia texted the question to someone. While we waited for an answer, I asked Kadar how long they'd stayed in the room.

"It didn't take that long, did it? A half dozen questions in English and then in Hungarian? Could've been five, maybe ten minutes. Not longer, anyway, because I got a text from my boss, someone threw up, I gotta change personalities from UN translator to janitor." He grinned nervously, hoping we would laugh with him.

I produced a sympathetic smile. "Anyone else in there with you? One of the nurses, or someone from the burn unit?"

"Hoo, boy, I am in trouble, aren't I? Maybe I need to get my union rep."

Cynthia looked at him in astonishment. "Why, Jan? I mean, of course, it's your prerogative, but I don't think Vic is accusing you of anything."

"You left, but the cop stayed, right?" I said. "It would be good to know what he said or did when he was alone with Jane Doe."

Kadar was scratching his arms, as if the conversation were giving him hives. "There was the gal in the other bed, but the cop, he sent her out of the room. She's a surgical patient and it took her a while, what with the drips and so on, but she went down the hall. I can't tell you anything else, honest. And I gotta go, I'm behind as it is."

He left the room so quickly he knocked over Cynthia's wastebasket. "Sorry," he muttered, picking it up, putting papers back into it.

"What was that about?" Cynthia said when the door had shut behind him.

"Something was said or done in that room that wasn't right," I said. "Can you check with his boss about him needing to clean up a patient room? I'll see the police in the ER to get the name of the officer who went up to Jane Doe's room. Can you print out something to show that I'm working for the hospital? Otherwise no one is going to talk to me."

While she was typing up a form, something else

occurred to me. "What was she wearing? If she left under her own steam she can't have been in a hospital gown."

"I'll ask the ward head. But hang on while I get this done, okay? You're as bad as Lotty, firing out multiple commands in one breath."

I grinned. "It's always easier to give than to receive, especially with Lotty. Are you hiring me? I mean, are you paying me?"

Cynthia made a face. "I'll ask Max. I know I blurted that out to Jan Kadar just now, but I don't have the authority. So don't go spending thousands of dollars that I can't reimburse. And now, *please*, Vic: shut up so I can type this for you."

6

Desperately Seeking

All big-city hospitals have a police detail these days. Sometimes patients are having violent drug reactions when they come in; cops try to protect the staff. People come in with bullet or knife wounds; cops on the scene try to find out who inflicted the injuries. A hospital like Beth Israel usually has four officers on duty for all three shifts. Beth Israel's unit reported out of the Twentieth District, which happened to be where Sergeant Pizzello was assigned these days

Midmorning is a busy time in the ER because it's when mothers with no access to a pediatrician bring in their sick children. However, it's not a population that needs a lot of police involvement. The officers didn't mind talking to me. They weren't enthusiastic, but I represented a break in the routine.

They already knew that Jane Doe had disappeared—Jan Kadar had been to them while Cynthia was typing up my official agreement. They didn't know the name of the man who'd gone up to talk to the girl.

"Not anyone from the Twentieth. We figured he was with SIU, looking for a juvie," said the oldest man in the quartet, thick through the middle, with a husky voice. The Special Investigations Unit handles missing persons and juvenile offenders.

"Did he think she was wanted for a crime?" I asked.

There was an elaborate group shrug. They weren't withholding information: they were miffed that SIU had sent someone in but hadn't checked with them, the keepers of the law at Beth Israel.

"Did he have the girl with him when he left?" I asked.

"He didn't stop here on his way out," the spokesman said. "We didn't know the girl was gone until Kadar told us just now."

I went up to Jane Doe's ward to see if the nursing team could tell me more. Of course, like every other civilian, I didn't belong on the patient floors, but with a mask and a protective bonnet I'd picked up in the ER, no one challenged me.

None of the nurses on Jane's floor had paid particular attention to the man with Jan Kadar.

"It was during shift change, Ms. Warshawski," the floor head said. "We're busy getting everyone's vitals, the dieticians are on the floor, transport is here from radiology or therapy units. The one thing I can tell you is your Jane Doe helped herself to her roommate's clothes. The jeans she was wearing when she came in were too burned for her to put back on, so we'd thrown them out. Jane stole a pair of jeans and a T-shirt with the Linda Lindas on it."

"When I found her, I wrapped her in my own jacket. It's red, basket weave, with big black buttons. Did she take that with her?"

"I'm running an overcrowded ward, not a fashion show," the ward head said. "But no one saw her leave, so I'm guessing she wasn't wearing anything that eye-catching."

"She must have made a speedy recovery if she could get dressed and out of the hospital without help."

"She wasn't out of the woods by any means." The nurse was looking at Jane's chart on her tablet. "She had a couple of bad burns on her right thigh and right forearm, as if she'd been crouching next to a fire. Second-degree and requiring a serious course of antibiotic ointment. If she's out on the streets on her own, she's at high risk for infection. The other problem she came in with was dehydration and malnourishment. I guess thirty-six hours of fluids gave her enough strength to go on with, but I wouldn't expect her to get very far."

"Jan Kadar said she just stared at the ceiling when the cop was questioning her. Did anyone check her hearing?"

"You can't do a clinical test of hearing on someone who's refusing to respond to you, but the resident who was in this morning blew a whistle; the girl jumped at the sound, from what they told me."

"So she speaks a language none of us knows, or she's determinedly mute, or she's still in shock."

The ward head hesitated, then said, "I didn't spend much time with her, but my diagnosis was fear. She may have stared at the ceiling when Kadar's cop was interrogating her, but I bet she looked at him out of the corner of her eye. She did that with me. It looked to me as though she decided she couldn't trust me and retreated into a protective silence."

Nurses are skilled observers, and they see more patient behaviors than doctors do. That was a likely diagnosis, given that the girl had run away as soon as the cop had left. She'd seen a crime? Committed a crime? At any rate, she couldn't afford to be caught up with the law.

I asked if the hospital gown she'd been wearing was available. The gown had disappeared, but no one had changed the bedding yet. I asked to take the sheet, to help Mitch focus his search. The nurse begged me to return it when I was done. "We are stretched so thin here, we can't afford to replace linens."

Jane Doe's roommate was watching television when I went in to collect the sheet. I introduced myself. She was reluctant to leave her show, so I had to sit through the overwrought emotions of some reality combatants until the commercial break.

While I was waiting, I looked in the lockers, but my jacket was gone. Jane must have been wearing it, but in the shift change, looking at their tablets, catching up with each other, the nursing staff hadn't noticed. *A vulnerable girl is missing, Warshawski,* I lectured myself. *Don't make your wardrobe the first thing you care about.*

The roommate had seen me searching. As soon as she muted her show, she said, "She stole my clothes. I'm making the hospital replace them, you better believe that. But I never heard her say anything to anyone. She was like a department store what's-it, the statues they put in the windows to show off clothes."

"Mannequin?" I suggested.

"Yeah. Girl-e-quin." She laughed at her play on words, and I smiled obligingly.

"Did you happen to hear what the policeman asked when he came in?"

"Yeah. He happened to ask if I would go down the hall to the patient lounge so he could be private with the girl-e-quin. I told him it was my show time, but he was kind of insistent and so I went."

I asked if she could describe the man. She shrugged. He'd been big. White. Wearing a warm-up jacket, she thought with the Blackhawks on it, but maybe it had been the Bears.

"The guy who was with him, he worked for the hospital, I think, because he had on one of those outfits they wear. When I saw him come out of my room, I started back up the hall. I just had surgery yesterday, I can't walk that fast, and before I got to the room, the hospital guy, the one wearing, like, the janitor outfit, he went back into the room, or at least, he stood near the door, so I waited down the hall until they both left."

"They left together?" I asked.

"Nah. The hospital guy, he left first. Pretty fast, and the big guy, he came out, looked around the hall. He saw me and waved, and so I came back to bed. He wanted to know, did that crazy girl say anything and I said I never heard her talk. And then he took off."

The commercial was ending; she turned the sound back on. I stuffed the sheet into a sack and went back to my car to collect Mitch.

Mitch hasn't been trained as a tracker dog, but he has a good instinct for the work. I took him to one of the hospital exits, let him sniff the sheet for a few minutes, then asked him to "find" our girl. Too many people had passed through the door; he couldn't identify our Jane, and he became anxious, pacing up and down the walk.

"It's okay, boy. A long shot. Take your time, don't let it rattle you." I'd been going to check all the exits, but they would likely all frustrate him in the same way.

The hospital was on Lawrence Avenue, a couple of miles from the lake. New high-rises, with matching rents, were going up close to the lake, but housing around the hospital was a mix of gentrifying bungalows and run-down two-flats. Many of the storefronts were standing empty. People, mostly men, were camped out in the doorways, but when I peered through the grimy windows, I saw squatters in some of the buildings. The economic recovery hadn't trickled into Uptown.

Mitch and I scoured a six-block radius of the hospital, checking alleys, bus stops, laundromats. I showed Jane's photo in all the businesses that were still open, but, as one convenience store manager said, "Everyone on this street looks like that. You know, drugged or drunk. Tired, hungry. It's that kind of street."

I stressed she'd been wearing a bright red jacket with black buttons, but that didn't help.

Mitch and I muscled our way into several squatters' hangouts. One of them had been turned into an ad hoc women's shelter, housing half a dozen infants and toddlers and their mothers or big sisters. I showed everyone in the room Jane Doe's picture but could barely get anyone to focus attention on her face. Mitch frightened some of the children. I had him show off his tricks, including taking a treat directly from my mouth. This emboldened a few of the kids to give him a tentative pat but didn't bring me closer to the missing girl.

By the end of the afternoon, we were both worn out. Wherever our Jane Doe had gone, she'd disappeared completely. I called Cynthia to report our failure. She commiserated, but was also relieved I hadn't put a lot of billable hours into the search. She had told Max about bringing me in, and he had not been pleased.

"I hate to say it, but from a nickel-and-dime standpoint, we're better off that she's left. He said we can't afford to find her." She was apologetic, but that was the reality of health care in modern America.

I'd missed lunch. I stopped at a diner for a bowl of soup and bought Mitch a hamburger. Good dogs get rewards. The burger came with fries. I kept the fries for myself, comforting myself with grease after our dispiriting day.

It was after five when I got Mitch home. I so wanted to stay there with him, watch the White Sox with Mr. Contreras, drink a glass of wine, but to keep my conscience happy, I needed to install the cameras at the synagogue.

I drove over to the Parientes' and explained what I was going to do, but that I needed a ladder. Emilio wouldn't trust me with the keys to the synagogue. At first Donna Ilona and I tried to talk him out of coming with me, but then I realized it would be better for him to feel he was playing a role in protecting the building. And in the bustle of getting inside, finding the utility room, unearthing a ladder, which he reluctantly let me help carry, he gradually became more focused, less fragile.

The streets near the temple, like the area around Beth Israel, held a mix of two-flats and small businesses, interspersed with vacant lots and abandoned buildings. We began to draw an audience: many of the shop owners knew Emilio and his friends from their years of stopping for coffee or going to the dry cleaners after their morning prayers. While I was bolting in camera mounts and programming the devices, I asked questions, but no one had seen the vandals. Or, at least, no one admitted seeing them. If I had time and energy later in the week, I'd come back to canvass the apartments, but I was depleted. It was past seven. I'd earned my glass—or two—of wine, although what I was drinking wasn't nearly as good as Max's Brunello.

7

They're Serving and Protecting—but Why?

In the morning, I drove by the synagogue before I went to my office. The camera feeds hadn't shown any attacks, but I wanted to double-check that the cameras hadn't overlooked something important.

The front of the building was still covered with vile graffiti. That had to come off as soon as possible. While I was double-checking my installations, Emilio Pariente emerged with four of his friends. They looked anxiously up and down the street before shutting the synagogue doors, but relaxed when they saw me. It was painful to see how the vandals had upended their tranquility, but I was glad the men had decided to get out instead of huddling at home.

"The window must be fixed, Victoria," Emilio said. "It isn't good to have it covered in wood. And also those terrible messages. We tried to keep our minds on our prayers, but always, this is in our heads."

I promised him I'd get it all taken care of. He clasped my hand between both of his and thanked me for being a good friend. I grimaced: I couldn't do much to protect them. Still, the men were reassured; they headed to a bakery up the street where they often went for pastries and coffee after morning prayers.

I took an hour to canvass the apartments and shops that overlooked the synagogue, but no one had seen anything. The woman who owned the dry cleaners across the street said she'd arrived at her shop at six, and the damage was already done. That was the best I could come up with.

Back in my office, I had to put the synagogue's problems to one side and concentrate on my biggest client's drug problem. I was deep in shipping routes and time stamps when my landline rang. Caller ID said it was Klondike Financial Services.

When I answered, a hearty baritone bellowed, "Is this Vic Warshawski? Corky Ranaghan."

I'd never worked for Klondike, but they're always in the news. Their managing partner, Brendan "Corky"

Ranaghan, sat on boards that gave money to high-profile charities. He was often photographed in a hard hat at ground-breaking ceremonies, and was also often a marshal at the St. Patrick's Day parade.

"Mr. Ranaghan. How can I help you?" I tried to sound cool, brusque even, as if a call from Klondike's senior partner was all in a day's work.

"You've been all over the news, Vic. A real heroine. I know those rocks you navigated; I've seen them from my boat. I wouldn't have tried it, but people who know you say you're quite a risk taker."

"Only when I have to be, Mr. Ranaghan." His tone was admiring, but I was sure there was a subtext. "Is there a risk you're hoping I'll take on your behalf?"

He let out an eardrum-shattering guffaw. "Not at all, not at all. You certainly understand the fundamentals of business: get to the point, don't beat around the bush, because time is money."

"Indeed it is," I said enthusiastically. "Did you want to buy some of my time?"

"I know Darraugh Graham trusts your judgment, but Klondike has our own staff of investigators. No, this is something small. I understand you know the old folks who worship at that Jewish church on West Lunt."

I didn't say anything, not to demand how he knew or to tell him that the building was technically called a synagogue or a temple.

"It's a beautiful little building, at least on the outside. That Calumet brick, not much of it around anymore. A shame that it got defaced like that."

"Yes, indeed."

"Word on the street is that vandals are targeting people in that part of town. I heard there's been some trouble at some of the Asian businesses, too."

He paused, but when I didn't speak, he said, "I'm sure these old men could use some help."

"Do you want to bring a group of volunteers out to scrub the building? They'd be most welcome."

He produced a barking noise. Laughter, I guess. "Nothing that hands-on, I'm afraid. But I could get them some first-class professional help."

"And why would you do that, Mr. Ranaghan? Do you have family that belong to Shaamar Hashomayim?"

"No, no, just my fondness for old Chicago buildings and people who take their faith seriously. And Klondike needs to invest in some of Chicago's needier communities. I heard the synagogue folks let their insurance lapse. It's the kind of mistake old people often make, but it may be hard for them to pay for repairs when the time comes. I'd offer to be a silent partner. I know they trust you. You could sell them on the idea."

"A silent partnership?" I echoed. "You mean you'd like to take over ownership of the building?"

He barked again. "Blunt, direct. Just like Darraugh described you. Not ownership, but help them keep their property going. That derelict house next to them could be housing gangbangers, druggies. I could help make that a safer area. You talk it over with the old folks."

"My opinion is that they wouldn't want to sell. There's a lot of family history in that building, not just Lake Calumet clay. But I couldn't begin to speak for them."

"See what you can do. There'd be a nice commission for you, if you helped broker the deal."

He hung up, leaving me looking at my phone, utterly baffled. Despite his exalted words about helping the city, Corky wanted the synagogue. Wanted it enough to try to bait me with a commission.

Klondike is one of those connected companies. If you want to do business in the metro area, you'll have a better chance of getting a contract if you work with Klondike. You want a piece of a big city or county project, say resurfacing all the roads in the forest preserves?

Or a completion bond for a new skyscraper, or even special parking concessions for your museum? You buy your insurance through Klondike. They don't just broker the coverage, they smooth your relationship with City Hall or the boards of the six counties in the metro area.

I wrote up a detailed summary of Ranaghan's call. His remark about the abandoned house next to Shaamar sounded like a threat. *Let me have the synagogue or I'll make sure we have thugs next door ready to beat up fragile old men.*

In Chicago, aldermen have the final say over what gets built in their wards. It's how they keep their coffers filled. Developers give to aldermen's campaign funds, all open and aboveboard, and if they give enough, their projects get approved. Pay to play, Illinois's favorite game.

Shaamar was in the Fiftieth Ward. I looked up development proposals in the inner recesses of City Hall's proceedings. If the city had given a green light to a development near the synagogue, there was nothing in the public records, either of the council or the Fiftieth Ward, to show it.

Maybe Corky just wanted access to some Lake Calumet brick. It's so highly prized by Chicago builders that people have been known to steal it by dismantling garages in the middle of the night when the owners are out of town.

I called Ilona Pariente to see who had the title to the synagogue. "We have all the papers here," she said. "Estella gave them to me before she went into that dreadful nursing home."

"Can you give them to me, or to Mrs. Coltrain at Lotty's clinic, so that we can lock them in a proper safe?"

"You're making me nervous, Vittoria. Is there a problem with our papers?"

"I just want to keep them safe," I said.

"Because I let the insurance lapse, you think I cannot be trusted with the rest of the documents?"

"No, Donna Ilona." I tried to soothe her, but she was sure I thought she was too old to handle synagogue business. I finally had to tell her that I was afraid someone might take drastic action to damage or destroy the synagogue.

"If you let me put the papers in my safe, then no one could steal them or harass you over them."

She sighed. "I will talk to Istvan. Our lawyer. I think you met him with Emilio at the synagogue. Perhaps he can hold them for us. That way if we need them quickly I don't have to disturb you or Mrs. Coltrain."

I had to be satisfied with that. I had a hard time

turning my mind away from Corky's strange call, but by the end of the afternoon, I had put together a detailed plan for Darraugh Graham. I emailed it to him and was preparing my invoice when Sergeant Pizzello rang my doorbell. I pulled on a mask and went down the hall to open the door so that I could check the size of her entourage before letting her in. She was alone.

"Sergeant, twice in one week. You're making me feel like one of the popular kids."

"Don't let it go to your head," she advised. "I'm taking a risk coming here. I hope I don't end up regretting it."

Neither of us spoke until she was in the alcove I set aside for clients.

She turned down offers of a drink. "I want to talk about your Jane Doe."

"Funny—I was debating coming up to the Twentieth to talk to you. Not about her so much as about the mystery cop who tried to interrogate her. You know she vanished, right?"

Pizzello nodded. "Our hospital unit reported it at the shift change yesterday afternoon. They helped the in-hospital security team search the building, but no one spotted her. Of course, Beth Israel is the proverbial rabbit warren—so many old corridors and staircases, you'd be searching one while the person you were hunting popped up on the other side and then doubled back through some damned tunnel or other."

"Jane Doe is not in marathon shape. If she were running around Beth Israel, the first tunnel would have done her in."

"Manner of speaking," Pizzello said. "Our guys at the hospital said you had a formal agreement from Beth Israel to look for her. Did you find her?"

"Is that a prelude to some kind of charge, obstruction or whatever?"

"No, it's a hope that she hasn't disappeared. It's a hope that if you have her on ice you'd let me know, unofficially, off the record."

"She's disappeared. My dog, who was her rescuer four days ago, didn't pick up a whiff of her scent in a six-block radius. That doesn't mean she wasn't in one of those alleys or abandoned buildings—it's not like I had a search-and-rescue team on the case. Anyway, your in-hospital unit said someone from SIU had gone up to her room."

Pizzello started fiddling with her hair and her mask loops. "That's the problem: my watch commander called over to SIU and they say they don't know anything about it."

"Could've been Bomb and Arson," I said. "Jane had second-degree burns on her."

"My commander said that, too, but B & A say they don't know anything. So—who was it?"

"I didn't see him, and I don't have the authority to look at the hospital's security cameras. Your crew at Beth Israel could do that, maybe get an ID."

She made a disgusted gesture. "You'd think. But a number of the cameras are broken. The one in the stairwell they used, the dude kept the janitor—the Hungarian speaker—between him and the eye."

"Deliberate, do you think?"

"Hard to tell from the video."

"You're in a position to bear down on Kadar," I said. "Of course, the real question is why the department is spending resources on Jane. There are what—twelve, fifteen thousand violent crimes committed a year in this city? And you clear only forty percent of your homicides and fewer than that of all the others? Who's leaning on you to find one teenage girl?"

"That's the trouble. We don't know. It was Lieutenant Finchley's idea for me to come see you, and he didn't do it through my command, which is why I'm out on the longest limb of my life right now."

The Finch and I have been crossing paths for years, not always happily. He holds me responsible for a bullet an ex-lover of mine took. He's a good cop, though, when his judgment isn't distorted through the lens of anger with me. Like all cops slated for top jobs, he was frequently rotated through different districts. He was currently chief of detectives out of Area 2, which had authority over Pizzello's district.

"The Finch doesn't trust your watch commander?" I asked.

Pizzello shifted uncomfortably in her chair. "He hasn't confided in me. Believe me, Warshawski, this is hard. First of all, I'm being disloyal to my command. On top of that, I'm being asked to trust you instead, which violates the code I live by. So—please—think of me as one of your annoying, whining clients that you'll risk your life for. Tell me what you know about this girl."

"I don't know anything about her, but I spoke to her roommate after she fled." I told Pizzello about the roommate seeing Kadar leave and then return to hover outside the room.

"You think maybe he was trying to blackmail the mystery man over something he overheard? I suppose, but it's thin." She paused. "You get the roommate's name?"

Ariadne Blanchard. I'd copied it from her chart on my way out.

"I'll talk to Blanchard, but as for Jane, are you sure you didn't end up with something of hers? Did she say anything besides that one word?"

"Sergeant, if you didn't believe me three days ago, I can't change your mind today. But I really, truly know nothing about Jane Doe. I found her through a complete fluke. You realize she'd be dead if my dog hadn't run off on me?"

"Coincidence. I just don't believe in coincidence, especially not around you." She slapped the chair arm. "It's a good story—it's a great story—but when V.I. Warshawski's dog runs off into the mountains, I have to believe his owner already knew there was someone trapped there by an avalanche."

"I didn't know your imagination was so poetic," I said. "It makes the conversation more beautiful, but doesn't make me less annoyed that you won't believe me."

She smiled. At least, I thought she did—the mask made it hard to tell. "I told you, I'm not comfortable with this assignment. It makes it hard for me to be as smooth as I need to be to persuade you to share information."

"I don't have information and therefore cannot share any. Imagine your Saint Bernard snuffling through the snow and finding an empty cave. That's me. By the way, the Shaamar Hashomayim synagogue—I installed surveillance cameras there. I canvassed some of the neighbors, but no one has seen anything, except that the damage was already done by six in the morning."

I told her about Ranaghan's strange phone call, but Pizzello didn't understand it any more than I did. She hadn't heard of any major construction planned for that stretch of Lunt that would have gotten Klondike involved.

She got to her feet. "We're increasing patrols, but if your cameras turn up anything, I hope you'll share."

"My Saint Bernard will gallop up to the Twentieth with the information inside his brandy barrel."

She hesitated in the doorway, came back to my desk, and scribbled something on a business card. "My private phone number. If you learn something, text me, don't call the station."

I followed her down the hall, watched her get into her car. Her own car, a Corolla Hybrid, not the department-issued sedan.

I stayed in the doorway, staring at nothing, wondering what was so important about Jane. The Finch didn't trust the watch commander at the Twentieth. That was a worry. I finally went back to my desk and called him.

"The Jane Doe at Beth Israel," I said. "You can always ask me anything, Lieutenant; you don't need an emissary."

"That a fact? And you'd tell me the truth?"

"Let's say I wouldn't tell you a lie. I hope that's a street that runs both ways. Are you free to talk?"

"I'm always happy to listen," he said. He was keeping a light tone—someone was in earshot.

"Then here is everything I do not know: the girl's name. Where she got those burns on her legs. Who came to interrogate her yesterday morning. Where she left, how she left, if it was on her own, if she was taken by force. Okay?"

"And what you do know?" he said.

"Nothing but questions. Is there a high-profile arson you think she may be involved in?"

"That's always a possibility, but I couldn't say."

"Is there a high-profile missing person you think she might be?"

He paused. "That's an interesting suggestion. This is the first I've heard of it. Do you have a candidate in mind?"

"Just trying to figure out why the department is spending valuable resources on a girl whose name no one knows. Oh—did they run her prints or DNA through juvie records?"

"Another interesting suggestion. Stay in touch, Detective."

He cut the connection. I made notes on a legal pad.

Longhand, which sometimes helps me think. It was after five. I needed to get home and go for a run, clean my
brain after a wearying day, but I still wondered where
Jane got those burns and whether there was a powerful
family whose kid was missing.

I went through all the Amber Alerts for the last six
month, for the metro area as well as the small towns up
and down the Michigan and Indiana shorelines where
Chicagoans had vacation homes. An astonishing number of children had gone missing. Even when I win-
nowed out boys and children under twelve, I still had
close to a hundred names. I concentrated on the photos. At the end of an hour, I had five possible matches,
but when I contacted the families and sent them the
close-up of Jane Doe's face, she wasn't a match.

Those were painful conversations—hope raised,
hope destroyed, within five minutes.

8
Childhood Friends

I shut down my system, set the alarms, and texted Mr. Contreras to say that if he hadn't already eaten, I was stopping at Farinelli's for pasta.

I was getting into my car when a teenager emerged from the bus shelter on Milwaukee and moved hesitantly toward me. He was chubby but tall, with wiry curls, sloppily dressed in a black bomber jacket and worn jeans. He'd fill out the shoulders of that jacket in a few years, but right now it hung on him. The sides of his running shoes had collapsed, and like a lot of kids his age, he was walking with the laces untied. The sun was setting, but there was still enough daylight for me to tell that his hair was red—not auburn, but that rare vivid carrot color.

"Are you—you are—the detective?" he stammered.

"I'm a detective, yes."

"The lady that's been on the news? I can't tell—your mask—"

I stepped a few feet farther from him and removed my mask. "I'm V.I. Warshawski. What do you want?"

"It's—it's something private."

"An entire lobe of my brain is filled with private somethings that I never mention to a living soul," I assured him. "What is it you want?"

He scrunched his eyes shut, afraid of the water but needing to jump from the high dive. "You have to promise you won't tell anyone I came here."

"I won't," I promised. "Mostly because I have no idea who you—" I cut myself off, struck by his resemblance to someone I used to know. Fatigue made me indiscreet. "Only Donny's hair was black. And he was short."

"You can't tell him I was here," the boy cried. "He'll kill me."

"Why?"

"He says you're worse than a cop, that you'd turn in your own cousin to prove you were Saint Victoria of the Mills."

The title forced an unexpected laugh out of me. "That was definitely Donny Litvak speaking. Unless it was Sonia."

"So it's true, you knew them growing up?"

"It's true that a Litvak family lived down the street from me in South Chicago. We didn't stay in touch as adults. Are you Donny's kid, or Sonia's?"

"Donny is my dad. Aunt Sonny, she never had any kids. I—you—" He broke off, biting on his knuckles.

"Young Litvak, I've had a long and wearying day. Can you let me know why you came here?"

People were passing by on foot, giving us curious glances, but not lingering. Perhaps they thought it was a mother and son having an argument.

He flushed a painful red, almost the shade of his hair. "I know I seem stupid. Maybe it was stupid to come here."

I remembered sixteen. My mother died that year, and I had done my share of stupid things to prove to her I needed her in my life, not in the cold ground where she lay.

"If you put on a mask, we can go into my office and talk in private. The street's no place for this kind of conversation."

He fumbled in his backpack for a mask and followed me into my office. I pulled my mask back over my face and settled him in my client alcove. Floor lamps and fabric-covered dividers are supposed to make it seem cozy. You're not supposed to notice the ceilings sixteen feet overhead. I switched on the lights and the air exchanger I'd invested in for the pandemic and tried to radiate an aura of empathic interest.

"I looked you up, and they said you solved some amazing cases. Fraud, all kinds of things."

"Some of that is even true," I said.

"I—I need help. Not with fraud, it's more complicated, just— Oh, I'm such an imbecile!"

"Have you killed anyone?"

His head jerked up. "No!"

"Injured them terribly so they're in the hospital?"

"Nothing like that!"

"Armed robbery? Hacked into the Koch brothers' accounts and used their money to pay someone's hospital bills?"

"I didn't commit a crime." He was indignant.

"In that case, if it's in my power, I'll do my best to help you. Although I'm disappointed about the Koch brothers. Why don't you start at the beginning. Which would be with your name."

It took another minute of prying, but he finally revealed that he was Brad Litvak. "At least, I will be in two years."

I opened my mouth to ask what was magical about

two years, then remembered you have to be eighteen in Illinois to change your name. My estimate of sixteen had been right. Maybe I am a great detective.

"I will call you Brad," I promised. "I can search on-line for your birth name, but why don't you tell me."

"Branwell Litvak," he muttered, so softly I had to strain to hear him.

"Branwell? Like Charlotte Brontë's brother?"

"My mom is, like, addicted to *Wuthering Heights.*" His voice was sour. "She has all the videos, and she watches them whenever she's depressed, which is every day, practically. She wanted to call me Heathcliff, but Dad put his foot down, only he couldn't stop her from Branwell.

"At my middle school they called me 'Bran flake' and then 'Shit flake' because bran, you know—so I made her send me to a different school where I said my name was Brad. And then one of the teachers, he said nicknames weren't acceptable in his classroom, and it all began again. The one good thing about Covid: virtual school. No more of that crap in the lunchroom or the hall. Dad keeps trying to teach me how to fight, but . . ."

His voice trailed off. I could picture Donny Litvak, impatient with a son who didn't know how to land a punch.

"So what's going on that you need help with?"

He pawed the earth a few more minutes, but I finally coaxed the story out of him.

"My folks, they're, like, always fighting. I don't even know why they got married. I don't know why they don't get divorced, except then I'd have to live with one of them and at least if they stay together, it's not so bad. My mom is worse, in a way, because she wants me to take her side, only I don't think she has a side. Anyway, there's not a lot of money, I guess that's one problem, so them having a trial separation means Donny is living in the basement."

"Next to the boiler?" I asked.

He was startled into a half laugh. "He fixed up a family room when I was little. There's a pool table—he's a really good player. I play some. It's one thing we do together. There's a sofa bed and a bathroom and fridge. He still has dinner with Mom and me sometimes, but mostly, unless he's out, which he is a lot of the time, he's in the basement. I hate thinking of him by himself down there, so I go down to shoot the shit, shoot a few balls . . ."

I tried to listen patiently as he circled the subject.

"My mom, I think she's having an affair. She goes out a lot at night, dressed up, makeup and everything. When I ask, she'll say she has an evening showing, not to wait up if she gets home late. She thinks I'm, like, five years old, ready to say, *Oh, Mommy, you're so pretty,* and swallow whatever lie she spits into my face."

"Is that why you're here?" I asked. "I can't intervene in anyone's private life, especially not your dad's—he'd ram a pool cue down my throat and rightly so."

"No, no. It's—she was getting ready to go out. She said she was off to show a house, at eight at night, like I would believe that. She's a stager."

"She works for a theatre company?" I asked, side-tracked.

"No, no. For Tricorn & Beck, the big real estate company. She gets houses ready to show. Like laying books out—pretending someone stopped reading *War and Peace* halfway through and left the book open next to an armchair while they went off to have a serious conversation about Russian history with their wife. She chooses artwork for the kind of buyer they want to impress. That kind of thing."

"That seems sad for someone who's in love with Heathcliff," I said.

"Maybe," he said, uninterested. "She even uses pictures I drew in kindergarten to put on the fridge. Like a hidden message to families with children—buy this house, have happy children who draw cute pictures! I hate that, I hate her exploiting me to sell houses."

A father who wanted him to throw punches, a mother who wanted him to be a cute kid. Poor Brad, what a stressful set of dueling expectations.

"So she was going out and you went down to the basement to see your dad?"

He nodded. "Only he was on the phone, he was shouting at someone. He said, 'Don't you understand, my ass could end up in Joliet, or in the Sanitary Canal.' And then the other guy—he was loud, too, I could hear him. Not the actual words, you know, but his voice. And then Dad said, 'I didn't do that. You won't pin that on me.' And then Dad was pacing around, and he got so close to the stairs I could hear the guy on the other end say, 'Sonia bailed you out back then, but she can't get your ass out of this sling. Play ball or roll over and play dead.'"

Brad's Adam's apple was working. He was having trouble getting the words out.

"And that was so awful, I made a kind of noise, so he whirled around and gave this fake hearty laugh. 'Gotta go. The boy is here, and we're getting pizza and knocking around a few balls.'"

Repeating the words brought them back to life. He began shivering and wrapped his arms around himself, rocking in the stiff client chair.

"That sounds truly frightening." I kept my tone

matter-of-fact—it might be frightening, but it didn't knock me off balance. "When was this? Last night?"

"Like, two weeks ago." He was talking to his feet, mumbling so that I could barely hear him through his mask. "I've been worrying and worrying, but there's no one I can ask. Like, if I tried talking to Aunt Sonia she'd get all huffy. *It's your dad, how dare you accuse him.* Stuff like that. So when I saw you on the news . . ." He stopped again and stared at his feet.

"Any idea who he was talking to?"

"I tried to ask him, but he laughed it off, said it was some guy from work trying to wind him up. I asked what trouble Aunt Sonny got him out of, and he said, all kinds of shit, all kinds of shit that Saint Victoria and her holy family tried to pin on him." He gave me a sideways glance. "Is that true?"

"My dad was a cop," I said. "Your dad ran with a rough crowd, and he thought I snitched on him to my dad. Which I never did. Donny wasn't subtle and there was a lot of talk in the neighborhood. Tony, my dad, could have heard about him from anyone on the street.

"I don't think your grandparents paid too much attention to what your dad and the twins got up to. Sonia had to look after all of them. And there was a baby, too, that she took care of."

"Uncle Gregory," Brad said. "He works in a liquor warehouse. Shelving bottles. He's, like, the bad example I'm not supposed to follow."

I didn't want to investigate Donny Litvak, but his son's anxious eyes made me remember the terrible fights in the Litvak house. Everyone on Houston could hear Mrs. Litvak. She was drunk eight nights out of seven, screaming abuse at her husband and her children, with Mr. Litvak bellowing back on the rare times he was home.

He ran a general store on Exchange Avenue, mostly clothes for women and children. Word was that he had another family with one of the fitters who lived on the East Side, but that didn't stop him shouting that none of the Litvak kids were his. When I thought of the steadiness in my own home, the respect between my parents, I knew I had been incredibly fortunate.

"What is it you hope I would find out?" I asked.

"If—if my dad is doing something—" He fumbled for words, not wanting to come right out and accuse his father of heinous behavior.

"Something not quite kosher?" I suggested.

His ready color flared up, but he nodded, relieved by the euphemism. "I don't want him going to jail, or my mom gloating over him."

"I can't make any promises," I said. "In the first

place, one phone call with an unknown person would be pretty hard to track down, especially one from two weeks ago. And besides, I have clients who pay me. I need to work for them so I can make my rent and pay for my phone and all those good things."

"I can pay you something," he said gruffly. "Not what you charge, maybe, but I had a job, before the pandemic, I have five thousand dollars saved, and my nana, she might—"

"You keep that money," I said. "The pandemic is dying down. If the global situation keeps improving, you will want to go to college or travel around the world. Give me a dollar to seal the deal, and give me your phone number. It would help, too, if you had the names of any of the people your dad hangs out with."

He didn't know any of them. "The person he's closest to is Aunt Sonny. That's one of the things that drives Mom crazy. She says he pays more attention to Aunt Sonny than to her, which is sort of true, I guess."

He found a grimy dollar in the recesses of his backpack. I gave him a receipt and took his phone number and address.

"Your dad has a day job?" I asked, getting to my feet.

"Yeah, he works for a big developer or insurance company or something. In the stockroom, like he did when he met Mom, only then he was working at the U of I bookstore. He won't take a broker's exam, which Mom says he could ace if he cared more about his family. Only, because of the pandemic, they laid him off, since no one is in the office, so no one needs him ordering supplies."

"What's the name of the company?" I asked.

"Klondike."

I saw him to the door, offered him a ride home, which he turned down in horror—if I dropped him off, then his parents would know he'd been to see me.

9
The Boys in the Hood

D onny and his twin brothers had been the leading hustlers of my childhood. The only time I saw my dad hit someone was the night he learned my cousin Boom-Boom was running with Donny and the twins.

My dad used to say the Litvak boys would all end up in prison if it wasn't for Sonia. That wasn't because she kept them on the right side of the law, but because she ran interference with the cops. By the time Donny was in middle school, he and the twins were boosting booze and cigarettes from delivery trucks and selling them out of the Litvak garage. They gave a cut to the local Mob boss, who in turn handed them part of the numbers concession at the gates outside the steel mills. This was when the mills were active, and before state lotteries did in the numbers racket.

The Litvak boys sported the coolest bikes in South Chicago. Donny was fifteen when he got his first motorcycle, and Boom-Boom was practically dying with envy. To be honest, so was I.

The night the desk sergeant called Tony to tell him they'd picked up Boom-Boom and Donny with a dozen cases of Crown Royal, my dad woke me and made me go to the station with him. My mother didn't protest, even though it was after one in the morning. She stood at the door with her worry face on: Was I doing something that would break her heart?

My uncle Bernie was waiting at the station. He and the charge sergeant both watched Tony punch Boom-Boom in the stomach hard enough to make him gag.

"If you ever do anything this stupid again, I will draw a line in front of my home and in front of Victoria that neither of you will cross," he said in a voice I'd never heard before. "I'm not going to lecture you on being stupid enough to blow your chances with the NHL. That's your choice alone. But the Litvak boys are headed for the joint, and if you want to travel there with them, you will *not* do it with your cousin. I know you and Victoria violate a hundred rules a week. I don't like it, but I let it ride. The day you move into crime is the day you will never see your cousin again. And if you join in, Victoria, you will be on the first plane to Warsaw to live with your grandmother's sister Veronika."

Boom-Boom and I were both terrified. Neither of us had ever seen my father angry, at least not that angry. I couldn't remember another time when he called me Victoria.

After that night, I steered clear of the Litvaks. If Boom-Boom didn't, he managed to hide it, from me as well as from the beat cops keeping an eye on us both. Sonia and Donny taunted me on the streets and in the halls at school—*cop's kid, snitch, turn in your own cousin*—and I turned the other cheek. I did not want to go to live with my great-aunt Veronika in Warsaw.

In the end, to everyone's surprise, the twins straightened out their lives and headed for college. I'd heard that one had decamped to Arizona, where he apparently lived on roots and berries and meditated under the stars. Gossip from my old neighborhood said the other twin, Reggie, was turning into a second Steve Jobs.

Reggie worked for one of the big electronics firms, but he also tinkered around with drones in his home workshop. At any moment, my old neighbors were sure he'd come up with a drone equivalent of the iPhone.

As I'd told Donny's son, everyone in the neighborhood talked about what the Litvak boys did, but I couldn't remember anything so horrific someone could threaten Donny with it today. And what did the mysterious caller want him to do in the present?

No one could send me to a contemporary equivalent of Aunt Veronika if I let myself get sucked into the Litvak gravitational field. I had only my own judgment to rely on. And my judgment said that a teenage boy with anxious eyes was not a good enough reason to be in Donny Litvak's orbit. I shut my office down again and went to Farinelli's to collect dinner.

I'd accumulated a screen full of texts from Mr. Contreras. Had I been mugged? Had my car broken down? I assured him I was fine, that a troubled kid had shown up, I'd tell him about it over supper.

Klondike, twice in one day. It could be a coincidence. Sergeant Pizzello said she didn't believe in them around me, and I didn't believe in them around Corky Ranaghan. Donny had worked in their stockroom, and Klondike wanted to buy Shaamar Hashomayim. It seemed like a major stretch to think Donny wasn't somehow connected to Corky Ranaghan's strange proposal.

I squinted at my phone under the streetlamp while waiting in the food pick-up line. Peter had phoned while I was wading through my conversation with Brad Litvak. That added to the frustrations of the day.

By now it was almost two in the morning in Malaga. I didn't call, just sent a text that I'd catch up with him tomorrow.

At least Farinelli's pasta was satisfying: Bolognese sauce for Mr. Contreras, decadently rich gorgonzola with walnuts for me. Mr. Contreras had been napping in front of the television when I dropped Mitch off earlier. I'd been happy to sneak out without a time-consuming conversation, but while we ate, I filled him in on Mitch's and my fruitless search for Jane Doe.

"The strange end to the day was the Litvak kid. It's a family of con artists, so he must be a disappointment to them, with his agitated conscience."

I regaled Mr. Contreras with some of Donny's exploits and Sonia's ingenious way of extricating him and the twins from the consequences. These made Mr. Contreras recount his own wild teen years, before the army and marriage settled him down. Even while I laughed over our memories, the stories I dredged up all dealt with petty thefts and cons, not big crimes.

According to Brad, the family was short of money. I could check on that tomorrow. Maybe Donny had a secret stash in the Caymans; his son wouldn't have any reason to suspect that. I'd find out everything tomorrow, or perhaps the day after, but tonight I didn't have energy left to do more than wrap up the leftovers and take the dishes to the kitchen.

Mr. Contreras had put on the Sox game while we were eating. I hadn't felt able to watch games with empty ballparks in last year's strange Covid season, but now, with the new season a week old, the rhythm of the game caught me again. At nine-thirty, I was nodding off. I left with the tying run at the plate.

When the phone woke me a little after two, I was sure it was Peter, with news of a disaster or a discovery.

"You find Hannibal's helmet?" I mumbled into the phone.

"Vic? Is this V.I. Warshawski?" It was a woman, frantic.

I sat up. Cynthia Dijkstra's name was on the screen, but she was so distressed I hadn't recognized her voice.

"Vic! Something awful has happened."

"Max? Lotty?" I flung the bedclothes aside and started pulling on clothes.

"No, not them, but—you know the janitor? Jan Kadar? Vic—he's been killed. Murdered. One of the housekeepers found him. He was in the tunnel between the main building and the radiology building. Vic, they made me come to identify him. It was terrible—his throat had been cut. There was blood everywhere!"

"Cynthia, how horrific. Where are you?"

"ER. Nurses station. I tried—to drive home—but I was shaking too much."

"I can be there in ten minutes. I'll drive you home," I said.

"That isn't why I called." She had clenched her jaw to stop her teeth rattling; her speech was muffled. "The police. They want to talk to you. They were going to you from here."

"I'll still be there in ten minutes."

Two-thirty in the morning, the ER was almost empty. A handful of people slumped in the uncomfortable plastic chairs, dozing in front of the TV. The stale air, the bright flickering lights from the screen, the droning announcements over the loudspeakers, the dull yellow walls, badly in need of paint, made me feel as though I'd been sucked into some circle of hell. I winced at my reflection in the mirror behind the nurses' station—hair sticking out at wild angles, purple-circled eyes above my mask. I had joined the undead.

I announced myself to the woman at the counter, and her face softened. "Cynthia told me to expect you. But this is terrible! We can't be safe in our own building. I told Cynthia that Mr. Loewenthal will have to provide an escort for any staff member going to and from their cars. Otherwise, how can we come to work?"

I nodded somberly. One more stress to pile onto frontline workers who were already stretched past the breaking point. I listened for several minutes while the woman poured out her agitation, but finally interrupted to ask for Cynthia.

"Cynthia, yes, of course, you're here to see her. I guess it's okay for you to go back, even though normally it's off-limits to the public, but what is normal? We lost that ship a long time ago."

There was a small cube of an office behind the station, with lockers for the ER staff and a table with three chairs. Signs taped to the wall by the door reminded us of social distancing, to wear masks, where to report a violation of human rights.

Cynthia was huddled in a blanket at the table. She didn't look up when I came in, so I went to sit next to her and put an arm around her, a natural gesture from the time before we lost the normal ship.

"Hey, girlfriend, Vic here. Let me take you home."

She produced a ghost of a smile. "Hey, Vic."

I maneuvered her out of the hospital to my car, which

I'd left in a loading zone near the ER entrance. The cops were much too busy at the crime scene to ticket errant vehicles.

Cynthia lived with her mother in Evanston, about a twenty-minute drive from the hospital. I took the slow route, following city streets.

"You must think I'm a crybaby, not to be able to drive myself," she hiccupped.

"I think it was bizarre, if not outrageous, for them to make you come to look at the body. Didn't Kadar have a family to make an ID?"

"Kadar's wife left him a long time ago. As far as I can tell from his file, they had one daughter, and she went out west with the wife—they ended up in Utah. We'll have someone in human resources get in touch tomorrow. Later today, I guess I mean."

"They couldn't bring in the head of housekeeping to do this?"

"Don't badger me, Vic, I don't know."

"Sorry, babe," I said. "My outrage is sticking up its angry head. Didn't mean to add to your discomfort. What about Max?"

"They couldn't get hold of Max, not until I called his private cell. He came in, but they have him in the office, going over other stuff with him, hospital security, logistics. They also brought in the hospital's head of security. And they had your name. I don't know why, unless the cops told them that you'd been asking about Jan. But you talked to Jan in my office, not with the cops, so that doesn't make sense. I can't make sense of anything."

"No," I agreed. "It's so horrible that we can't make sense of any of it. I know you're past your limit, but did they think there was any connection to our missing Jane Doe?"

Cynthia stared at me, wide-eyed. "Oh, Vic, no! If Jan was killed because I asked him to interpret—"

"Don't even start on that path, Cynthia. Jan was killed because someone wanted him dead. That someone was not you." When she didn't respond, I repeated, "You are not the person who wanted him dead. Agreed?"

She made a heroic effort and produced a smile. "Agreed . . . The woman at the ER station thinks we have a maniac on the loose in the hospital. If everyone starts thinking that, we won't be able to keep staff, and we're shorthanded already. I don't know what we'll do."

I didn't try to answer that, but asked why Kadar had been in the hospital in the middle of the night. "Was he working the graveyard shift?"

We were turning onto her street; she directed me to a white-painted frame house halfway up the block.

"No, he had super seniority. He only worked the day shift."

"So the fact that he was there means he was invited there," I said. "His killer may be a maniac, but I still think Kadar was targeted specifically. Even if I'm right, it won't hurt to beef up security. No using the tunnels unless you're in pairs, that kind of thing. I'll talk to Max about it. He can issue a directive."

She thanked me, but told me to stay in the car when I offered to escort her to the house. I stood on the parking strip until she reached her front door. Her mother had been waiting for her. She had the door open as soon as Cynthia reached it and took her daughter in her arms. Cynthia turned to wave, a tiny gesture with one weary hand. I waved back and took off.

After her night of horrors, it was fortunate Cynthia had a mother to hold her. Their embrace filled me with a deep yearning for my own dead mother, even more than for Peter. The old Jill Sobule song went through my head. *Wish I had my mother to rock me to sleep.*

I wondered if I'd been too dismissive of the idea of a killer on the loose in the hospital. Cynthia had said that if the staff were terrified, they'd quit, with the implication being the hospital would have to close.

I couldn't help thinking of Beth Israel's CFO, the

man Lotty had railed against. If he couldn't get the hospital to turn a profit, maybe forcing it to shut down would be a good second choice in his mind. I shook my head, trying to clear it, irritated with myself for giving in to the national craze for conspiracies.

Jan Kadar had been present when a mystery man interrogated Jane Doe. And then his throat had been slit. If those two events were connected, the mystery man had said or done something alarming in that hospital room. He'd been afraid Kadar might repeat it. As I pulled into the alley behind my building, I fingered my throat, that space just below the hyoid bone where a knife could sever your head. Ugh.

Since I'd parked in the alley, I came into the building through the back. As soon as I reached the door, I could hear the dogs barking. Ferocious, angry barks: *We're under attack, we're under attack.* Blue strobes were streaking the hallway walls, a bright light shone through the front door, and all the neighbors were on their different landings.

I'd forgotten: Cynthia had told me the police were on their way to interrogate me.

Mr. Sung, leaning over the second-floor railing, cried out, "Vic, this is terrible. What is going on? The police have arrived, looking for you! Where have you been?"

"At a hospital. I'm sorry they were so thoughtless as to wake your family, but you can go back to bed. No one's going to be shot tonight; you're not in danger." I hoped. So many bullets had been flying around America this past year that anything might happen.

10
Bull With a Horn

M r. Contreras was in the front vestibule, magnifi-
cent in his maroon dressing gown. Mitch and
Peppy were flinging themselves against the door. Three
cops stood on the other side, all with their guns in their
hands. My stomach turned over. Someone might be
shot tonight after all—me, for instance.

"We are here to talk to Victoria Warchosi. Are you
Victoria Warchosi?"

One of them had a bullhorn. No wonder everyone
in the building was awake. Every now and then, one of
the other tenants starts a campaign to evict me. With
this chaos, it was hard to blame them.

Between the dogs and the bullhorn, there was no
way to make myself heard. I told my neighbor to call
Freeman Carter, my lawyer, if the trio outside carried

me off. I opened the outer door just wide enough to slip through sideways, and pulled it shut behind me. I leaned against it, arms stretched wide, crucifix angle. Someone beamed a high-powered flash at my face. I shut my eyes, but the light was so bright that it shone orange through my lids.

"I'm V.I. Warshawski. And you don't need three people with weapons to talk to me. What is going on that made you wake up everyone in this building? Why couldn't you call me? My phone number is easy to find."

I squinted, trying to see past the flashlight. One of the trio seemed to turn and give a signal to the squad cars at the curb. I shut my eyes again, focused on my breathing, imagined the high violin fading at the end of *Spiegel im Spiegel.* I was almost successful.

"Warshawski?" A baritone. It's hard for tenors to get promoted in the police or in corporate life.

The flashlight holder moved his light away from my face, but the bright light pointed at my retinas had left behind rings of orange like smoke puffs. "Present. And you are?"

As far as I could make out, he was a white man of perhaps forty. Six feet or so. He flashed a badge, too fast for me to read even without the smoke puffs.

"I didn't take the speed-reading class. Please tell me your name."

"This isn't a formal interrogation. I want to talk to you about Jan Kadar."

"That won't be possible until I know who I'm speaking to."

I could feel the tension in the trio who'd roused the house. They were staring at something in the sky—they wouldn't be able to testify if the guy in civvies hit me. Or shot me. In the vestibule behind me, the dogs clawed at the door, whining to protect me.

Civvies seemed to be debating how tough to be, but he decided to play good cop, at least for starters. "Scott Coney. Feel better?"

"Exuberant," I agreed.

"Talk to me about Jan Kadar."

"I met him once, two days ago, for five minutes. Maybe you knew him better?"

"He's dead, murdered. Did you know that?"

"I was *told* that. In this world of QAnon and other conspiracies, I don't know if it's true."

Coney pulled out his phone and held it under my face. It was a crime-scene photo, a close-up of a blood-bath. A bathtub of blood, the tub the size of a human neck. The remains of the trachea floated in it. Other things that I couldn't identify. I was glad I was already leaning against the front door. I didn't want Coney to see that my legs were trembling.

"Satisfied?"

"That is the throat of a dead person," I said, "but I don't know if it is Jan Kadar."

"I was told you were a wiseass. And I don't need wiseasses blocking my investigation. What did you and Kadar talk about in those five minutes you shared?"

The ugliness in his voice made my own hackles rise. "He told me he came to this country from Hungary as a child. He spoke Hungarian at home but these days he understands it better than he speaks it. Understood. Spoke. Do you think someone from the Hungarian secret police killed him? That severed throat looks like the work of a professional. Was Mr. Kadar spying for the Orban government? If this is an international incident I can understand why you need to move as quickly as possible. Are you with the FBI?" I spoke with the earnestness of a patriot eager to help her country.

"This is a local crime, Warshawski. I'm with the CPD, so don't worry your pretty head about international conspiracies."

"I'm glad you think my head is pretty, Officer," I said, same earnestness. "It would be so easy to look haggard when the police arrive in force in the middle of the night."

The trio of doorknockers seemed to take in a collective breath. Coney's jaw was tight, and he was flexing his right hand, as if getting ready to slug me.

"We already have a statement from Cynthia Dijkstra, Warshawski. She says you spoke to Kadar about the Jane Doe you brought into the hospital."

"The Jane Doe whom the fire department brought into the hospital. I'm the person who found her, but I didn't make the decision on where to bring her for care."

"You may think of yourself as a wit, Warshawski, but you aren't funny. You are merely annoying, like a fly. And not one with a pretty head. I misspoke there. You're as ugly as a cockroach."

"That's unfair, Coney. Just when you had me preening."

He hit me, so quickly that I couldn't duck from his hand. My head banged against the glass door panel. That was enough for Mr. Contreras. He shoved the door open and surged out along with the dogs.

"I don't know what slum you grew up in, but you don't hit people like that. You don't hit ladies, ever," Mr. Contreras roared. "What kind of manners did your ma teach you?"

I grabbed the dogs' collars a nanosecond before they sank their teeth into Coney.

"I will tase those dogs if you don't get them back inside on the count of three," Coney said, his voice more frightening now because it was level. "One."

I couldn't hold the dogs and unlock the outer door. I begged Mr. Contreras to unlock the door, but he was incensed and letting rip. "When did you let a two-bit punk like him tell you what to do? He don't get to come around here like some Nazi in an American uniform."

Coney yanked his taser from his belt. I was leaning over the dogs, trying to shield them with my own body, when a cool, clear voice spoke from behind Coney. "I don't think tasing is necessary under the circumstances, Lieutenant. Especially not with an audience out here recording what we're doing."

We all turned to look at the street. Even at this hour there were joggers and dog walkers, too restless after the long lockdown to stay inside.

"You checking up on me, Finchley?" Coney said. "We're in Lakeview, not Lawndale. Your *particular* expertise won't be needed here."

The racism was overt, Lakeview being a mostly white, affluent part of town, Lawndale Black and poor. And Finchley being a Black cop.

"You never know, Coney, you never know." Finchley's tone was light, but there was menace underneath it. "What did Warshawski tell you about Kadar?"

"She was dancing around like the prom queen, refusing to tell me anything."

"Yeah, well, you hit her, out of the blue. I seen you, it was like you thought you was going ten rounds with Joe Louis, except Louis would've flattened a coward like you," Mr. Contreras said.

"Will someone put a muzzle on this old guy?" Coney demanded. "All I want is answers to some questions, and instead I get a cunt with an attitude, an animal show, and a guy who should be in a nursing home."

"Is there some reason we're out on a sidewalk where everyone in Wrigleyville can hear the conversation?" Finchley said. "Remarks like yours on the record can prejudice a jury."

"I don't want him in my home," I said to Finchley. "And I don't want to be in his home. If he hits people and insults them out where God and everyone can see him, I can well imagine what he does when he's snug in his own station."

"Let's move this conversation away from playground insults. What did you hope to learn from Warshawski, Lieutenant?" Finchley said.

Coney glared at him but answered. "I need to know what Kadar said to her about the meeting with Jane

Doe. You were with him at the hospital, Warshawski. You did not meet with him to talk about his sad-little-immigrant-boy childhood."

I spoke to the Finch, my back to Coney. "Someone who claimed to be with the CPD came in to interrogate Jane Doe. The one word she said when I found her might have been in Hungarian, so the hospital put out a call for Hungarian speakers, and Kadar answered. When Jane went missing, I was afraid the alleged CPD officer had kidnapped her. I hoped Kadar had gotten the officer's ID, but he hadn't. And neither had the cops from the Twentieth who were stationed in the hospital. The mystery visitor was smart enough not to show up on the cameras." I turned to look at Coney. "That wasn't you, was it?"

"Don't fuck with me, Warshawski. I don't give a rat's asshole how many friends on the force you have."

"Which translates to 'I have fifty-seven excessive force complaints and none of them has ever amounted to anything'?" I said.

He gave a smile that showed off his incisors. "Only forty-three. And none of them has ever amounted to anything. So fucking answer the question."

I'd lost track of the question, but I was worn out and I was never going to win a game of "Poke the rattlesnake to see if you can jump before he bites" with Coney.

"I'm trying to understand why everyone and their dog Rover is focused on this Jane Doe." I tried a gentle poke. "As a citizen, I love to see my police department spend resources on a mute and injured teen, but look at the tax dollars at work here: you, your three-man advance team, and now Lieutenant Finchley has arrived as well. Overtime, since it's the midnight shift."

Coney scowled, stared at the ground, took another breath. "We think she witnessed a major crime. We need to get her on ice. That is all you need to know."

"If you know what crime she witnessed, you must know who she is," I said.

"I just said, 'That is all you need to know.'" Coney bit the words off like cigar ends and spat them out. He stomped down the walk. The three men followed like well-trained sheep.

"Warshawski," Finchley said softly. "Coney operates out of Homan Square. I wouldn't yank real hard on his chain, if I were you."

Homan Square. Old friends from the public defender's office had been talking about it for the last few years—the CPD's enhanced interrogation facility, they claimed. And apparently those reports were true, if

Finchley was warning me to play nice with Coney.

"Thank you for showing up when you did," I said to Finchley. "He would have tased the dogs and Mr. Contreras. Maybe a bullet for me."

"Yeah, he wanted to muzzle me. Means I was getting under his skin." Mr. Contreras was complacent.

Finchley rolled his eyes. "Getting under his skin is easy. Getting out from under it, not so much. I'd been called to the scene at the hospital, since it's in my jurisdiction. And one of the uniforms there told me Coney had come to interrogate your pal Loewenthal's PA, and that he'd announced you as his next port of call. You're a pit dog, Warshawski. You'll go into the ring with anyone, as long as they're at least three times your size. You and Contreras don't know how to draw a line."

"Could be. But it still doesn't explain why Jane Doe is such a high-profile person of interest. Who is she?"

"I don't know." He held up a hand to forestall my protest. "If I knew and couldn't tell you, I'd say that. I don't know. All I know is, I don't like the setup."

He was walking down the sidewalk when something occurred to him, and he came back to us.

"Joe Louis?" Finchley said to Mr. Contreras. "What century are you living in?"

"I seen him fight," my neighbor said. "He was entertaining the troops and did exhibitions. He'd a' taken that Coney fella apart like a cheap watch and crushed him."

"And who takes watches apart these days?" Finchley said, but he was whistling under his breath as he walked to his car.

11

A Cry in the Night

Jane Doe and Ilona Pariente were floating in a deep well of blood. They were trying to speak, but when they opened their mouths, blood poured out. I knew they were reproaching me. They had come to me for help and I had not protected them.

The ringing phone, dragging me up from the depths, was a merciful release. I picked it up without opening my eyes, commanded Siri to answer, but she told me no one was calling. The ringing went on. My landline, my fatigue-thickened brain figured out. It still stood on my bedside table, where periodically some robocaller tried out a new scam.

"'Lo." My voice was hoarse. A quavering voice asked for "Miss Warshawska."

I sat up, pulling my wits together. "This is V.I. War-shawski. Who is this? What do you need?"

"Yulchia. You must find her before—"

"How did you get this phone?" It was a man, speaking in the background, his angry voice so loud I heard him clearly. "You stole it, didn't you? And why are you creeping around the hall? You belong in bed. In re-straints."

I shouted frantically into the phone, demanding to know who was speaking. My caller's voice, now remote, cried, "No! Don't—" and then the line went dead.

I turned on the light and looked at the little display bar on my landline, which showed the last number that had called this phone. I dialed it, but it went straight to an impersonal voicemail. Subscriber 279 couldn't take my call right now.

I got up, thick-legged, thick-headed, and went into the dining room for my tablet, so I could look up the number in my reverse directory database. Subscriber 279 was Gisela Queriga. She lived on Twenty-Seventh Street, west of Damen, in Pilsen, a largely Mexican neighborhood. She was married, she was thirty-seven, she had three children. Had she lent her phone to my caller? Or had the woman somehow filched it from her?

"You belong in restraints," the man had said.

That made it sound as though my caller was in a hospital, perhaps on a psychiatric ward. She'd sounded old. Who would threaten an old woman with restraints? That was a stupid question. The country was awash in cruelty. You read all the time about hospitals and nursing homes that tie elderly people to their beds to avoid caring for them.

"I don't know anyone named Yulchia," I said to Peppy. "Do you think that's Jane Doe's name? After all, the woman asked for me as 'Ms. Warshawska,' so she understands Eastern European last names, even if she's not Polish. Jane Doe thought I was *Nagyi*, her Hungarian granny—at least, Max guessed it was her Hungarian granny—and now Nagyi is asking for Yulchia. All we have to do is find them both, reunite them, and see them live happily ever after."

I couldn't think of any way to trace either the old woman or her Yulchia, not without a surname.

Peppy had gone back to sleep, taking up two-thirds of the bed. I didn't have the heart to dislodge her. Anyway, I needed her warmth. I lay down, an arm across her soft fur, and tried to relax my rigid muscles, tried to pretend I was a golden retriever who fell easily asleep. I tried not to imagine an elderly woman tied to her bed for the crime of phoning me.

Too many things had happened today. Yesterday. Starting with hunting for Jane Doe. Donny Litvak's kid's fear that Donny was being pressured into taking part in some unpleasant act, most likely criminal. On top of that, Jan Kadar's murder and my confrontation with a bully cop. And now a call from a woman, beseeching me to find Yulchia before—before what?

I lined up a to-do list in my head. Find someone in South Chicago who could tell me what dreadful thing Sonia had bailed Donny out of. Go to Gisela Queriga's home in Pilsen. Inspect the cameras on Shaamar Hashomayim. That reminded me of yet another event of the day—Corky Ranaghan's strange wish to be a silent partner in owning the synagogue.

Could a private person, or a for-profit company, be an owner of a house of worship? I drifted back into sleep, into dreams of Donny Litvak with my cousin Boom-Boom. They were holding up a bank, and Lieutenant Coney was saying, "You think you're getting away with murder, but it will come back to haunt you."

Peppy woke me at nine, licking my face. She needed to get outside. Last night's worries and disruptions had left me as stiff as I'd been after climbing up and down the rocks six days ago. While Peppy explored the garden, figuring out what creatures had wandered through in the night, I took a mat out to the back porch and did a warm-up. Ran the dogs, drank a double espresso, created a worksheet with all my outstanding inquiries.

Jan Kadar's death was not one of my problems. That was police business. Except Scott Coney's irruption into my life was making it my business.

I wrote in block letters, FIND OUT WHO WAS QUESTIONING JANE DOE WITH JAN KADAR. And underneath it, GET GISELA QUERIGA TO TELL ME WHO USED HER PHONE. AND WHAT THAT PERSON WAS AFRAID OF. WHO IS YULCHIA? FIND JANE DOE.

I'd taken a course last year for private investigators called How to Manage Your Practice. It included a module on "growing into success." We were taught how to get clients to pay bills without resorting to violence, and also that the key to a good investigation was a well-defined goal. Here I had three goals all defined at once. I definitely was growing into success.

Before setting out, I downloaded the images from the cameras I'd installed on the synagogue. They hadn't recorded any attacks, but they had shown a group of people in masks working on the building. When I drove up there, I saw that the masked crew had vanished. Whoever they were, they'd gotten most of the paint off. Here and there a line or a letter remained, but the facade was essentially clean.

Rana Jardin in the dry cleaners across the street was repairing a jacket. She took the pins out of her mouth long enough to report that the business owners on the street had banded together to hire a firm. I gathered they were motivated in equal measure by pity for the old men who worshipped there and fear that the monstrous images facing the street would frighten away customers.

"With Covid, already we are losing half our customers. We can't afford for the other half to stay home," Jardin said.

"You ever see anyone coming in or out of that abandoned house next to the synagogue?" I asked.

Jardin started pinning the jacket's armhole so vigorously that she stabbed herself. She gasped when a drop of blood landed on the jacket.

I stared at her. She knew something or she'd seen something, but she was afraid to tell me what.

"I can't do alterations with you staring at me. Maybe you don't have to work for a living, but I do. You need to leave."

I put one of my cards on the counter. "Call me when you feel up to talking."

I went from there to the Parientes'. I'd made a detour to an Italian deli, where I bought a bag of the imported coffee beans Donna Ilona loved. Locally roasted beans might be fresher, with a richer taste, but Italian air was sealed into these bags, Donna Ilona told me, giving it a special flavor you couldn't find in America. Nostalgia, the seasoning beloved by homesick immigrants.

She and Emilio knew that the synagogue had been cleaned. They tried to act hopeful that the cameras and added attention from the cops and local businesses would end the vandalism. I hoped so, too, but the poison in the air these days didn't make me overly optimistic.

I sat for close to an hour with the Parientes, listening to their worries and their memories, but finally detached myself to drive to the address I had for Gisela Queriga. The Pilsen neighborhood runs mostly to two-flats and bungalows, but her stretch of Twenty-Seventh also held storefronts with apartments built above them. Queriga lived in one of those.

Although it was midmorning on a school day, kids were out, skateboarding or on motorized scooters, weaving around cars, and then jumping up onto the sidewalks to harass the pedestrians. A couple of girls were in the mix, one lugging a toddler. That was how

Sonia Litvak had always dressed when I knew her—with Gregory, the baby, as an accessory, like a handbag that she always carried on her hip.

Most learning in Chicago was still remote as the teachers union fought with parents and administrators over reopening. The kids should have been in their homes plugged into Zoom lessons—assuming they had enough screens in the house for every child, and that they could afford Wi-Fi, and that an adult was at hand to cajole or order them to sit in front of those screens, instead of working for minimum wage to feed them.

The street door to Queriga's building hadn't shut properly. I found her apartment number on a directory above the mailboxes and climbed the stairs to the fourth floor. There was an elevator, but I didn't want to share it with however many puffs of a virus it had received today.

When I knocked on the door to 4K, it was opened the length of a chain by a solemn-eyed child of six or so.

"I'm looking for your mother. For Gisela Queriga."

"She's not here," the child said.

"Can I leave a message for her? It's important that I talk to her."

The child shouted, "Jazmin!" and a girl of about

eleven appeared. Her black hair was down to her shoulders, with two little braids on the left side and bangs cut straight across her forehead. Her expression was fierce.

"We are not talking to you, so take your nasty questions to someone else."

"I'm not with the government," I said. "Your mother's phone was apparently stolen. The person who took it phoned me in the middle of the night. She seems to be in trouble and I'd like to know where your mother works—"

The girl shut the door, swiftly. I heard three sets of bolts click into place. I tore a piece of paper from a small notebook in my bag and printed a message to Queriga.

I am not with ICE or any other agency. I want to find the woman who used your phone early this morning. I think she's in danger. Can you please tell me her name? If you don't know that, can you at least please tell me where you work? I will not mention your name to anyone.

I signed my name, wrapped the paper around one of my business cards, and slid it under the door. "Please see that your mother gets that," I called.

As I walked back down the hall to the stairwell, I could hear the doors crack open behind me. Despite my dark hair and olive complexion, I was an Anglo and an outsider. No reassurance would persuade the people in this building that I wasn't an agent with ICE.

12
A Blast From the Past

A red Navigator stood at the curb outside my office, motor running. I was rattled enough by the events of the past few days that I didn't pull into Tessa's and my parking strip but parked halfway up the street and walked back, staying in the road.

A man and a woman were in the SUV, but I couldn't make out their faces. The man saw me looking and jumped from the car. He was short, about my own height of five-eight, but with broad shoulders. His dark curls were flecked with gray.

"What the fuck were you doing, Warshawski? You in charge of the Fascist States of America's Chicago branch?"

I backed away, alarmed more by the spit flying from his mouth than his fury. "Donny Litvak," I called loudly. "If you want to talk to me, put on a mask and take it down a few decibels. Otherwise I'm out of here."

That infuriated him so much that he ran toward me, fist ready to slam into my face. I dropped to the street and rolled to the curb. Donny fell heavily against his car, knocking the wind out of himself.

"Damn you, Warshawski, damn you!" he choked.

I was scrambling to my feet, backing away from him, when a woman spoke, her voice languidly contemptuous.

"Donny, I told you not to be stupid, but here you are, the reigning king of stupid."

She was standing next to the passenger door, auburn hair styled so carefully it was clear she braved Covid and went to a salon.

"I'm V.I. Warshawski," I said. "Are you with Donny? Can you explain why he's screaming at me?"

"I'm Ashleigh Breslau. Donny and I share a child, whom you spoke to last night." Her voice remained cool. Sharing a child, my speaking to him, all not terribly interesting.

"Your child is Brad Litvak?" Asphalt fragments had caught in one of the scrapes I'd gotten from climbing around the rocks. I picked out the fragments; the wound began to ooze blood.

Ashleigh looked on, eyebrows raised. I wondered what might faze her. "My son is named Branwell."

"And I'm *Brad's* father, which you never seem to remember. Stupid fucking name. Kid hates it. Stop using it." Donny stayed next to his car door, kicking the rear tire as a substitute for my shins, or perhaps Ashleigh's.

"He'll grow into it," the woman said with serene confidence. "If you didn't harp on it—"

"Have you listened to him any day in the last sixteen years?" Donny landed a particularly savage kick, which made him yelp in pain. "Or me, or anyone but your own—"

"Can you save the fight for your reality show?" I said. "I'm not interested. Why are you two here?"

Ashleigh folded her arms and turned away, staring at Elton, the homeless man who sells *StreetWise* on my stretch of Milwaukee.

"I want to know why you sicced your buddies in the CPD on my boy," Donny said. "You always lorded it over every other kid on Houston Street because your dad was a cop. You thought that made you in charge of everyone else's life. Well, you are goddamn not in charge of my life or my son's life. If you *ever* talk about him to the cops again, it'll be the last time you talk to anyone about anything."

"Donny, that sounds awfully like a death threat. Which leaves me completely unwilling to talk to you."

I walked past Ashleigh to my office door. She was still staring—not at Elton, who'd skittered down the street when he sensed her gaze—but at the spot where he'd been standing. However, when I'd typed in the code and pulled open the door, Ashleigh called to me to wait. I turned, but kept the door open with my right heel, in case I needed to flee another assault by Donny.

"Last night, the police snatched Branwell off the street and interrogated him without notifying me, even though he's a minor. I thought perhaps Donny had involved my son in one of his stupid schemes, but it turned out they wanted to know why you were talking to Branwell."

"To Brad," Donny snapped. "And could you remember he's *my* son? It's like you think you own him. Brad came down to my dungeon last night after you finished boo-hooing over him. I told her royal painness here I was going to have it out with you, Warshawski. You do not get—"

I didn't wait for the end of his sentence. Someone had been watching me and I hadn't noticed. Hadn't noticed when I saw Brad waiting at the bus stop while I got into my car. Had I lost all my detecting instincts?

Surely it hadn't been Finchley or Pizzello who tailed Brad and ambushed him. Maybe Lieutenant Coney? Except he hadn't known me before he showed up early this morning.

Donny was still talking, Ashleigh still sprinkling him with contempt, but I went back into the street, walking a block north, crossing Milwaukee and turning around, going as far as the Polonia Triangle, inspecting the parked cars.

Donny was so taken aback that he stopped yelling. He moved closer to Ashleigh, who kept her arms crossed disdainfully.

When I circled back to my office door, I said, "I don't see any obvious surveillance, but they must have had someone watching my building last night. Your son arrived around five-thirty, without an appointment. Until that moment I didn't know you had a son, and I had never heard of Ashleigh."

"Yeah, we're married. Stupidest goddam thing I ever did."

"The one subject we agree on," Ashleigh said.

"I'd like you to agree on something else: that your son's welfare is more important than your battles with each other or with me." I paused.

Donny looked at Ashleigh. When she nodded fractionally, he muttered, "Deal."

"People in my space have to wear masks," I added. "I have a supply in my office."

"I've been vaccinated," Ashleigh said.

"As Mr. Dooley used to say, 'Trust everybody, but cut the cards.' People in my space wear masks."

Donny made another remark about the Fascist States of America, but softly enough that I could pretend I hadn't heard him. Ashleigh gave an elaborate shrug but pulled a mask from her handbag, a green one that matched her top. When Donny had a mask on, I led them into my workspace so that they could watch the footage from the cameras that monitor the doors to my building.

I only survey front and rear doors and the parking strip on the building's north side; any cars lingering near the building would have been out of range. That also meant we couldn't see Brad/Branwell until he was actually talking to me in my doorway. The audio isn't great, but Ashleigh and Donny grudgingly agreed their son had sought me out on his own, not that I'd summoned him.

"What happened to your son after he left here?"

"Let's start with why he wanted to talk to you. He won't tell me," Ashleigh said.

"Because you—" Donny started.

"No," I said coldly. "Blame game and out you go. Your son saw my name in the news story about the girl I found in the rocks. He wanted advice on a personal problem. Please tell me what happened to him after he left here."

"A personal problem?" Ashleigh's poise cracked slightly. "Something he couldn't talk to me about?"

"Of course he couldn't talk to you about it," Donny snarled. "What sixteen-year-old cries to Mama when he has a personal beef? He should have come to me."

He cast a malevolent glance my way. "Why'd he come to *you*, of all people? He knows you're an enemy."

"For sure he knows you and Sonia don't like me, but he's getting old enough to make up his own mind about people."

"So he's made up his mind to trust Saint Victoria of the Mills? Life plays one fucking joke on us after another. What could you help him with that I couldn't?"

"Yes," Ashleigh said. "My son should feel that he could confide in me, not in a stranger, even if the Better Business Bureau does give you an A-plus rating. You need to tell me what Branwell wanted. We can talk privately, away from Donny, if you're worried that he'll overreact."

Donny made the sound that I imagined you'd hear in a bullfight when the bull wants to destroy someone.

I shook my head. "The privacy of sixteen-year-olds matters as much to me as that of sixty-year-olds. If he didn't confide in you, I'm not going to break his confidence. Please tell me what happened to him last night."

Husband and wife looked at each other, nodded sourly.

"I work for Tricorn & Beck," Ashleigh said, "but I work from home unless I'm actively setting up a house."

"She's a stager," Donny supplied. "Creating phony homes. Perfect for a phony—"

"No," I said, before Ashleigh could respond to the bait.

She sighed loudly but went on. "My office is in the back of the house. I can't see Branwell come and go, although since his school is only doing remote learning I do check periodically to make sure he's attending his classes. I didn't even know he'd been out until I texted him at seven, saying I was putting supper on the table. He said he was on the bus, coming up Milwaukee—we live in West Ridge—"

"In the house *I* pay for," Donny couldn't resist snarling.

Ashleigh sailed past the interjection. "He should

have been home by seven-thirty, but at eight he hadn't shown, so I texted and didn't get an answer. I kept texting. Of course, Donny wasn't home, he was out with his *business* associates, spreading Covid far and wide, but when I called, he told me not to treat Branwell like a baby. When Donny was his age, he was doing every illegal thing you can imagine; why he thinks that's a good model for—"

"No," I said. "When did your son get home?"

"After nine. He said the cops picked him up as he got off the bus on Devon. He said they claimed you had given him something that you got from the girl in the rocks. The cops even accused him of being her boyfriend. He kept telling them he didn't know the girl, and you hadn't given him anything, but they wouldn't listen. They even kicked him in the stomach."

Her perfect poise cracked at that: she squeezed her eyes shut, fists clenched in her lap.

"He didn't tell me that," Donny growled. "If he had—"

"You'd have been the Emperor of Stupid, not just the king," Ashleigh said.

"Did he know the name of the cops who picked him up?" I asked.

"No," Donny said. "I asked him last night when he came down to tell me about it. He said he was too scared to ask for ID. Ashleigh has him so—so sheltered, like he's made out of eggshells and she has to keep him wrapped in flannel blankets, he doesn't know how to stand up for his own rights."

"Just as well," Ashleigh said. "If he'd told you, you'd have tracked down the cop and beaten him up and then spent the rest of your life in jail."

"Wouldn't that have made you happy as ten clams," Donny jeered. "Get me the guy's name and I can make all your dreams come true."

"Enough!" I slapped my desktop. "If you want to spend the day on your domestic drama, take it outside. I don't have time for it, and it doesn't help your son."

Someone had staked out my office in the wake of Jane Doe's disappearance; they'd killed Jan Kadar, perhaps because he'd heard them say something to Jane that needed to be a secret. Everyone and their dog Rover thought Jane had something of value, and they wanted it badly enough to attack a kid who came to my office. I didn't like this story at all.

"I want to talk to Brad," I said. "I'd like to show him photos of some cops and see if he recognizes any of them from last night."

The pair argued over it some more but finally agreed I could talk to Brad tonight. They bickered over the time, but settled on seven-thirty, when Ashleigh would have finished designing a room where happy families could picture playing board games with their eager, well-mannered children.

The location was another sore spot. They weren't going to come to me. Klondike and Tricorn were both opening back up to vaccinated staff, but neither partner would go to the other's office. We finally agreed to meet in their house in West Ridge. And that everyone would wear a mask. I'd never appreciated how hard diplomats have to work. Getting the Breslau–Litvaks to the table took more patience than working out a nuclear test ban.

About half an hour after Donny and Ashleigh left, Donny reappeared at my office. I went to talk to him on the sidewalk, not sympathetic.

"Warshawski, tell me what my boy came to see you about." It wasn't possible for him to be placating, but he'd abandoned his earlier fury.

"Donny, I won't betray Brad's confidence. All I can tell you is to be open with him. When people second-guess each other, the guesses are invariably wrong."

He smashed a fist against the other palm. "He talked about me, didn't he? Tell me!"

"You don't have a difficult illness you're hiding from him?" I asked. "No? Are you doing something you don't want him to know about?"

He gave a fake laugh. "Of course not. I'm not the Donny Litvak your cousin hung out with. I have a family to care for."

"Of course you do," I agreed. "So if there's nothing that you need to hide from him, encourage him to ask whatever he wants to know."

"You sound like fucking Ask Amy," he said bitterly. "What about Ashleigh? Did he talk about her? Tell you who she's fucking?"

"You actually could use Ask Amy. The three of you need to talk to each other, not to me."

13
Home Deliveries

Back at my desk, I could see Donny on my monitor. He lingered on the sidewalk for a bit before walking slowly up the street, head down. I never would have expected to feel pity for one of the Litvak boys, but Donny was in over his head, with his family and with whomever Brad had heard him speaking to.

I called Sergeant Pizzello. "Did somebody from the Twentieth drift down Milwaukee Avenue last night to check up on me?"

"You getting paranoid, Warshawski? We have better things to do than pay attention to a PI who can't solve her own problems."

"You know what they say, Pizzello: just because you're paranoid doesn't mean someone isn't after you."

"You sure someone's following you?"

"Not me, Sergeant. A kid came to see me yesterday afternoon. A pair claiming to be cops trailed him as he left and picked him up for questioning. They beat him, to try to get him to confess to having something that belonged to my Jane Doe of the Rocks."

"Oh, they beat him, did they?" She sounded bitter. "These days, every person in this town who gets stopped by the police gets to claim brutality. It doesn't matter if we've found them over a body with a gun in their hands: they were beaten and so the murder doesn't couht."

"I realize that's a serious problem for law enforcement. It's not one I can solve, which won't surprise you, since you don't think I can solve my own problems. Just tell me if someone from your district was assigned to keep an eye on any visitors to my office."

She muttered what might have been an apology and put me on hold. After a good quarter hour, when I wondered if she were stiffing me, she came back on the line.

"You know I'm the newbie in the district, so I can't be asking awkward questions. However, I made a surreptitious check of the duty logs, and I put in a call to Lieutenant Finchley. If—and that's a very big *if*—some client of yours was picked up by the CPD, it wasn't on orders from here. Now you go detect something yourself. It will do you good."

I thought of Coney, showing up in the predawn to interrogate me about Jane Doe. With his small hold on his temper and his outsize fists, he'd be a good candidate for going after Brad. But why?

I fiddled with a bronze paperweight on my desk, a lump Tessa had removed from one of her sculptures. "Did the cops pick up Brad because they're on Donny's tail, because they're on my tail, because they're after Jane Doe? Or because Brad is dealing and is in over his head?" I asked the bronze.

Like all oracles, it returned an enigmatic smile that could mean anything.

Data. My undergraduate physics professor, Mr. Wright, had instilled in his students a mistrust of fact-free theories. I needed to shelve speculations about Brad and focus on something else. Like who from South Chicago might know an ancient secret of Donny's, a crime Donny had committed that could be held over his head in the present. Assuming that the conversation Brad had overheard was connected to something that went that far back.

Maybe someone who'd worked at Litvak's, the store

Mr. Litvak had owned on Exchange. Of course it was long gone, muscled out by the big-box stores, as well as by the deterioration of a neighborhood where unemployment was double the national average. But someone who'd worked there might have heard rumors about the boss's son.

I looked for news of the store in old newspapers and found a piece celebrating Litvak's fiftieth anniversary. Donny's grandfather had opened the store as the country entered World War II, and they were appropriately patriotic, carrying flags along with basic dry goods and clothes. They would take a picture of your son or spouse heading off to the Armed Forces. The picture was free, but you could buy a frame decorated with stars and stripes for fifty cents.

The story in the *Herald-Star* included a photo of the original staff—owner, wife, and Donny's father in a baby blanket (also in red, white, and blue, for sale in the store's infant and children's department). More helpful for my immediate needs, they had a group photo of the 1990 staff. I copied out their names.

Dorothea Jenko was eighty-one now and living with a daughter in Munster, Indiana, just south of Chicago's southern boundary. In so-called normal times, I would have driven down there to see her in person, but in the plague years, I couldn't risk infecting an older woman.

When I called and introduced myself, she said, "Oh, yes, I remember your mother. She gave piano lessons to my Melanie, and was very patient, even though my poor girl never could learn to count time. I follow your investigations with great interest. Really, all of us from the old neighborhood do. It's nice to see someone from South Chicago who's made a success of her life."

We chatted for a few minutes about the old days in the neighborhood. I asked if she also kept up with news about the Litvaks.

"Oh, those children!" I could picture her flinging up her hands. "They ran so wild, you'd think they didn't have a mother. Or a father, for that matter. Donny used to come in to help with heavy work—unloading crates of shoes and clothes and knickknacks, that kind of thing. Some of his friends came in sometimes, and we ladies who worked there were always tense, because they had that edge, you know, that edge that makes you think a boy can be dangerous."

"Did Donny seem dangerous?" I asked.

She paused for a moment. "You know, that's a good question. He was a rough boy, but we all liked him. He was more daredevil, trying to get attention from his parents, than downright wicked. He'd help if he could, even if he was sulky about it. People said he and his friends stole, and that they did jobs for Valentine Tommaso, but Donny didn't have that ugly attitude."

"My cousin sometimes hung out with Donny," I said awkwardly.

"No one in South Chicago would ever think Bernard Warshawski could be a thug. He was just young, letting off steam, but he wasn't hanging out in Tommaso's back room the way Donny and some of the other boys did."

Val Tommaso had been the local Mob boss who Donny and the twins stole liquor for. As had Boom-Boom, the night my dad confronted him at the police station.

"Why I called, Ms. Jenko: Donny has a son who's about sixteen. He thinks Donny may be in hot water because of something he did back then. The boy doesn't have details, just a fragment of a conversation he overheard. Was there ever talk of Donny or the twins taking part in a major crime? Something bigger than stealing cases of Crown Royal?"

She was quiet for so long that I wondered if she'd hung up on me.

"There was one time when Donny took the store's van," she finally said. "I heard about it the next day from Moira Lonergan. She lived alone in one of those studio apartments that used to be above some of the small shops on Exchange, and she saw everything that happened on the street. She said the boys showed up in the middle of the night, maybe two in the morning. They were making enough of a racket to wake her.

"Moira said your cousin was there, and Donny and the twins, and another boy, Stosh Duda's son. Your cousin was arguing with them; she could only hear bits of what they said, but your cousin said he wouldn't rat them out. It's such a funny expression, it's stayed with me all these years. The Duda boy accused him of being a sissy, so your cousin punched the Duda boy, knocked him down, and the Duda boy came after him with some kind of weapon. Moira thought it might have been a tire iron, something like that, from the junkyard. And then Donny said, if—I can't remember the Duda boy's name."

"Tadeusz—Tad," I supplied. I remembered him and Donny buzzing the neighborhood on their motorcycles. Sometimes Boom-Boom joined in.

"Yes, that's it, Tad. Donny said if Tad wanted his help moving the load, he'd better stop fighting and get in the van. They drove off, and your cousin walked away. Moira couldn't sleep. She sat there all night, watching for the van, which Donny drove back around six in the morning. It was dented along the front fender and covered in mud. We all went to look at it the next day. There was gravel in the front bumper, and even some bits of grass. Of course, Mr. Litvak was beside himself, but none of us let on we knew anything about it."

"They lived five doors down from us," I said, "and we could hear his yelling in our kitchen. But his anger never seemed to have any effect on the kids."

Dorothea Jenko gave a dry laugh, like wind rustling autumn leaves. "He was too angry all the time, which made him uncomfortable to work for, although he could be charming to his customers. I don't think any of his children paid much attention to him, but when Donny brought the van in, all damaged, it was a different story. Mr. Litvak sent the van off for repairs, and took away Donny's motorcycle until he'd worked off the cost of the damage."

"What about the twins?" I asked. "They'd been involved, too, right?"

"Oh, yes, the twins. That was the end of their life of crime. They buckled down to study. I believe they both went on to college, and one of them is doing well for himself in computers, or at least that's what the neighborhood says."

Chicago neighborhoods are like individual small

towns, where people follow each other's life stories. Even though she'd moved miles farther south, Dorothea Jenko continued to keep track of her old friends.

"And Donny?" I asked.

"Yes, that night had an effect even on him. Not as much as it did on the twins, but he saved up his money, moved out of the neighborhood. I heard he got a job at one of the downtown schools. Roosevelt, maybe?"

"University of Illinois," I suggested.

"That sounds right," she agreed. "I always thought it was a pity, a pity really for all of them that their parents weren't more attentive. They were bright kids, even the baby, but no one ever pushed them to be disciplined or think about their futures. Sonia could have been a lady lawyer like Justice Ginsburg. She had the smarts, and she could argue a table into standing on two legs if she set her mind to it, but Reba—Mrs. Litvak—never wanted her daughter going to school. Reba was happy to have Sonia looking after the baby and the housework."

"What about Tad Duda?" I asked.

"I guess he got his life turned around, too. Stosh's bar didn't last, not after the mills shut down, and maybe Tad had enough of liquor by the time he grew up, because he took over the cement company Val Tommaso used to own. He kept Tommaso's name on the business. His ma lives in a retirement home near to here, so I hear about him from her.

"It's so hard to picture these wild boys as grown men working jobs, paying mortgages." She gave another rustling laugh. "Of course, your cousin is the one we all brag about knowing. Fire on ice, how we loved to see him play."

That was Boom-Boom's nickname in the sports pages, *Ice on Fire,* until he wrecked his ankle hang-gliding in the off-season.

We chatted for a few minutes about other people in the neighborhood, schoolmates of mine who were mothers now, some even grandmothers. I extricated myself gently, with a promise I'd visit once the virus was no longer so big a threat.

The Litvak delivery van, damaged, and with gravel and grass in the front bumper. They'd driven off the road in it, that much was obvious, and dumped something for Val Tommaso. I tried to think of what it could be besides a dead body, but I couldn't imagine anything else that would shake up Donny so badly that he'd wriggle away from Tommaso's organization.

The twins, too. They'd only taken part in stealing and hot-wiring and so on because Donny was their older brother and they followed him like ducklings. Whatever they'd seen had sobered them faster than any lecture my dad or another cop could have given them. I wondered if I could persuade Reginald, the twin who'd stayed in Chicago, who did something with computers, to confide in me.

Of course, there was also Tad Duda. His father had owned one of the neighborhood bars that stood open twenty-four hours a day, where steelworkers could drink going on or off shift.

In those days, in that neighborhood, bars didn't have fancy names. Stosh's was owned and run by Stanislaw "Stosh" Duda, a weedy-looking man with bad teeth and a worse temper. In those days, people—men— went into a bar to drink, not to unload their troubles onto the bartender. The men who drank thought Stosh was entitled to his bad mood and the occasional black eye he gave his wife or son. Life was hard and a man needed respect at home. I was pretty sure that Stosh's was one of the places that took delivery of liquor that Donny and the twins hijacked.

According to Dorothea Jenko's account, Tad had a temper every bit as ugly as his father's, at least as a teen. He'd gone after Boom-Boom with a tire iron.

People change as the testosterone storm subsides. Maybe Tad had become an easygoing family man, running the old Mob chief's cement business with genial goodwill. Hard to believe. Tommaso's Mob nickname had been the Viper. If Val the Viper thought Tad Duda deserved his company, it meant Tad had kept doing favors for the Mob.

I looked up Tommaso Cement. Their operation was at the south end of Goose Island, that odd chunk of land in the middle of the Chicago River that holds a lot of warehouses and factories.

My financial databases told me the company wasn't thriving. Of course, a lot of big construction had been on hold during the pandemic, but even the four previous years showed Tommaso running in the red. In fact, right before the pandemic, a condo board had sued Duda, claiming that Tommaso Cement was responsible for the collapse of a garage floor. There was a sealed settlement, but Tad's personal finances were also rocky.

He was making payments on a house on the Southwest Side, he was making payments on a car he'd bought for a third party, maybe a girlfriend, and he was struggling with payments on his own luxury pickup. If Tad wanted something from Donny, he could be desperate enough to do any number of ugly things.

Tommaso himself had dodged both federal prosecutors and rivals. He'd retired to Florida a dozen or so years ago, and even had a Facebook page that showed him splashing in a pool with his grandchildren. I was tempted to post a query: *What did Donny Litvak and Tad Duda get rid of for you thirty years or so ago? And where?* But just because the Viper had retired didn't mean he didn't still have pals in Chicago who'd be glad to shut me up for him.

14

Who's Afraid of Virginia Woolf?

I t was four in the afternoon, and I still hadn't done any remunerative work today. However, I needed to prepare for tonight's meeting. I created a photo array to show Brad Litvak, to see if he'd seen his attackers' faces clearly enough to identify them. I included a couple of African American cops I know—Finchley and Conrad Rawlings, the ex-lover who'd taken a bullet for disregarding my advice. I didn't think either of them was responsible for beating on Brad, but I wanted to see how Brad would react to the possibility.

I put in a random mix of other white faces—cops, non-cops, even Robert Mitchum at his most menacing. I found Lieutenant Coney in a video on his daughter's

TikTok account. He was playing with a Boston terrier, too fiercely for my taste. His daughter had posted it to a soundtrack from *Cop Block.* I wondered if Coney knew he was out in cyberspace to that particular music.

I packed up my office and collected the dogs. It was early April and lake temperatures were in the low fifties, but the dogs didn't mind. They swam while I sat on the rocks, throwing balls for them and letting my mind drift away from South Chicago and the sins of Donny's youth. I finally, reluctantly, leashed up the dogs and went home to shower and change for my front-row seat at *Who's Afraid of Virginia Woolf?*

Donny and Ashleigh lived in one of the white neighborhoods close to O'Hare, near the remnants of the North Italian neighborhood where my mother used to go when homesickness overwhelmed her. There was a particular grocery on Harlem that carried the dried figs she loved. We'd go there by bus, L, another bus, and spend the afternoon. Gabriella would speak Italian with the owners, a couple in their sixties who gave me strawberry gelato and always pressed a little extra cheese, a few more oil-cured olives on my mother as we left. I looked for it on my way, but it was long gone, its narrow space part of a giant auto-body repair shop.

I cut across on Devon and promptly got lost in the cul-de-sacs and angled streets, so I was ten minutes late when I finally found the Breslau–Litvak house. It was typical of this part of the city, a tan brick bungalow on a half-lot, with an extra room added at the back. Presumably that's where Ashleigh created stage designs for houses she might wish to own herself.

The red Navigator was pulled up next to the garage door. A nondescript Honda was parked behind it, along with a motorcycle, one of the big Suzukis.

I parked on the street, behind a Jeep—Donny's. That wasn't a guess: he got out as soon as he saw me in his rearview mirror.

"So what do you think, Warshawski? You think the cops are such good law-and-order folks that they'd never rough up my kid?"

I started to say I'd talked to the cops and believed they hadn't picked up Brad, but that would confirm that I was a liar and cop collaborator. "I think anyone can do anything, given the right provocation. I want to hear directly from Brad what happened and where it happened."

Ashleigh was watching us from the doorway, arms akimbo. When we reached her she said to Donny, "Of course you called Sonia. You can't take a shit without support from your big sister."

"Fuck's sake, Ashleigh, I need someone who cares about me and the kid. Sonia knows Warshawski, she'll be able to tell in a blink of an eye if War-shawski's lying."

"And Reginald? Why is he here?"

"Good evening, Ashleigh," I interrupted. "Is Brad here, or just Sonia and the twins?"

"The twin," Ashleigh said, voice cold enough to freeze an egg on a sidewalk. "Stanley's communing with the vortex down in Arizona, so it's just Regi-nald, but Gregory's filling in. Gregory, the most use-less person on the planet, trailing Donny by a good five lengths."

Ashleigh was blocking the doorway, but she stepped away when I started to sidle past. "You might as well come in and join the South Side Gangster Disciples. Disciples of Sonia Litvak, I mean."

"Geary." Sonia's harsh South Side accent carried to me from a room on my left. "I did get married, Ash, and unlike Warshawski, I kept the SOB's name when we divorced. The gay divorcées, we should meet for a fun night on the town, isn't that what the movies show? Warshawski and Geary, let's have a drink and salute the old days. Or should we wait until Ash here gets her decree so she can join us?"

I followed the voice into the room. The Litvaks weren't tall, but they were broad, and they filled the small space to the point of suffocation.

When I'd known Sonia, she'd been sloppily dressed in her mother's hand-me-downs, frizzy hair cut at home into unruly coils, like broken mattress springs. In middle age, the wild halo of frizz had been clipped close to her skull and dyed an eye-popping magenta-orange. Her eyes above her mask were lavishly made up.

Gregory was sitting next to Sonia. He'd been the baby, Sonia's special charge while their mother drank herself into incoherent rages every afternoon. He was slouched over, shuffling his feet. As Ashleigh had intended, he'd heard her spiteful comment. Reginald, the computer whiz, was standing by the window, fiddling with his phone. Brad had moved into a corner as far from his family as possible.

"Hey, Sonia, hi, guys," I greeted the room. "Brad, we need to talk. Do you want to do it with all your relatives around you, or with me alone, or with me and your folks?"

"Branwell," Ashleigh hissed behind me. "I will not have you South Chicago thugs demean or diminish my son."

"You stay in here with us," Sonia directed Brad. "Warshawski will cheat you out of your shorts if you're not looking. We need to make sure she doesn't trick you into saying something that will be used against you in a court of law."

"If I wanted to spend my life in court, it wouldn't be on your nephew's account, but because I'd sued you and Donny for the twenty different slanderous remarks you've made in the last twelve hours," I said. "Brad, can we go somewhere to talk?"

"Not alone." Ashleigh, Donny, and Sonia all spoke at once. This was going to be an exhausting night.

Reginald looked up from his phone. "Can we begin with why Vic and Brad were talking yesterday, before we figure out what to do tonight?"

"Donny said you refused to tell him what Brad wanted. So what are you trying to cover up?" Sonia, to me.

Neither Brad nor I said anything. His face was in shadow, so I couldn't gauge his expression, but I could tell he was twitching.

Sonia let the silence last for about half a minute before she said, "If Warshawski refuses to cooperate I don't think there's anything else we need to talk about."

"You could be right," I said, "but before I leave, I'd like Brad to describe what happened last night. How many cops were there? Just the one?"

Sonia started to object, but Brad said, "No, I can tell her. There were two."

"Men? Women? Hard to tell?"

"Two men, at least, I think they were men. Their voices, you know, and they were pretty big."

"They grabbed you when you got off the bus?"

I could see his head bob up and down in the shadows.

"They try to rob you? Did they think you had something valuable, like, I don't know, the newest iPhone?"

"It happened so fast. It was crazy," he said. "I was scared. I knew Dad would've stood up to them—"

"And gotten himself killed!" Ashleigh intervened.

"Did you have something valuable?" Reginald cut in, voice harsh. "Exactly what were they after?"

"I don't know!" Brad's voice cracked into his upper register. "They were in an SUV. When I got off the bus, one of them yelled, 'You, kid! Come here a minute.' I knew not to do that, but then they got out of the SUV. I tried to run, but I tripped on my shoelaces."

I could see his feet. His high-tops were still unlaced.

"I thought it was, like, a mugging, I didn't know they were looking for me specifically. And then they grabbed me and pulled me into the SUV. The one guy, he said they were cops looking for what the girl had on her. He kept yelling, 'Don't lie to us! We know you have it. Talk or get the shit beat out of you.'"

He was hovering on the brink of tears. I interrupted in my calmest voice. "I know you didn't get a good look at them, but can you describe them at all? Tall, short, fat, thin?

Brad shook his head, but my interruption had helped him; his voice was steadier. "Big, like I said. They weren't in uniform, but they both wore these big jackets, like warm-up jackets."

"Any logos?" I asked. "Like for the Bears or the Sox?"

"I think the one guy, his jacket might have been for the Blackhawks."

That was the only detail he could remember, so I asked him what happened next.

"I—I said I didn't know what they were talking about, I kept saying that, they kept saying I was lying, and I—I was, like, crying, like a stupid baby. So then they pulled into this alley and took me out and searched me—it was gross—they pulled—pulled down my jeans and—"

"It's okay," I said. "Strip searching is horrible and degrading. I've been through it."

When Sonia objected to my torturing her nephew, I said, "Be quiet, Sonia. He needs to talk. Get him some water and stop interrupting."

Sonia sucked in a breath, ready to expel flames, but Reginald interrupted again, telling her to let Brad finish talking. He went into the kitchen and came back with a glass of water for his nephew.

When Brad had drunk enough to regain some composure, he said, "They dumped out my backpack and went through everything, and said, okay, I—I was telling the truth, I didn't have it, whatever it was, and they said, in that case, why had I gone to see Warshawski?"

"Yeah. We'd like to know that, too," Donny said.

"Damn straight," Sonia chimed in. "Why did you go see a woman who no one in your family trusts?"

Brad didn't speak. He drew a circle on the floor with his toe.

"Is this something you'd like to tell me privately?" I asked.

Brad nodded, still mute, but Sonia and Donny and Ashleigh all said, oh, no, I wasn't going to get away with that, alone with Branwell, or Brad, putting words into his mouth.

"Whatever you said, Branwell, it's okay," Ashleigh said. "No one will blame you for saying something to save your life."

It took more prodding, but he finally blurted, "I said I was afraid you were—were—were fucking someone and could she find out."

Sonia gave a hoot of ribald laughter, but Ashleigh turned on me. "You knew this this morning, and you said nothing? Nothing?" Her voice rose an octave on the second "nothing." "What kind of prize bitch are you? Is this loyalty to the old neighborhood no matter who else gets damaged?"

She whirled around to face her husband. "Did you put him up to that? You knew about this all the time we were at her office this morning? You—you *bastard,* you!"

"Don't scream at me," Donny said. "This is the first I heard about it. Kid said nothing to me. But if you are fucking one of those suits you work with, by God, there's nothing—"

"Enough!" I shouted. "I told you this morning that Brad spoke to me in confidence and I respect his privacy. This isn't about you. This is about someone beating up your son because they thought he knew something or had something they wanted. Can any of you get your faces away from your own reflections long enough to come up with an idea of what that could be?"

"Yep," Reginald said. "I'd love to know what a couple of thugs, cops, whatever, thought a teenage boy would have."

Brad was trembling. "I don't know, Uncle Reggie. Maybe they thought I was some kind of computer whiz, like you, instead of the biggest loser in the family."

"You forget. That's me." The hoarse baritone silenced everyone. Gregory had been so quiet that we'd forgotten he was there. "Stop beating on him. Just because Mom and Dad beat on each other and on us doesn't mean you have to go beating on him. It's like Warshawski said—he got attacked and all you want to do is scream at each other or at him."

Ashleigh and the other Litvaks stared at him, slack-jawed. Brad crossed over from the shadows where he'd been hiding and muttered an apology to me.

I stepped into the hallway, and he followed. "That was quick thinking, very impressive. And close to the truth, which is what you want in a reliable lie. Maybe a little too close for family comfort."

Ashleigh stood in the doorway, clenching her fists. "*Now* what are you getting him to do?"

"Yeah, Warshawski." This was Reginald again. "You've stuck your stick in the hive, gotten all the bees buzzing and stinging. Is that why you came here? If you've gotten the honeycomb you were after, you can go home now."

"Very soon," I said. "This family lovefest has worn me out. I have one more question for Brad—"

"Branwell," Ashleigh snapped. "Although why I should try to instill a sense of pride in him I don't know."

"—for your son." I looked at Brad. "I have a photo array that includes some cops who might have been in the SUV last night. I'd like you to look at them, see if any of them might be your assailants."

"It was dark," Brad muttered. "I didn't get a good look at them."

"Still—"

"Only if I see them, too," Donny growled.

Sonny and Reggie chimed in. Brad took me into the dining room so he could see the pictures under the overhead light. I had fifteen altogether and dealt them one at a time. He studied each carefully but kept shaking his head. I'd had great hopes that he'd pick out Coney, but he didn't recognize him any more than he did Conrad Rawlings or the Finch.

As he rejected them, I laid them in a row on the far side of the table. The elder Litvaks eyed me suspiciously: What was I up to? But they lined up behind the table and started inspecting the photos. The ninth one made Donny swear.

"What the fuck is he doing in there? If you're trying to connect my son to him, my God, Warshawski, you've been crossing a line all night long, but this is one you won't get away with!"

Reginald and Sonia elbowed Donny out of the way. "Isn't that Tad Duda?" Reginald said.

"Duda?" Sonia echoed. "Is he one of your pals,

Warshawski? If he is, you're a bigger prize bitch than I thought."

Ashleigh had stayed in the living room, still bruised at her son's perceived treachery, but Donny's and Sonia's outbursts brought her in to see the photos. She picked up Duda's picture. "He's a good-looking man. Don't tell me he's a friend of yours."

"Donny and the twins used to hang out with him," Gregory said unexpectedly. "They used to do stuff together. Steal liquor. Siphon gasoline out of cars, I guess for kicks. I think they even beat someone up once or twice."

"How can you possibly know crap like that," Donny said scornfully. "You were a baby."

"Everyone called me the baby, the afterthought." Gregory took a deep breath. "The mistake, that's what the parents called me. The rest of you were the right answer, but I was the mistake. So they left me to Sonny, and Sonny took me everywhere. You and Sonny talked about everything. You didn't even notice I was there. I was four or five. You talked about Boom-Boom the hockey player, and what you'd done together."

No one spoke. After a moment, Gregory added to Ashleigh, "I'm not stupid, even if I never went to college and work in a warehouse, okay? So stop saying I'm the most useless person on the planet, okay?"

He walked away, his gait shambling, shoulders hunched. Sonia cried out, a howl of grief or remorse, and ran after him, but he shook his head, said something to her in a low voice, and made his slow way out of the house.

15
Encore

Sonia was standing in the middle of the walk when I left.

"Why'd you have to bring Tad Duda into this?"

It was typical Sonia: aggressive, demanding, but she'd been crying and her words came out as a muffled sob.

"Sonia, what did he and Donny get up to the night Donny trashed your father's van?"

"You really are the total snoop, aren't you? Boom-Boom was there that night, too."

"I'd need a medium to talk to Boom-Boom. Besides which, he walked away before they set out. He flattened Tad, if I remember correctly, and Tad came after him with a tire iron."

"If you know all that, then you don't need me to tell you anything."

"I could ask Gregory," I said. "He said Donny and the rest of them beat people up for Valentine Tommaso, right? Did a beating get out of hand that night? The van looked as though it had gone into a gravel pit when they brought it back. They wouldn't have dumped someone for Tommaso, would they?"

"Don't you go tormenting Gregory." Her fierceness returned. "His life has been hard enough. I tried to take care of him. I tried to protect him from the stuff that went on at home, but it didn't do any good, did it? Look at him. He was such a smart baby. I used to read my homework to him, and then he learned to read himself just from following along with me. Believe it or not, you weren't the only person on the block to study, even if you had your name up in the halls and I didn't.

"Down in South Chicago they act like you and Boom-Boom were king and queen of the neighborhood, like no one but you ever learned how to take the ACT test. I could have gone to college, easy, but I couldn't leave Gregory home alone with Larry and Reba. And it didn't do any good. It didn't save him."

"Maybe it did," I suggested awkwardly. "He can support himself, and he can speak up for himself when he really wants to. You gave him that."

"Don't patronize me, Warshawski!" she screamed. "You don't have any idea! Larry and Reba, they weren't like your parents, treating you like a little princess whose every wish was met with a bow and a curtsy."

"Oh, Sonia, it wasn't like that," I said, but she gave an outraged cry. Whatever I had to say she didn't want to hear. She stormed up the walk and into the house.

Maybe, anyway, it had been like that, or had looked like that from the outside. Not that my parents' lives revolved around me, but they paid attention to me. They made me set goals, they made me work, they gave me praise when I earned it, they gave me love, abundantly. Sonia had four younger brothers, all elbowing each other, crying for attention that their parents wouldn't or couldn't provide.

I lingered under the streetlamp for a few minutes, wondering if one of the other Litvaks might want a few private words. However, it was Ashleigh who appeared, wanting to know why I hadn't told her this morning about Branwell trying to hire me to follow her.

"Ashleigh, it's what I said to you and Donny in my office. You need to talk directly to your son. I can't be the mail server for messages you two want to deliver to each other."

We argued the point for a few minutes. She didn't admit to an affair, but she did blame Donny for upsetting Branwell by making their marriage an intolerable situation.

When she finally gave up, I got into my car. The afternoon respite by Lake Michigan seemed a hundred years in the past. I was longing for the leftover pasta from last night and a glass of Amarone, and was just pulling away when Reggie tapped on my window.

I cracked it open. "Yes?"

"Will you get out of the car? I want to ask you something."

I left the engine running but climbed out.

"What did Brad really ask you to do?" he said.

"You don't believe the Ashleigh story?" I asked.

"You grow up in a family like mine, you learn every sentence has a double meaning. Brad may be worried about his parents splitting up, but kids don't hire detectives to follow errant mothers. They worry, they talk to their friends, they act out, but they don't hire detectives. What did he really want?"

I shook my head. "He's my client, and he gets the same privacy as all my clients. My turn. What did you guys do that night with your dad's van? Everyone in the neighborhood says afterwards you and Stanley walked clean away from the Viper. You started studying and went off to college."

"None of your business, Warshawski. Stan and I are entitled to our privacy, same as Brad. My turn again. What did the girl give you?"

I almost said, what girl? I'd been so focused on the Litvak family drama, I'd forgotten that part of the story. Brad had been beaten up because his assailants were trying to find an unspecified thing that my Jane Doe had. Or they thought she had. And thought she'd offloaded onto me.

"This." I rolled up my sleeve and showed him the deep scrape on my forearm. Under the streetlamp's cold light, it looked like a brownish-gray island in my skin. You couldn't see the lurid yellows and purples. "She didn't have anything to give. The hospital went through her clothes, looking for an ID, and found nothing."

"Which means she gave it to you before she was put in the ambulance."

"Reggie, way too many people in America are living in a world of lies, secrets, and delusions. I am sick of all of them, big and small, including the delusion that my Jane Doe had something and that she gave it to me. She was unconscious the whole time I was with her except for five seconds, when she opened her eyes and said '*Nagyi.*' Does that word mean anything to you? Does it sound like something from the tech world you inhabit?"

He eyed me narrowly, but between my mask and the streetlamp's pale light he couldn't read my expression.

"You could be holding a straight or you could be bluffing; I can't tell."

"Neither, Reggie, but it sounds as though this Jane Doe isn't a stranger to you. What's her name?"

"I don't know. Before I came over this evening, I looked at the photos Global ran after your dramatic rescue mission. I didn't recognize her. But she wouldn't have been targeted if she didn't have—well, vital information of some kind."

"And that information would be?"

"If she gave it to you, you know already. If she didn't, you don't need to know." He spun on his heel and climbed onto the big Suzuki in the driveway. He made a show of revving the engine long enough to excite most of the dogs on the street, then took off at a ferocious speed.

I got back into the Mustang. I hadn't expected to end the evening feeling sorry for Sonia, pity and embarrassment at the knowledge that I and my parents had loomed so large in her adolescent mind. Her father had owned a clothing store, but he hadn't bothered to see that his own daughter was decently dressed. She'd tried to protect her brothers, but no one looked out for her.

That was a tragedy, but not relevant to the problems of the moment, which included the attack on Brad, and

Jane Doe's fate. People thought both teens were carrying some object that was small and important. Their lives didn't seem to intersect, but it also seemed like a mighty big coincidence.

Reggie's interest in Jane Doe's object had me confused. If the Litvaks knew who Jane was and what she supposedly had on her, that would mean Brad knew her. He hadn't mentioned her when he came to see me, except to say he'd seen me on the news. Brad hadn't seemed interested in her, and he didn't seem like a skillful liar. Yet here was Reggie, implying that he knew what Jane reportedly had.

Brad's attackers had strip-searched him. A cavity search meant we were looking for something small, a thumb drive, perhaps, although I wasn't sure one that had been stored in a body cavity would still be usable.

At any rate, perhaps the attackers had been following Brad, not staking out my office. But if Reggie, not Donny, were the connection to Jane Doe, then why had they followed Brad?

I'd been disappointed that Brad hadn't picked Lieutenant Coney out of the photo lineup. Or Tad Duda, for that matter. Of course, it was a long shot, a scared kid identifying two men whose faces he'd only briefly glimpsed in the dark.

The Litvak melodrama was just that: melodrama.

The scary story was Jane Doe's. Who was she, what had Jan Kadar heard when he'd been interpreting that meant he had to die? And where was she? A teenage girl in precarious physical shape, alone in a big city, could be in danger even without people like Coney hunting her.

I hadn't gone back to the rocks where I'd found her because I'd assumed anyone looking for her would already have searched there. Maybe it was worth a visit, though. If she'd returned there, thinking she'd be safe, and someone had already found her—I couldn't bring myself to finish the thought.

And if someone thought she'd given me something, I'd be a target, too. When I reached home, I parked up the street and walked around the block, but I seemed to be clean.

16
Caught in the Act

The dogs and I set out at first light. This time I had on tight-fitting shoes with good gripping soles, spandex clothes, fingerless gloves, headlamp. In my backpack I had rope, water, sugar cubes—in case I found Jane Doe and she needed her blood sugar raised quickly—dog treats, a couple of bananas—for my own blood sugar.

The April air had a knifelike edge of cold, a reminder that the Chicago winter still lurked. At this hour there was little traffic; we covered the route in under fifteen minutes. The sun was just bobbing its head above the horizon. I hoped we'd be early enough that the eager crime spotters across the street would still be in bed.

Mitch and Peppy were straining at their leashes, whimpering a little, as we crossed the handkerchief park next to the rock fall. Early runners were already out; I waited until we'd climbed over the barrier to the rocks to release the dogs. They skittered down the steep incline and started snuffling around.

I couldn't remember exactly where we'd found our Jane Doe, except that it was close to the south end of the rock hill. She'd been between two concrete blocks, the opening wide enough for my shoulders. Mitch and Peppy were hunting in circles, in efficient dog fashion. While I edged my way around boulders and concrete, they concentrated on the scent they wanted, ignoring rotting fish, a soiled diaper, and the empties that cover even the rockiest part of Chicago's lakefront.

The dogs found the crevice when I was still inching my way along the section above them. Mitch gave a couple of sharp barks and disappeared into it, with Peppy close behind. I slid down to their level, heart beating uncomfortably hard, calling to them to get out so I could see in. They backed out and looked at me, puzzled. They'd found the hiding place, but there was no girl inside it.

I knelt and switched on my lamp. I inspected every square inch of the crevice, but I didn't find anything that showed the girl had ever been here. If it hadn't been for the dogs' certainty, I would have thought we were in the wrong place.

There were a dozen or so openings that were about the same size, and I looked at all of them, in case she'd parked whatever her pursuers were looking for in one of them. By the time we crossed back over the barricade, I was sweating, and the sun had risen, baking off the nighttime chill.

A patrol car was at the curb. A uniformed man was leaning against it, waiting for us. He didn't want to hear anything about why I'd violated city ordinance 604-33 forbidding people from climbing on the rocks, looking for missing Jane Does. He demanded my ID and wrote me a ticket, a nice even two hundred dollars.

I was fuming but impotent. You can't argue against ordinance-based tickets in court, which seems like a total denial of citizen rights, and I didn't even have a client to whom I could bill the fine. I didn't waste energy on a useless argument, just snarled and stuffed the ticket into my backpack.

I swung past Shaamar Hashomayim before driving home. My cameras were all in place, all still communicating with my computer, and there hadn't been any new graffiti. I waited until the morning service ended, and saw that most of the regulars had returned, but I didn't offer to drive Mr. Pariente home—the car was too full of dog.

I was making the turn onto Racine, three blocks

from my building, when I got a panicked call from Tessa Reynolds, my lease mate.

"Vic! There are two cops at the door. They say they have a warrant to search the premises."

"Have you called your mother?"

"She's sending a lawyer down, but it's your office they want to search. Call Freeman! You know my mother doesn't handle criminal law."

"I'll be there ASAP, but I have to leave the dogs at my building. I'll call Freeman on the way."

I had Freeman Carter's secretary on speaker as I raced down Racine. I was telling her about Tessa's call when I reached my building. Two squad cars were in front, strobes flashing.

"Rhiannon, it's worse than I thought. They've got my building staked out. I'm going in through the alley with the dogs before I try to deal with the cops."

I drove past and parked on the nearest side street. Ran down the alley with the dogs. As soon as I got the back door opened, Mitch and Peppy roared down the ground-floor corridor to the front, barking with full-throated fury. Coney stood on the other side of the glass door, flanked again by three uniformed cops. Mr. Contreras was on the cops' side of the door, florid with a rage of his own: they'd cuffed him.

Coney saw me and spoke through his bullhorn. "I

have a warrant to search you and your premises, War-shawski, and another warrant to take you into custody if you resist."

I was choking with fury myself, but I couldn't give way to it. *Breathe it out, breathe it out enough to be coherent.* Rhiannon was still on my open line; she was calling to me.

"Don't know if you heard him. He has warrants, I need to let him in. Call Murray Ryerson, tell him to get over here at top speed, with any kind of camera—phone in a pinch, camera crew would be better." I was panting. "And get someone to my office to support Tessa Reynolds."

I pulled the dogs back from the door and forced them into Mr. Contreras's apartment.

Coney was impatient. "We're going to break the door down on five, and your shiny detective isn't here to stop us."

I gritted my teeth but also had to ignore the racial slur. "I need to see the warrant, Lieutenant," I shouted.

He cocked his head at one of the uniformed officers, who held up the documents. A Cook County judge had determined there was probable cause to search my home, my car, my office, and my person for items re-moved from Jane Doe, either in her hideout near Lake Michigan, or in her room at Beth Israel hospital, or directly from her person in the days since she'd gone missing.

I opened the door. "Good job, cuffing an old man, and a veteran to boot. You'll get some great press out of that, Coney."

"No one cares what a cock-sucking cunt like you has to say." He backhanded a slap across my face. He was wearing a ring, and it caught in my mask. He yanked it free, tearing the mask from my face. I backed away, put the ear loops back on. He and two of his crew shoved their way past me into the building

Above me doors slammed shut. The neighbors were all working from home; they must have been hanging over the railings while the drama unfolded, but now that the cops were inside and violent they didn't want to be in the cross fire.

"Help!" I shouted. "Help! The cops are here, they're hurting Mr. Contreras. We need pictures!"

Coney's henchmen grabbed my arms and half dragged me up the stairs. I didn't resist but kept screaming for help. The dogs were barking hysterically inside Mr. Contreras's apartment, slamming themselves against his door.

"We're calling the police!" The couple who lived across the hall from me had cracked their door open. "You can't make this kind of racket."

"These thugs are the police!" I bellowed. "Take their pictures!"

The door slammed shut. We were outside my own door, but Coney wouldn't let me get my keys out of my backpack. He had one of his officers yank it from my shoulders and empty it onto the floor.

They went through the contents an item at a time. "I knew you'd be crawling around those rocks, Warshawski. I knew you couldn't resist the chance to go back, once you thought interest in your runaway had died down. So whatever you found there, we'll take charge of it from here."

Coney took my keys and let himself into my home. He took one of his men with him and left the other to make sure I "didn't try to run or phone anyone." At least they hadn't battered the door down. At least I wasn't shot in my own bed. It would be harder to get away with murdering me in the hall, with the Clingmans peering through their peephole. I hoped.

"What's this?" My guardian had found the sugar lumps.

I didn't answer.

He slapped me, same spot as Coney had, same violence. "I asked you a question."

I took a deep breath in—breathe in calm, breathe out fear. Breathe in the Tuscan hill town where my mother grew up, breathe out the Chicago apartment where cops were trashing my home. Every muscle in my body was tight. I heard glasses ringing together, pots banging. If Coney broke my mother's Venetian wineglasses, I would shoot him myself.

"Hey, Looey," my bodyguard yelled. "Found drugs in her pack."

"Pack 'em and label 'em. We'll get the lab to analyze them."

I still didn't say anything as the cop made an elaborate charade of pulling out an evidence bag and putting the sugar lumps into it. He hadn't bothered with gloves; one of the pieces crumbled between his fingers. White flakes floated to the floor.

I squinted at his badge. "My dad wore this uniform, Tillman. He would be ashamed to know you."

"If he was anything like you, bitch, that cuts both ways. We don't need libtards in the force."

"Are you wiping your hands on your legs?" I said, incredulous. "Now those pants have to be bagged and entered into evidence. And the evidence lab is going to make you a laughingstock, wasting their time analyzing sugar. Or do you have a horse you have to feed?"

He moved toward me, fist back, but a clamor at the bottom of the stairs stopped him. Swearing, shouting, front door banging, and then, "Get the fuck out of my way or get flattened."

Murray Ryerson had arrived.

The cop left to guard Mr. Contreras was protesting, but Murray's voice booming up the stairwell drowned him out. "Picture of this old man in handcuffs is already in the cloud. And your name and badge number are right next to him. So uncuff him."

Murray was puffing by the time he reached the top. His press badge had rotated around his neck. He straightened it with one hand, held up his phone with the other, and started photographing Tillman, me, my belongings on the floor, the open door.

"Warshawski, this time tomorrow you're going to have a big black eye. You run into a door?"

"This guy," I said. "Officer Tillman. On top of a blow from Lieutenant Scott Coney, who is inside, ransacking my belongings."

"You can't take pictures in here," Tillman snarled. He lunged at Murray, grabbing at the phone, but Murray had a good four inches on him and held it out of reach.

I ducked around them and went into my apartment, my phone out. Tillman pulled his gun, shouted a warning to Coney, who erupted from the kitchen with his own gun drawn.

"Murray Ryerson is a reporter," I said. Voice quiet, trying to lower the room's temperature. They'd knocked music from the piano, but I ignored the scattered paper, ignored the overturned bench. Focused on the moment, not on the weapons. "Photos he's taken are already in the cloud. They may already be on Twitter, so let's not up the ante, Lieutenant."

He hated stepping back. He probably hated any situation where he didn't make the decisions about what happened next. Each spoonful of cereal his daughter ate for breakfast, where the Boston terrier peed would be under his command and control.

He lowered his gun arm and said to Tillman, "She didn't have time to hide it here. Tell them they can stop searching her office. We'll take her to Homan Square so a female officer can explore her interior parts."

Tillman cuffed my hands behind my back and shoved me toward my front door.

"Call Freeman," I yelled at Murray.

17
Lost Property

The four-mile trip along Jackson Boulevard was like a time-lapse sequence of urban culture. Closest to downtown were high-end condos and chic restaurants that had taken over the old wholesale food district. New buildings were packed in so tightly that you couldn't drive on the narrow side streets any more. Tillman put on his lights and his siren, but we still had to inch through this stretch.

Beyond this money belt lay a stretch of old bungalows and three-flats. These petered out into junk-filled vacant lots and boarded-over buildings. It's in that mix of storefront churches, bars, and, incongruously, an urban farm that the Homan Square police building stands. If you look it up on a map, you'll see it's called the Police Evidence and Recovered Property Section.

You don't see a label for Bomb & Arson. You definitely don't see a sign for Enhanced Interrogation Facility, the euphemism for "torture" we all learned from America's time in Iraq.

The building itself is constructed in late neo-bureaucracy, five stories of featureless redbrick covering most of a city block. It seems ordinary until you're right up next to it. All the ground-floor windows are bricked in, and the building itself is wrapped by razor wire, surveillance cameras, and searchlights that look like the set for *Stalag 17.*

A handful of protestors stood across the street in Homan Square's scrap of a park. They carried signs that read DEFUND HOMAN SQUARE, along with SAY THEIR NAMES and NO MORE GEORGE FLOYDS.

Cops in riot gear stood between them and the building. It was hard to see how people in Ts and jeans could breach the razor wire. In fact, it was hard to see how anyone could get in, even if they made it past the riot gear and the wire. There was no public entrance, except for a door marked RECOVERED PROPERTY.

We were buzzed in through a door labeled POLICE, which opened only from the inside. Coney turned me over to a female officer with instructions to give me a cavity search and to inspect every item of clothing. "She's creative. She might be hiding it in a denture."

As I told Brad Litvak, I know how demeaning a strip search is. There's no way to survive it except through dissociation. I worked through one of my mother's favorite Handel arias, *Vieni, o figlio*. In my head I changed son to mother. *Come, o Mother, and console me.*

In a detached second part of my mind, I was grateful that the female who searched me wore a mask and gloves. Coney, Tillman, and the other punk hadn't worn masks, and I had to worry about infection on top of humiliation.

In a third part, I thought that Coney or his henchmen had been Brad Litvak's assailants. Murray had recorded them when he was photographing them at my apartment. Brad hadn't recognized their faces in the photos, but maybe he'd recognize their voices.

When I was dressed again, women officers escorted me to a room designated for lawyers and clients. Freeman Carter was waiting for me, as was my personal thug, Officer Tillman. Freeman had persuaded the police to let me go, which I suppose is why Coney wasn't there—he wouldn't want me to see that he'd been forced to back down. Officer Tillman walked out with us, to make sure we didn't roam the halls, freeing people from unmarked interrogation cells.

Neither Freeman nor I spoke until we were in his

car, on our way back to the North Side. I gave him a thumbnail of the last few days.

"After going through this horror show with Coney, I have to believe his guys were the team that attacked Brad Litvak three nights ago. But why is the CPD intervening in such a heavy way? If Brad is to be believed, someone was threatening to expose Donny's involvement in an unknown event, in order to shame Donny into taking some other equally unknown action."

I told him about Tad and Donny's adolescent escapade with the Litvak shop van. "I included Tad Duda in the array I showed Brad last night, and Donny erupted like a reliable Etna. And then there's the murder of Jan Kadar."

"Could have been a random attack."

I explained the connection I saw between his presence at Jane Doe's interrogation with the mystery figure in the hospital.

"Could be he was targeted for a completely different reason. May I suggest, V.I., that unless someone is paying you to find out why Kadar was murdered, you leave that to the homicide detectives? Despite the cretins at Homan Square, many Chicago cops know what they're doing. And there are thirteen thousand of them, versus one of you. You could hire some assistants, but then you'd need paying clients even more than you do now. Your quixotism is charming, but it doesn't pay your bills."

"I hope you're not worried about your own bill; you know I make payments every month to keep it under control. And I have life insurance dedicated to paying you. Along with my tab at the Golden Glow."

He laughed. "Vic, I trust you. I'm not worried about that, but you get in over your head faster than Houdini in a water tank. I'm one of the people who will be grieved beyond bearing if you die in the line of something that only you would see as a duty. And Jan Kadar's murder is way beyond anything you need to take on."

"Agreed," I said, but slowly. "Something the cops don't seem to have pursued is Jane Doe's roommate. The guy who used Kadar to interrogate Jane in Hungarian sent the roommate down the hall while they talked. She saw Kadar leave the room, and then he returned to eavesdrop."

"You're suggesting he heard something, tried to put the bite on the mystery interrogator, and was killed for his pains?" Freeman said. "Share that with the police, not with me. If—please see that 'if' in caps, boldface, underlined—that's what happened, all the more reason to make it police business."

I nodded. "I've done that, but it's another wrinkle

in this wadded-up fabric." I told him about Pizzello's sub-rosa visit to my office.

"They're on the case, then," Freeman said. "Leave Kadar to them."

"Okay," I said. "But the attack on Brad Litvak cuts close to me personally for a whole bunch of reasons. The one crime I turned up that could have been used to pressure Donny goes back to South Chicago and the errands Donny and his pals used to run for Valentine Tommaso. One of those pals is Tad Duda. Does that name ring any bells?"

"No. Doesn't mean he isn't a player, just that he isn't a player who's needed my expert advice. But if Duda crawls around the same rocks as the Viper, he is not a good man to know. I know the Viper retired to Florida, but his stock dividends aren't what pay for his beach-front estate. Stay away from that crowd. If you value your life, I mean."

He slipped between a semi and an outsize SUV and got off the Eisenhower. Traffic was supposedly lighter in the Covid era, but the Ike was always jammed.

"I'm going to file a formal complaint with the Police Review Board. As you know, that is unlikely to lead to any action against Coney, but it will put him in the public eye and make it harder for him to come after you again."

I nodded. It's why I use one of the city's most expensive lawyers: the name on his letterhead makes cops and states attorneys pay attention.

"There is one other thing," I said. "I've been trying to help a synagogue keep vandals at bay."

I told him about the attack on Shaamar Hashomayim. "Corky Ranaghan called me himself. He knew the synagogue had let the insurance lapse. He was offering to clean and repair the building in exchange for part ownership.

"Donny Litvak works for Klondike, in their supply and stockroom. He was laid off during the pandemic, but I assume they'll recall him when their office is running again. A day after Donny's son is roughed up, Corky calls me. Doesn't that seem strange?"

Freeman smiled sardonically. "If you do business with Corky, you'll be able to pay off my bill in no time. Unless he runs afoul of the feds. Rumor is, the Northern District prosecutor is sniffing around Klondike's reserves, but a clever solo op like you could probably save him."

Freeman pulled up in front of my office—I wanted to stop there first to see how much damage the search party down here had wrought. He drummed his fingers on the steering wheel.

"Kidding aside, Vic, Scott Coney could be doing

dirty work for any number of people, not just Corky. For Christ's sake, don't deliberately bait Coney. Today was painful and humiliating for you but not life-threatening. Stop before it is."

He came into the office with me, where he talked to Tessa about what the officers had done. He and Tessa's mother did pro bono work for the same civil rights organization, and so he knew Tessa personally.

"They mercifully left my studio alone," she said, "thanks to my mother showing up to make sure they followed the letter of the warrant. I think Mom kept them from doing damage to your office, too, Vic. It's a hard day at work when you'd rather see the robbers than the cops."

She was right. They'd opened a few drawers in my office but had left my computers in place. I'd have to sweep the machines for malware, but at least they hadn't impounded them.

I needed to get home, take a long bath to wash away the humiliation of the body search. Freeman dropped me at my apartment.

"I'm not billing you for the rescue, Vic. Like everyone with a criminal defense practice, I'm disturbed by the reports coming out of Homan. I wanted to see the place for myself." He got out to open the door for me.

"And, Vic, if you know where Jane Doe is hiding, get her someplace where she can be protected."

"If I knew, I'd tell you, but I truly do not, and I am truly scared about her safety."

"And the object the cops are hunting?"

"Scout's honor, Freeman, I have no idea what it is, let alone where it is."

Inside my building I found Mr. Contreras and the dogs, still agitated. I glossed over what had happened in Homan Square, but the mere knowledge that Coney had taken me away by force had only increased my neighbor's distress.

I went upstairs to bathe, and to make a stab at reorganizing my apartment. I collected all the sheet music. Much of it had been Gabriella's, and it enraged me that Coney had touched paper that she had handled. Thankfully, he hadn't gotten as far as the cupboard where I keep her Venetian wineglasses, but the kitchen was a mess. Flour, sugar, coffee, all spread on the countertop, where they spilled over onto the floor.

As I swept it up, I remembered Tillman bagging my sugar lumps as possible drugs. It would be so easy to plant something in my kitchen, among the cannisters or frozen food—anything Coney could use as an excuse to come for me down the road.

Or a listening device.

I went back down to Mr. Contreras. He was happy to share a late lunch with me—grilled cheese sandwiches. I used his phone to call a bug-sweeping company that I've used in the past, to arrange for them to inspect both my apartment and my office, and to deal with possible malware on my machines.

Since I'd gotten home, my phone had been dinging with texts, but I'd been too bruised in spirit to look at them. Now I finally opened my message app. Murray had been busy, posting the story of the assault by Coney and his crew, mostly through a dozen key photos he'd taken.

Friends had written, outraged on my behalf. Mr. Contreras's grandsons were horrified at seeing their grandfather in handcuffs. Another seven media outlets wanted comments from me. I started with Beth Blacksin at Global Cable News, since she'd covered my rescue of Jane Doe.

I had told no one about my middle-of-the-night phone call, the old woman who'd asked for Yulchia, and I didn't reveal it now. *You belong in restraints,* a man had said. If I publicized the call without knowing who she was or where she'd been calling from, she might be punished with even greater cruelty.

I did tell Beth that an entire posse of law enforcement agents wanted something that Jane Doe had. "No one believes the ER team at Beth Israel when they say they searched her clothes looking for a way to ID her and found nothing on her. And they don't believe me when I say she didn't speak to me or give me anything. You were there, Beth, when she was put into the ambulance; you have footage. Can you let the world see she was unconscious?"

"I can't believe you're asking that, Vic. When millions of Americans think Covid-19 is a hoax, how do you expect them to believe you and your Jane Doe aren't involved in some elaborate plot together?"

"Got it, Beth. I live on the wrong planet, the one that's spherical instead of flat. But whatever it is Jane Doe might have had, enough people want it that a kid who visited my office three days ago was beaten up by some toughs who were sure I'd handed him something."

That excited Beth: it was news no one else had. I gave her the broad outline, told her because the kid was a juvenile she needed the parents' permission to talk to him, and sicced her on Ashleigh.

My brain was as weary as my body. I lay down on my living room couch. A call from Ashleigh Breslau woke me about an hour later. She was predictably furious. Really, she was justifiably furious. I should have let her know that I'd given her name to Beth Blacksin. Really, I should have gotten her permission first. I lay still and let the tide of her anger wash over me, murmuring, "You're right," "I shouldn't have," "I won't do that again."

"Are you letting her interview Brad?" I finally asked.

"His name is Branwell. And no reporter is going to talk to him. Why did my son come to see you, really? Reggie said I shouldn't believe what Branwell said last night, but Branwell won't talk to me. Donny is so angry that he's moved into a studio apartment. Thanks to you, my family is falling apart."

"Yep, you all were humming along like Marmee and the March sisters until I entered your lives." I saw that Peter was calling from Spain and hung up with enough gracelessness that she could keep believing the worst of me.

18
Something's Bugging Me

My bug sweepers arrived while I was talking to Peter. I let them in and went down to the garden to be private with him. After Peter and I reluctantly ended our conversation, I drove down to Pilsen, to Gisela Queriga's home.

When Coney jumped me this morning, he knew I'd been at the rocks on Sheridan Road. This meant he'd put word out to patrol units to notify him if anyone saw me there.

In case he was still tracking me, I parked in the lot of a rehabilitation hospital on California Avenue. I wished I had time for some good physical therapy to restore my sore joints, but I stuck my phone in the trunk and walked the mile to Queriga's building.

When I knocked at her door, the door across the hall

opened. An enormously fat woman stepped into the hall. She looked at me with loathing.

"You're the person who is persecuting Señora Queriga? Thanks to you she moved away, quickly. And before you ask, I don't know where she went. She works hard, she looks after her three children. Her husband, he died of this corona virus, but that isn't good enough for you, is it? No, you have to go after her like a hunting dog." She bared her teeth and snapped them together, imitating a dog.

"Ma'am, I don't know your name, and I don't know any way to persuade you that I am not with ICE or any other government agency. I'm a private investigator. A woman—an old woman, by the sound of her voice—called me in the middle of the night, desperate for help. She used Señora Queriga's phone, and so I want to find out where Señora Queriga worked. Not to report her, either to her boss or to ICE, but to help me identify the frightened woman who phoned me for help."

I stopped, out of futility. The woman was continuing to make snapping noises, and when I set off down the hall to the stairwell, other people had come out of their apartments. I heard calls of "Shame!" And "Never come back to this building. We know how to treat informers here. Snitches get stitches."

The cops hated me, Ashleigh and Donny hated me.

So did Sonia. And now Gisela Queriga's neighbors hated me, too. Good thing I had my dogs. And Mr. Contreras. And Peter and Lotty and Sal. *Yeah, a lot of people depend on me. And like me. So there.*

The walk back to my car seemed depressingly long. I tried to take my mind off my worries by studying the mosaics glued to the sides of some of the houses and buildings. They were beautiful, intricate, jaguars and other Mexican images, but I wasn't in the mood for art appreciation.

When I finally reached home, I found a handwritten message from my bug sweepers. They'd located voice-activated trackers inside the lid to the piano and screwed into my bedside lamp. WE DIDN'T DISABLE THEM IN CASE YOU DIDN'T WANT YOUR EAVESDROPPERS TO KNOW YOU'D FOUND THEM.

It was an interesting suggestion. I didn't want Lieutenant Coney sleeping with me. I moved the bedside lamp into the bathroom and brought one in from the living room. Singing is a good exercise for spirit lifting. I stood next to the piano and worked on vocal exercises for twenty minutes, and then picked my way through *Vieni, o figlio* a dozen times, phrase by phrase. By the time I'd finished, Coney should have been able to sing at least the first twenty measures.

I had a recording of my mother singing it, a disc

created for me by yet another former lover. While I settled down at the dining room table with my laptop to finish an overdue report for an actual paying client, I played my mother's version and then another by Lorraine Hunt Lieberson.

As I was hitting the SEND button to whisk my report to my client, Murray called. I thanked him profusely for coming to my aid this morning.

"Thanks are great, Warshawski, but they don't pay the rent. What was Coney up to?"

"I'll call you right back," I assured him, hung up, flushed the toilet for verisimilitude, and went into the garden, where I sat on a little stone bench I'd given Mr. Contreras for his birthday.

I explained about the bugs I'd found. "I hope they haven't loaded malware onto my phone. I hope Coney didn't come prepared to be that invasive, so here's what I know."

I told him everything, except for the mysterious call from the woman begging me to find Yulchia. I even told him about Brad and Donny, about Brad's fears that his father was being pressured into doing something dangerous, and the ancient episode with the Litvak store van that had unnerved Boom-Boom and the twins.

"Tadeusz Duda?" Murray said. "He's not on my radar, but I'll do some digging. Cement is a wonderful front for Mob action. By the way, I know Mr. Contreras doesn't like me, but I love him. My photo display of him in cuffs, plus the recording of him haranguing the cops, has been around the globe a few times. It also landed me a big assignment with a British newspaper. They enjoy the chance to show what barbarians we are. I need more detail on Homan Square, though."

I told him about being propelled down a series of long dark corridors, hands cuffed behind me, at a speed designed to make me trip on the rough spots in the flooring. About the tiny room, the angry female officer who searched me, the weary overweight one who stood at the door to make sure I didn't bolt naked down the hall.

"Sorry I don't have intimate photos of the officer with her fingers inside me," I said drily.

Murray said it was a pity, with more wistfulness than a friend should display. I hung up and went down to check in with Mr. Contreras. When I told him his heroic stance in front of our building was now global news, he was greatly cheered. We found some of the links online, which he mailed to his buddies from his old machinists local.

"They keep saying you turned me into a communist or anarchist, so this will give them some new ammo," he chortled.

He wanted to feed me dinner, but I couldn't keep awake long enough to eat. I took Peppy upstairs with me and fell instantly into a deep sleep.

Peppy's frenzied barking yanked me awake at five the next morning. I pulled on jeans and followed her into the kitchen. She stood next to the door, hackles raised, tail up, sniffing, growling deep in her throat.

I grabbed a flashlight from the wall by the door. Undid the locks, crouched low, opened the door and rolled onto the deck. Peppy leapt over me to a corner of the deck and gave two sharp barks. She'd cornered the intruder and was waiting for my command.

"No!" It was a child, clutching the railing, looking over the side to see if it was safe to jump. "Don't let the dog bite me!"

I squatted next to Peppy and put an arm around her neck, shone my flashlight on the child.

"Is it Jazmin?" I asked. "Señora Queriga's daughter?"

She nodded, trembling.

"This is Peppy. I'm going to take her back into my apartment and put a leash on her. You're afraid of her, but both of us were afraid when we heard someone outside the door. Now that she sees you haven't come to hurt us, she won't try to hurt you. Okay?"

Jazmin nodded again, slowly, uncertain. I went back into the kitchen and leashed up the dog, took masks from a stack of disposables by the front door. After another nervous moment, checking to make sure Peppy wasn't going to break away from me, the girl followed us into the kitchen. I put on a mask and handed one to Jazmin, who took it in surprise but put it on.

I turned on my stereo, playing my mother's disc again, switching on a speaker I had in the kitchen. I wasn't sure how sensitive Coney's transmitters were, but I hoped he'd assume I had insomnia.

"Jazmin, is your mother in trouble? Is that why you're here?"

"We moved in a hurry. We thought you were ICE. When I read your note to my mother, she was scared, and Tía Renata, the lady across the hall, she said we should move out fast before you came back with police."

I'd put Jazmin in a chair by the door so that she knew she could leave if she didn't feel safe, but she was still gripping the edges of the seat, watching me with eyes made large by fear.

"I understand," I said reassuringly. "These days in this country, it's hard to know who you can trust."

Her grip on the chair eased slightly. "Then we saw you on the news. We saw the police take you away in—" She fumbled for words, lifting her hands to circle her right wrist with her left hand.

"Handcuffs," I supplied.

She nodded. "We watched all the stories they told about you, a man and a woman both telling stories, how you are a detective who helps poor people, not someone with the police. And finally, my mother, she said we should tell you what you want to know. We should come before she goes to work, come while it is still dark and people can't spy on us."

"Where is your mother?"

"She is waiting. Outside your garden. She doesn't speak good English, so I am here."

I nodded. "My mother also didn't speak English very well. I often did what you are doing, translated for her."

She smiled shyly, glad to meet an adult who understood something of her world.

"How did you find my apartment?" I asked.

"In the pictures, you can read the number of your building behind the old man in the handcuffs. And so I came first to the front door to see which floor you are on, which side of the floor, and then we came around to the back, so that I didn't ring the bell."

"You are a very smart girl," I said. "That was very clever."

She didn't smile, but sat a little straighter and produced a piece of paper out of her jeans pocket. "If you didn't come outside with the dog, I was going to leave this message. My *mami* works at the Archangel Senior Living Home in Northfield. She is the person who looks after old people who have lost their—their memories. It is sad work, and also hard, but it is a job that American peoples don't like to do, and so we can eat. My *papi*, he drove a truck, which is better money, but he died from the virus, and so it is just *Mami*, and the little boys, and me."

"I'm very sorry you lost your father. This is a cruel disease."

She shrugged. Why state something so obvious?

"Someone at Archangel called me using your mother's phone. Does your mother know who that was?"

Jazmin shook her head. "They don't tell her. She gets home, her phone is missing. The next day she goes to her supervisor—she thinks she leave—left—her phone maybe in the toilet. The supervisor tells her *Mami* gave it to a patient and she should be fired, but because of the virus they need her to still be working. And then they put her phone on the table, take a hammer, and—bam!—they smash her phone. So now she has my phone, but she cannot call me because I have no phone, so I don't know, is she safe, is she coming home? Now I have to leave. It takes her one hour and one half to get to her job and she cannot be late."

My mouth twisted, involuntary response to brutality. Even the smallest person with the smallest kingdom can revel in cruelty.

"Okay, Jazmin, let's get you back to your mother. And get you safe to your new home. We'll be quiet walking down the stairs so no neighbors come to see us."

We made it to the back gate without rousing anyone, not even Mitch, who was in Mr. Contreras's apartment. Señora Queriga was waiting in the alley with the two younger children. She had a whispered exchange with Jazmin in Spanish, adamantly refused my offer to drive her to work or take the children to their new home. I waited with Peppy until they reached the mouth of the alley, then followed at a discreet distance, staying in the shadows until I saw them safely onto the L platform at Sheffield.

19
Closing Ranks

Dawn was sticking her rosy fingers through the cloud cover when Peppy and I returned home. I pulled some espresso shots and looked up the Archangel Senior Living Home in Northfield. They were part of a chain of private nursing homes and senior centers, a sprawling empire that covered much of the northern half of the United States, with a thick cluster of locations in Chicago's affluent suburbs.

At Archangel, we welcome the chance to show you how exciting a new beginning in Life's Journey can be, their homepage proclaimed. The website showed a white couple whose faces were radiant with joy at the chance to live in an Archangel facility. They were golfing, while a Black couple, in a smaller photo, were gardening in front of a town house.

If I was ready for a new beginning at the Northfield complex, I could move into one of the town houses or condos at the facility's west end. These overlooked a golf course and were connected to the outside world, where all the shops you might desire were a short distance away.

If my journey took me to a place where I needed extra support, I could choose from a variety of floor-plans in their assisted-living units. If I injured myself in one of the strenuous outings they organized for seniors, doctors affiliated with St. Helena's would see I got world-class care, followed by a stay in Archangel's nursing home.

On the east end of the complex, close to the express-way, was the "memory care" building, where every effort would be made to keep me going in the most vibrant way possible. The progression from golf to grave seemed profoundly depressing.

I opened a map app and looked at a satellite view. The facility covered a lot of ground, what with the golf course and everything. While the whole complex was enclosed by fencing, with guard stations at four entrances, it should be relatively easy to breach such a sprawling place—especially with a golf course that allowed public memberships in addition to Archangel residents. Trouble was, I didn't know who I was looking for, beyond an elderly woman who'd recently been threatened with restraints.

I knew it was a leap, but I kept imagining that the woman who'd called me was Jane Doe's Hungarian *Nagyi*. If I could get a patient roster, I could research the backgrounds of everyone on it and find the Hungarians.

Lotty called as I was mulling over the problem. Like Señora Queriga, she had seen Murray's and Beth Blacksin's reports of my detention. I took my coffee out to the garden so I could speak freely. Having those bugs in my home made me feel as though I had been invaded by rats and roaches at the same time.

"That was a shocking sight to wake up to, Victoria. Thank God you're safely back home. Were you harmed in any way?"

"Psychically bruised but physically fine. I'm angry about the whole event, but baffled, too. Why are the cops so focused on Jane Doe and some item they think she had with her? Someone in the city with a lot of power must have enlisted the police to pressure me, and to find the girl, but since I have no idea what they're looking for, I can't begin to guess who's applying the pressure."

Lotty and I hadn't spoken for several days. I also told

her about the middle-of-the-night call from a woman at Archangel.

"Is there any way you could get me a patient list from that place?"

"No. There's no pretext that could justify my asking for it. Find someone you know in the Illinois Department of Health—someone who's willing to violate HIPAA laws for you."

"Right. You're right, of course. What about the Jan Kadar murder? Have the police made any headway?"

"I don't know, Victoria. There's a surfeit of horrifying deaths in the world, and I avoid the details as much as possible. Cynthia will know. Poor thing, she can't afford my delicate news appetite."

We agreed to meet for dinner this evening in her condo. Max would provide wine and a meal prepared by his housekeeper.

When we'd hung up, I called Cynthia. It was after eight; she was at her desk. Like everyone else, she'd seen me on the news and asked if I was okay.

I repeated the reply I'd given Lotty, but said I was calling in the hopes that she'd show the video footage to the cops assigned to the ER. I wanted to find out if Coney or one of his team was the person who'd used Jan Kadar as a Hungarian interpreter when he interviewed Jane Doe.

"I don't know, Vic. If I talk to them, they'll assume the request comes from the hospital and this could cause bad will between us and them."

"From looking at pictures?"

"From looking at pictures of other officers. There's a lot of protest against having cops in the ER, and some of it's justified, but sometimes, too, someone comes in trying to attack a patient who was injured in a fight. Or they want to hurt a doctor who they think didn't look after their family right. We need that police backup, and we need them on our side."

She was right. It was frustrating to have so many friends who were so law-abiding, but there was always Murray. I called to see if he would play the videos from my assault for Brad Litvak.

"He didn't get a good look at his assailants," I said, "but he heard them talking. Maybe he can recognize their voices. It's worth a try—it's hard to believe there are two sets of weasels running around town attacking people connected to Jane Doe."

Murray was delighted to get more deeply involved in the investigation. It would make his piece for the *Edge*—the British journal that had commissioned his story—more intimate and so more compelling.

"You're on his mother's bad side," he added, "which gives me a good entry point. We'll have fun dissecting your recklessness. I'll tell her how I almost died last spring because I signed on to one of your ideas. No, maybe I'd better not go that far. She's likely to put her precious baby into a carriage and wheel him across the Canadian border. We'll stick to how you trample all over other people's feelings."

"I guess that's supposed to be funny," I said sourly. "Anyway, whatever gets the job done."

I made another stab at cleaning up the mess Coney had created in my kitchen. I was going to abandon it again when it occurred to me that he hadn't been wearing a mask or gloves. I needed to do a deep clean. I hoped I hadn't picked up a nasty germ from bouncing around in his squad car, but at least I could sanitize my home.

I took Peppy down to Mr. Contreras so she wouldn't have to breathe in disinfectant and put an hour's hard work into sweeping and scrubbing, making my kitchen sparkle and smell of Clorox. It was strangely satisfying. My friends and I couldn't meet for basketball these days. Perhaps I could take up housework as a competitive sport.

Before I left for my office, I locked the laptop into the wall safe in my closet. Coney hadn't plunged that deep into my home. There'd been nothing subtle about him, and the shoe bag that hangs in front of the safe hadn't been disturbed. I keep my mother's diamond drop earrings in the safe, plus my condo title and my Smith & Wesson.

I looked at the gun for a long moment but locked the safe back up without taking it out. Right now, the only person on my tail whom I could ID was a Chicago police lieutenant who would face no repercussions if he shot a civilian, especially one who was carrying a weapon.

Cynthia called as I was driving to my office. "Vic, I decided to talk to the police in the ER, to see if they had any leads on the Kadar murder. A lot of the staff are badly scared, and I wanted to see if they had made an arrest. The group on duty last week had been rotated out, and this new batch didn't know anything."

She'd asked the ER administrator for the names of last week's roster, under cover of wanting follow-up on Kadar's death. "She said that the cops check in when they come on duty, but we don't log their names. The police are responsible for keeping track of who's here. If you want to talk to last week's group, you'll have to call the station yourself."

I called Sergeant Pizzello at the Twentieth.

"This is the police department, Warshawski, not the library. We aren't a public information service."

"Sergeant, if my local library could tell me which

officers were on duty at Beth Israel last week, I'd be talking to them, not to you. You know we're trying to ID the man who took the janitor with him to interview our Jane Doe. He talked to the cops on duty at Beth Israel when he arrived. They're the only people who saw his face. I have some photos of possible suspects for them to look at."

This made her angry. "You are the most arrogant PI I've ever met. You and you alone can solve a homicide with no DNA, no fingerprints, no security camera intel? Don't call me again unless you have real information, not a wish list. Besides, we don't work homicides out of the Twentieth. As you'd know if you knew anything about policing in Chicago."

She hung up. I paced around my office. I'm the daughter of a man who served forty-two years with Chicago's finest. I grew up with cops. *You think I don't know Chicago policing? I spent two hours at Homan Square yesterday and I know way more than I want to about Chicago policing.*

That kind of venting doesn't solve anything. I sat down at my desk to answer emails, but I couldn't put my anger away. My lawyer had urged me to leave the Kadar murder to the police, but despite their superior numbers, I had a big advantage over them: I wasn't nervous about fingering someone in the CPD if he was the guilty party.

I could see Cynthia's point, though. If an outsider to the force tried to get the crew at the hospital to finger another cop, they'd all close ranks and become thirteen thousand hostile people with guns and tasers.

With that helpful thought, I set to work on the photos of Coney and his two officers. I didn't doctor their faces, but I changed their clothes—took the uniformed men out of uniform and put them in jeans and Ts. I gave Coney a gangster-wannabe look, black jeans, black bomber jacket. Like cleaning my kitchen, it was hard work, but it was even more satisfying.

I sent them to Finchley with the suggestion that his homicide investigators show them to the cops who'd been at Beth Israel when Kadar was taken up to try Hungarian on my Jane Doe.

Finchley called back within the hour. "Vic, what are you trying to do? Get the entire force on your butt instead of three or four of us?"

"I'm trying to eliminate possibilities in the Kadar murder. Why is a senior officer so invested in tracking down a missing girl? Or rather, why is he so invested in some object she might have been carrying that he was willing to beat me, subject me to a cavity search, and trash my home? He's violent enough to kill anyone who crosses him. He's had forty-three registered accusations of excessive force, and who knows how many people were too scared to come forward with additional accusations?"

"That's my point, Vic. I don't know why I care whether you get beaten so badly that you spend the rest of your life as a vegetable, but that happened to someone who got in Coney's way three years ago. Yet here Coney is, not just on the force, but heading a special unit. If he was involved in Kadar's death, showing his photo around a district is not going to get him arrested and convicted. It's only going to goad him into going after you with a bigger, heavier weapon than his bare hands. And may I point out, Kadar's death is a CPD investigation. We have the resources for this—not just the technology, but a dozen cops trying to keep a hospital safe. Go work on the crimes that require your unique brand of creativity."

He hung up before I could answer. At least he hadn't told me to play with dolls, although the last comment veered in that direction. He was right about Coney, though. My unique brand of creativity often involves stirring a pot hard enough to see what rises to the top, but in Coney's case, I already knew what was there.

20
Wet Blanket

Dinner with Max and Lotty got off to a bumpy start. When I told them about my conversations with Pizzello and Finchley, they came down hard on the police side.

"Victoria, I've met with Chief Superintendent Eckhardt every morning since Kadar's murder," Max said. "They are working hard on this. If you get involved it will be like—like sticking a spear through the spokes of a bicycle in the Tour de France. Everyone will collapse in disarray."

"It's shocking, and deplorable, that you and this young man were molested," Lotty said. "But, Victoria, please be realistic. If the police are really covering up a major crime, you can get yourself seriously wounded physically, on top of the degradation of a strip search."

She put her hands on my arms. "Please remember that I love you, and others do as well, and take yourself out of harm's way."

That was an unanswerable argument. I nodded acquiescence, a lump in my throat, and helped myself to the dinner laid out on Lotty's sideboard.

Max's housekeeper was a fine cook. Over roasted halibut with spinach and a dry Ligurian white, I calmed down, listened to Max and Lotty's music talk, contributed Peter's progress exploring the Phoenician ruins at Malaga. Only over dessert did I revert to my questions about Jane Doe. I'd told Lotty about the call from the woman at Archangel, but Max hadn't heard.

He shook his head, troubled. "We try not to send our patients to Archangel for nursing care. Actually, to any for-profit home. The f-ps don't staff as well as the public homes. They also have almost double the Covid deaths as public facilities. Archangel caters to a wealthy set of seniors in their retirement homes and assisted-living units, but for their nursing homes, they go after Medicaid patients aggressively because Medicaid will pay the bills without auditing the services.

"I'm sorry if you heard from a woman in distress in their Northfield office, but you absolutely must not violate patient privacy in your efforts to find her. Thinking you're justified because an old woman called you out of the blue means you think your judgment is better than the law. And we've just gone through four years of seeing how dangerous that attitude is."

"Besides, Victoria," Lotty chimed in, "you have to imagine other possibilities than the one you want it to be. You were in the news, rescuing the girl. This could be a patient with cognitive issues who was alert enough to steal a phone, alert enough to get your old landline number out of directory assistance, but is having delusions about needing to be rescued."

"It was the anger in the voice of the man who took the phone from her," I protested. "Putting her in restraints for making a call."

Max nodded sympathetically. "People with power can be gratuitously cruel. But this is a situation where you have no information. For everyone's well-being, unless you have concrete proof, you need to step aside."

They were right, of course they were, but their duet of criticism left me feeling depressed and isolated. I'd walked to Lotty's, since Max always brought delicious wine and I like to drink it. I walked home, hurt by the criticism and confused about my own judgment. If Max and Lotty both opposed me, maybe I really did have an outsize sense of my abilities.

One of the problems with working alone is you don't have colleagues to bounce ideas around with.

Murray was kind of a teammate, though, and he was eager to be involved. As I walked, I called him to see how Brad had reacted when Murray played the recordings for him.

"Frustrating," he said. "Ashleigh sat in on the interview and kept hijacking it, wanting to talk about her son's lack of trust in her. In her head, you encouraged him to turn on her. When I finally was able to play the recording all the way through, Brad said the men confronting you were scary enough to be his attackers, but he couldn't be sure the voices were the same."

"I guess that's just as well." I told him about my dinner conversation, including Max's fear that I'd derail the police investigation by interfering—and Finchley's and Pizzello's trenchant statements on my arrogance.

"Warshawski, I won't disagree. You're arrogant, you trust your judgment more than you trust the cops. Hell, you don't trust me enough. But look at the numbers: the CPD has a forty percent homicide clear rate. I've been working with you and against you for years, and I can count your failures on one hand. Okay, maybe seven fingers. Just don't be stupid in this situation. Coney is not a good person to bait. But don't start second-guessing yourself too much. *Capisce?*"

"*Capisco*," I said, smiling a little.

"Oh, before I go—Donny's old pal, Tadeusz Duda,

who took over Tommaso Cement from the Viper? Tommaso isn't doing well."

"Yeah, I saw that when I looked at Tad's financials. He was threatened with a lawsuit over a garage floor that collapsed." I was walking along Addison, but the traffic noise made it hard to hear. I turned onto a narrow side street and sat on the bottom step of one of the old graystones there.

"The uptick in construction right now is giving him some breathing room," Murray said. "Everyone needs projects finished by yesterday, so he's getting jobs he wouldn't usually have access to. I talked to a guy I know at Suntasch, and he said someone had pressured them into taking a bid from Duda. They're not happy, because his quality is uneven."

Suntasch was one of the biggest contractors in northern Illinois. "Your source doesn't know who applied the pressure?" I asked.

"No. Of course I pushed hard on that."

"Do you think the Viper is still a player?" Construction, particularly cement, is a perennial Mob front.

"Could be," Murray said slowly, thinking it over. "But whether or not the Viper is still Duda's godfather, Duda is in trouble. And guys in trouble do mean and ugly things."

"Noted," I said. "Donny Litvak is in financial

trouble, too. Mostly because he's been laid off, not because he's running up big bills. He worked at Klondike, though, and he probably stays in touch with his old coworkers. Maybe Duda is pressuring Donny into giving his cement company early access to new projects."

"This is shaping up to be a great story," Murray said. "I can smell the Pulitzer committee reading my prose. I will dedicate the prize to you, O High Empress among all the detectives in the six counties."

I got up again. "Put it in a moving speech at my funeral. That might make Peter Sansen or even Lotty less cross with me."

Murray laughed, but as I headed west again on Addison, I felt a prickling at the base of my skull, the sensation you have when the Mob is painting a bull's-eye there, right before the bullet hits. Since I couldn't imagine a new career, I'd better start thinking harder, faster, better.

I had four undeniable facts: Brad had been attacked by thugs looking for a mysterious something. I'd been attacked by the cops looking for a mysterious something. Jane Doe had run away from Beth Israel after being interrogated, with Jan Kadar translating. Jan Kadar had been murdered, and in a terrifying fashion. Jane was still missing, and with every passing day, the odds she was still alive were shrinking.

I didn't see the point of trying to get Brad to remember more about his father's phone call. It's rare for anyone to remember the exact language another person has used, even ten minutes after hearing it. We were almost four weeks out from what he'd overheard, and he'd layered plenty of emotion over it in the meantime.

I was about a quarter mile from home when my phone dinged. An incoming text from Mr. Contreras. Where are you? Get home right now!

I didn't take time to reply, but sprinted the last few blocks. I stopped across the street from my building, checking for signs of trouble—squad cars, Coney, men in ski masks lurking in the shrubs along the walk. I didn't see anything. Ran up the walk, keys out, but my neighbor had been on the watch.

"You get in here, doll. This boy is in trouble and he says you're the only one he'll talk to."

He propelled me into his living room. Brad Litvak was in the mustard-colored armchair, wrapped in blankets. His hair was wet, and he was shivering, despite the blankets. The dogs were nuzzling him, heads on his lap.

I knelt next to the chair. "Hey, Brad. What's going on? How'd you get here?"

"Bike." His teeth were chattering; he squeezed out the one word.

"He's been like that since he got here. He was ring-ing your bell and the dogs were barking. Of course that new couple across the hall from you, the Clingers or whatever they call themselves, they're shouting down the stairwell to shut the dogs up before they call the cops. Anyway, I go see what's going on and here's this poor kid, soaking wet. I got him dried off, put some clean clothes on him, but he's kind of in shock. Said he'd talk to you but not anybody else."

"Something hot to drink," I said. "Tea? Hot milk?"

"Should've thought of that myself. Hope I ain't get-ting old or nothin'." Mr. Contreras disappeared into his kitchen.

I started chafing Brad's hands, rubbing some warmth into them. I didn't ask him anything, just kept up a line of quiet chat, the history of how I got Peppy, the time Mitch had jumped up after a squirrel and landed in the crotch of a tree, six feet off the ground.

"He was still a puppy, and he was terrified to find himself up there. I had to get a box to stand on so I could lift him down."

Mr. Contreras returned with a cup of hot milk. "Honey in it, that's what my wife used to give our girl Ruthie when she was sick. You drink it up, son, and tell Vic here what's got you so upset."

The warmth of the blankets, the unchallenging attention my neighbor and I were paying him, the sweet hot drink calmed him down. He stopped shivering and let the blanket around his shoulders fall open. Mr. Contreras had given him one of his flannel work shirts, which was too wide in the shoulders and a good three inches too short in the wrists.

"How did you get wet?" I asked.

"The river," he said. "I was pushed into the river."

"The Chicago River?" I repeated. I shut my eyes, trying to visualize the river's path through the northwest side. "Over in Forest Glen?"

"No, not up by me! Why would anyone push me in up there?" He was shouting, impatient at my slowness. "I was down in the city. At Chicago Avenue."

"Take me through it, a step at a time," I said. "Assume I know nothing, because, in fact, I know nothing."

"It's my mother," he muttered. "You know, that reporter came to talk to me today. I don't remember his name, but he said you were friends."

"Murray Ryerson," I supplied.

"Did Ryerson push you into the river?" Mr. Contreras was always willing to believe the worst of Murray.

"No, no," Brad said. "It was this man, I don't know his name."

"Your mother," I said. "She wouldn't let you talk to Murray?"

"She was okay with that at first, but then she wrecked it. The reporter, he had this recording, the one of the police arresting you. Of course, I already saw it, it was all over the Net yesterday. And my mother, she said you deserved to have cops beat you up. If you were soliciting business from minors, you should be arrested. So everything got more confused. You know the reporter, Murray, he wanted me to listen to a video?"

I nodded. "I wondered if those were the men who assaulted you four days ago. You didn't get a good look at their faces, but I thought you might recognize their voices."

"Mom kept interrupting, and so it took a while, but when the reporter finally played it all the way through, I couldn't tell. You know how angry guys all sound pretty much alike, so after all the interruptions and everything I wasn't sure of anything. When Murray left, I had this big fight with my mom. I didn't want to tell her the real reason I came to see you, especially now Dad moved out, so I yelled at her to mind her own business. She's always all over my business without paying any attention to what I say, or what I want, like with my name!"

His face flushed with indignation and it took a few minutes to get him back to the main story.

"Yeah, well, then we didn't talk the rest of the day. But tonight—I told you how she gets all dressed up to go out at night, right? So she got dressed up, and I thought this time I'd follow her. Like if I got a photo of whoever she was meeting, I could get her to shut up about all this stuff, about Dad, and calling me Branwell, and everything."

"On your bike," I said. "How'd you manage that?"

"The app where you can track people who are in your pod, and of course both my parents are in mine. So she took off, and I followed. It took me forever! Like over an hour, even pedaling hard. I kept losing her, because she was on the expressway, but she got off at Chicago Avenue, and then I found her car outside this house, this amazing house right on the river."

Mr. Contreras let me use his computer to open a map app. Brad showed us the route he'd taken from his home down to Chicago Avenue, and then to a thumb of land that stuck into the river underneath the Chicago Avenue bridge.

All that part of town used to be an industrial hub because it was on the river and close to the central city. These days, the area is a funny mix, with industry and transit depots on one side of the river, while the old warehouses on the other bank have been turned into high-end condos. I saw from the map that the industrial side of the river housed a number of cement factories, including Tommaso's.

The mansion Brad had visited faced Tommaso's across one arm of the river. The house seemed to have a substantial garden around it, separating it from old industry and new development both. Brad showed me on the map a small private drive that led from Halsted Street to the house.

"There were lights on inside, on the ground floor, so I crept up to look. I thought it would be a house Mom was staging. You know, everything cleaned and painted with fancy artwork and shit. But this place was kind of, I don't know—it was someone's home, but not real well looked after. Like, things could have been expensive when they were new, but no one was taking care of them. So I thought maybe the guy was showing Mom the house so she could start making her staging plans.

"Anyway, Mom and this guy had the curtains open, because the room faced the river. I guess they liked the view and they figured no one could see them. They were drinking wine and laughing, and then they started—he took her—anyway—I lost it, I took a picture, and the flash went off and the guy came out—it all happened so fast—he said he knew how to deal with scummy private eyes and he grabbed me and shoved me into the river.

"Some homeless man, he showed up and helped me get out. He thought I should call the cops, but I was afraid—of everything. And anyway, I lost my phone in the river. The lights in the house were turned off, too. So I got on my bike and came here because I didn't know where else to go."

He was making a massive effort not to cry. I didn't touch him—that could make him feel belittled.

"There's a lot to be afraid of," I said calmly. "What if the cops who took the 911 call were the same ones who attacked you? Or what if they went after your mother? You're fighting with her but you don't want her arrested."

He nodded, gulped back his sobs. I put the mug of milk into his hands and he obediently emptied the cup.

"How did you find me?" I asked. "I didn't think I told you where I lived."

Like Jazmin Queriga this morning, he'd seen it on Murray's video.

"I had to keep asking directions on account of I didn't have my phone," he added. "So after everything I went through, I don't even have the picture of the man with Mom."

21
Parental Notification

Mr. Contreras and I agreed that Brad should spend the night in my neighbor's place. I could have driven him home, but he was worn to the bone and didn't need a long confrontation with his mother.

Brad said Ashleigh's back had been to the window, so he didn't think she'd spotted him outside the mansion. Even so, he didn't want to try to explain to her what he'd been up to. Since he'd lost his phone in the river, I got him to use Mr. Contreras's to send his mother a text, which said succinctly, Spending night with friend. See you tomorrow.

Mr. Contreras's daughter used to send her two sons to stay with him, and he had bunkbeds set up in a side room for them. While he found a spare toothbrush and clean pajamas for Brad, I took his filthy clothes down to the basement and put them in the washing machine.

When I brought his bike inside, Mr. Contreras told me that Ashleigh kept calling, wanting to know Mr. Contreras's name, and whether her son was safe, and demanding to talk to Branwell.

"I don't want to lie to the lady," he said. "He's her boy, after all. She should know he's safe."

Mr. Contreras was right, but before I could think of a way to convince Ashleigh her son was safe and yet to leave him alone, she called me.

"Do you have my son? Have you kidnapped him as part of your plan to turn him against me?"

"Ashleigh, hi. I just got home. Your son showed up at my place while I was out. He had an exhausting night. He rode his bike all the way from your home into the city. He had an accident, fell into the river over by Goose Island. When he got out, he came to me for help. Right now, he's asleep in my downstairs neighbor's spare room."

There was a long silence at the other end of the line, and then she said, "Did he say why he was at Goose Island?"

It was revealing that she asked that before she wanted to know how he'd gotten out of the river.

"You'd have to ask him that," I said. "All I can tell

you is he was wet and frightened. He lost his phone when he fell into the water, so he borrowed one from Mr. Contreras—my downstairs neighbor—to text you. It didn't occur to him to give you a long story, but he really is fine."

"A doctor should see him. He could get typhus or cholera from that river!"

"If these were normal times, I would take him to a hospital ER," I said. "But in these times, since he has no symptoms, he could wait as long as ten or twelve hours to see an overworked nurse or doctor. He also could easily be exposed to Covid while he waited. Would you like me to take him to my doctor in the morning?"

"I don't trust any doctor you would visit. Bring him home now and I'll get our doctor to see him."

"His clothes are still wet, Ms. Breslau. It will be after midnight by the time they've gone through the dryer. He had a pretty big shock tonight. You're his mother, of course, but he's sleeping soundly and it would be best for his health if he got a full night's sleep. Do you want to come here to see him right now, to make sure my neighbor is a safe person for him to stay with?"

She paused again, possibly debating a second cross-town drive tonight, but decided to trust Mr. Contreras; she'd be at my building first thing in the morning to collect her son. Before she ended the call, she asked again if Brad had said what he was doing down by the river.

"I was more concerned about how he landed in the river," I said. "He thinks someone pushed him. I guess homeless people live there. Maybe he got too close to someone's hideout."

I heard a sharp intake of breath, but she didn't speak. I added soothingly, "Mr. Contreras made sure Brad took a hot shower to wash off the river grime. And your son says he has a few bruises, from banging into the stanchions as his good Samaritan pulled him out, but nothing broken or bleeding."

I cut the connection and blocked her number. I'd unblock it in the morning, but I didn't want her calling me every half hour, trying to find out if her son had seen her in the mystery man's arms.

It occurred to me that Donny also had a right to know about his son's traumatic experience. I expected another dose of vitriol from him, but he surprised me by his resigned, almost depressed reaction to my call. He gave a short riff on how I'd been butting my nose into Brad's business and making him distrust his parents, but it felt like a pro forma performance.

Donny said he'd seen me on TV, he didn't like seeing anyone beat up by the cops, but maybe now I understood why Donny and Sonia didn't trust Chicago cops or their daughters. The words were angry, but his rant lacked conviction.

Like his wife, Donny also wanted to know why Brad had been over by the river at all. "Someone lured him down there, didn't they?"

"I don't know, Donny. He said it took over an hour to bike there from your house. Who would have a powerful enough hold on him to get him to make that trip?"

"That's what I want to know," he said roughly. "Did you?"

"No, Donny. Brad riding to Goose Island, going into the river—that was a big surprise to me. He's asleep now, but you can ask him all that in the morning."

Unlike Ashleigh, he didn't question the wisdom of having Brad spend the night with my neighbor. He even gave me a grudging thanks for taking care of his son. "If he'd gone home, Ashleigh would have driven him round the bend with her questions and accusations. I'll be by in the morning to pick him up."

I didn't tell him Ashleigh was also coming in the morning. It would be good for Brad if both parents showed their concern. Maybe Brad's dousing would lead to one of those Hallmark moments, where the family embraced each other and realized how lucky they were to have one another. Or maybe not.

I put Brad's clothes in the dryer and went up to my

own place. I took my laptop from the safe and looked up the house where Brad said he'd seen his mother. It had been built in the 1880s by a Rudolph Zigler, whose glass factory had been on the island. While most of the robber barons built mansions near the lake, Zigler liked to be in walking distance from his works, but his house was still a statement of wealth and power. Three stories, built of granite, five fireplaces framed with hand-painted Dutch tiles and walnut mantels, five bathrooms with a complex water filtration system that allowed him to draw directly from the river.

When Zigler died, the house passed to his only child, a daughter who'd married a man named Augustus. Augustus had taken the Zigler name, apparently because in those days the glassworks were internationally famous. The family fortune disappeared in the Great Depression, and neither his daughter nor her husband had much of a head for business or interest in maintaining the property, but they clung to the house and left it to their eldest son, Augustus Junior.

The article didn't tell me much more about the family, but a title search showed that the current owner was a Silvia Zigler; the house had stayed in the family.

22
Return to Manderley

In the morning, when I brought Brad's clean clothes to Mr. Contreras's apartment, Brad was still asleep, or at least still in bed. I warned my neighbor to expect the warring parents and drove to the Zigler mansion with the dogs.

The Chicago Avenue bridge went right over the house, so I'd driven past it thousands of times, but I'd never noticed it. I crossed the river and bumped my way down the pitted access road, passing under heavy-duty pylons and over old trolley tracks that had been used to roll goods on and off barges. My Mustang stood out in the knot of cement trucks and delivery vans. A couple of drivers honked and gave me a high sign, admiring my muscle car.

I drove cautiously to the house, not wanting to wreck my tires on the rubble that littered the island. The house stood alone, surrounded by a circular garden. The property was large—house and garden must have filled the best part of two acres. In the beginning, the garden had probably been carefully thought out. You could see the remnants of bushes and paths, but neglect had taken a major toll. Branches torn by storms hung at crazy angles from the trees. Vines crawled up the pillars of the portico over the front door. I found a driveway leading to an underground garage. That, at least, was clear, showing that someone was using it. I wondered how the Ziglers kept water out of the garage and the basement. The original Mr. Zigler must have used some advanced engineering when the house was constructed.

I left the car on the tarmac at the south side of the property. All along the east and north sides, a fence left a gap of no more than a yard between the garden and the Chicago River.

The river split like a Y at the lip of land where the house stood. The east arm of the water ran past high-end condos on the east bank. The Greyhound bus depot stood on the east arm, directly across from the north side of the house.

Next to the station stood the Tommaso Cement Works. A billboard attached to the top announced CHICAGO RIDES ON US. It was so old that the phone number didn't include an area code.

I skirted the garden fence, edging along a narrow lip of concrete until I could look directly into the Tommaso works. A green Ford pickup stood in the yard, with SUNTASCH stenciled onto the side. A sunburned man with sun-bleached hair was in the yard, talking to someone out of my sight range. I didn't think that was Tad Duda; I remembered him as being dark.

Suntasch was big enough to handle the massive projects Klondike underwrote. Interesting that one of their crew was in Duda's yard. It made me wonder again about whether Duda had pressured Donny into feeding him early information on Klondike projects.

I made my way back along the river's edge to the mansion's front gate. The greenish-gray water looked viscous. Styrofoam slabs and plastic bottles on the surface might have been suspended in half-set cement rather than water. I shuddered, thinking of Brad landing in this cesspool. The concrete path between the garden gate and the water was so narrow that it would have been easy to knock him into the river. In several spots I had to walk heel-to-toe to stay on the path.

Just south of the house, the Chicago Avenue bridge

crossed the river. All the time I'd been looking around the perimeter, I'd been aware of the sound of traffic, and of the bridge itself, which was old and rusty. The joins shook noisily, and the roadbed bounced under the weight of the traffic. I hoped the Chicago Department of Transportation had performed recent stress tests on the bridge.

Like all the river bridges, it had originally been a drawbridge, which accounted for the number of seams in the girders. A disused tender house, overgrown with moss, was built into the southwest corner of the bridge. It might have been the model for a castle keep in an old history book. A little house stood on top, but down at ground level, you could see the concrete cylinder that housed the bridge gears.

The banks on both sides were lined with thick concrete overlaid with corrugated iron. It probably hadn't looked this depressing when Zigler built the house, but why had his heirs stayed here, amid the growing grime and noise, instead of joining the rest of the plutocracy on the North Shore of Lake Michigan?

The dogs were whining and pawing, eager to get into the garden to pursue its wildlife. When I opened the unlocked gate, I was surprised to feel a sense of peace, despite the tangled vines and overgrown shrubs. I hadn't expected this wilderness to feel like such an oasis, with the expressway overhead and industrial wasteland all around. I could even hear birds calling to each other from the heavy tree branches.

A flagstone path led to the house. I tripped several times on the roots that had grown through the stones. I passed unclipped rosebushes, dead plants, and more of the island's detritus.

The dogs found the scene rich with promise. I let go of their leashes, and they took off into the bushes barking at each other. *Here's a water rat! Here's a mole hole!*

Brad hadn't mentioned seeing anyone except his mother and her companion. I wondered where Silvia Zigler was. It's possible she'd been there, not visible from the outside, but I didn't think so: the house had the unmistakable feel of a place that's standing empty.

Ashleigh was a stager for the Tricorn & Beck real estate company. Maybe last night's meeting really had been part business—an inspection of the premises so Ashleigh could decide how to tart up the place. I didn't see a For Sale sign anywhere, but that didn't mean anything—you'd have to be told the house was here before you'd know to arrange for a viewing.

Brad had looked into the windows facing across the river to the east bank, which was dense with high-end condos. In daytime, the path on the east side was full of joggers, dogs, toddlers and their minders, coming in and out of the condos. Ashleigh and her pal had run a risk, cavorting in full view of the mansion's bare windows.

I found a wooden crate amid the junk and brought it to the windows where I could stand and get a good look inside. The room was furnished, but sparely, with pieces that appeared to be a century or more old. As Brad had said, they might have been expensive when new, but they were shabby now.

The main entrance was on the house's north side. The bell still worked—I heard it over the traffic, a rich alto like a clock chiming the half hour. After a decent interval, when no one answered, I tried the door. Locked, but easy to unlock. The wild shrubbery kept the dog walkers and child minders from seeing me squat with my picks and work the tumblers.

Mitch and Peppy appeared as I found the sweet spot that opened the door. They had been having too good a time in the mud and brambles for me to bring them indoors.

I stood in the foyer, looking into the big front room. The Dutch tiles had cracked since Rudolph Zigler installed them around the fireplace, and the walnut mantel needed polishing and repairing.

I tried a light switch, but the power had been turned

off. I wondered what they'd used for light last night, then saw a cordless lamp in front of the fireplace. I turned it on, but a message on the base told me the battery needed charging. Ashleigh and her friend had also lit a fire. They hadn't banked it properly; it still let out some acrid smoke.

The dogs were barking at the door, demanding to join me, but I wanted to tour the house now that I was inside. Maybe there'd be some clue to Silvia Zigler's whereabouts, or the identity of Ashleigh's pal.

Although the windows were dirty, enough light filtered past the expressway and the high-rises that I could see my way. I wondered what Zigler or his wife had in mind for the rooms when the house was first built. The dining room was obvious. Portraits of Victorian figures hung over a long dust-covered table.

I passed from there into what must have been Zigler's study. A grand desk full of drawers and pigeonholes was placed so he could look across the garden to his glassworks. The trees and bushes wouldn't have blocked the view back then the way they did now.

The bookshelves held old encyclopedias, chemistry and philosophical works in German, published in the nineteenth century. On the bottom shelf, where a child could reach them, were illustrated books, some in German, most in English. The covers were well worn, read and cherished over the years. It was easy to stand in here and get caught up in a vicarious nostalgia, but I pushed open a pocket door that led to a smaller room.

One wall was lined with built-in shelves that held books on twentieth-century politics and economics, most in English, but many in other languages as well.

Among the books were a few ceramic pieces and some family photos: a couple dressed in formal clothes, a baby in the woman's lap. It made me think of my Warshawski grandmother's wedding photo. The subjects had the same solemn faces, the same look of discomfort, as if the dressy clothes were so alien that they chafed the wearers. Other pictures showed more recent, more relaxed family events—weddings, school pictures with gap-toothed children grinning at the camera.

A desk, placed at an angle to overlook both the garden and a fireplace, held a USB spreader, with a few cables dangling from it, but no sign of a computer. Curiouser and curiouser.

I looked in the drawers, which held all the things that people stick in drawers—theatre tickets, rubber bands, a bundle of old letters, handwritten, in a language I didn't recognize. The deep bottom drawer was set up with file folders for Silvia Zigler's business affairs. She'd kept years of credit card and bank statements, recent ones printed out from the Internet.

When I flipped through the pages, I saw that over the years she'd disputed a number of four-figure charges to her credit cards. She'd changed cards several times. Her statements from the past eight months were apparently all in order. Her most recent paid statement was for January, three months earlier. If Silvia Zigler was still paying her bills, she was doing so from somewhere else.

I left the room by a door that opened onto a hallway. As I made my way toward the back of the house, I smelled charring again. I followed the smell to the kitchen, where a door had burned so thoroughly that the bottom panels were gone. The scorching ran along the frame, and into the walls, but someone had put out the fire before the whole house went up.

Fragments of charred wood lay on the floor around the door. I switched on my flashlight and squatted to look through the hole. At first all I saw was blackness, but as I rotated my phone, the flash picked out a set of steep steps. The kitchen had been used recently, even if not in the immediate past. Clean dishes stood in the drainboard, but the fridge held milk that was long past its shelf date. Had Silvia Zigler set a door on fire and burned herself so badly she'd been hospitalized?

It was a very odd place to have an accidental fire, not close to the stove or any kind of electrical appliance. I pulled the basement door open, cautiously, in case it came away from its hinges, and took a tentative step down. The top riser splintered under my weight, the second creaked ominously, but when I took a giant step down to the third, it held me. I gripped the banister and went halfway down, shining my flashlight around.

Paper was strewn across the floor. Not pieces of paper, but foot-high piles of paper. I crept to the bottom so I could see what Zigler had stored. Newspapers. Tax receipts. Blank Zigler company invoices. The dates on papers near the top went back a century. Silvia apparently had married into a hoarding dynasty. I didn't try to wade through the mounds but retreated up to the kitchen, one careful step at a time. However the fire started, Silvia Zigler had been extraordinarily lucky that the whole house hadn't gone up.

The doorbell chimed, a noise so loud and unexpected that it made me jump. I'd forgotten the dogs, but now I heard them barking in outrage as I sprinted through the rooms to the front door.

A heavyset man stood there, wearing a bomber jacket

with the Chicago Fire Department logo on the sleeve. He was holding both dogs by their collars while they barked and growled.

"Sorry!" I cried. I'd dropped their leashes inside the door when I came in. When I had the dogs hooked up, the firefighter let them go.

"I'm glad to see you," I burbled. "I was walking the dogs along here and smelled smoke—I left them outside so I wouldn't have to rescue them if the house was burning."

He stared at me, face twisted in a mix of disgust and disbelief. "If there was a fire, why didn't you call 911? My station is so close to the off-ramp that one of my guys heard your dogs."

I ignored the question but moved back to the living room fireplace. "Someone lit a fire here—you can still see some red in the ashes."

He went to the fireplace and kicked at the wood with a booted foot. The half-burned pieces fell apart, sending up sparks.

"And then I found remains of another fire in the kitchen that left a lot of charring."

He eyed me narrowly, but followed me and the dogs into the kitchen, where he shone his powerful work flashlight along the charred door panels and frame. He knelt and sniffed the wood, fingered the sharp edges of the busted panels.

"Fire's been out for a while. Can't say how long ago it was set, weeks probably, but this was arson. I can still smell kerosene in the wood. Whoever set this fire wanted to torch the house. That you?"

A reasonable guess—arsonists like revisiting their work. I sidestepped the accusation. "How come the whole place didn't go up?"

"Fire extinguisher, I'd say at a glance. Whoever came on the blaze had a household extinguisher, although I don't see it—they must have thrown it out."

He spoke into his lapel phone. "Carlton here. Any arson reports from the crazy house on the island in the last month?"

Someone on the other end told him to wait. After a short delay, his contact confirmed that no one had called in a fire. Carlton and his buddy chatted a few minutes—the two barking dogs belonged to a strange female who'd smelled the charring and gone into the house. "Of course I told her. Civilian idiots, think they're flame-retardant."

Mitch started whining and pawing at the damaged door. Peppy joined him. The two were straining to get into the basement.

"I may be a civilian idiot," I panted, "but the dogs smell something. I need to take them down there."

"Probably rats," Carlton said.

"Rats would get them excited, but not like this." I pulled the leashes close to my chest to hold them, but I couldn't budge them from the door.

Carlton looked at me skeptically but put in another call, asking for help. "Hold them for another five," he said to me. "I don't want even a civilian idiot tumbling down those stairs. Too much paperwork if I have to rescue you."

I was sweating by the time his crew arrived. They pounded on the back door, which got the dogs even more excited. Three people came in, carrying ladders and battery-powered work lights. They pulled the basement door from its hinges, knocked out the rotten top two risers with an ax, set up a ladder alongside the stairs, and climbed to the bottom, all in under a minute. It was impressive.

They created a sling to lower the dogs, whose legs flailed in fright at the loss of ground underneath. I went down the stairs after them.

As soon as they were set down, Mitch and Peppy started making a channel through the mounds of paper. They seemed to know exactly where they wanted to go.

"Sheesh, Carl—you should have told us to put on waders," a woman officer said, slipping on some of the paper as she followed the dogs.

The basement was full of paper, but most was in boxes or paper bags. It was only the area around the bottom of the stairs where it had been upended into such a mess. I stuck a hand into one of the piles, checking for damp, but Rudolph Zigler's engineering had held up for a century and a half. Everything was dry.

The basement underlay the whole house. As we followed the dogs away from the stairs, the boxes gave way to racks of clothes. The firefighters' lights picked out long skirts, frock coats, shawls. We passed through the mechanicals room and a workroom where a long bench was covered with dusty tools. One of the men shook his head sadly. "These should have been kept oiled and hung up. There's stuff in here I'd love to have."

"We don't plunder the houses we're saving," Carlton said. "At least not in front of civilians—especially one who's only part idiot."

Mitch and Peppy came to a halt by a door that was almost shut. Mitch shoved his muzzle into the crack but couldn't push the door open enough to get his shoulders through. He came to me, barking a command to deal with it.

Carlton shone his beam along the frame. We saw a

hefty padlock and chain anchored to the door and adjacent wall. At a signal from Carlton, the woman swung her ax a couple of times and broke the links.

She pulled the door open, and the dogs ran in. They nosed into a nest of blankets, came away baffled, and started circling the small space, sniffing and whining.

The room held a stinking slop bucket, empty water bottles, and granola bar wrappers, but no one was there.

23

Danger Is Double and Pleasures Are Few

Carlton sent two of his team out for additional lights so they could search the basement more easily. He also called the local police station. The dogs and I slipped away while he was describing the scene to the cops . . . *someone held prisoner there, fire in the kitchen, owner missing.*

"She's an elderly woman," Carlton added. "I've seen her over the years, working in the garden or going out for groceries. Don't know if she was held prisoner. We may need to drag the river, but let's see if we can locate her first."

It wasn't an unreasonable assumption, but I didn't believe it, because of the dogs. I was sure they had been smelling my Jane Doe down there. *Arrogant again, Warshawski,* I mocked myself. *Building a theory from one data point?*

It was a good piece of data, though. Both dogs had spent time with Jane at close quarters, and Mitch had been actively hunting her only a few days earlier.

The chained door had opened wide enough for a skinny girl like Jane to slip through. Had she set fire to the basement door and barreled through it? That would explain the burns on her clothes and legs. I wished I could explore the disused tool room. She might have found kerosene and matches there. A terrifying second scenario: her captors had started the fire, hoping to burn down the house and her with it.

My theory didn't cover everything. Where was Silvia Zigler? One of the firefighters said she was an elderly woman. She could have been held captive in the basement as well and be recovering in a hospital or nursing home. Was she Jane Doe's *Nagyi?* Was she the woman who'd called in the middle of the night, looking for Yulchia?

Enough speculations. I needed to leave quickly, before someone came out to demand my name. No time to look for Brad's phone, or to make my dogs more agreeable travel companions. Their coats were matted with burrs, mud, and stuff I didn't want to analyze, and they smelled as bad as the rotten milk in Silvia Zigler's refrigerator. I bundled them into the Mustang with a pang. I'd have to do a deep cleaning of the car as well as the animals.

I bumped my way back to the access road. There was a backup of trucks at the bottom—a cop was holding all traffic so the emergency crews summoned by Carlton could get in. They were flashing their lights, pushing on their sirens: *crime scene, we're important, get out of our way.*

A Crime Scene truck led the parade, followed by squad cars, both CPD and Fire Department, and two unmarked sedans. They couldn't move fast through the tangle of industrial vehicles, and so I was able to see Lieutenant Coney's face in one of the sedans. I sat like a pillar of salt, not even blinking. What was he doing in this group? Of course he was with Bomb & Arson, and Carlton said the kitchen fire was definitely arson, but Coney's presence still seemed an ominous sign.

My place in line was below the old bridge tender house. The play of light and shadow on the windows made it look as though the bridge keeper was still inside, monitoring the river traffic.

A goose honk behind me startled me back to the present. The traffic cop was signaling our lane forward.

When I got home, Ashleigh and Donny were in Mr.

Contreras's place, arguing at full throttle about coming home. When they saw me, they turned their fury my way. The parents didn't like each other, but they were united in wanting to know Brad's real mission at the Zigler mansion.

"Maybe he went to shoot craps," Mr. Contreras suggested. "Used to be a floating game under the bridges along the river. I went sometimes myself on Friday nights."

That further divided the parents. Donny hoped his son was manly enough for craps, but Ashleigh said Branwell couldn't stay with an old man with immoral habits—which brought Mr. Contreras steaming into the fray. As the battles intensified, I took the dogs to the basement. Brushing out the burrs, shampooing them was not a simple job, but it was soothing. Brad came down when I was partway through the process.

"Vic, I don't know what to do. Uncle Sal says I can stay with him, only Mom is totally against it. And what am I supposed to tell them? If I tell them the truth, Dad will use it against Mom, but I don't know a good lie."

"The other night at your home, you already said you came to me because you thought your mother was having an affair. Tell them the truth, that you wanted to see who she was meeting."

"I can't do that!" he cried. "She'll be mad and he'll use it against her and I'll be in the middle between them like some Ping-Pong ball."

"Trouble with lying is you have to keep building the story up bigger," I said. "But you do what works for you. If you want to stay with Mr. Contreras for a while, I'll try to get your mom to agree to that. If you do stay here, you could help me walk these beasts, which would be a good deed."

He didn't go back upstairs but set to brushing out Peppy's matted fur while I concentrated on Mitch. While we worked, I told him about my own expedition to the mansion. "I don't think anyone is going to be doing anything in that house for some time to come, now that it's an active crime scene."

In his agitation, he pulled too hard on Peppy's fur. She yelped and moved away from him. While I was showing him a gentler way to work, his family trooped in—not just his parents, but Sonia, Reggie, and twin teenage boys, Reggie's sons. Sonia waved at a space between the pair and announced that they were Finn and Cameron. Finn and Cameron had the Litvak shoulders and wiry hair, but they also had the kind of expensive orthodonture that makes your teeth look iridescent under bright lights. I blinked and looked away.

The cousins greeted each other with every sign of

dislike. Brad muttered, "Stuck-up assholes," under his breath and Reggie's sons said, "Loser mommy's boy," more loudly.

Reggie took Brad away with him to a corner of the basement near a stairway that led to the garden. The basement windows don't open, as an anti-burglary precaution, but I noticed a long crack in a pane to the left of the stairs. I try not to get involved with the condo board, since they'd like to evict me, but that glass would have to be replaced.

Reggie spoke too softly for me to hear, but we all saw Brad's skin turn its treacherous red. He yelled, "That is a fucking lie! You can't blame that on me!"

He broke away from his uncle and ran up the stairs. Reggie and Sonia followed, but the twins stayed in the basement with me and the dogs. Through the laundry room windows, I saw Reggie grab Brad by the arm. Donny moved in on his brother. The two started bellowing at each other. Ashleigh was on the perimeter; I couldn't see enough of her to tell if she was joining in the fight or merely watching.

"He's such a loser," Finn, or Cameron, said.

"Yeah, he'll run into a truck, or be hit by a scooter and lie in the street crying for his mommy."

"He seems to be crying to get away from his mother," I said.

"Won't last," the one I thought was Finn said.

"Any idea what your dad said to set him off?"

The brothers traded glances, shrugged. Finn, unless it was Cameron, said, "Dad works for Metargon, in their drone unit, but he fiddles around in his shop at home. He keeps thinking he'll be a unicorn. His newest, bestest idea on the planet was something he attached to a drone. He's calling it a Skyrocket, so you realize it's way cooler than an ordinary drone. It has to be a secret so that Metargon can't claim a patent on it before Dad registers it, but he couldn't help showing it off to the family. Which meant Branwell was at the demo and saw it all."

"When was this?" I asked. "Last week?"

They shrugged. "Ages ago. A month? Two? We didn't know the date would be on the test." They both laughed to prove they'd been hysterically funny.

"Where did he do it? At his shop?"

"No way. Our street is too crowded. We all had to get up at, like, sunrise, and go to a park so we could see it in an open field. Everyone was there, even Aunt Ashleigh, who hates all the Litvaks. She and Mom mostly stood in a corner drinking out of a thermos and insulting Aunt Sonny and Uncle Donny."

"And that's when it disappeared?" I asked.

"Nah. Dad brought it back to the shop. So-called.

It's a shed in the garden where the lawn mower is the most successful invention. It was supposedly locked up, but when he went to look at it, like three days ago, maybe, it was gone. Branwell is the best suspect since he imagines he knows how to operate drones."

The other twin said something about Brad's inability to operate a zipper, let alone a machine. "But he's been to Dad's shop a few gazillion times, pretending like he knows something about electronics."

I finally finished with Mitch. He went to the door that led to the garden, begging to be let out. I ignored him and hefted Peppy into the sink. "If Brad biked out to your home to steal the rocket, he couldn't have broken into the shop without someone seeing him."

"Branwell's such a fucking loser, skulking around in corners, no one notices him even though he's got the biggest feet in Chicago. Probably he took it to try to buy friends with it. You know, 'I've got the coolest game, before it's even on the market.' Maybe he'd attract some loser girl."

Mr. Contreras came down the stairs, troubled by the Litvak family fight. "Do you know what it's all about?" he asked me.

"These kids think their dad accused Brad of stealing some kind of drone prototype. Reggie's an inventor in his spare time."

"That boy ain't a thief." Mr. Contreras had added Brad to the roster of people he cared about, which meant he would ignore or deny any of their shortcomings.

"He could be a thief," Finn said earnestly. "You wouldn't think it to look at him, but it's a good disguise, being a clumsy slob."

Mr. Contreras started to protest, but I said, "They're just trying to get a rise out of you. They're about kindergarten age emotionally, so best to ignore them."

The twins were briefly silent, then decided that was a joke, too, which they began milking. I turned my back to them, concentrating on my dog. Mr. Contreras prudently joined me at the sink.

Before his family descended on us, Brad had combed most of the burrs out of Peppy's fur. She didn't need much work. I hosed her off and dried her and headed outside to see what the Litvaks had decided about Brad's sleeping arrangements.

The argument hadn't progressed that far. Donny and Reggie were still fighting over whether Donny's son could have stolen Reggie's invention.

"How about I come over and search your house?" Reggie said. "Five bucks says he's hidden it in a comic book."

"They call them graphic novels these days," Ashleigh

said, at her most languid. "Branwell doesn't read them. In any event, my house is not open for you to search."

"Because you know what Reggie will find?" Sonia said.

"Because I value my privacy," Ashleigh said. "If it will make you happy to watch me sort Branwell's dirty underwear, you can stop by later tonight. I have work to do this afternoon."

She sauntered over to the Navigator and drove off. Brad and Donny stared at her, and then Brad ran into the building. He came out a minute later with his bike, and took off, pedaling at a ferocious pace.

"He's going home to get the rocket out of his filthy jock," the twins crowed.

"Will you get your brats to shut up?" Donny roared at Reggie. "For all you know, they're the ones who made off with your precious rocket."

"My boys know better than to screw around in my lab," Reggie said.

"Can you explain what it is you've lost?" I asked. "Your children told me you think Brad stole something called a Skyrocket from your shop. How big would that be? Are we talking about a thumb drive, or a bigger piece of equipment?"

I was wondering about the attack on Brad. I'd assumed it had to do with Jane Doe because people kept asking me to hand over what she'd been carrying when I found her. I'd thought Brad's attackers had jumped him simply because he'd been in my office, and they wanted to see if I'd handed something off to him. But the Skyrocket wrinkle meant the assailants might have targeted him for that.

Reggie sighed. "I work with drones at Metargon. I don't create drones, but I work on the cameras and spyware they carry. A couple of years ago, I had an idea for a piece of hardware that would allow drones to become flying computers, instead of following commands from an operator. I finally finished a prototype this past winter. The hardware itself is unique, and if you saw it, you could dismantle it and see how to— never mind that. It isn't big—size of a couple of thumb drives, I guess, but only about five microns thick.

"When I conducted the demo, I found, well, call it a major design flaw. Someone with a bigger lab, more resources could take what I've done so far and make a fortune out of it. And I don't want Metargon to get wind of it. I'm doing this on my own time, with my own resources, but they have the financial and market muscle to bring it into the company workshops. In which case I'm screwed."

"So you're trying to keep it secret."

"My own damned fault for showing it off for the

family," he said bitterly. "It obviously isn't as secret as I'd hoped. I'd been redesigning the specs, and when I went to my shop to reprogram it two days ago, it was missing from the fireproof safe where I'd locked it."

"Had the lock been disturbed?"

He shook his head. "Whoever broke in either knew the combination or had a key."

"And you think Brad took it and is trying to sell it? He doesn't seem to have the savvy to find a buyer for high-tech gizmos."

"You don't need savvy these days," Reggie said. "A photo on TikTok or Instagram and people will flock to him. I'm betting that's why he was at that deserted house last night. He'd lined up a buyer."

"Maybe he lost it when he went into the river," I suggested. "It could be in the mud on the bottom."

"And then an Asian carp would eat it," Finn said, "and some fisherman would catch it, and when he cooked it, there it would be. Cameron and me, we can do something on TikTok to alert all river fishers."

"Damn it, this is not a joke!" Reggie roared. "Get the fuck into the truck."

The Litvak temper, the one reliable part of this family. Mr. Contreras said, "You ain't in your own home, son. Don't swear like that in front of women and children when you're in mine."

Finn and Cameron snickered.

"They're not children," Donny said. "They're space devils, carried to earth on one of Reggie's drones."

Reggie had started for his truck, but he whipped around to look at me. "Of course. If Brad had it on him, he's stowed it here. I want to look at your apartment, and the old man's."

"Not my place," I said. "I'm past due at my office. I'll take a look around when I get home tonight."

"Yeah, we're up to our eyeballs here with cops and other jerks pawing through our stuff," Mr. Contreras said. "You take your family and go home."

Reggie scowled more deeply, but he stomped off to his truck. As he was shutting the door, we heard him threaten to dump the boys on the Kennedy if they said one *fucking* word on the way home. One of them said, "Don't use that word in the old guy's home, son," and both of them laughed.

24
Grandma Firebrand

Donny and Sonia were the only remnants of the family party. Donny asked Mr. Contreras and me where Brad would have gone.

"I don't know," I said. "If he has friends, you're in a better position than me to know who they are."

"You'd think. I guess I'm just as bad a father as my own old man."

Sonia put an awkward arm around his shoulders. "No one could be as bad a dad as Larry Litvak. Brad's a good kid, and that's more thanks to you than Ashleigh."

Donny produced an unhappy smile. "Thanks, Sonny. Maybe I'll drive around, see if I can spot him."

Sonia followed him to the Jeep.

"You believe that Reggie?" Mr. Contreras fretted when they'd taken off. "Brad wouldn't have stolen nothing, I'm sure of it."

"Me, too," I said. "Brad is not a subtle person. I wouldn't put it past those two delinquents of Reggie's, though."

"What, you mean those boys? Why would they steal from their own pa?"

"To seem cool. To raise money. To hurt their old man. All of the above—if they did it. I don't think Brad took it, but you might have a look around. Reggie said it's about the size of two thumb drives, only it's going to be thin, like a piece of film."

I left the dogs in Mr. Contreras's apartment and headed to my office. My most urgent project was to try to locate Silvia Zigler, but I was curious enough about Reggie that I looked him up first. He'd done a degree in aeronautical engineering at the University of Illinois. He'd tried going into business for himself as a drone and computer consultant, but he'd finally signed on with Metargon Electronics around the time the twins were five. Melanie, his wife, was a counselor at a suburban middle school. Her sons must give her plenty of practice in working with disruptive kids.

The financial databases didn't show any buzz about whatever unique hardware Reggie had created. It could be that he was successfully keeping a lid on it. Or maybe, despite his bold speech, his Skyrocket had proved a dud.

Reggie's name cropped up in drone chatrooms. He wrote open-source navigation code that a lot of recreational drone users respected. But neither on those pages nor on social media were people talking about unique hardware.

I put everything I'd learned about Reggie into a folder in case it became relevant. I also wanted to explore Freeman Carter's comment that federal prosecutors might be looking into Klondike's affairs.

I started with Jonathan Michaels, an old law school friend who was on the staff of the Northern District's federal prosecutor. After we'd caught up on life after lockdown, Jonathan said, "Come on, Vic. You know I can neither confirm nor deny that anyone is under investigation."

"Corky made a puzzling offer for a stake in a Rogers Park synagogue—at least, in the building. He says he cares about preserving Lake Calumet brick."

"A surprising number of people are passionate about that brick. You might as well tell me the synagogue's name, though. Never hurts to have information."

He took down the details but said that people were reporting plenty of unsavory financial acts generated by the pandemic. "They're nasty but not necessarily illegal. Everyone's brain is fuzzy these days, including mine. I wouldn't send Corky Ranaghan to Leavenworth because he's drooling over a house of worship."

"Would you buy insurance from Klondike?" I asked.

"Please, Vic. I'm a salaried civil servant. I can't afford the kind of projects Klondike underwrites."

"Say you could. Do you think they'd be around long enough to make good on any claims you filed?"

"You belong in the courtroom, Vic. You definitely have a litigator's brain."

"Word on the street is that someone is putting the screws to contractors to give preferential treatment to Tad Duda. He's running the Viper's old cement company, Tommaso. Is the Viper pulling the strings from down in Florida?"

"Really?" Michaels said. "That could be good news. We couldn't touch the Viper during the Outfit trial. If he's still active, we'd have a crack at him. However, this is the first I've heard about it, so it may be coming from some old Tommaso rival, not from anything reliable."

"What about Klondike, then?" I persisted.

"What, indeed?" Jonathan's tone was urbanity itself as he ended the call.

I tried unsuccessfully to access Klondike's company books. Although Klondike is best known for underwriting big developments, they are also insurance brokers. As with their construction underwriting, their brokerage is for big projects, usually on the financing end. But as insurance brokers, Klondike had to file reports with insurance commissioners in every state where they did business—all fifty, in their case. But because they are closely held, they don't file with the SEC. Unfortunately, Klondike had firewalls too sophisticated for my low-grade hacking skills.

I did learn that Corky got his nickname from his college fraternity brothers—he could outdrink them and still carry on a semi-lucid conversation.

I put Corky to one side to look up Silvia Zigler. No death certificate had been issued. If she'd been injured badly enough in the kitchen fire, she could be in a hospital or nursing home. If she had adult children, she might have moved in with one of them.

She wasn't on social media, which made her somewhat hard to locate, but I learned she'd been a social worker. She'd retired, but recently enough that she still had professional listings online. Her degree was from the Jane Addams College of Social Work at the University of Illinois. I searched their degree rosters and didn't find her, but I checked for people named Silvia or Sylvia; she'd gotten her degree as Silvia Elek.

Silvia had been a social worker at a refugee resettlement organization. When she retired, her coworkers held a party for her that got written up in the organization's newsletter; they included a bio, which explained that Elek came to the States after the 1956 uprising in Hungary.

> Silvia's parents fought in the Hungarian Resistance during the Nazi occupation of Hungary in World War II. She inherited her parents' passion for justice. As a high school student she took part in the uprising against the Communist regime in Hungary. Her leadership role, even as a young student, made her a target of the government when the Soviet Union put down the uprising. She managed to flee Hungary with the clothes on her back, and made her way to the United States. She has been a lifelong advocate for people on the margins of American society.

Silvia Elek had been naturalized in 1968. She'd been born in Pécs, Hungary, in 1940. I sat back in my chair. *Nagyi*. My Jane Doe had cried for her Hungarian granny.

The woman who called me in the middle of the night, crying for her Yulchia, was Jane Doe's grandmother. *Maybe you're arrogant, V.I., but you were right*. Yulchia. In Polish, your family is always giving you a pet name. My Polish granny had called me "Vikusha." I was guessing it was the same in Hungarian. The *J* would be pronounced Y, so Yulchia would be Julia. I could name my Jane Doe.

It seemed incongruous that a young revolutionary had ended up in that decaying house in the middle of an industrial zone. Now that I had a name, though, it was easy to get more of her personal details.

She married Augustus Zigler Jr. not long after she got her social work degree. Zigler had a position with a refugee resettlement organization, which I guess is how they met. The couple had two children: Augustus III, born in 1981, and Emma, born in '86. As to which was Jane Doe's parent, that was easy. Augustus didn't have any children, Emma had one daughter, Julia, born in 2007. As far as I could see from going through a long chain of public records, Emma had never married. She died when Julia was seven. I couldn't find a cause of death and couldn't see who had custody or provided child support.

Silvia's husband died in 2001. I imagined Silvia driving home from resettling refugees to the Goose Island home, alone, night after dark night. Her children were grown, probably on their own; she'd be there by herself, with the floating crap game and the rats and the Tommaso cement works for company.

Why had she stayed in such an isolated place? Maybe after a day dealing with needy people, she was happy to have time alone. Perhaps she even shot craps. A bold, risk-taking woman would have enjoyed gambling with the men who hung out under the Chicago Avenue bridge.

I drew an outline of the house. *Yulchia, Julia, was it you who was locked in the basement? Or your granny? Did you burn down the door to help her escape and get burned yourself? Surely you weren't trying to hurt your* nagyi.

Silvia's son, Augustus III, lived with his wife, Lacey, in Glenview, one of the cluster of suburbs northwest of Lake Michigan. Augustus was self-employed, as a contractor, which could cover anything in the building trades, from subcontracting on big projects to building a kitchen extension on a neighbor's house. Reviews on sites like Craigslist were tepid. He got jobs done, but the work was often sloppy.

Like Tad Duda, he was in financial trouble. His wife worked for one of the North Shore hospitals, St. Helena's, but they had two mortgages on their house and they seemed to be kiting their bills through a dozen or so credit cards. Every now and then, there'd be a deposit into one of the bank accounts, sometimes quite a big one. It had all the earmarks of a gambling problem.

Augustus was active on Twitter, where he spoke resentfully about minority contractors taking jobs that he, Augustus, should have had.

His wife, Lacey, had a Facebook account, which showed her and Gus, as she called him in her posts, enjoying maskless get-togethers with neighbors at the pandemic's height. No Masked Bandits Allowed she'd posted under a picture of a barefaced crowd at last year's Fourth of July party.

Lacey had posted a few moments in life with her mother-in-law, including photos of the mansion and of Silvia standing in the overrun garden. Creepy mansion, creepy old lady, and the kid is like a walking advertisement for why kids need to be smacked for talking back. Of course, considering her gene pool, anything is possible.

I enlarged the photo, looking at Silvia Zigler's face. There was strength in it, but also guardedness. She wouldn't reveal herself to her daughter-in-law.

In February, Lacey wrote, My mother-in-law broke her hip. Supposed to be the kiss of death for old people, but they're doing a good job with her at St. Helena's— hey, hope my boss is reading this! They're sending her over to Archangel for rehab. Thank God for Covid—I can't care for her myself in case I infect her. Downside is, we get the brat!

Lacey worked in collections at St. Helena's Northfield facility, which was across the street from the Northfield Archangel complex.

Remembering Max's concerns about the standard of care in for-profit homes, I looked up Archangel's file with the Illinois Long-Term Care Ombudsman's office. Families of people in Archangel's long-term care had filed a staggering number of complaints, over neglect, filth in the long-term care unit, lack of bath or shower opportunities, and excessive use of restraints in the memory care unit.

You belong in restraints, the angry voice had thundered at the old woman on the phone. Silvia Zigler, surely.

The ombudsman fielded complaints but didn't handle litigation. I went into LexisNexis to explore lawsuits against Archangel. There were several dozen in various stages, from discovery to dismissal. A persistent problem the litigants had was in identifying the owners of the facility whose poor care they were contesting. This was apparently a problem with complaints to the ombudsman as well. Unless a lawsuit or complaint named the owner, judges tended to rule against the complainants. But the nursing homes had elaborate layers of ownership, making it impossible for ordinary citizens to find who was actually behind the red curtain.

This problem was apparently not unique to Archangel. It seemed to be true with all complaints against for-profit nursing homes. I skimmed through reports of endless failures to bring charges or change because of the sophisticated layers of ownership the homes hid behind.

The more I read, the more depressed I felt. What kind of country were we, anyway, to deprive people of the last shreds of dignity and comfort at the end of their lives?

25
The Loving Son

It was time to pay a visit to Silvia Zigler's son and his wife. She was not a fan of her mother-in-law, but maybe Augustus III felt warmer, or at least responsible, for his mother.

Before I could get out the door, though, Brad arrived, hot and sweaty but triumphant. He had cycled all the way to his home, had a confrontation with his mother, and cycled back.

"You were right, Vic. The best thing was to tell her the truth. I said I wanted to see what she was doing, so I followed her to that house."

"Good for you," I said. "What was her reaction?"

"She was pretty upset, but mostly she wanted to know exactly what I'd seen. I—I kind of flubbed it there. I didn't want her to know I saw her with—

with—this guy. So I said I'd been pushed into the river before I saw much." His shoulders slumped. "I guess I really am a chicken, aren't I?"

"No, kid, not at all. You were following your mother, not some random stranger." I'd been about his age when I'd worried my own mother was romantically involved with her voice coach. I'd never seen them embrace, but if I had, I would never have dreamed of mentioning it to her, and certainly not to an outsider. I would have buried the image in some deep tunnel of my mind.

"You going to stay with Mr. Contreras for a while?" I asked.

He nodded. "I did tell her that, and Dad, too. I said I needed a vacation from family. I know I'm lucky to have Dad, and Aunt Sonny, maybe even Mom, but sometimes it's too much."

I nodded sympathetically. I told him I had to run up to the northern suburbs, but that I'd drop him at Mr. Contreras's apartment on my way. He strapped his bike to the back of the Mustang.

I left Brad with Mr. Contreras and swung by Temple Shaamar Hashomayim. I'd lost transmission from two of the cameras, the ones above the front doors that were easy to spot. Someone had removed them, which was worrying. It might mean the vandals were preparing to attack again. In the meantime, though, the facade was still clean-scrubbed, the rose of the brick Corky coveted glowing in the fall sunlight. I surreptitiously checked the cameras I'd hidden under the eaves and in a hole in the mortar; they were still intact.

From there I headed over to the Edens Expressway, for a run up to Augustus and Lacey Zigler's home in Glenview. It was late afternoon. In ordinary times the Edens would have been packed with homebound commuters, but in the Covid-verse, with the city reopening only slowly, traffic was moving fast.

It was a gamble, of course, as to whether the Ziglers would be home, come to the door, talk to me, but I didn't want to try to reach Silvia Zigler at the Archangel facility until I had a sense of her son's involvement in her care.

The Ziglers lived in a modest ranch house on a street of tiny, treeless lots. A green Ford pickup was in the drive, with the slogan SUNTASCH: BUILDING A BETTER WORLD FOR YOUR FAMILY stenciled on it. That was interesting, since Zigler's online profile listed him as an independent contractor.

As I went up the short walk to the door, I saw a Hog parked in front of the pickup, next to a Kia Soul. Gus and Lacey were certainly prepared for the road, in case they decided to flee their creditors.

I rang the bell. After a minute, the door opened partway; a woman in her thirties, with tawny hair falling around her face, peered out.

"Didn't you see the sign? No soliciting allowed in this neighborhood."

"Then it's good I've come on private business. I'm V.I. Warshawski, the person who rescued—"

She shut the door firmly. Who could blame her, a complete stranger in front of her house about to launch into a long story?

I took off my mask so I could launch my story at full volume. "My name is V.I. Warshawski. About ten days ago, I rescued a girl who was hiding in the rocks along Lake Michigan. She ran away from the hospital where the EMTs took her, and I've been trying to find her. Someone told me she was Augustus Zigler's niece. I'm hoping this house belongs to the right Augustus Zigler, and that his niece is safe."

A woman had gotten out of a car in the driveway next door and was staring at me with frank curiosity. A man walking a dog stopped on the sidewalk to look.

The door opened again, and a man stood in the doorway, his face ruddy from outdoor work, his hair bleached by the sun. I stared at him, then turned to look at the pick-up. He and his truck had been in Duda's cement yard when I was at the Zigler mansion this morning.

"Sorry Lacey shut the door on you," he was saying. "So many scam artists around these days, you can't be too careful. If you're the woman who rescued my niece, thank you. She needs to return home, so please tell me where she is."

"Sorry, Mr. Zigler. I came here hoping you could answer that question for me."

He produced a rueful smile. "Call me Gus. My niece has been running wild for years. We knew it was only a matter of time before she got into serious trouble. Thank God you were on the spot to save her, but I'm not surprised she ran away from the hospital. If she channeled all her running into something productive, she could be a track star."

That was supposed to be a joke, but I couldn't bring myself to produce a smile.

"When did you last see her?"

He stepped back into a narrow hallway. "Come in and talk to Lacey. She remembers details better than I do."

Lacey appeared from a doorway on his right. She'd pulled her hair into a knot, wrapped with a gauzy pink scarf.

"If you want to talk to me, you need to take off that mask," Lacey said. "People come around pretending they're scared of a virus, when all they want to do is spy on you."

"No spies here." I took off the mask. Surely I could trust the vaccine, and I didn't want to start the conversation on a hostile note. There'd be plenty of time for that later. I went into a room off the narrow hallway and sat on a floral-print armchair. Husband and wife followed me in and sat on a couch, bodies touching, holding hands.

The furniture was shabby, but they had some important artworks. An oil painting on one wall looked like Monet, and a modern sculpture in a corner might have been a Louise Nevelson.

Gus stiffened when he saw me looking, but Lacey said, "Those are some of my mother-in-law's things that we're keeping safe for her. They don't have anything to do with Julia."

I nodded. Point taken. "Your niece's disappearance is extremely concerning. The hospital she ran away from hired me to find her. I was hoping she'd found her way to you, since her grandmother seems indisposed."

I put two business cards on the glass table in front of them.

"A detective?" Lacey said. "And you say you're not a spy?"

"A detective looking for your niece. She was all over the news after I found her. You didn't go down to Beth Israel to collect her?"

"That was Julia?" Gus said. "I saw the news, but, gosh, that girl was so beat up, I never guessed it was her."

Lacey nodded and squeezed his hand. "Her mother died when she was seven. I love Gus's mom, she's an amazing person, but she's never been interested in discipline. You'd think being a social worker, she'd have seen the damage done to children when they don't have structure in their lives, but Emma, Gus's sister, she ran wild just like Julia does. And that's why we have Julia in our lives. Emma ran wild with a boy from Brazil. He was deported when Emma was five months pregnant. We thought maybe she'd take off for Brazil after him, but no such luck— Ooh, sorry, honey, that slipped out."

Augustus squeezed her hand in turn. "It's been a challenge. When Emma found out she was dying, she made my mother Julia's legal guardian. We protested. Mother was already seventy-two, not the right person to look after a child, but you never met two people more stubborn than Mother and Emma. Maybe just as well. Lacey and I both work full-time. Before Covid, we couldn't be home to supervise a child, especially not someone like Julia."

"It does sound challenging," I said. "You say she *was* living with your mother. What happened? I hope your mother didn't die?"

Augustus paused. "Mother fell and broke her hip. She lived alone, except for Julia, who didn't call 911 as fast as she should have, and the break got infected."

Lacey nodded, so vigorously that the ends of her scarf bobbed like a cottontail. "Mother had to have surgery, and now she's in extended care, trying to get back on her feet. We hope to persuade her to sell the house and move into a facility, but like Gus said, she's stubborn. No one knows anything better than her. She said as long as Julia helped out she didn't need a care home, but look what happened when she fell! She's quite a ways from being able to leave the nursing home. And paying for that, now that her Medicare has run out! Selling that white elephant on the river would solve so many problems!"

"You don't want to move in with her? If it's a big house—" I spread my hands suggestively.

"She won't let us," Lacey said. "She blames Gus for—"

"This detective doesn't want to hear our family

troubles," Gus cut in warningly. "Anyway, the house is falling to bits. Best thing would be to tear it down. Or sell it to someone with the money to fix it up."

"I don't suppose you could put out feelers, just to get an idea of the market until your mother recovers," I said. I wanted to ask if he was working with Tricorn & Beck or if he'd been having sex with Ashleigh Breslau in his mother's front room, but I couldn't think of a subtle way to put it.

"The key is to persuade her to sign—" Gus cut himself off, remembering that I was a detective who shouldn't hear their family troubles. "Anyway, the long and the short of it is that we're Julia's only family. She's been with us for almost three months, and all we've done is fight with her."

"Yes," Lacey said. "Nothing makes you feel more helpless than shouting your head off at a teenager who's deliberately winding you up."

"She's in school?" I asked.

"Sort of," Lacey said. "Of course, it's still remote right now, but getting her to pay attention to her coursework is impossible. All she says is, by the time she gets out of high school there won't be any jobs left except packing boxes for Amazon so why should she study when she can do that right now."

"Your mother's in a nursing home?" I asked Gus. "Would they let Julia visit her?"

"Not during Covid. Besides, they tell me my mother's mental function has gone downhill since her fracture. But we need to find Julia first, anyway. You really don't know where she is?" He looked at me with a kind of earnest, puppy-dog expression.

"I really don't," I said.

"When you found her over by the lake, she didn't give you anything that would help you find her?"

I looked at him steadily. "Sadly, although everyone, from the hospital staff to the Chicago police, have been all too literally on my butt about whether your niece gave me anything, the answer continues to be no. What were you hoping I had?"

Gus spread his hands wide. "A letter, a thumb drive, a favorite toy. Anything that might tell a person who knew her something that a stranger couldn't interpret."

"Not even a scrap of paper, Mr. Zigler. If you know the names of her school friends, or her school counselor, I could talk to them, see if they could help me locate her."

"If she has any friends, we don't know their names," Lacey said. "Believe me, we've been to the school and they couldn't help. That didn't surprise me. Julia isn't the kind of girl who makes friends or talks to counselors."

"Would she have tried to find her father in Brazil?"

The couple looked startled; that hadn't occurred to them. "Although I don't know how she would have found him. He was deported for associating with some group we have on a watch list, so he can't come back into the country," Gus added. "Anyway, can Americans travel to Brazil these days? I heard the virus is way out of control there."

"Julia had burns on her legs when I found her," I said. "Do you have any idea how she acquired those?"

Gus and Lacey were full of sympathetic noises and glances. What terrible news. If the burns were serious, all the more reason to track down his niece.

"Someone came to the hospital to talk to her," I said. "She ran away right after he showed up. No one at the hospital can identify the man. Was it someone you sent?"

"No," Lacey said. "Like Gus said, we didn't even know that was Julia in the news. Gus, honey, who could that be? Some friend of your mother's?"

He shook his head, his unhappy puppy face on again. "You think it was someone she knew, someone who encouraged her to run off?"

"I don't think anything. No one knows what the conversation was about." I got to my feet. "I hope your mother recovers. That's a hard business, for her, and

I'm sure for you, too, to have her in a place where you can't see her. And if her mental condition is deteriorating, that must make it a hundred times tougher. I hope it isn't the kind of place where they put elderly people in restraints, just for the sin of wandering the halls at night."

"She's getting good care at Archangel," Lacey said stiffly. "But paying for good care when Medicaid runs out, that is our nightmare."

"I'm sure. What with mortgages and trucks and all those other things needing payment, hospital bills are the last thing you need."

I paused in the doorway. "I saw the Suntasch logo on your truck. I thought you were an independent contractor."

Zigler grimaced. "I was. But it's a tight economy. Easier to sign on with one of the big boys. If we ever get the Chinese to take their virus back, maybe I'll be able to work for myself again."

"I grew up in South Chicago and used to know the guy who runs Tommaso Cement these days. Tad Duda. I don't suppose you know him."

"So you know Duda," Zigler said, after a pause. "Does he know you're talking to me?"

"I haven't seen hide nor hair of him in thirty years.

Anyway, I didn't run with his crowd, although he knew my cousin Boom-Boom."

"The hockey star," Zigler said. "So you and Boom-Boom Warshawski are cousins. Well, well."

He held out a hand, but I managed to slide past without touching him.

26
Bracing for Trouble

Silvia Zigler was in the Archangel nursing home, spitting distance from Gus and Lacey. In the Covid world, I wasn't expecting to see her myself, but a personal conversation with an administrator might both give me an idea of her condition, and let Archangel know Silvia had a lawyer in her corner.

Gus and Lacey's dislike of his niece, and their contempt for his mother had depressed me. The meeting had also left me with a bucket full of questions. His relationship with Tad Duda, for one. Duda had debts, likely from gambling.

Gus's finances were also shaky, and he looked like a gambler, too. Silvia Zigler's credit card statements, the big charges she'd queried over the years, could easily have come from her son. Maybe that's how Tad and

Gus met—shooting craps under the Chicago Avenue bridge.

If Val "the Viper" Tommaso were bailing out Duda, that meant he was also a player in this game. That raised the risks for an outsider—me, for instance. I hoped no one cut my tongue out before I died. That was a favorite Mob punishment for someone who spoke too much, one of my shortcomings going back to kindergarten.

My throat contracted at the thought. *Move on to less-threatening ideas.* Gus and his mother. Gus resented his mother's seemingly preferential treatment of his dead sister. Then there was something he wanted his mother to sign, something connected with the house on Goose Island.

I was liking the idea of Gus as the person Brad had seen last night with Ashleigh. If Ashleigh's real estate firm did joint projects with Suntasch, the contractor Gus was working for, she could have met Gus while she was staging some Suntasch development.

The Zigler house itself, or at least the land it stood on, was getting more valuable by the day. Now that the east bank of the river was filled with high-end housing, I guessed developers were eyeing the west bank. Something to check on, but it must be maddening to Gus and Lacey that his mother refused to consider leaving. It must have seemed like pennies from heaven when she fell and injured her hip. Park her in a nursing home where she couldn't stop him doing—whatever he was trying to do.

I tried to fit the granddaughter into the scenario. She had something Gus needed, or Lieutenant Coney, or the mystery interrogator at Beth Israel, but what? There was Coney, too. Why was an officer of his rank so involved in the small affairs of the Litvak and Zigler families?

I'd reached Harlem Avenue, which was near the eastern edge of the Archangel complex. I was starting to feel protective of Silvia Zigler. I wanted to try to check up on her, but not without looking over the facility's security first.

Driving around it confirmed what I'd seen on the satellite map. Eight-foot-high fencing surrounded the place. Four roads went in, one on each side. They all had barriers and surveillance cameras to protect the inhabitants. I parked up the street from one entrance and watched as cars and delivery trucks went in and out. Residents apparently had a pass card that they swiped. Visitors called in through a squawk box. The barriers didn't look that sturdy. If someone wanted to plough through them at high speed it wouldn't be impossible.

As I watched the inbound traffic, I saw flashes from the cameras posted on the far side of the barrier. From the camera angles, I was judging they got both the driver and the front-seat passenger, along with the license plate. Good to know.

The golf course had its own entrance for non-residents using the course. As the flashes went off to record an entering SUV, I walked in, skirting the squawk box, following a path that led to one of the holes and from there into the heart of the compound.

The golf course and town houses were at the west end; the memory care unit at the east. I passed the Wellness Center, where people were sitting at outdoor tables in groups of two or three, chatting happily over drinks, as if advertising the vitality that could be yours if you signed up for a home here. I peered in through the window at the exercise room and saw a sign directing people to physical and occupational therapy.

From the Wellness Center, the path led to the nursing home and the memory care unit. I chose the nursing home, although it was called the Road to Wellness Pavilion. It was a determinedly cheerful structure made of glass, with tan brick struts. People in wheelchairs were lined up inside a brick verandah, staring straight ahead like pigeons on a wire. They were wrapped in blankets against the chilly April air. A couple of aides were nominally watching over them, but both were on their phones.

The glass front doors slid open at my approach, but beyond them a second set of doors remained shut. A sign on the panel told me to ring a bell to speak to an attendant, but that no one was allowed to visit family members. And anyone entering was subject to Covid protocols: masked, temperature taken on entry, no outside food or drink.

I rang the bell. There wasn't a response at first. While I waited, one of the attendants arrived from the verandah, wheeling in a woman whose head was drooping onto her chest. The attendant swiped the inner door lock with a magnetic key. I was tempted to follow, but I'd been with Gus, Lacey, the Litvaks, and the fire department today. I could well be covered in ugly germs. I didn't want to be the person who infected the entire nursing home. Besides, cameras were mounted on either side of the interior doors.

A voice finally spoke to me through a loudspeaker overhead, asking my business.

"Checking up on Silvia Zigler," I called out.

The voice said that they did not give out patient information.

"I am a lawyer with a connection to Ms. Zigler's granddaughter," I said. "I'm not going to bellow confidential details about the granddaughter into your loudspeaker."

After a longer silence, a woman appeared, wearing protective eye gear and a paper bonnet in addition to her mask. Her name badge identified her as R. Thatcher. She started to ask me who I was, but another patient was being wheeled in, someone else was exiting. She took me out to the verandah, on the far side from where the inmates were lined up in their chairs. We stood six feet apart, which meant with our masks and all we had to shout to hear each other.

I leaned into our safety zone to hand her a card, one which identified me as a member of the Illinois bar, which I am, but not as an investigator.

"You know that Ms. Zigler has custody of her granddaughter?" I said. "The girl is quite concerned about her grandmother's well-being, but because she's a minor, she doesn't have standing to raise questions. However, she overheard a family conversation where the adults were discussing the need to keep Ms. Zigler in restraints. That shocked her, since her grandmother is here for rehabilitation from a broken hip. I promised I'd check up on Ms. Zigler."

"A child hired you?" R. Thatcher was skeptical.

"I have a connection to her," I corrected. "And there is no law spelling out how old someone has to be to consult an attorney. Restraints seem counterindicated for someone who needs to keep moving after breaking a hip."

Thatcher's eyes narrowed behind her protective glasses. "The only person who's authorized to ask questions about Silvia's care is her son."

"Yes, Gus," I said. "I was just with him and Lacey. My responsibility is to the granddaughter. Ms. Zigler calls her 'Yulchia.' Does that ring a bell with you?"

"I don't interact directly with the patients," Thatcher said, "so I've never heard her talk about her granddaughter. But in any event, a visit from a minor is out of the question, even if Silvia's son and her doctor gave approval. And even if Silvia were still here."

"You released her?" I said. "That's excellent news."

She shook her head. "She's been moved to the memory care unit."

Something inside me crumpled. "But—she's been living on her own, caring for her granddaughter, paying her own bills—"

R. Thatcher looked past me to the people in their chairs. They were watching us avidly—we were live entertainment in a place that didn't offer much. R. Thatcher turned partway around, which forced me to move away from the spectators so I could still hear her.

"Old people can decompensate very quickly," Thatcher said. "She became abusive to the staff, and delusional. We had no choice but to make the decision.

If there's anything else, Ms.—uh—" She looked at my card and struggled with my last name.

I shook my head, then remembered a key question. "Yes. Did Ms. Zigler have burns on her body when she came in?"

"Burns? How on earth would she have gotten burns?"

"I wondered if she broke her hip running away from a fire."

R. Thatcher stared at me through her protective eye gear. After too long a pause, she said, "HIPAA regulations prohibit my sharing details of any patient's physical condition with you. In any event, we're not a provider of medical care. If she had burns, they would have treated her at St. Helena's when they repaired her hip."

I was starting to argue the matter, since the nursing home staff would have been treating any skin problems, and then realized it was pointless. She was going to stonewall me, no matter what I said. If I became too abusive, perhaps R. Thatcher would whisk me off to the memory care unit.

I thanked her for her time and left, almost running to get away from her. I felt an irrational grief over Silvia's situation, and a fury I could barely control at the lack of interest R. Thatcher seemed to have in Silvia's well-being. I was hurrying past the people lined up in their chairs when a man tugged at my jacket. He said something to me that I couldn't make out through his mask; I squatted, perforce, despite my anxiety to be gone.

"You a friend of Silvia?" the man said.

"I never met her," I said, "but even so, I guess you could say I'm a friend. Do you know her?"

He gave a phlegmy chuckle. "Only in the way you meet people around here. There was nothing wrong with her, except she wanted to leave and they wouldn't let her. Something wrong with them." He jerked his head toward where R. Thatcher was still standing. "I don't know why they tied her to her bed and moved her to the other place, but don't believe what they say about her."

Thatcher moved over to us. "Dr. Azernov, you've been out here quite long enough. And you, Ms. Wacharsi, you cannot sit so close to the patients."

"This gal and I go back a long way," Dr. Azernov said brazenly. "Recognized her the minute I saw her. Her mother used to bring her in to have her braces changed. You don't forget a pretty girl's teeth. You keep brushin' 'em, like I taught you, and you'll still have 'em when you get to my age."

"Yes, sir, thank you, I will." I got back to my feet.

"And your mother. She was a beautiful woman, I remember that, but not her name."

"Gabriella. Gabriella Sestieri. Yes, she was beautiful. She died not long after my braces came off, but I'm touched you remember her."

Against all regulations and security protocols, I squeezed his hand. The kindness of strangers should not be mocked. My panicky feelings subsided. I walked at a normal pace, following the path to the memory care unit.

I had never worn braces. They were way outside my parents' budget.

27
Ariadne Auf Chicago Parks

If I'd been asked to design a memory care unit, I wouldn't have placed it close to a busy cross street. I also would have concealed the chain-link fence behind some greenery that was restful to the spirit. Still, Archangel's bare design let me see through the fence into the grounds around the building itself. And to do Archangel justice, the occupants had a strip of Astroturf where they could walk.

A few people were in wheelchairs on a patio. Others were walking restlessly around the area. A woman was carrying a large doll, which she kept patting and crooning to, a man had a stuffed animal in his arms, but most were just pacing.

One of the men came over to where I was standing. "Rachel? Rachel?"

"I'm sorry, sir, I'm not Rachel," I said, feeling helpless. I saw an attendant on the patio in Archangel's maroon uniform. "That lady can help you. Go ask her for Rachel. She knows where Rachel is."

He followed my pointing arm and shuffled toward the attendant, but his attention wandered halfway there and he moved toward a bright pink plastic bench. The attendant had seen him talking to me and came over to the fence to check me out.

"Visitor?" she asked, her accent heavy, and then she looked at my face and gasped with fright.

I was momentarily puzzled, until I read her name badge. Gisela. Gisela Queriga, whose phone Silvia had swiped.

"I'm not here to see you," I said. "I hoped I could see Silvia."

She shook her head, not understanding my English. My Spanish wasn't up to even a simple sentence. I pulled up a translation app, while a supervisor came out to see what was going on. *Looking for Silvia Zigler. No one knows your daughter spoke to me.*

The supervisor came over to the fence and demanded my business. She spoke a few sharp sentences in Spanish to Gisela, who scuttled back to the patio and to the patients in their wheelchairs.

"Sorry." I produced a smile from some ashpit in

my heart. "I was visiting my old dentist in the nursing home and passed the memory pavilion on my way out. It's everyone's fear, isn't it, a loved one or oneself needing to be in a locked facility."

"This isn't the zoo where people can gape at the animals."

"You're absolutely right," I said, sincerely. "It was very wrong of me to do so."

I moved back to the path, but she called out to me to stop: she wanted my dentist's name.

"Dr. Azernov," I said. "Be sure to let me know if he has to be moved here. I want to keep up with him. He was a good friend to my mother."

She wanted my name, but I kept walking. Let her get it from R. Thatcher. The class system at work: the administrator was R. Thatcher, the attendant was Gisela.

When I was out of her view, I circled back so I could walk the perimeter of the memory care unit. The outer fence had two gates. One faced the gardens and paths of the main complex. There was also a bigger service entrance, which opened onto the access road. For both, you could either swipe an electronic card or be buzzed in.

Once inside the memory unit, the building's door was also opened by card or buzzing, but the service entrance didn't seem to be locked. As I watched, people bringing in supplies or carrying out trash could just open the door. It seemed like a safety risk to have an open door in a unit where people wandered, but as I watched the vans and cars move in and out, I supposed it saved everyone's time to keep the door unlocked.

As soon as I had an idea of the unit's layout, I left quickly, jogging down the service road to the outside world. The street where I landed was at the opposite end of the facility from my car, but it was a relief to be in the open air, to be with people doing ordinary things.

I passed the stop for PACE, the bus that traveled between city and suburbs. I wanted to try to speak to Gisela Queriga, to see if my app could help me communicate well enough to ask her about Silvia. I didn't know what time Queriga's shift might end. I would have expected her to be off work at three, and it was past four now. Maybe she had to take a double shift, leaving her daughter, Jazmin, in charge of the little ones.

I fetched my car and drove back to the bus stop. I'd been sitting there for about ten minutes when Beth Blacksin phoned.

"Just picked up something on the scanner, Warshawski. There's a dead woman in Warren Park. A jogger called it in."

"I'm still alive," I said.

"There isn't time for fun and games, Warshawski. The person who called 911 did what everyone does these days, posted on Instagram. You know that red jacket you gave the Jane Doe you pulled out of the lake? The dead woman has on one a lot like it. Where are you?"

I sucked in a breath. "No."

"What do you mean, 'no'? I want you to come look at her before the cops get there and block us off. If it's your Jane Doe, I have the scoop to end all scoops. I need you."

No, I did not want Jane Doe to be dead. Nor for her life to be distilled into the scoop to end all scoops. I had feared this ending ever since she disappeared from the hospital, but the distance between fear and reality is great.

"Are you there, Warshawski? It's a matter of minutes before the cops arrive."

"Where?" I managed to croak out the one word.

"I told you, Warren Park. Oh, southeast corner, inside the Albion Avenue entrance."

My hands were shaking, but I managed to get back on the road. *Pull yourself together, V.I. Who gave you permission to have a panic attack?* I floored the car, weaved around traffic at stoplights, slid through inter-sections on red lights, roared onto the Edens, and drove with a horrible recklessness. I should have been pulled over a dozen times, but I made it to Albion and Damen without hitting anyone or getting stopped.

I texted Beth. She directed me to a spot a few hun-dred yards from the entrance. I found a parking space in an apartment lot and ran to where Beth was stand-ing, next to a clump of bushes. She was on the phone, demanding a camera crew *now*, not in the following millennium.

"Warshawski's here. I'm filming her with my phone, but what kind of newsroom are we running?"

I grabbed her phone and tossed it aside. "You are *not* filming me, Blacksin."

The body was lying almost concealed under the bushes. If it hadn't been for the jacket, it might have gone unnoticed longer, but the red jumped out. I knelt and parted the overhanging branches. She was curled up, fetal style, her back to me. Had she crawled here to die?

"It's okay, Yulchia," I whispered. "I wish you could have trusted me, let me look after you. Maybe it's just as well your *nagyi* can't see you now."

I put my fingers on her carotid artery. There were

no pulses. The head flopped in a sickening way when I pulled my hand away. Her neck had been broken. She hadn't crawled into the bushes to die of exposure. She'd been killed. The body had been posed to look like a natural death, but the arms were broken, the humerus at a crazy angle to the ulna. My jacket, with tears now across the back, had been half pulled from her shoulders.

I could hear the police approaching, the sirens, the loudspeaker commands for people to get out of the way. I scooted around on my knees so I could see her face without moving her.

Sucked in a breath, sat back on my heels. This wasn't Jane Doe. I managed to get my phone out, shine the flashlight. That was my jacket, definitely, the big black buttons, the basket-weave on the bias. But the face above the big sailor collar wasn't Jane Doe's. It was Jane's hospital roommate. Whose name I couldn't remember. "Strauss" popped into my head, but that couldn't be right.

Some wild impulse drove me to slide my jacket from her broken arms. I had a primitive fear that sending my clothes to the morgue meant that a part of me would be lying dead on a metal gurney.

The woman's limbs were in segments, like a mannequin's. Girl-e-quin. Her joke, her macabre laugh, rose in me with a mouthful of bile.

Her shirt was hiked up, her jeans unzipped. I could see her raw surgical scars, the staples black against her paler skin, ants crawling where pus had oozed from the wounds.

I slid away from the bush with the jacket in my hands as the cops arrived on the other side. They were demanding information from Beth, who was showing her press credentials. I scuttled further from the undergrowth, got to my feet, sauntered. A fast move would attract attention. They probably would have spotted me, anyway, but just then, the Global Mobal van pulled up next to the cars. A camerawoman jumped out.

I didn't try to watch what the press and the police did or said. I could imagine it pretty well, and I wanted to be away from the scene. I made it unaccosted to my car, where someone was leaving an ugly note on my windshield.

I apologized, got in the car while the ugly note was translated into ugly speech: *How dare I, the sign clearly says, a tow truck is coming.* I lay back in the driver's seat, eyes shut, letting the words wash over me.

"Don't you have anything to say?" the man shouted.

"Yes." I struggled to sit up. "You're right. It was

unconscionable, about the worst event of the year. I'm terrifically sorry, and if you'll move, I'll get out of here so that you can have your space."

"It would serve you right if I made you wait for the tow truck," he grumbled, but he moved, and I backed up the Mustang, turned onto Damen Avenue. My arms felt like the roommate's, as if the bones were broken, not connected to muscles and tendons. I could move them just enough to drive a few blocks, but then I pulled over to the curb.

Sent a text to Beth. That isn't Jane Doe. It's the woman who was her roommate in the hospital. The traffic moved past me. I was in a bubble, an insect locked in amber while the hive buzzed around me. Shock—the clinical part of my mind knew that, but the knowledge couldn't get my arms moving again.

Ariadne auf Naxos, that was why I thought the roommate's name was Strauss. Ariadne something. I could look it up in my case notes but that would have meant moving my girl-e-quin arms.

My phone was ringing. Beth. She, too, was angry. *She'd done me a favor, calling me ahead of the cops, and I'd bailed. What was she supposed to say to the officer on the scene when they asked how she knew it wasn't Jane Doe under those bushes? And what about the jacket? What had I done with that?*

"All good questions, Beth. I'm at rock bottom. You can feed me to them if it will make you happier."

"Just tell me how you knew it was the roommate."

"I talked to her the day Jane disappeared." My words came out slowly, like ketchup from a cold bottle. "Her name is Ariadne . . . Was Ariadne . . . She had abdominal surgery, maybe a week ago . . . Don't know when she was discharged. Don't know where she lived . . . How she got under those bushes . . . Dead before she got there. Dying, anyway . . . Both arms broken."

"This is brilliant, Vic, thanks. What did she say when she talked to you?"

"Later, Blacksin. I'm done."

"The jacket. Why did you take the jacket?"

I hung up and turned off my phone. Lay back in the seat, thinking about nothing. The jacket. Inevitably Beth would tell the cops about the jacket, or they'd question the person who phoned 911. They would come demanding the jacket.

I was only a few blocks from Shaamar Hashomayim. I sometimes used the dry cleaners across the street when I was visiting Donna Ilona. I wasn't sure who actually owned the business; a woman named Rana Jardin was there most mornings and was still on duty now.

Jardin laid the jacket out flat and shook her head over the ruins. "This dirt, we can try, but it will always leave a stain. And these rips—we can try to mend, but this wide-weave fabric, very expensive—each strip must be sewn separately."

I fingered the fabric sadly.

"What do you want to do?" Jardin said sharply. "It is time for me to close the shop. Do you want to leave it or take it?"

It seemed futile to try to repair it. I put it into my bag. I turned to leave, but paused to say, "You know I'm the detective who's trying to keep an eye on the synagogue across the street?"

She nodded, warily.

"The cameras I put over the front door are gone. Did you—"

"I didn't take them!"

"But you were watching when someone else took them, weren't you." I made it a statement, a certainty that she knew something. "Can you give me a description?"

She looked at me with something between fear and loathing. "The shop should be closed by now. You must leave!"

I stumbled out the door. I was so weary, I was branded on my feet. It astonished me to think I'd already been on this street today, on my way to interview Gus and Lacey Zigler. I walked outside, swaying slightly.

I felt a sadness, a kind of embarrassing grief over my jacket. It had been on sale, but still expensive; I'd worn it the last time Peter and I were together before he left for Malaga, and he'd enjoyed undoing the great black buttons. *Enough.*

I'd been distressed by learning Silvia Zigler's fate, and shocked when I thought her granddaughter had been killed, but I hadn't stopped to think about her roommate, Ariadne. Blanchard, that was it, not Auf Naxos.

Jane Doe had stolen Ariadne's jeans and Linda Lindas T-shirt. She'd abandoned the jacket because—I could only speculate. She needed to be inconspicuous? At any rate, when I looked in the hospital room lockers, the jacket wasn't there, so Ariadne must have taken it and hidden it in her bed. She thought it was Jane's and she was entitled to it, payback for Jane taking Ariadne's jeans.

And then what? Ariadne had been released from the hospital and ended up dead in Warren Park. I crossed the street and sat where Mr. Pariente and his pals often did, on the curb in front of the synagogue. I turned my phone on, planning to see if I could locate Ariadne's home address. Instead I saw multiple texts from Beth Blacksin. A CPD lt. named Coney came along as I was packing up to leave. He's looking for you, knows the jacket is missing, says you tampered with a crime scene.

And Mr. Contreras had left a voice message: *You better call me, doll. That ugly cop's been around looking for you.*

28
Coney, Round Three

My first impulse was to get into the Mustang and drive out of town at top speed. However, I've never invested in a GPS jammer. If Coney wanted to find me, the CPD had access to surveillance drones that would locate my car easily enough. Fleeing a crime scene, tampering with evidence, fleeing jurisdiction— the state's attorney wouldn't blink twice before issuing a warrant.

I heard the cop cars before I saw them. Their goose-honk horns were warning drivers to get out of the way as they barreled down Lunt. I looked around wildly for a place to park the jacket and saw the synagogue's mail slot. I stuffed the jacket through it a nanosecond before a squad car and an unmarked SUV screeched to a halt near the synagogue. The SUV had its butt in the road, blocking oncoming traffic, an arrogance that belonged to Coney.

His support thugs—Tillman and the other guy, whose name I never got—emerged from the squad car.

"Warshawski, hands in the air, down on your knees," Coney barked.

The thugs had their hands on their service weapons. A homeless woman in a doorway next to the cleaners was watching with greedy interest. Arrests are always exciting, trebly so when a white woman is ordered to her knees.

Rana Jardin paused in the act of locking the dry cleaners. A guy on an electric scooter stopped to video, but passersby on my side of the street scuttled past as quickly as possible.

I raised my hands but stayed on my feet. Coney marched over to me and grabbed the lapels of my blazer, shook me. "What did you do with the jacket?"

"What jacket?" I asked.

His right hand swung back, ready to slug. I went limp and he took my whole weight with his left hand. He swore, dropped me, pulled out his taser. I performed an awkward cartwheel and backed away.

"Warshawski!" It was Sergeant Pizzello. I'd been focused on Coney and hadn't seen her squad car pull up behind the thug twins. Her rookie, Officer Rudy Howard, was a few steps behind her.

"Don't make the lieutenant give you an electric ride. Tell us what you did with the jacket."

"I don't know what you're talking about," I said. "Coney here smeared grease on this jacket, so it's going straight to the cleaners."

"Don't be a wiseass, Warshawski," Pizzello said. "It's never attractive, and when you hold no cards at all, it's pathetic. The victim in Warren Park. The person who called it in identified her as wearing a red jacket. The gal from Global News said you were there, that you looked at the dead woman. By the time we got there, the jacket was missing and so were you."

"Sergeant, Beth Blacksin from Global News phoned me when she got the tip about the dead woman. She'd been listening to the 911 scanner and she was sure the dead woman was the Jane Doe who's been missing all week. It wasn't Jane. I told Blacksin that and left. I don't know about the jacket. People are desperate in these hard times. Someone must have taken it before you got there."

"Why'd you leave the scene?" Coney snarled. "Even a cunt like you must know you don't leave a crime scene until you've talked to us."

I looked at the place on his neck where I could stun him with an upward chop. "There are crime scenes all over this town. This synagogue is one of them. It was vandalized. Someone stole the cameras that I'd placed over the doors to watch for whoever attacked the building. I'm right here, right now, at this crime scene. I'd love to know that the CPD has resources to protect a house of worship. If you want to deploy Tillman and his buddy to watch over the synagogue, I'll go back to Warren Park and hunt for your jacket."

Coney started to take another swing, saw the kid on the skateboard with his phone out, and held back.

"Search her car," Coney said to Tillman. "She didn't have time to get home or to her office before she came here. It'll be in the car."

I should have insisted on a warrant, but I wanted to sleep in my own bed tonight, not in a cell in Homan Square. They emptied my handbag onto the hood of one of the squad cars, took my car keys, opened the Mustang, and went through everything in the trunk as well as the interior of the car. Pizzello ordered her rookie to help.

As they dumped my belongings onto the street, I realized I should wash the dogs' beach towels more often. And stay on top of the trash. A couple of used masks, empty water bottles, and receipts from coffee bars fell out of the towels. My picks were in the glove compartment. I was sure those would earn me at least a citation, but it was the rookie who found them. Coney had his head inside my trunk. Pizzello took the picks and tucked them into a vest pocket. When the jacket didn't surface, Coney made the rookie lie flat in the road and look under the chassis.

"Where'd you leave it?" he snarled at me.

"If I didn't have it, I couldn't leave it anywhere," I said.

"You said the dead woman wasn't your Jane Doe," Pizzello intervened. "Who was she?"

"I'm pretty sure it was Jane's hospital roommate. Poor thing, she had abdominal surgery the day before Jane disappeared. How did she end up under that bush? When I saw her in the hospital, she could barely walk because of her incisions."

"She was killed someplace else and carried there," Pizzello said. "Probably dead for at least eight hours. That's as much as the ME could tell us at the scene."

"Which you don't share with a civilian." Coney turned his anger on Pizzello.

"No worries." I figured I owed Pizzello the return courtesy of getting Coney off her back. "Nick Vishnikov is an old friend. He'll tell me when they've finished the autopsy. You reckon the jacket will show how she was murdered?" Vishnikov was the county's deputy chief medical examiner.

"I *reckon* you don't need to stick your nose into police business."

"What about the synagogue?" I asked. "Is it police business, or is it okay if I keep an eye out for the vandals?"

Coney stuck out a hand, twisted my left ear so hard I saw spots. I sucked in a breath but didn't cry out. His face was so close to mine I could count the blackheads on his naked nose. He finally released me and stomped back to his SUV. The thugs followed him, but the one whose name I didn't know took the time to tell me to watch my step.

"He's right," Pizzello said when Coney pulled away. "I keep telling you not to provoke him and you keep bringing him to the boil."

"He brings himself to the boil. What is it with the jacket—which was mine, originally, before I wrapped Jane Doe in it when she was as cold as last year's open cases."

"If the roommate—did you get her name? Ariadne Blanchard?—was killed in a hit-and-run, the jacket probably has traces of paint or metal from the car that hit her. Our lab can track those back to the make and model."

"Right, Pizzello. The CPD has so little on its plate, they're happy to act like CSI and investigate each hit-and-run as if it's the key to who shot JFK. And Coney's zeal for justice is what keeps him crawling out of that rat burrow on Homan to attack me. What is it he's really looking for?"

She glanced at Officer Howard, who was looking as though he wished he'd chosen a career cleaning toilets at Wrigley Field instead of police work. He was too green to know that such a look from his boss meant he was supposed to back away, so Pizzello beckoned me to the curb.

"I don't know. And Finchley doesn't know. They were hoping whatever it is was on the dead woman's body. Someone phoning 911 to report a body under a bush doesn't get every squad car in the district racing to the scene. Most of the time it's a drunk sleeping it off. The jacket, and the rumor that it was your Jane Doe, brought out enough cops to work a presidential visit. I was late to the party, so the looey sent me here. Partly to protect you from the consequences of your own indiscretions."

She paused; I told her I was grateful. Which I was.

"Mostly the looey wants a whiff of what they're looking for. Something small, portable, could have fit in a jeans pocket. They searched poor dead Ariadne in a gross way."

I could feel the heat from my jacket radiating through the synagogue door, but I didn't look that way. I shook my head in genuine puzzlement. The jacket was torn, the fabric, even the facing that held the buttons, too flimsy to hide something.

"Jane might have eaten it," I suggested.

Pizzello made a face. "If she did that, she'd better be able to retrieve it herself."

I laughed. "On the down low, though, I'm ninety-nine percent sure I have an ID for Jane."

I told her about my visit to the riverfront mansion, my discovering the dungeon in the basement, as well as the family tree of the current owner. "Silvia is the grandmother, Yulchia the kid. They want to be together, but the divider in the middle is Silvia's son, Gus."

"Social work one of your skills, Warshawski?" Pizzello said. "You going to patch that unhappy family back together?"

"Pizzello, don't keep blowing cold and hot on me. Whatever Coney and the mystery man in the hospital are looking for, they think Jane/Yulchia has it. She's been living with her uncle and his wife. She ran away, they say; on the other hand, someone was held prisoner in the basement of the Zigler mansion. She burned her way to freedom, and Jane had burns on her legs when

I found her, which makes me think the uncle and aunt had locked her up."

I hesitated. "One of my sources thinks the Viper may be involved."

"And you see him connected to Jane Doe and to Coney?" Pizzello made a swatting gesture—I was a buzzing fly in her ear. "If you remember where you put your jacket, and if you find out what Jane Doe has that Coney and his buddies want so badly, give me a call. Rudy!"

The rookie straightened his back.

"Time for us to serve and protect some other Chicagoans."

She stopped on her way to her car. "I almost forgot— these are yours, although they shouldn't be." She tossed the picks in my direction.

29
Taking the Plunge

I collected my belongings from where the cops had dumped them. My bottle of hand sanitizer had rolled under the front wheels. I worked it into the crevices between my fingers, poured more of it over the backs and palms, repeated it twice, and still felt contaminated.

I took off the mask, which was filthy with Coney's spit, and dumped it in a trash bin on the corner. I worked more sanitizer into my face and my left ear, which was throbbing from where Coney had twisted it. I've been vaccinated, but I still felt vulnerable, as if Coney were so violent he could wipe out my antibodies.

My phone was pinging. I had many voicemail messages. Mr. Contreras wanted assurance that I hadn't been arrested, Murray Ryerson wanted to know why he had to hear about me from Global, Beth Blacksin wanted more about Ariadne, actual clients wanted to know if I was ever going to do any work for them. And Gus Zigler wanted to talk about my visit to Archangel. The day had started sometime in the previous decade and didn't show signs of ending anytime soon.

The homeless woman who'd watched my encounter with the cops still had her eye on me. When I bundled the dirty towels into the trunk, she called out in a hoarse voice, asking if I needed all of them.

"Nope." I took the two least filthy ones over to her. "They're not clean, but you're welcome to them."

"Not clean, ha-ha. I'm not clean. I was washed in the blood of the lamb when I was thirteen, but dirt built up since then. Those cops was plenty pissed at you. I thought they was going to carry you off in handcuffs."

"Me, too," I said. A rich mix of stale sweat and beer rose from her. As soon as I'd handed her the towels, I backed away.

"What are they so mad about?"

"I'm a private detective. They don't like me solving crimes that they can't figure out themselves."

"Ha, Five-Oh don't like to look bad, 'specially not that big guy who was beating on you."

"Right you are. I'd like to know who's painting ugly words on the synagogue there. You ever see anyone doing something like that?"

"You do your detecting for free?"

"Sometimes."

"You a fool, then. I don't watch this street for free."

I dug in my bag for my wallet, found a couple of tens.

"I can't leave my stuff. I don't have a fancy ride to hide it in. You go down the street to that chicken place. Dinner with everything. And some Remy to wash it down."

I sighed, wondering if she'd seen anything useful, but I finished picking up my stuff, scrubbed my hands again. I needed a clean mask to get the chicken, but a drugstore on the corner had a free stack near the entrance. As a thank-you, I bought the Remy Martin there.

While I waited in line for the chicken, I called Mr. Contreras. He was predictably, reassuringly angry on my behalf when I described Coney's behavior.

"I'll be home soon—half an hour. Is Brad doing okay?"

"Yeah. He's a good kid. He took Mitch and Peppy out, so don't you worry about him or the dogs."

When I brought the chicken back to my homeless friend, she turned out not to know much about the vandals. "They come on motorcycles. Five of them, maybe six." She thought they were all white, but she wasn't a hundred percent sure.

"Although what Black man is going to go around with a bunch of white bikers, huh?"

"Good point," I agreed.

A man had joined her as we were talking. He wanted some of the chicken, and he definitely wanted some of the Remy. As he wheedled, he called her Olive. At least I had a name for her now. I left Olive to sort it out. She seemed tough enough to handle street hustlers, way tougher than I felt at this point.

I wanted to retrieve my jacket from Shaamar Hashomayim, but the woman was watching me, even if she hadn't paid much attention to the vandals. If she'd seen me stuff the jacket through the mail slot, I think she might have mentioned it. I didn't want her to see me in action with my picks. She'd probably sell me to the cops for a pint. I'd have to come back tomorrow before Mr. Pariente arrived for morning prayers.

I called Murray as I drove home. I cut short his jokingly delivered sense of injury.

"There's a lot going on and I'm happy to give you the details that no one else knows, but I have to rest for an hour, maybe two." I looked at the dashboard clock. Six-thirty. "Meet me at nine on that spit of land across from the south end of Goose Island. There's an abandoned mansion there, built by a robber baron named Zigler. It probably has crime scene tape around it, but I'm betting they didn't leave any kind of guard in place."

That stirred him into a frenzy of questions, but I interrupted him. "Can you see if anyone's making buy or sell moves on the mansion away from the radar? Maybe presenting plans to the commission as if its sale were a done deal?"

"Anyone who builds housing on the island or the land facing it has to commit to twenty percent affordable units," Murray said. "That was the original agreement, and I don't think anyone's been able to budge the local alderman on the ratio. The requirement made some investors back off, but the site is hot. It's begging for condos and lofts."

"Then developing the mansion would make developers' mouths water, wouldn't it? The mansion could be grandfathered in ahead of the affordable housing guidelines. See what you can snuffle out."

I hung up. I was starting to see shimmering lights around the cars in front of me. I needed to get to my bed before I hit someone.

At home, after catching up Mr. Contreras on my day, and getting a blow-by-blow from him and Brad on theirs, I dismantled the bugs in my apartment. I was spending too much physical time with Coney; I didn't want him in my home as well.

I put all my clothes in a plastic bag and left it on the porch. I'd take them down to the laundry later, but for now I didn't want anything he'd touched anywhere in my home. I took a long shower, washing that man out of my hair, my skin, my mind—almost.

I got in ninety minutes of sleep. When I got up, I saw Gus had phoned three more times. It's possible Coney wanted me badly enough to track my phone and my car, so I left both at home. I stuffed a stack of twenties into my pocket along with my house keys, put gloves, picks, and an industrial flashlight into a fanny pack. I took a cab to an electronics outlet where I paid cash for more burner phones, and hailed a second to Goose Island. I was left with seven dollars. Murray would have to drive me home.

The Zigler mansion and garden were dark. I shone my flashlight on the gate. Crime scene tape dangled from the handle.

"Murray?" I called in a low voice.

"Yo, Warshawski."

Dark is relative in a city. The bus depot across the river and the apartments on the opposite bank gave off enough light to show the outline of the house, the looming arms of the trees, and Murray moving cautiously along the flagstones toward me. He'd been trying the door, but it was locked, with a police seal across it.

"Your turn to be the criminal," he said. "I cut the crime scene tape at the gate."

"I'm thinking my boy may have put a mike or a camera at the front door," I murmured to Murray. "Let's see what Zigler's study windows are like."

I found the box I'd stood on to stare through the front windows and carried it around to the south side of the house. The heavy undergrowth meant we couldn't make any pretense at stealth. Murray got his feet tangled in a creeping vine and almost fell over. After that we decided using a flashlight was less risky than a bad fall.

Murray shone his flashlight on the catches while I worked them. Even with the box, these were above my head, which might be why none of the homeless population had broken in this way.

Once I'd gotten the windows unhooked, Murray gave me a boost in. I went around to the kitchen and opened the back door for him. He wanted to see the dungeon. I didn't think we should waste time on it, but he wanted photographs for the piece he was working on for the *Edge*.

When he came back up, I told him about my conversation with Gus and Lacey Zigler, and my visit to the Archangel facility. I didn't mention Gisela Queriga. Murray might promise to respect her privacy, but if he decided she would jazz up his piece for the *Edge,* all promises would fly out the window.

I did tell him about seeing Gus Zigler across the river in Duda's yard, and my speculation that they were gambling buddies.

"You're like the little pig building a house out of straw," Murray said. "I'm not saying you're wrong, but it would be a help if you had a firm foundation under any of this."

I agreed gloomily.

I wasn't sure what we were looking for in the house, but I was hoping there was some kind of trail linking Ashleigh's real estate company to Silvia Zigler. Better yet, something proving a connection between Gus and the Viper. It was an impossible job. The chaos in the basement, the century and a half of accumulated newspapers, magazines, clothes, tools, would require a team of expert searchers to sort out.

I went through Zigler's desk. Her computer was gone, but she might have a printed document showing someone trying to pressure her to sell. Murray hunted the upper floors. He'd been upstairs for about twenty minutes when he came thundering down the central ornamental staircase.

"Warshawski, we have to clear out. Fast. Three men, maybe four in the garden. I saw them out the window."

I turned off my flashlight, flattened myself against the wall by the window, and peered out. Movement in the shrubbery and then four figures in hunting camouflage, including night-vision goggles, emerged. One of them signaled to the others the way they do on cop shows, sending two to the front door, two to the back.

"We have about fifteen seconds to get out the windows in Zigler's study," I said. We heard the stealthy opening of doors fore and aft.

The study windows screeched loudly as we shoved them open. Straddled the ledge for a second to get a handhold, swung the legs down, and jumped.

We made it into the garden seconds ahead of the hunters. They came through the window after us, boots thudding hard on the ground. We froze, listened to them curse thorns and vines as they crashed through the old rose bushes; one of them shouted to turn on flashlights—night-vision goggles couldn't see through the underbrush.

"Separate," Murray mouthed into my ear. "I have a cover: I'm a journalist working a story. Save yourself."

We timed our movements to the noise the hunters created thrashing through the undergrowth. Murray headed toward the front of the house. I wormed my way along the ground to the far end of the garden. I slid under the fence. Got to my feet. And a figure in camouflage loomed over me, pointing a rifle.

I grabbed his ankle with both hands, jerked hard, pulled him over. The rifle went off, too close to my head. Ears ringing, but I was up and running along the lip of cement between the garden and the river. I saw the light bobbing behind me, turned my head as he lifted his weapon. Launched myself over the metal-lined riverbank.

30
View From the Bridge

The mask was choking me. I'd sucked in a breath as I dove, and the water pushed the mask into my throat. I thrashed blindly, pulling cloth out of my mouth, pulling loops away from my ears. Gulped a mouthful of rank water, choked. *You're a water animal, you're a seal, you've done this in the Calumet River, lie on your back, move your arms.*

I bumped against the metal barrier, grabbed at it, looked up. Hunter pointing rifle straight at me. I dove. Not enough air to stay underwater. Surfaced upriver, saw the hunters on the bank. I was in the water's widest place, the arm of the *Y* where the river split. I lay on my back, kicking as best I could with my waterlogged clothes, pointing myself toward the east bank.

A bullet spat into the water by my head. I flipped over, dove again, underwater, praying I was still heading to the east bank. *Not far, you've done ten times that distance in Lake Michigan.* My sweatshirt was weighing me down, but I couldn't get out of it. I surfaced to breathe, saw marsh grasses ahead.

I turned over again, slowly, a Galapagos tortoise, not a seal. Moved my heavy flippers, landed in mud.

People were leaning over the edge of the bank. I saw their lips moving, but my ears were still ringing from the bullet fired close to my head. They were conferring, gesturing, getting out phones. I didn't want a police presence, didn't want an ambulance. I struggled to my feet. My shoes were thick with sludge.

I'd disturbed some goose nests, and the birds were circling angrily. "Yeah, guys. I want to be out of here as much as you want me gone."

I put my hands up to grab the top of the iron that lined the bank. I did not have the strength to lift myself. Blue strobes caught my eye. Squad cars were crossing the Chicago Avenue bridge. If Coney was after me—I squatted, jumped, caught my midriff on the metal top. Someone grabbed my wrists, pulled me all the way up.

I was cold, my ears were whining from the bullet, and I stank. I backed away from my rescuers, who were crying out in what I guessed was a concert of concern.

"I can't hear," I said. "But thank you. I have a car over there." I lied, pointing toward the Chicago Avenue bridge.

My rescuers gestured at the blue-and-whites. I thanked them again and moved away on my heavy muddy legs. The riverwalk is a pedestrian path between condos and water. It isn't wide enough for cars, and there are passageways to the street only every hundred yards or so, which meant the police would have to park and approach on foot. That gave me a few minutes to leave the area before the cops worked their way down. I staggered along the walk until I came to one of the passageways. I stood behind a pillar and watched three blue-and-whites pass on the far side of the passage, then shuffled my way through the arcade to the street.

If those were ordinary squad cars, ready to help a citizen in distress, I'd be stupid to run—shamble—away from help. But if the hunter who'd shot at me was connected to Coney, then I'd be stupid to stay.

When I got to the street, I was only a couple of blocks from the bridge, but my clothes were so heavy on me that I couldn't move fast. Down one block to Chicago. West on Chicago to the bridge. This stretch of Chicago Avenue is built on pylons that lift it across the river, the expressway, and freight tracks; the street rises steeply to meet the bridge. When I got to the first girder, I squatted behind it to look at the riverwalk below me.

The cops had arrived at the place where my Samaritans had pulled me out of the water. Some dozen civilians were gesturing at the riverwalk, at the bridge, flinging their hands in incomprehension—why hadn't I waited for help? The police would assume I was fleeing a crime scene. Or maybe just homeless.

I knew Mr. Contreras would be worried sick, but my fanny pack had somehow come undone in the water, and with it my new burner phones. I couldn't summon a ride, even if a driver would let me into their car. I hoped Murray was safe. I hoped he'd see the cop activity on the east bank of the river and figure I was safe. And then he could notify Mr. Contreras. In the morning, I'd walk home, but I couldn't manage it tonight.

I looked across the bridge, praying for a hiding place. The old tender house stood there, moss covered, windows thick with grime.

The sidewalk across the bridge was wedged between the bridge's girders and an iron railing. I started across, holding the railing tightly. The bouncing of the old iron slabs underneath made me feel as though I might be jolted back into the water.

A late-night dog walker passed me, turning his head

conspicuously away. I looked like the most derelict person on the street tonight, even more than a homeless man propped in a sitting position against a girder. The traffic bouncing across the bridge seemed perilously close to his head, but he was sharing his thoughts with a bottle and didn't seem to notice.

The tender houses had been out of commission for decades. The city hadn't bothered to keep them up, at least not ones where tourists didn't visit. The houses typically had three stories, with the top at street level and the bottom level with the water.

I inspected the house but couldn't see a way in from the top. There was a new door, with a solid lock and a bolt over it. I'd lost my picks when I lost my pack, and anyway, my hands were too numb for the nuance of picking.

The high windows, which would have given the bridge tender a view of all three arms of the river, were out of my reach. A metal staircase, closed off by a tall, padlocked gate, led to the bottom levels. Maybe I could just squat on the sidewalk like the other homeless people I'd passed, wait for morning light, hope I didn't greet the dawn with pneumonia or cholera.

I heard Boom-Boom's scornful laugh. *You going to turn chicken now, Vic?* We'd been standing on the high concrete bank above Lake Calumet, an oceangoing

freighter approaching, daring each other to jump before it passed in front of us. He dove; I followed. *I am
not a chicken, Boom-Boom.*

I peered over the sides at the water below, at the
disintegrating wooden logs meant to keep boats from
ramming the metal banks. The gate was bolted to a
concrete sleeve. I stripped off my sodden sweatshirt.
I couldn't be any colder in my thin T-shirt, and now
I could move my arms. Sort of. I dug my fingers into
holes in the house's concrete base, knelt on the narrow
top of the railing. Pulled myself standing. Stuck a leg
out onto the concrete sleeve.

My hearing was returning. Cars were honking at me
from the bridge. For pity's sake, do not call the cops.

Second leg onto the ledge. Left leg down to a lip at
the bottom of the base. Don't look down, don't think of
water, wooden pylons waiting to impale me. Hold the
ledge with cramping fingers, right foot down to the lip.
Scoot around. Reach the stairs.

See, Boom-Boom? No chickens here. On the landing, I disturbed another homeless man. He brandished
a broken bottle at me. Cried that he would gouge out
my eyes if I tried to steal his spot. I gave him a salute
and moved away.

Below me, where the house's outer wall seemed to
sink into the bridge, I saw a half-open window. Finger

holds in the crumbling concrete, right foot on the ladder, left foot seeking toe holds in the concrete. Left foot secure, right foot on stairwell, lower my trembling arms. Repeat once, twice, right knee on windowsill, hamstrings spasming, couple on riverwalk with dog, do not scream in pain. The masonry around the windows was thick. I pulled up my left leg, pushed up on the sash. Fell gracelessly onto the floor inside.

I was on the bottom level, where no light came in. My flashlight was in my fanny pack at the bottom of the river. House keys and seven dollars were all I had in my jeans pocket. No way to see where I was.

I'd landed on wood, soft wood by the feel of it. I didn't dare walk on it in the dark, in case it had rotted away in the damp. I took off my shoes and socks, massaged my cramped toes, massaged my hamstrings. Stood, gingerly, and pulled the window shut. I lay down on a firm piece of wood, so tired I fell asleep, despite my cold wet clothes, my stench, the hard floor.

31

Tender Is the House

Ascreeching woke me. I sat up, panicked, forgetting where I was, and then realized the window I'd used was opening. I got to my feet, unsteady, muscles frozen from the cold and wet. A pinpoint of light picked me out. A voice cried, "Who are you? What are you doing here? I have a gun, and I'm not afraid to shoot you."

A girl, young and terrified.

"If you have a gun and want to shoot, aim for my heart." I tapped my chest. "If you miss, I'll be bleeding and feverish. I will die slowly, and it will be horrible to share this space with me."

The light jumped around, bright but narrow, coming from a phone. I could see the floor now, and the drawbridge machinery, large gears with giant chains wrapped around them.

I could play hide-and-seek with this child. Could probably tackle them. I just didn't have the energy or even the desire to fight. I sat back down, knees drawn up to my chin, arms clasped around them, and waited.

"Who are you? What are you doing here?"

"I'm V.I. Warshawski. I landed in the river trying to get away from a man with a rifle. I am too worn out to walk home tonight. I need a safe place to rest. I found my way into this tender house. Your turn."

"V.I. Warshawski?" the voice cried.

"You know my name?" I asked.

"I saw you on the news. I know you're hunting me. If you try to catch me, I really will shoot."

My hands fell to my sides. "Yulchia. Julia. I don't want to catch you. I want to keep you safe."

The light wobbled more. "How do you know my name? Is Unc—is someone outside, waiting to catch me?"

"It's true I've been looking for you, but only because I want you to be safe." Fatigue made it hard for me to shape thoughts, let alone words. "I know you can't be safe with your uncle and aunt. I also know you're in a terrible bind. Your granny is in a nursing home; they won't let the two of you see each other. Did your uncle lock you in your granny's basement?"

"In *my* basement," she said fiercely. "I live in that house with my *nagyi*. Did Uncle Gus hire you to catch me?"

"No one hired me to look for you. I went into your grandmother's house searching for something else. I didn't know then that Silvia Zigler was your granny. And then I smelled the remains of the fire, and saw the burnt panels on the kitchen door. How did you get out of the dungeon? How did you set the fire?"

She had been alone too long, her fears and her story locked inside. After a few minutes of more suspicions and accusations, she found herself spilling the details, an urgent geyser of words.

Gus and Lacey had locked her in the basement. They came every now and then to toss a granola bar at her, but the day she escaped, they hadn't pulled the chain tightly enough across the door; Julia slipped through sideways.

"The door from the basement into the kitchen was locked, but that old workroom, I knew there was kerosene, because *Nagyi* told me they used to use it for their lamps in my grandpa's father's time. He kept everything, old clothes, old newspapers, those old lamps because they were made in his glass factory. I found matches, too. I threw kerosene at the door and set it on fire, only some kerosene landed on my jeans, and I caught fire going through the door."

"How did you end up in the rocks all the way on the Evanston border?"

"I don't know what you're talking about." She was tense again.

"It's where my dogs and I found you." I described Mitch's heroism. "How did you end up so far from home?"

It took more prodding, but the rest of the story finally came out. She'd been trying to see Silvia in the Archangel nursing home.

"She fell and broke her hip. Only, I think my aunt and uncle pushed her down the stairs. I went off on my bike that day, because I knew they were coming over, and I hate being around them. They want our house. They hate my *nagyi* and they're rude to her, even though she's Uncle Gus's mother. My mother's mother, too.

"When I got home that day, it was January, but no snow, which is why I was biking. Anyway, *Nagyi* was lying on the floor. She was barely awake. I called 911, and then Uncle Gus popped up, pretending he hadn't already been there. He said, what a terrible accident, why was she still lying on the floor, didn't that prove she couldn't live alone and that I wasn't fit to look after her? That's what he said to the judges and the doctors and everyone, like he cares about her when he wants her dead."

After her grandmother was taken to the hospital—"Uncle Gus made them go to St. Helena's, where Aunt Lacey works, even though it would have been so much better to take her to the closest hospital"—Julia tried to stay in the Goose Island house.

"It's my house, too. *Nagyi* says when she dies it will be mine, and this makes Uncle Gus super mad. He thinks because he's her son, it should go to him, only he did something terrible—I don't know what, exactly, something Uncle Gus did before I was born, even. Something about money that he owed my dad."

Gus and Lacey had mentioned that Julia's father had been deported. I didn't know how that connected to Gus owing him money, but I couldn't sidetrack Julia's narrative with that question.

"Anyway, Gus got some special legal paper, like what Britney Spears's father did, and that gave him power to turn off the gas and the electricity in the house, and of course the house turned into an iceberg. I wanted to stay there even without heat. I have plenty of blankets, but a family court judge made me move in with them. I told the judge my aunt and uncle were riffraff, and the judge said I needed an attitude adjustment and some discipline."

She fell silent for a moment, reliving her anger. "I kept running away, and Uncle Gus would get blockhead cops to bring me back. Him and Aunt Lacey, they're trying to make my *nagyi* give them the house. And if she won't, then they want me to sign some form, something they got from a lawyer, saying if she dies I'll give up my right to the house. They said if I don't, they'll sue me or some bullshit, and no court will believe that a wild child like me could be trusted with a house like ours."

"Is that why they locked you in the basement? To force you to sign?"

"I was stupid," she said bitterly. "I was so mad at them! See, I know about this because I heard them talking one night. Aunt Lacey was saying she couldn't live with me one minute longer, and why couldn't Uncle Gus just sign my name, he was good at that kind of thing, and he said *Nagyi*'s lawyer would challenge that, because of his history, and then Aunt Lacey said, what would they do if *Nagyi* died and never signed? So that's when Uncle Gus said about suing, and me being a wild child.

"So I ran into the room and said they were right. *Nagyi*'s lawyer had all her papers, and she had proof what a loser and criminal and jerkface he was. And they were locked up where no one could get them. So that's when they locked me in the basement, they were trying to starve me so I'd tell them where her lockbox was."

"She put her papers in a bank's safety deposit box?" I asked.

"No, not in a bank. Her lawyer is keeping the box for her. But when the ambulance came to get her, she told me where the key was. Uncle Gus and Aunt Lacey started going through all the papers and everything looking for the key. I could hear them, and I told them they'd never find it in a million years. Which was so stupid, because then they knew I had it!"

"Do you have it?"

"I—" She stopped speaking. "It's not in the house. They can open every box of papers and go through every one of Great-Grandpa's tools and they won't find it."

She refused to tell me more about the key. She said she'd talked too much already and what if I really was working for her aunt and uncle.

I changed the subject. "Gus said your grandmother's lawyer would challenge Gus if he forged your signature. That sounds as though Gus has a history of doing stuff like that."

"What, you mean he was signing someone else's name? Like *Nagyi's*?" Julia thought for a minute. "I know he lost a ton of money gambling. Him and

Nagyi, they fought about it every time him and Lacey came over."

"So he'd want your grandmother to sell the house and let him have the money to cover his debts. They locked you in the basement to make you relinquish your right to inherit? Or to tell them where you'd hidden the key?"

"Relinquish?" she repeated.

"The form they wanted you to sign, giving up your potential inheritance."

"What do you mean, 'potential'?" she demanded, voice fierce again. "My *nagyi* is leaving it to me. She's said it hundreds of times."

"Then I'm sure she is." No point in mentioning chickens and hatching eggs. "So they locked you in the basement, but you're tough, you're innovative. You managed to escape."

"I really thought I was going to die. But I kept remembering how *Nagyi* stood up to Russian tanks when she was my age, so even though they were mostly starving me, I wouldn't sign what they wanted.

"That day I burned my way out, I hitchhiked up to the nursing home. I thought I would see my *nagyi* and we could escape together. But the nursing home people wouldn't let me visit her. I was begging with them, and they fooled me; they made me think they were talking to their boss about letting me visit, only really, they called Uncle Gus.

"He came and tried to grab me, and I ran off and got on the back of this truck that was driving out. And when it got to the lake I jumped off and climbed down the rocks."

She'd turned off the phone light. In the dark, her narrative was a strange mix of childishness and an adult who's experienced too much.

"You're a heroine," I said. "I will do my best to help you and your grandmother survive this mess. After you ran from the hospital, did you come here, to the tender house? How did you know about it?"

"This is where my grandpa, my *nagyi*'s husband, used to play when he was a little boy. He was dead before I was born, but my mom told me, before she died. She used to play here, too, as a little girl, but she said Uncle Gus never came here, so it's always been my secret place. How did you know about it? Were you spying on me, after all?"

"I didn't know you were here. I didn't even know you could get into this place," I said. "I was desperate to hide from the police. They're after me because they think I can lead them to you. Someone tried to shoot me tonight, outside your grandmother's house."

"That was you? I was watching the house from the

windows upstairs here. I saw two people going in, and then these men dressed like soldiers went in after, and then they shot someone and dumped them in the river."

"That was me," I said. "They shot at me and I jumped into the river. I'm still wet and filthy. And I would consider it a great favor if you would let me use your phone. Not to call the cops, but to let the neighbor who looks out for me know I'm safe."

She was reluctant, understandably, but I drew on all my powers of persuasion. "You can shoot me if you hear me talking to the police."

She hesitated. "I don't really have a gun."

"I didn't think you did. But I really am not going to call the police."

She finally moved close to me in the dark space, the phone lighting up and showing me her own thin, vivid face. I made my call, assured my frantic neighbor that I was safe but too tired to move another foot tonight. Murray had called him, hoping I'd made it home, which had made my neighbor blow up at him—"He's that kind of guy, Cookie, kind who'd go off getting his newspaper scoop and not caring if you drowned or nothin'."

He wanted to drive the Mustang down right now to pick me up, but I didn't want to leave Julia on her own. And I didn't want to navigate the tender house window and the river in the dark, not after the night I'd had. I told him we'd connect in the morning.

When I hung up, I hit the photo button. And saw a woman with a cloud of auburn hair flowing down her back. A man was embracing her, his face buried in her curls. That was Ashleigh Breslau's hair. All I could see of the man was a mass of dark curly hair and his bulging traps.

32

My Cup Runneth Over

"**I** thought this was your phone!" I cried. "It belongs to Brad Litvak."

"Aunt Lacey smashed my phone. And then they cut off the service, so I can't use it anyway. I never heard of Brad Litvak, so what do I care about his phone?"

"He's the kid who went into the river, night before last. He was watching his mother through the windows at your granny's house."

"So what? He dropped it in our garden. That means it's mine. Finders, keepers."

"Maybe for a lost dollar bill. But phones are registered. The Litvaks haven't gotten around to reporting the phone yet. If they had, the service would have been turned off. But it also means that the carrier can locate exactly where you are. The carrier will be delighted to share that information with the authorities. This could happen at any second. I'm too tired to move, but I'm absolutely not going to wait here like a rat in a barrel for a monster lieutenant named Coney to shoot at me. Come with me or stay here, your choice, but I'm gone."

I found my shoes and socks and started to pull them on. My feet were raw and sore. They wanted to be soaked in hot water and have liniment rubbed into them. They did not want wet socks and shoes and more climbing around the outside of the tender house.

"The key to your grandmother's box: if the cops come in here and search, they're going to find it, no matter how carefully you hid it. If you give it to me, I promise I'll keep it safe."

"It's none of your business what I did with it," she said fiercely.

She became agitated when I tried to press her. I dropped the topic, but urged her again to come with me. She only replied that I was not the boss of her.

My eyes had adjusted enough to the dark that I could make out the windows, lighter oblongs in the masonry walls. I found the one Julia and I had used, shoved the sash up, moved on clumsy feet back to the thick sill. Swung my legs over, grabbed the metal stairwell rail. For a perilous moment I swayed over the water and the spiked wooden bumpers, and then I managed to make the stairwell.

I started up the stairs on trembling legs. One step, stop, rest. A second step, stop. Rest. I was level with the sidewalk when Julia caught up with me.

"I don't want to be a rat in a barrel for Uncle Gus," she whispered. "I'll take the phone back to the garden where I found it."

"They'll still trace it here. They can see every place it's been. Toss it in the river, but understand that your hideout is not safe."

We were at the top now. I reversed the grueling crawl around the masonry. To the railing. To the street. Julia followed.

"Now what?" she whispered.

"Now you get rid of the phone, or stay away from me."

In the light from the cars, I could see her face, hollowed out by hunger and pain. She drew her lips into a pout, but took the phone from her jeans and dropped it over the side. It landed with a clatter on the bottom step.

"Now we need to rest and get warm." If I'd been on my own, I would have forced my bones to march the three miles to my apartment. Julia's thinness made me fear she couldn't make such a journey. The options without money or a smartphone were limited. We made our way down the service road to her grandmother's house. I'd seen the time on Brad's phone when I used it, past three in the morning.

We moved slowly, fatigued, cautious, but the hunters hadn't left a lookout. Julia knew her way through the garden to an entry into the house behind a shrub so thick you couldn't tell there was a door there.

"They used it in the olden days for deliveries into the kitchen, when they had a gazillion servants," Julia explained. "*Nagyi* says the cook would go out through this door and a barge would unload supplies right at her feet."

We crept up to the second floor. Gus had turned off power and gas to the house, but the water was still running. I bathed gratefully under a cold-water tap and found some warm clothes in Silvia Zigler's closet. I wrapped Julia in blankets on her own bed and brought blankets in from Silvia's bed so I could stay on the floor near her. If someone came after us, I didn't want Julia on her own.

"What have you been doing for food?" I asked her.

She'd eaten all the dry breakfast cereal her first few days on the run, and now was eating out of the cans in the pantry. Cold soup, cold beans, uncooked macaroni. "I come, like, around the middle of the night, when I know the workmen in the cement place across the river won't see me, and Uncle Gus won't be hanging around.

But I stay in the tender house because no one knows to look there. Even if the phone was there, they couldn't get in and find me."

I didn't try to argue with her but sat on the bed until she seemed to be asleep. I worried about the burn wounds on her legs but couldn't do anything about them in the dark.

I lay in my cocoon of blankets, where I slept, but uneasily, unwilling to surrender awareness. I woke when the room was flooded with light. Impossible to tell the time of day, but the graininess in my eyes and my throbbing hands and feet told me I hadn't slept much.

I carried the blankets back to Silvia's bed. Her room overlooked the river and the bridge. Where I could see cop activity around the tender house.

I went back to Julia's bed. She was heavily asleep. I put on a pair of Silvia's socks and my own wet shoes. Silvia was smaller than me and the pants I'd taken didn't quite zip, but they were better than my own soiled clothes. I dug my house keys and my seven dollars out of my jeans pocket and stuffed them into Silvia's jacket. I found my picks as well. I hadn't remembered sticking them into my pocket when I finished opening the catches to the Zigler window last night, but I was glad I still had them. I hoisted Julia out of bed and over my shoulder.

Julia woke as I was going down the stairs, fretful, not wanting to come with me.

"Baby, the cops are all over the tender house right now. If I leave you here, they'll find you and take you to Gus, and your drama will start up again."

She tried to protest that she could hide in the garden until the cops finished at the tender house, but she clearly wanted my support. She put on her shoes and one of her grandmother's sweaters and let me help her through the garden.

We stayed on the west side of the grounds, out of view of the bridge and of the condos on the east bank, and walked up the access road to Halsted Street. Cement mixers, from Duda's yard and the yards farther north, were backed up at the light by the bridge, which made me think it was still early. They were preparing to head out to job sites.

We found a taxi on Halsted. The driver had a stack of masks. He handed us two without speaking. It was seven-thirty, according to his dashboard clock.

I was worried that my home wasn't safe, that Coney might be watching it, but I had to go there to get enough money to pay the cab. In the event, no one bothered us. The driver swore when I asked him to wait, but he wanted to be paid.

Mitch and Peppy heard us come in. They smelled

Julia, I guess, because they started a chorus of whimpers, not barks, loud enough to rouse Mr. Contreras. He opened the door, and Mitch and Peppy swarmed around Julia. They even paid a little attention to me.

When Mr. Contreras started fussing over Julia, I lumbered up to the third floor to get enough cash to pay off the taxi. I caught a glimpse of myself in the bedroom mirror. My cold bath had smeared mud around my forehead, and my hair looked as though I'd glued a clump of steel wool to my head. The unzipped pants showed about five inches of my belly. It was a miracle that the taxi had picked us up. I added a five to the meter total.

"We need baths," I told Mr. Contreras, who was in the kitchen with Julia, starting to make a batch of French toast. "And Missy here needs the burns on her legs attended to."

"She needs food, doll. Doesn't take a math professor to count the ribs on a kid this skinny."

I had to agree. Her eyes were glittering with hunger, and a spool of drool seeped from her mouth as he started to fry the bread.

Before going back upstairs, I asked about Brad. My neighbor said he was still here, still sound asleep. Maybe Mr. Contreras and I should register formally as a halfway house for runaway teens.

"His dad came around last night," Mr. Contreras said. "I was hoping maybe Litvak would want to patch things up with his boy, but they had a fight and Litvak stormed away, mad as usual."

Donny Litvak couldn't draw a breath of air without fighting someone for a bigger share of the oxygen, but I wondered if this was a continuation of the argument that had sent Brad running away from his family yesterday morning. Unfortunately, even though the contestants had been in full throat, Mr. Contreras only picked out a few phrases.

I left Julia pouring a quart of syrup over her French toast and went up to wash the Chicago River out of my hair. While I massaged my feet with one hand, I scrolled through my messages. Gus Zigler had left a total of seven, some voice, some text, most wanting to know why I had gone to Archangel prying into his mother's state of health.

The last one had come in twenty minutes ago. The police had been at his mother's house and there was every sign that Julia had been there, with an adult who had left filthy clothes behind. If that was me, I had a lot of explaining to do.

Sergeant Pizzello had called. The dry cleaners across from Temple Shaamar Hashomayim had reported a break-in. Someone had made off with two carts full of uncleaned clothes. Did I know anything about that?

Murray wanted to know what happened to me after I jumped into the river. And he wanted to tell me what had happened to him.

Lotty wanted to know that I was safe. Max Loewenthal wanted to talk about the woman I'd identified yesterday afternoon in Warren Park. Had that been yesterday afternoon? It felt as though it belonged to some universe I no longer had access to.

The message from Gus was the most alarming. It meant I needed to get in motion and find a safer place to stash Julia. I taped the open blisters on my feet, put on clean socks and shoes, dressed in clothes that fit me, and put together a day pack, including a change of socks and bandages, a couple of bottles of water, and a cheese sandwich. If I was going to be on the move all day, I needed to make sure I had food. I kept my smartphone with me but wrapped it in foil to block its signals.

I drank a fruit smoothie and took a triple espresso downstairs with me, where I explained to Julia and Mr. Contreras why she couldn't stay here.

"I'm not leaving," Julia said. "Mitch will cry. And Uncle Sal will take care of me."

She was sitting on the floor. Mitch was sprawled

across her left knee, his big head filling her lap. Peppy was wedged against her right leg. Both dogs would clearly cry.

"Besides, I can't go anywhere until I have a bath and clean clothes, and I need a cup."

"She can stay down here with me," my neighbor said. "I got a bathtub and I got a whole bunch of cups."

"Menstrual," the girl said. "My period started this morning."

My neighbor turned a shade of puce that Renoir would have envied. Julia giggled.

"I can get her a cup," I said, "but Lieutenant Coney is sure to show up here today. Her uncle Gus, too. They both could be on their way right now."

"Coney can't come in here without a warrant," Mr. Contreras said. "And no reason for this Gus to bother with me."

I didn't like it, but I also didn't have the energy to fight Julia, especially when she had not just my neighbor but the dogs backing her up.

"Tell Brad she's your great-niece. We need to limit gossip about her in the building. I'm going to be on the run all day, but I'll go to a drugstore and get Julia a few necessities."

I turned to her. "Don't go outside unless you go into

the garden with the dogs. Remember: if Brad asks, this is your uncle Sal. Of course, Brad calls him that, too, but you tell anyone who asks that you're Clara's sister's granddaughter. Got it?"

"Clara's sister's granddaughter?" Julia wrinkled her nose. "Who are all those people?"

"Uncle Sal will explain."

33

Button, Button, Who's Got the— What?

A drugstore near my building had a few clothing basics. I got those for Julia along with the cup she needed. I also bought more burner phones. I went home on foot, nervous about trackers, not knowing if I needed to be this nervous.

The building didn't seem to be under surveillance, but these days, with drone technology, you could be watched by a hundred eyes without knowing it. Like the drones Reggie Litvak worked on for Metargon. And the Stingrays law enforcement departments all over America deploy to keep an eye on us. I stood in the middle of Racine, staring up at the sky, but all I saw were pigeons, sparrows, and bits of unidentifiable fluff.

Julia was on the living room floor with the dogs. I handed her the bag of toiletries and clothes and took her upstairs to my place to change. Mitch and Peppy tagged along. While she bathed, I went back to Mr. Contreras's to talk to Brad.

"Your uncle Sal says that your dad came over last night and that the two of you fought. I thought he was cool with you staying here?"

"It wasn't that." Brad was in the kitchen, finishing a fifth piece of French toast. "He thought maybe I really had Uncle Reggie's specs, that I'd loaded them on to my phone. He wanted to see the phone, and then I had to tell him I'd lost it over by the river. So he blew up over that, like did I think he was made of money that I could throw away a smartphone that cost hundreds of dollars. Anyway, of course he canceled the service for the phone, so even if I can get a new one, I'll have to find a way to pay to use it."

He put his fork down, scowling at his plate. "I know I should get a job, but how can I, right now, when I don't even know where I'll be living?"

"We'll worry about that when we get this mess cleaned up," I assured him. "But it is a mess that will take a lot of work, so let's do this one day at a time. I'll give you a burner. They're cheap, but that's because they don't have apps and bells and whistles. Anyway, Julia Zigler had found your phone. The house where you saw your mother actually belongs to Julia's grandmother. Your phone landed in the garden, not the river. I saw your photo of the man your mother was embracing, but only from the back. I'm going to talk to her today and try to find out who he is."

Brad wanted me to give him back his phone and was angry when I said I'd discarded it.

I apologized, but said, "It was leading the cops straight to me, and I needed to stay ahead of them for a few hours."

I went back to my place to check on Julia, who was still soaking in the tub. Mitch was lying close by. When he saw me, he thumped his tail but didn't get up.

"Will you let me inspect your burns?" I asked from the doorway. "I want to make sure you are healing properly. If not, I need to get you some antibiotic ointment for them."

She frowned at me doubtfully but finally decided to let me come in. Mitch got to his feet and tried to stick his head between me and Julia's legs. He was definitely on guard duty.

I was relieved to see that the lesions were forming scabs. I rummaged in my medicine chest for some vitamin E ointment. "When you're out and dry, rub this on them, okay? Or let me do it for you."

She nodded.

"Last night you didn't want to tell me where your granny's lockbox key was. Do you think you could trust me with it now?"

She scowled more deeply, turned her head away. "The key wasn't with her lawyer. I put it in that jacket that the lady— Oh, that was you. The jacket you put on me. Only I forgot it. I was leaving the hospital so fast I didn't remember to bring it with me. How could I be so stupid?"

A wave of dizziness swept over me. The jacket. I'd completely forgotten the jacket in the mad running I'd been doing all night. I'd stuffed it through the synagogue mail slot. Would Mr. Pariente and his friends still be there?

And the break-in at the cleaners. Sergeant Pizzello had asked if I knew anything about that. *I didn't an hour ago, Sergeant, but I for sure know now.*

"Not stupid, baby," I said. "You were in danger of your life. That comes way ahead of remembering jackets and keys and all those things. You know your granny values your life above any house or any other object, right?"

She nodded, trying to rub away her tears with the washcloth. Mitch hovered over the edge of the tub, licking her face, which made her get to her feet.

I handed her a clean towel and left the room again. I waited for her to get dressed, curbing my impatience to get back to the synagogue while she played with my face cream. She wanted to stay in my apartment with the dogs, but I couldn't allow this. If anyone was looking for me, they'd come here, and I couldn't leave her by herself to deal with thugs. I gave her and Brad each one of the burner phones I'd just bought.

"One last thing," I said, as I was leaving Mr. Contreras's home. "I never asked you why you ran from the hospital. You should have stayed put until those burns on your legs healed. Who was the man who came in to interrogate you? What did he say that frightened you into leaving?"

"I don't know who he is." Her voice trembled, and she dug her fingers into Mitch's neck. He flinched but didn't move away. "First I thought it was funny that he was trying to question me in Hungarian. I only understand about ten words, but the janitor was having trouble with the language. I could tell he didn't remember a lot, and I think maybe I smiled, or did something that made the other man realize I could understand what was going on."

Her tears began to fall again. "He threatened my *nagyi*. He said if I didn't give him the key to the box, he'd make sure that *Nagyi* didn't leave the nursing home alive. And then I ran and left the jacket. Maybe in my secret mind, I hoped they'd find it. Then she'd be safe."

"Okay, doll, okay." Mr. Contreras was speaking to me, but he handed Julia one of the big cloth handkerchiefs he still carries. "This gal don't need any more stress. You take care of these creeps so she can stop having nightmares, but don't keep banging on her head."

I squatted briefly to look Julia in the face. "You behaved with great bravery and presence of mind. You stood up for your granny as best you could when you were alone in the world. I'm going to do what your uncle Sal said, do my best to find the creeps and get them out of your life. You do your part. Stay inside. Don't go peeking out the window if the doorbell rings. Got it?"

She gave me a watery smile and a nod. I took off, Saint Joan of Chicago, ready to put the grandmother back where she belonged, in her own home. If she truly had developed dementia under the strain of her captivity in Archangel's memory center, I'd get Lotty to help fund in-home care for her.

Assuming I could sort out who the dragons were. I drove over to Lunt Street, to Shaamar Hashomayim and the cleaners. The synagogue was still intact. That was a mercy. I'd been so overloaded by Julia and recovering from my time in the river, I'd forgotten my obligation to the Parientes. I'd forgotten that the cameras were missing from the entryway. And I hadn't looked at the feeds from the ones that were still in the eaves.

Across from the synagogue, the cleaners had boards in place over their broken windows. Olive, the homeless woman, was asleep in a heap of towels and blankets in the adjacent doorway, an empty bottle of brandy near her head. It wasn't the eighteen-dollar pint of Remy I'd bought her last night, but a fifth of the kind of alcohol brewed from old shoes in a dirty bucket. Even someone whose body was used to a lot of liquor was going to be sleeping it off for a long time.

I stared at Olive, reconstructing the previous evening. She'd seen me go into the cleaners with my red jacket. She assumed I'd come out without it, because I'd rolled it up into my bag. She hadn't seen me force it through the Shaamar Hashomayim mail slot. If she had, she'd have told whoever bought her the rotgut, and they would have hacked their way into the synagogue.

A handwritten sign on the cleaners' door announced that because of the damage the shop would be closed today. I peered through a crack in the boards. Lights were on and I could see the shadow of movements. I unwrapped my smartphone and called their number. The call went straight to voicemail. I identified myself and said if Rana Jardin wanted to talk to me about the break-in, I'd be in the area for a few more minutes.

I was too late for the conclusion of the morning service at Shaamar Hashomayim, but I found Mr. Pariente and his cronies in the bakery up the street, eating poppy-seed cake at a table on the sidewalk in front.

"You know?" Mr. Pariente cried, getting to his feet.

"Know what?" I asked. "Was there another attack on the building?"

"It feels that way," he said. "We were just talking—we don't know what to do."

I assumed they were talking about finding my jacket inside, and I was starting to explain when he pulled a document from his jacket pocket.

It was a report of a building inspection, conducted yesterday. It said that the boiler was old, it was leaking carbon monoxide into the building. The stairwell railing to the women's balcony was loose, and the balcony needed to be shut until it was repaired. Some of the brickwork was damaged, making the building unsafe. The report concluded by saying that Shaamar Hashomayim had thirty days to get the repairs completed and to request a reinspection, or the building would be shut permanently.

"We hoped Istvan could take care of it," one of the men said, "but he says he can't."

"I never had many connections at City Hall, and now I have none." The speaker was a short man with a thin, intense face and mournful eyes. "When I was a member of the bar, I specialized in estate planning and wills. If my office had to deal with property inspections, it was for the valuation of a bequest. I called my former colleagues, but they don't know how to bribe an inspector, nor do I, even if I wanted to.

"But this is the most troubling thing of all. When we went inside, it looked as though the inspectors had searched the building. Prayer books were out of order. When we opened the Ark, we could see that the Torah scrolls had been moved."

"Two of the crowns are valuable," Mr. Pariente said, "but they didn't take those. We don't understand what they could have been looking for."

"The damage was from the vandals!" cried another of the group. "We will repair it. Although where we will get the money, since we let our insurance lapse—" He flung up his hands in despair.

"I'm taking the paper home to Ilona," Mr. Pariente said miserably. "Maybe she can show it to Dr. Lotty, and Dr. Lotty can help—but to repair the railing—

and—look, loose boards in the balcony—even if Dr. Lotty would lend us the money, how would we find workmen who could repair this in thirty days? Do you think—do you know—"

"I'll look into it, certainly," I said. "But when did they make this inspection? And how did they get into the building?"

The men looked at each other, shrugged helplessly. "After yesterday morning's prayers, between then and now. That's all we know. None of us let anyone into the building. Maybe they broke in."

"Yes, and they left behind a woman's coat, all torn up," Istvan Reito said. "It's red. We thought it was a symbol. Blood, you know, accusing us of the old blood lie."

My face turned hot with shame. "I'm so very sorry. That was my jacket." I told them about the police coming to search me while I was checking on the cameras I'd put on the synagogue. "I meant to phone you this morning, before the service, but I ended up running from the law all night long. I apologize, again and again. I completely forgot about the jacket. When you picked it up, did anything fall out? A key?"

They murmured among themselves, but agreed there'd been nothing on the floor when they got rid of the jacket.

"We looked," Istvan said. "We normally don't look at the floor, but as Emilio said, we were afraid of a bomb. We made sure the intruders left nothing behind before we began to pray. But this inspection—we could barely pay attention to the Sh'ma."

"We thought that perhaps the jacket had been soaked in gasoline or had a bomb in it," another man said. "We put it in the garbage can on the corner. I know we should have called the fire department, but the inspection made us feel we couldn't trust the city authorities. And we were right. You, too, were fleeing from the police."

I felt an urge to sit on the floor and weep. These old men had survived terror, they now felt unsafe in America, and I had added to their fears.

"You know that cleaners across the street?" one of them said. "They were attacked in the night. Was it by the same people who harmed our building?"

I started to say no, because I was sure it was someone looking for my jacket, but I was swimming in a sea of ignorance. "It's possible. I don't know enough right now to answer that."

Our whole country was so awash in conspiracies that I didn't want to add to them. But what is detective work if not assuming conspiracies by murky groups, out to make money from other people's troubles?

I jogged back to the synagogue and dug around in the corner garbage can. I was in luck: I was out ahead of the street people who searched the garbage looking for discards from the affluent. Part of a sleeve was sticking up over a Styrofoam box with the remains of an eggy breakfast. I put the box, plastic bag, newspaper and other leavings on the ground so I could lift the whole garment out without tearing it further.

I held it up to the light, baffled by where Julia could have stashed the key. The basket weave itself didn't offer hiding places; the pockets were empty. I began to think the key had been lost when the unfortunate Ariadne Blanchard was killed. Maybe it was under the bush where her dead body had lain. But if the police had found it, Coney wouldn't have been on my butt last night.

I turned it over, looking at the placket. And there it was, wedged into the back of one of the buttons. The big black buttons that had been part of the jacket's charm when I bought it had edges that curved, creating a minute shelf. Julia had slid her key inside the button's rim.

What extraordinary presence of mind she'd shown, to protect this while on her way to the hospital. Perhaps growing up with a grandmother who defied an army with tanks had given her a well of courage and enterprise to draw on.

Gabriella had fled Italy alone, as a teenager, to escape certain death at fascist hands. Her own extraordinary courage was a constant reminder not to shirk a task merely because it looked dangerous or disagreeable. *Back unto the breach, Vic. Don't close up the wall with the bodies of these old men, or the teens now entrusted to your care.* I carefully tucked the key into an inside pocket of my jeans.

34
On the Seesaw

I needed to talk to Mrs. Pariente, and Sergeant Pizzello, and Murray, and Lotty, but first I drove to my mechanic. Luke Edwards is a human embodiment of Eeyore, Winnie-the-Pooh's lugubrious donkey. He knows disaster lurks around every corner, maybe because he sees the aftermath of so many car wrecks, but he takes an especially dim view of my own driving. He's often repaired my cars when they've been battered, and nothing can convince him that damaging a car when I'm escaping a murderer doesn't make me a reckless driver.

Today, all I wanted was for him to remove the Mustang's GPS signal emitter.

"You mean right now? This minute?" He gave a sigh as long and loud as a train whistle and waved an arm at the cars awaiting his attention. "I guess. When I've got this transmission gear installed on the Beemer there. You've been all over the news, Warshawski. Thought that was a good advertisement for a small business-person."

"Unfortunately, it's a reminder to my current clients that I'm not paying enough attention to them." I'd looked through my emails before driving over. Many of the midsize law firms who make up the bulk of my business were not happy with me. They were reading about me in the news and they wondered if I'd become a glory hound who didn't care about their problems.

I turned to the building inspection report. It had been conducted yesterday, at one in the afternoon, long after the men had finished praying for the day and before I'd found Julia. That made it seem independent of the problems I was stirring up, and yet, and yet . . .

I called the city building department. While I was on hold, I finished writing a report for one long-suffering client and began the tedious process of searching social media for information on a potential hire for another. While I was copying some extreme statements he'd posted on Parler, I was finally connected with a clerk in the inspections department.

These are patronage jobs, despite the Shakman decrees, which theoretically outlawed patronage jobs, and so the people who answer the phone don't feel an obligation to help the public as much as the public might like. However, after a tedious amount of backing and forthing, my mentioning being a member of the bar and asking if I needed to issue a subpoena or whether it would be better for me to approach Beth Blacksin at Global for a human interest story (*Holocaust Survivors Victimized by City Building Department* would generate a lot of views, I suggested) the woman on the other end gave a mighty sigh of her own.

"We had an anonymous report of the building being a danger to the old people who use it. We got permission from one of the titleholders to enter, and he met our inspector at the door." She spelled the titleholder's name: Raamah Calabro. "Anything else, you can read in the report they left at the building. The church has thirty days to show they've put in a new boiler and repaired the stairs and so on."

I thanked her as politely as I could. I'd been planning on going to see Ashleigh when Luke finished with my GPS, but I'd better visit Mrs. Pariente first to see if she could identify Raamah Calabro.

While I was jotting down a to-do list, putting in order all the people I needed to talk to today, Rana Jardin called me from the dry cleaners. "Are you still in the neighborhood? Do you know anything about our break-in?"

I told her I'd moved on, but that I didn't have any leads on who'd broken in. This was technically true, but it still made me squirm, since I was pretty sure I knew why the break-in had happened.

"There's a homeless woman who sleeps in the doorway next to you," I added. "She won't confide in me, but I have a feeling she's aware of everything around her."

"Oh, no, I can't talk to her. She stinks of booze and a thousand other things I clean out of people's clothes all day long."

"That's all I can suggest, although you might post a reward around the neighborhood for getting the clothes back. I imagine your insurers want each stolen item valued."

"Yes, if I had coverage."

In hard times, small businesses often let insurance lapse. I assumed that was what had happened here. Rana said she'd only bought fire and water damage coverage, for the building and the clothes.

"I knew it was a gamble, not insuring the inventory, but that added so much to the premiums! Who expects someone to break into a cleaners and steal dirty clothes?

They didn't take any of the pieces we had hanging up, ready to collect."

I commiserated with Jardin. I even said I'd check with Olive myself the next time I was visiting the synagogue. The best she could hope for was for the thieves to dump the clothes someplace accessible when they didn't find what they were looking for, but I kept that depressing idea quiet.

When the call ended, I sat for a moment with my eyes shut tight. I felt like someone on a seesaw. As soon as I focused on one thing, like the synagogue's problems, someone dropped a five-hundred-pound weight on the other end of the board and flipped me into the air. By the time I landed I had no idea what I needed to focus on.

My phone rang. I opened my eyes to squint at the screen. Sergeant Pizzello, asking what I knew about the break-in at the cleaners.

"Just that it happened, and the place didn't insure the inventory against theft," I said. "There's a woman named Olive who sleeps in the doorway next door to them who is pretty aware of what happens on the street. She was sleeping off a fifth of rotgut when I was there an hour or so ago—a fifth someone brought her after she'd drunk the pint of Remy I bought her."

"You bought her brandy? Jesus, Mary, and Joseph,

Warshawski. A woman like that belongs in a shelter and in rehab. What goes on in your head that you'd buy brandy for a drunk like her?"

"I could have given her money, hoping she'd answer questions about who she'd seen around the synagogue, but she wouldn't leave her spot in that doorway, and she was willing to talk to me for a pint. Which is why I think she didn't buy that slivovitz herself. Someone brought it to her. Someone wanted to know whether anyone had gone into the cleaners with something they wanted."

"This isn't an action flick, Warshawski, where we try to second-guess Father Brown. Tell me who wanted something at the cleaners. And what it was."

"Coney could have come back," I said. "He was ten kinds of mad when you showed up and stopped him whacking me. He could have come back, hoping to catch me on my own, then noticed the cleaners and seen Olive next door to them. She'd be an ideal witness if she was awake."

"And sober."

"Oh, I expect it's been years since she was sober," I said. "She may not be able to walk or talk very well, but she still notices what's going on around her."

"Okay, Warshawski, I'll bite. I don't believe Coney was hovering around nearby, but let's say there was a mysterious someone who wanted dirty clothes. What garment was he—or she or they—looking for?"

"Suppose someone had a red jacket that needed cleaning and repairing—"

"Are you telling me you interfered with a homicide investigation?" Pizzello cut me short with a voice like a knife blade. "That you took a garment from—"

"Sergeant, I am imagining a story. I am not describing a real event at a real crime scene. Do you want me to continue?"

She breathed heavily in my ear for a beat, then hissed, "All right, continue."

"Suppose someone who looked like me had a red jacket that needed cleaning, and since that someone was at the synagogue, checking camera feeds, she took the jacket into Rana Jardin's shop. Olive knew what this someone looked like. Olive could have told an ugly police lieutenant about the jacket. That red would stand out, even after being in the dirt under a bush."

"It's a very long stretch," Pizzello said. "And it assumes that some brainless arrogant private investigator left her jacket at that particular cleaners. And that an ugly lieutenant wanted it badly enough to smash down the door and make off with all the dirty clothes."

"It's a stretch," I agreed. "Probably none of it happened."

"If it happened, Coney didn't do it himself— he'd farm it out. But if all these clothes that were stolen show up in an alley near your office, I'm taking you in for questioning."

"I'd expect no less," I agreed.

She was right, though. It was a long stretch. It presumed that Coney—or someone, anyway—Gus, maybe?—guessed that the jacket held the object they were so desperately seeking. Which in itself was a stretch.

Gus wanted that key to his mother's lockbox. But if his mother's lawyer held the box, what good would the key do him? All he needed to do was go to the lawyer's office and say Silvia was asking for the box. Or get the probate court judge who'd given him control over Julia's affairs to issue an order giving him Silvia's box.

I kept circling back to the question of why Coney was involved in this mess. Was he off-duty muscle for a connected person? Perhaps for the Viper? Certainly not for Julia's uncle Gus. Gus was a wannabe, not a player. And he was deep in debt. Ditto for Tad Duda.

Corky Ranaghan was a pretty connected guy. If Klondike was interested in developing Goose Island, Corky could have cops like Coney on tap to frighten people into selling their land.

I wondered if there was a traceable connection between the Viper and Corky. If I found that, Murray would get his Pulitzer, Jonathan Michaels would get indictments by the yard, and I would get—hopefully not a bullet between the shoulder blades.

Luke called me out to the Mustang. He explained in exquisite detail the steps he'd taken to free my car of surveillance. If I'd wanted to write a manual on the subject, I could have by the time he finished. "You know this means you can't use GPS yourself, Warshawski. You'll have to find out where you're going the old-fashioned way."

"I still have paper maps," I said.

"I meant by sniffing the air. That's how bloodhounds work. People are way too dependent on technology."

"Says the man who repairs cars for a living."

I paid him—cash, which he prefers—and drove over to the Parientes' building.

35

Sharper Than
a Serpent's Tooth

Even though Luke Edwards had removed the GPS
signal from the Mustang, and I had my phone
in its Faraday cage, I still parked a quarter mile from
the Parientes building. I turned onto a side street going in the opposite direction from them and sat in the
shadow of a stairwell for perhaps ten minutes. Worked
on my breathing, did a few soft vocal warm-ups, anything to keep from giving into the impulse to pull out
my smartphone and mindlessly run through apps, the
way one does.

A woman walked past with a stroller, talking animatedly into the ether, while the baby stared dumbly at the
street in front of it—marking time until it, too, could be

plugged into a device. A couple with a dog paid more attention to me, because the dog jerked on its leash to inspect me. I wasn't attracting an audience, but I still took a big circuit around the neighborhood, coming at the Parientes' building from the south instead of my usual route from the north.

Using a burner, I phoned when I was inside the lobby, apologized for dropping in unannounced. Mrs. Pariente buzzed me in.

"Victoria! Thank God you came quickly. Emilio told me about the building inspection. He's heartsick and we are both frightened. He went to bed; he is exhausted by his fear. Who is targeting us in this cruel way?"

I wanted to say something reassuring or heartening, that I would find the evildoers and track them to the ends of the earth, but I had already made her promises I hadn't been able to keep.

I did tell her I would do my utmost to protect her and Emilio from personal harm. "And when Lotty knows the synagogue needs a new furnace, she'll get someone there to install it ASAP."

"But we can't pay," Mrs. Pariente cried.

"Let's not worry about that now. Instead, tell me who Raamah Calabro is. He's the person whose name is on the title, and he let the building inspectors into Shaamar Hashomayim yesterday afternoon."

"Raamah Calabro? That isn't possible. Estella, my darling friend Estella Calabro—she died a year ago February—I think I told you. Raamah Calabro was her husband's father. He's been dead many years, many. He was one of the original founders of Shaamar Hashomayim. I can show you the title, show you the names of all the people who were named trustees and given power to make decisions about the building."

She moved to the small desk in the corner where the phone stood and carefully eased a gray cardboard box from its one drawer. Her swollen ankles and distended fingers made it hard for her to move, but I resisted the impulse to leap up and take over from her.

She set the box on the table in front of me and went to the stove to put on water for coffee. Even in distress, it wasn't possible for her to have a guest in her home and not offer refreshments.

The papers on top were current utility bills, all paid by check and receipted, and a list of the current members, thirty-two only. The check register recorded their monthly dues of fifty dollars. Most members were current. For those in arrears, Donna Ilona had recorded her efforts to collect in the European handwriting I knew from my mother: TELEPHONED FOR THE THIRD TIME, BUT LUCIA IS ILL AND HOW CAN THEY AFFORD TO PAY TEMPLE FEES?

It was barely a break-even figure. How could they ever afford a new boiler, unless Lotty, or some Jewish charity, came to their rescue?

Underneath the current accounts were documents about the history of the synagogue. It had been founded shortly after World War I by a mix of immigrants from the old Habsburg empire, some Hungarian, some Czech, some German. A newspaper clipping from 1921, showing the finished building, said almost five hundred families belonged.

The trouble was, after going through all the papers twice, I couldn't find the building title. The plat survey was in the bottom of the box, clipped to the architect's drawings, with a statement from the Fort Dearborn National Bank showing the mortgage had been paid in full, but the title wasn't there.

"If the title isn't in there, I don't know where it could be." Mrs. Pariente placed coffee in front of me, then went through the stack of papers herself, one at a time, fingers moving slowly through the documents.

"Donna Ilona, you said Mrs. Calabro gave up the title to her apartment to pay for the nursing home fees. Is it possible she also gave them the title to the synagogue?"

"Oh, no! She could never have done such a thing." Mrs. Pariente's eyes widened in horror. "Although it was her son, Robert, who actually gave the nursing home the title to her condo. He had that authority, as her son, you understand. It was so sad. She was a brilliant woman. She spoke five languages, she loved opera. And then her beautiful mind abandoned her.

"But Robert, he is lazy and, really, good-for-nothing. He didn't even clean the condo or take care of her special treasures before he gave away the title. We thought we should each take a few of her treasures. Adele Reito loved Estella's Crown Derby tea set, and I took the clock you see when you walk in the door. When I die, I suppose it will be sold to some greedy person, but for now I can see my friend every time I look at the clock itself."

I'd often noticed the pedestal clock, made of some kind of highly polished wood, with a gold face. It sat on a shabby deal table, but it suited Donna Ilona's personality.

"The nursing home, they were greedy—they wanted Estella's home cleaned out in two weeks. Adele Reito—she is also a member of Shaamar Hashomayim, and like me close to Estella—she and I took care of that. Adele's daughter, thank God, she came with their grandson to help clean out the condo. Otherwise, Robert or the nursing home people, they would have sold everything for their own benefit."

She shook her head, unhappy at the memory, but added, "Robert couldn't give away the title to the synagogue, though, because his name isn't on the deed. It belongs to the members and he isn't a member."

I shifted uneasily in my chair. It actually would be easier than that. American courts are thick with lawsuits over religious property. If Shaamar Hashomayim was like many small congregations, they'd never taken legal advice on changing the names of trustees on official documents. It's not so hard to claim you are one of the people named on the title—especially if you're dealing with a bored patronage employee.

"Mrs. Calabro's son turned over all these papers to you when she died?"

"No, no, it was very sad, but it happened a year before she died. She became so forgetful, you see, and the electric company actually turned off the power at the synagogue for one month. I saw that we needed to help her out. We wanted Istvan Reito to take over the books. He was an advocate—lawyer—very good and the ideal person, but at the time he was recovering from shingles. And so I took the books home with me. Robert was not interested at all, and perhaps that's just as well. He would have let all the bills slide even more than my Estella. She, poor soul, cared for the synagogue and wanted to look after it, but he—! He'd already installed her in a nursing home, against Adele Reito's and my expressed opposition. He wouldn't care for her himself, and Adele had her hands full with Istvan's illness. I couldn't look after Estella on my own, but putting her in the home made her deteriorate much more quickly."

Her face contorted with pain at the memory. "It was a terrible place. They had put her in a bed where they never came to change the sheets. Adele and I used to go once a week, all the way out to Northfield on the bus, and change the bedding, bring poor Estella a clean nightgown and clean sheets. It was terrible. She died right before the Covid began, mercifully, since we would not have been able to visit after the pandemic."

"Signora Calabro was at the Archangel place in Northfield?" I asked.

"Yes, as if an angel could be looking after a place like that. I have told Dr. Lotty, if my time for care comes, she must promise to give me morphine here at home, enough to send me peacefully to sleep."

"Lotty won't let anything bad happen to you, Donna Ilona, and neither will I. I need to talk to Mrs. Calabro's son. Perhaps he misplaced the title when he put all these documents together for you."

"Yes, it's possible he lost the title. The life of the synagogue means nothing to him—as soon as he put

Estella in that nursing home, he couldn't wait to turn all the paperwork over to me." She sighed. "Perhaps it was a mistake for me to keep paying our bills. I see I am too old for the job. I couldn't pay proper attention. I never even noticed the title was missing."

"Hey, hey, none of that." I pressed her hand, the contact we all need that we can't have right now. "Get me Robert's address and phone number. I'll go see him. We'll get this sorted out, no worries."

She walked back to the little table and took an address book out from under the phone. The leather cover was worn to a soft rose, almost the color of the synagogue bricks, and she wrote out Robert Calabro's address in a labored hand.

"You and Dr. Lotty, you are Emilio's and my angels." She stood on tiptoe to kiss my cheek. Another act prohibited by Covid, but one I welcomed.

36
The Pottery Barn

Chicago had kept libraries open during the pandemic. I had thought it was an irresponsible decision, giving people a chance to share a virus that loved meeting new people, but today I was happy about it: there was a branch half a mile away where I could use a public computer and sit safely distant from other patrons. Mrs. Pariente had given me Robert Calabro's address, but I wanted some background on him.

Before going inside, I sat on a bench to talk to Lotty. Today was one of her clinic days, so I was on hold for a time while Lotty finished with a patient. When she came on the line, she wanted an update on my health after my bath in the Chicago River.

I told her about finding Julia Zigler. "She's parked with Mr. Contreras right now, which can only be a temporary hideout. No one saw me bring her home, but the cops can readily guess we were together in the tender house."

"Tender house?"

"Those little houses at the ends of the drawbridges. Bridge tenders used to stay in them to raise and lower bridges. The Zigler family apparently used one on Chicago Avenue as a private playhouse. Anyway, Julia seems in pretty good shape. She's having her period, which means she isn't as malnourished as we feared. And I retrieved a key she'd hidden. I guess this is what her pursuers have been looking for. Before you hang up, I need to tell you about Shaamar Hashomayim."

"I know—Mrs. Coltrain told me about the inspection report. How was that even possible? Who would care enough?"

"Corky Ranaghan has been sniffing around wanting to take over the title, for reasons that make no sense to me, but I'm guessing he sicced the building department on Shaamar," I said. "They need to get these repairs done quickly to keep him from moving in. I thought maybe they could take out a line of credit, since they own the building free and clear. Only—I was just with Donna Ilona, and the title has disappeared. Donna Ilona is quite distressed, but I'm about to talk to the guy whose mother used to handle the accounts."

"Ah, yes, Ilona's friend. She often spoke of her. I'll try to see Ilona and Emilio before I go home, but there's a long day in front of me. It won't be until late. Max and I can pay for the required repairs, though. That will help ease the Parientes' minds."

There's an advantage to being a famous surgeon whose fees can run to seven figures.

In the library, I dug up some background on Robert Calabro. He'd been an only child. He was almost sixty now, living some three miles east of his mother's old home, in one of those parts of town that hover between decay and stability. He'd never married, had no children, but he currently lived with a woman named Virginia Wiggins.

On social media, he called himself an entrepreneur, but whatever he undertook was vague and hadn't yielded any significant income. Wiggins was an artist, which also covered a lot of possibilities.

Ceramics, I learned, when Virginia let me into the apartment half an hour later. She'd answered the call I'd made from the lobby, where I said I was a friend of Robert's mother with a couple of quick questions about the synagogue she'd belonged to.

A giant turquoise urn, perhaps for umbrellas, stood outside the door. Inside, pots, bowls, cups filled the shelves and were lined up along the baseboards.

Virginia saw me staring and gave a self-conscious laugh. "I had to close my shop because of the virus. No one was buying and I couldn't afford the rent. Now I do it all on Etsy and eBay."

I wondered where she did her work. She explained that she belonged to an artist's cooperative where she could store her supplies and rent time on a wheel and in a kiln.

"She ought to sell some of these first, before putting more money into making more stuff no one wants."

The voice came from a wing chair near the window. The ceramics were so overwhelming that I hadn't noticed Robert Calabro when I came in. He was a dark man with a receding hairline, so thin that the wings of the chair made a kind of cocoon around him.

Neither Virginia nor Robert offered me a chair. A stool holding a red-and-blue teapot stood in the middle of the room. I moved the teapot to the floor, ignoring Virginia's protests, and pulled the stool near Robert, positioning myself so that I could see Virginia as well as him. He fished a black cloth mask from a pocket.

"I don't know why Ginny let you in," he grumbled. "She knows I'm working and that I don't have anything to say to Mother's friends." A laptop stood open on his knees—proof that he was working, I guess.

"I was just visiting Mrs. Pariente," I said. "I gather she was a big help looking after your mother before her death."

He hunched a shoulder.

"She took over the synagogue accounts when your mother became too ill to manage them. Was that your idea, or your mother's?"

His eyes flickered from his keyboard to Virginia. "Mother was so impaired in the last years of her life that she couldn't make decisions. She didn't even recognize me. Zia Ilona—Mrs. Pariente—was the person in the community closest to my mother. She seemed to be the best person to pass the responsibility on to."

"You've been keeping up with news about the synagogue?"

He gave an uneasy laugh. "I stopped going to shul as soon as I left home. That place was like a graveyard for Jews who wanted to pretend they could live in the world that the Second World War destroyed. I'm even writing a novel about them. Drifters, I'm calling it, about people who've drifted into the wrong century and wrong country but don't know they don't belong where they've landed."

"I'm sure publishers will fall over themselves bidding for it," I said politely. "Have you seen the reports about vandals attacking Shaamar Hashomayim?"

Virginia gave a tiny headshake, as if warning Robert not to answer. Interesting.

"I don't read the news these days. It's all a load of crap—everyone is lying about something."

"You think I'm lying about the vandalism?"

He shifted in his chair. "One of the old men called me, thinking I'd want to give money to help clean up the building. Ginny and I can barely keep going. This economy may be good for someone like you, snooping into people's lives, but it's killing us artists."

"So you did know about the vandalism. Did the man who called explain that the city building department is giving Shaamar thirty days to replace their boiler and rebuild the staircases?"

"As I just said, Ginny and I don't have resources to help other people. And if we did, there are soup kitchens that come way in front of a synagogue with thirty-some decrepit members."

"One easy thing you could do to help them would be to let them have the title to the building. I want to suggest they take out a mortgage. That would give them the resources they need to keep the building going. They wouldn't be dependent on the whims of a powerful broker to get the money they need for insurance or to install a better furnace. But they need the title, of course."

He and Ginny became completely still. I could hear the traffic passing on Western Avenue outside, and a couple of men calling to each other about a cable.

"I gave Zia Ilona all the papers Mother had when she became too ill to manage her affairs or the synagogue's business," he finally said, in a voice that lacked conviction. "If she doesn't have the title, it's because she lost it."

"You and I both know that's unlikely," I said. "She has every other document connected to the synagogue, but the most important one, the title, isn't in her folder. This means she never had it."

"Get to whatever point you have," Robert said. "I don't know why you care about Shaamar Hashomayim's problems, but I have zero interest in them. And don't start rehashing Zia Ilona's complaints about Mother's condo. She couldn't look after it any more than she could look after the synagogue. Exchanging the condo for her care was a good deal."

"Except that she was badly treated, and, unless Donna Ilona is exaggerating, you didn't try to help make her more comfortable."

He pressed his lips together and looked out the window.

"Maybe you left the synagogue title on the kitchen counter in your mother's condo," I suggested. "After

Donna Ilona and Mrs. Reito cleaned it and disposed of her treasures, you took one last look around and left the title lying where someone else could pick it up."

"You have an imagination," Robert said, voice bored. "Just not an interesting one. I'm not learning anything from listening to you, except that you think you have a right to barge into my home and lecture me as if you were Istvan Reito or some other crony of my father's."

"What if I were a crony of Corky Ranaghan's?" I asked. "Would you tell me about the title then?"

He paused too long before saying, "Corky Ranaghan? Is he some kind of rock wannabe?"

"Uh-huh," I said. "He's exactly a rock who wants to squeeze people like you between himself and a hard place. Did he squeeze you to get you to hand over the Shaamar title?"

Robert yawned theatrically.

"What about Tad Duda and Gus Zigler?" I asked. "They pals of yours?"

"You're fishing," Robert said. "You don't even know what you're fishing for."

"And you do. That at least lets me know to keep looking into your affairs."

"I can report you," Robert said. "There are laws against stalkers."

"No laws against people using publicly available financial records," I said.

"We have work to do if you don't, so if you don't mind," Ginny said. "You've way outstayed your welcome."

I looked around the room, at the clutter of ceramics. If Robert had kept the title, it would take hours to search all those pots and bowls. Why would he have clung to the title, though? Maybe to raise money he needed himself, pretending he was one of the directors or trustees or whatever of Shaamar Hashomayim?

I got to my feet, resisting the urge to smash every vase and pitcher in the place. If you consort with vermin, you have to take every precaution to keep from becoming vermin yourself.

As I threaded my way through the pots and cups to the door, Ginny ostentatiously moved the stool to its original position and repositioned the teapot.

Robert started complaining to Ginny before I had the door completely shut. "My parents, not content with making me miserable in life, are haunting me from the grave."

I couldn't resist staying in the hall to listen.

"First my father leaves all his money to the synagogue except what he gave Mother. He was trying to pressure me into taking over his fur business. I was supposed to bury my nose in rich women's armpits as they came in to be fitted for their minks and sables! And then the old *putane* who couldn't stop lecturing me thought I should wear myself out looking after Mother."

"I know all that, Rob, you've repeated it about five hundred thousand times. But what about the title to the synagogue?"

"What about it?" he growled. "Are you going to start lecturing me?"

A woman with two children came noisily up the stairs. Ginny pulled the door open faster than I could move away. She swore at me—I, too, was a *putana*—and slammed the door. A *putana*, more "whore" than "bitch," a word my mother slapped me for using.

37

Jekyll and Hyde

I sat inside a bus stop and used my phone to request a copy of the title to Shaamar Hashomayim. For a dollar, I got a summary of the information I'd found in Donna Ilona's documents—year built, construction type, and so on. As the woman in the building department had told me, the name that popped up as titleholder was Raamah Calabro, a trustee of the synagogue.

You don't get a printable copy of the title online: for that you have to present the actual deed. It's a way of preventing people from printing out titles and committing fraud with them. However, the titleholder's name would be good enough for a building inspector writing up his report.

I went back to my car, where I could have a quiet

space to talk, and called Corky Ranaghan from my burner. I got his voicemail and left a message: *I know you're interested in the Shaamar Hashomayim building. I just met with Robert Calabro, and we had an interesting conversation about the building title. You're probably the most knowledgeable person in Chicago about property and titles and so on, so I'm wondering if he consulted you on how to handle the synagogue's documents.*

I was leaving the parking lot when Ranaghan called back. I pulled over to the curb.

"Ms. Warshawski, you're such a busy little beaver, or should I say mountain goat, leaping up and down rocks, jumping in and out of the river, climbing up and down bridge tender houses, it's amazing you still have time to think about a group of old Jews in a decaying building."

The language was deliberately offensive. He was trying to goad me into showing my hand, such as it was. "The building looks in good shape to me. A few bullet holes, as you know, but they didn't undermine the structure."

"That's not what I hear," Corky said. "In fact, the building might be condemned soon."

"Your sources of information are legendary, Corky, but they might have led you astray here."

"I don't think so, Warshawski, I don't think so. It would only take a little knock on the brickwork to show how unstable the building is. And that recent building inspection points to how decrepit the interior has become."

"Ah, yes, that building inspection. That was a masterstroke, organizing that so quickly," I said. "I can't help wondering why. Is one of your pals hoping to build on that site?"

"If the building comes down, I'm sure some developer will be interested, although it's not a part of town that feels ripe for development." His answer came quickly, smoothly—he'd spent a lifetime fencing with more skilled duelists than me.

"If the building comes down, I expect I'll see you out front with a little wagon, collecting those Calumet bricks you prize so highly."

He produced his loud bark of a laugh. "Wonderful image, Warshawski, and probably accurate. But my pals, as you call them, would love to acquire access to a particular item. You could call it the key to the synagogue property. You keep disclaiming all knowledge of it, but we both know you know what and where it is. If you give it to me to turn over to my associates, we'll make sure the Jews get a clean bill of health for their building at next month's hearing."

"Corky, I disclaim all knowledge, because it's the truth." At least, it was until this morning. "Your buddy Coney conducted a cavity search, inspected my car from u-joint to seat cover, and found nothing, there or in my home or office. You should trust your hirelings more."

"You should take it as a compliment that I trust your wiliness more than the CPD's skill."

"Would that it were true, Corky. If it were, I'd have had new cameras installed to see who was actually coming in to inspect Shaamar Hashomayim."

He laughed again, even more loudly. What was I missing? Cameras. Of course. They hadn't been taken down by whatever Oath Keeper or Proud Boy wanted to attack the synagogue; they'd been removed so I couldn't tell who'd let in the building inspector. Someone with a key, someone with access to the title.

"It didn't matter to your inspector that the person with the title wasn't actually Raamah Calabro, I suppose."

"Not my inspector, Warshawski." Corky's voice was gentle. "He works for the city, and he does his job with due diligence. So, yes, he made sure he was working with Raamah Calabro. Now, Warshawski"—and he spoke more briskly, as though he'd been slouching and now was sitting up straight—"I have a busy day, and

I'm sure you do, as well, so, much as I'm enjoying this conversation, I have to run.

"But there is one more thing—I understand that you and the Zigler girl were in the tender house together. We can make a deal over the synagogue, but the price is higher now. You're such a hyperactive mountain goat, leaping across so many rocks, it's hard to know why you haven't fallen to your death. I gather you've leapt onto the Litvak rock. Do persuade the boy or his father to give us the material we're looking for."

He paused.

"So you are pulling those strings, Corky. I wish I knew what you were talking about, but sadly, I don't."

"You're a little old for batting your eyes and pretending feminine ignorance, Warshawski."

"Corky, I think you're confusing me with Ashleigh Breslau. Eye-batting was never in my skill set."

"Keep singing that song until you lose your voice," he said sharply. "Oh, one other thing. Gus Zigler wants his niece back. He's entered a successful petition for guardianship. I understand he's hired a lawyer from Crawford, Mead to sue you if you keep her from him."

That was the firm where my ex-husband was a partner, where the hourly rate is north of a thousand dollars. Like Jekyll and Hyde, my ex and I find it hard to occupy the same space at the same time. Ranaghan must have chosen them in another effort to knock me off-balance.

"You do have good sources, Corky." I kept my voice steady, put a tinge of admiration into it. "I'm wondering which one told you about Julia Zigler, or for that matter why you care about her. Or about the tender house."

"Oh, I don't care about her, not personally. But I'm a father myself. I believe strongly that children belong with their families."

The pulse in my neck was jumping, making it hard for me to breathe, let alone think. "Whatever happened in the tender house wasn't in the news, because there was no one to report it. So you must have learned about it from Scott Coney. I'd been thinking the Viper was pulling Scott's strings. Thanks for letting me know he reports to you. I wonder if his commander at Homan Square knows that?"

"Vipers, strings, you're building a movie set, where you can create nonexistent crimes to entertain yourself."

I ignored that, but said enthusiastically, "You must really be in love with Gus Zigler, to put up money for his legal fees. Speaking of movie sets, it could be a Neil Simon flick, *The Odd Couple*—a two-bit contractor who's barely getting by and the power broker whose deals are so exciting that my sources tell me a federal grand jury wants to see them. You'd have to put in sex for today's viewer, but I'm sure Gus would do pretty much anything you asked of him."

"You're a small-time, two-bit operator yourself, Warshawski. It's amazing to me that people have let you get away with so much over the years. It would be easy to crush you, the way we do with cockroaches that invade our space."

I'd rattled him; that was good. "First a mountain goat, now demoted to cockroach. But you know what they say about cockroaches, Corky—along with Keith Richards, we'll be the only survivors of a nuclear war. We're just so darned hard to crush."

I cut the connection. My shirt was drenched with sweat. I got out of the car and walked around in circles, trying to stop the tremors in my arms and legs.

I was trying to put the pieces together. We'd been tracked to the tender house because of Brad Litvak's phone. For the police to arrive so patly, tracking Brad's phone signal, meant someone had reported that Brad's phone was over near Goose Island. Reported it to Corky? Or to Scott Coney? I couldn't believe Donny had done it. The Litvaks had survived South Chicago by banding together as a family. He might insult his son, but he wouldn't betray him.

Ashleigh was another story. If the dark-haired man in Brad's picture was her lover, Ashleigh could have confided in him. A polite way of saying she betrayed her son.

Zeroing in on Brad's phone so that they knew to search the tender house had happened at warp speed in a city where it took five years to repair a broken sewer pipe.

Brad and Julia's safety at Mr. Contreras's was a mirage. I needed to find another place for her, and quickly. I'd been keeping my smartphone under wraps so I wouldn't be followed, but until I could find a safe-house for Julia, I'd better reveal myself. The Pied Piper of Chicago, getting the rats to follow me in the hopes I'd lead them to her. I thought wistfully of my Smith & Wesson, safely locked in my bedroom closet. Probably best it stay there. Sergeant Pizzello and Lieutenant Finchley would not protect me if I started shooting at members of the Chicago Police.

38
The Count of Monte Cristo

When Ashleigh Breslau saw me on her doorstep, she launched into a full-throated harangue about the legal action she was planning against me for interfering with her minor child.

I cut her off. "You do know your son was outside the Zigler mansion two nights ago, right? That he saw you inside the mansion, in the arms and lips of a man not his father. That was a major shock to your minor child's psyche, and it's why he doesn't want to come home to you."

"Egged on by Donny," she said. "I asked Branwell over and over what he was doing there, and he finally admitted he was following me, which I had already guessed. Did Donny hire you to stalk me? And then you sent my own son to do your dirty work?"

"No and no. Brad is worried about both you and Donny, but it was his own idea to track your car all the way to the riverfront. He thought if he proved you were seeing someone on the side, you wouldn't be able to make a custody plea, and you'd stop trying to make Donny look bad."

"*Make* Donny look bad? *Make* him look bad?" She gave a shriek of theatrical laughter. "He does that all on his own with no help from me."

"Maybe. Point is, your son doesn't want to be the football you two are trying to spike. He doesn't like the way you were spinning him around, pretending you were dressing up to go to work in the middle of the night.

"He took a picture. And then your lover came out and threw him into the Chicago River. Your son almost died because of your lover. He didn't want you to know he'd seen you, so I held my fire for a couple of days, but we've moved past that now. That picture of you is up in the cloud, retrievable whenever Brad gets access to his photo album."

Ashleigh smiled, a private catlike smirk, but she only said that Donny had called her after he left Brad at Mr. Contreras's place. "Donny told me *Branwell* lost his phone over by the river and we agreed to stop his service at once. I told Donny if he wants to replace Branwell's phone, that's his business, but I'm not contributing one cent to a phone or to his phone service, not if he's going to use it to spy on me."

"But you called your boyfriend right away, didn't you? Telling him to retrieve the phone so you could delete the damning picture?"

She curled her lip in derision. "My boyfriend? That sounds as though we're in seventh grade."

"The whole setup sounds like seventh grade. Call him your new Heathcliff. You fell for Donny twenty years ago because he seemed like a romantic outlaw, but he couldn't deliver the creature comforts you crave. So now you've found a bigger bad boy. He hangs with big bad cops and does bold bad things. Your adolescent dream all over again."

"You don't know what you're talking about," she said.

"Back when you and Donny were close, did he tell you about an episode in his teens, something he did that he was embarrassed to admit to in public?"

"He was a punk. He told me that. He also told me he ran around with a bunch of losers in South Chicago, including your cousin, who you think walks on water. They used to commit petty crimes, a story boys in every neighborhood in the world could repeat. But Donny said he'd stopped all that. He didn't want to end up in prison or at the bottom of a quarry."

"You're right about Boom-Boom," I said. "Not that he was a loser, but he did walk on water. At least, he skated on it. Donny and Tad Duda ran errands for Val Tommaso, the local Mob boss. And then one night they ran an errand that frightened them into quitting. At least, it frightened Donny and the twins. Boom-Boom never took part in whatever it was.

"A few weeks ago, someone called Donny and told him he'd report whatever they'd done that night unless Donny did something for him. Do you know who called? Was it Val Tommaso? Do you know what he wanted Donny to do?"

"Donny takes on so many schemes and scams I stopped paying attention to them eons ago. And as you've seen, we haven't been sharing secrets lately, let alone our phone calls, so I don't know what you're talking about."

"Then let's talk about stuff you do know about," I said. "The house by the river where you and your non-boyfriend were making out. I hope you don't think you're going to make money from staging the Zigler mansion, because it isn't for sale."

"That house is in escrow, waiting for a buyer," she said. "I was there for a perfectly legitimate business reason, and my escort had a key to the house."

"Given to him by Gus Zigler, the owner's son, who had stolen it from his own niece. And the two of you were inspecting the property in the dark, in a house lit only by battery-operated lamps and a romantic fire in the front room. To go with the burned-out door in the kitchen."

"Yes, the last tenant was an old woman who has dementia." Ashleigh's voice was steady. "She couldn't keep track of what she was doing and so now she's in a locked ward. She won't be coming back to that house. It's on the market."

Violence is not the answer, violence only begets more violence. My parents had both said that to me, more than once. I repeated it, took one of those breaths that is supposed to calm you down. I still wanted to rip Ashleigh's head off.

"Your friends have been feeding you fake news. It's Gus's mother's house, she wants to return to it, and I am working to help make that happen. Ask your *escort* to show you the title. He won't be able to because it's in a lockbox at the owner's law firm.

"When you go back to the Zigler mansion to strew around copies of *Midnight in the Garden of Good and Evil,* go down to the basement. You'll see the dungeon where Gus and Lacey Zigler imprisoned their niece, trying to force her to give them the key to her grandmother's lockbox. It might inspire you to add *The Count of Monte Cristo* to your display."

"I've been in the basement," she said. "It's a rat's nest down there. Before anything can be done to the house, we'd have to bring in a dozen dumpsters to load up all the papers and everything."

"I was in there the day after your battery-lit tryst," I said. "With members of the Chicago Fire Department. Believe me, you go past all the papers and historical costumes, you find a dungeon with an opening just wide enough for a skinny girl to slip through."

She gave her theatrical laugh again. "Your imagination is amazing, Vic. I don't associate that with Donny and Sonny and the South Chicago gang, but maybe your musical mother developed it in you."

"Your own imagination is pretty impressive, Ashleigh. You should record yourself someday. Your bitterness, your cheap insults have turned your son from you. Just maybe Donny is not the sole party to blame for your desire to end the marriage."

Ashleigh had been shutting the door. She opened it again, eyes glittering with dislike. "You know a lot, Vic, but you don't know everything. I have a chance to be on the ground floor of a new real estate company. I can be a broker and get commissions, and the Zigler house is my springboard."

I stared at her, my jaw going slack. "Who's behind this real estate company? Corky Ranaghan? Is that who was with you in the Zigler mansion?"

"Corky Ranaghan?" she echoed. "Really, Vic, have you met him? I'd just as soon embrace a slab of bacon."

She started to close the door again, then opened it to say, "That's a good suggestion about *Midnight in the Garden*. Not the *Count of Monte Cristo*, though. I don't think sword fights will help sell the house."

"You're thinking of *The Three Musketeers*," I said, "The Count was locked in a dungeon where his enemies expected him to die. But—surprise! He escaped. Just like Julia Zigler."

I'd had the last word, but it didn't make me feel good. Ashleigh was the third person today to tell me I didn't know anything. Corky had insider knowledge I'd never be able to penetrate, but maybe Ashleigh's boyfriend-escort was part of his inner circle. Robert Calabro had also told me how ignorant I was, but he wasn't a player, just a bottom-feeder.

Ashleigh was right about one thing. If Donny was scared or worried, the person he'd turn to wouldn't be his wife but big sister Sonia.

39

The Big Box

Like the rest of her family, Sonia had moved away from South Chicago. She'd married a guy named Geary. It made sense that she'd landed in Bridgeport—it was the historic home of Chicago's Irish mayors and their cronies.

Time was when a Black person would be murdered for crossing the Eleventh Ward's boundaries, and if you were white but not Irish you might get beaten up. These days, it was one of the few truly diverse Chicago neighborhoods, which probably has old Mayor Daley's Hamburg gang spinning fast enough in their graves to split atoms.

Sonia had divorced Steve Geary eight years ago. They'd never had children. My databases told me she was a manager for Old Comiskey Auto Parts on Pershing Road. She was probably there now. Even in a pandemic, people need batteries and fan belts.

Today was a game day. The Sox have a hard time drawing a crowd, even when they're coasting into the World Series. This early in the season, on a chilly April day, traffic near the ballpark moved briskly. At Wrigley, even when the Cubs are in the sub-basement, the stands are full. Life is definitely not fair.

Old Comiskey Auto Parts, three blocks west of the Sox park, advertised battery jumps on game days: WE GET TO YOU FASTER THAN YOUR DAD OR AAA. They also offered fifteen-dollar parking, watched by Old Comiskey's security cameras. Today only two vehicles stood in the shop's parking bays, next to a truck with a generator and cables in its bed.

I parked in an empty bay and went inside. The front of the shop was a narrow space separated from the auto parts by a reception counter and a gate leading to the warehouse beyond. No one was in the front, but I could hear voices from the back. I went to the gate, which was locked.

A ship's bell sounded overhead. "Welcome to Old Comiskey. Say 'cheese' for our camera."

I was startled by the recorded voice and looked

up instinctively. A light flashed and the gate opened. Clever. Your face would be on file if you were inclined to help yourself to the merchandise.

"Someone's come in; be right back," I heard Sonia say from the back of the shop. She called out more loudly to let me know she'd be right with me.

"Hey, Sonia! It's V.I. Warshawski," I shouted. "In Aisle Fourteen."

"Warshawski! What the hell are you doing here? You need a jump, call Triple A. I'm not taking the truck out for you."

On the last sentence, she appeared at the top of the aisle. She was dressed for work in jeans and a green, man-tailored shirt with OLD COMISKEY stitched across the left pocket and SONIA on the right.

"Yes, what are you doing here, Warshawski?" Reggie had appeared on her heels.

"Reggie! Have you found your rocketship yet?"

"Skyrocket," he corrected me. "No. Have you persuaded Brad to tell you who he sold it to?"

"There must be a reason you suspect him and not your own sons, who seem like a very enterprising pair."

He stiffened. "My sons know how important the Skyrocket is, not only to me but to the whole industry. Its success will also make it possible for them to do anything they dream of."

"I don't think most teens care about the discounted net present value of a future stream of earnings," I said. "They like excitement and immediacy. Finn and Cameron have dozens of opportunities to be in your lab or in your computer. They're clever boys; they probably know all your passwords."

"She's right, Reggie." Sonia surprised me by agreeing. "They're much cleverer than Brad."

"Of course if it's Donny's kid, you'll stick up for him," Reggie said bitterly. "But Brad's a gamer, he *is* Donny's kid, so he's grown up knowing how to hustle."

"Brad isn't a hustler," Sonia said. "Who knows what he is under all that red hair and moodiness. He isn't like Ashleigh any more than he's like Donny, so maybe he was switched at birth."

Before Reggie could fight back, I jumped in. "Donny and his hustles, that's actually what I wanted to talk to Sonia about, so it's good that you're here, Reggie. I've been keeping quiet about Brad's reason for consulting me, because he was afraid if his parents found out they'd fight even more viciously than they do now, but he was worried that someone was pressuring Donny, blackmailing him with something from his past, into doing something he didn't want to do. I need to know what that was. I need to know who was turning the screw."

"What, is Ashleigh paying you to make Donny look bad?" Sonia jeered. "She needs to cover her own—"

"Please stop," I said wearily. "I have a teenage girl whose life is in danger, and your nephew, who was definitely assaulted—by whom, we don't know, but someone looking either for your Skyrocket software or for what my girl is hiding. Two teens, two life-threatening secrets—I have to assume they're connected somewhere, somehow, and I need to see if the paths lead through Donny."

Brother and sister both started to speak.

"Let me finish." I sketched the part of the phone call Brad said he'd overheard. "I talked to Dorothea Jenko, who used to work for your dad, and she told me about an episode with the store van on a night that you twins and Donny went out with Tad Duda. Boom-Boom refused to go, even though he'd run around with you and Donny on some of Tommaso's other errands. After that night, Ms. Jenko says you and Stan turned your backs on Tommaso and turned into academic superstars. Donny didn't start going to school, but he stopped being Val's errand boy."

Sonia and Reggie became completely still. In the silence, I could hear the blower for the furnace kick on.

My hamstrings were starting to ache from standing so long. "You guys were running an errand for the Viper that night, weren't you?"

"Errand? I guess you could call it that," Reggie said bitterly. "Donny'd been doing shit for the Viper since he was twelve or thirteen. Back then, Stan and I followed him around like he was some rock star. He was the big brother, he was cool. Stan and I, we were thirteen, Donny was sixteen. We saw he got respect in the 'hood, and that bike—we loved that bike of his. He'd boost cigarettes from the bars of people who wouldn't pay protection to Tommaso. Like Novick, who ran the convenience store on the corner—remember him? 'Novick's the enemy,' Donny would say, and Stan and me, we go, 'Oh, yeah, Novick's the enemy.'"

He spoke in a falsetto, imitating his thirteen-year-old self.

"That's how it happens," he went on. "You put a foot into the lake, then you're in up to your ankles. And pretty soon you're swimming without noticing your feet left the ground—that was what getting into Val's orbit was like.

"Anyway, that night, Val wanted us to ride down to the Guisar slip in Cal Harbor, collect a load that some guy was going to give us. Don't ask me who, because if I heard the name back then, it didn't mean anything to me.

"Tommaso told Donny that a freighter was going to be offloading at the Guisar slip, and we had to pick up one container. It was boys' adventure night. We had a password to get past security into the slip, we had a password we were supposed to give to the guy unloading the freighter. What could go wrong?"

He gave a mirthless smile. "Boom-Boom bailed. He and Tad Duda fought about that."

I nodded. "Dorothea Jenko learned about this from another woman in your dad's store. She lived in one of those little apartments above the shops on Exchange and she saw the fight."

"Yeah, Warshawski—your cousin, I mean—he must have smelled a rat. He was already going off to those NHL training camps, hoping one of the farm clubs would recruit him, so he didn't want to be caught doing something criminal.

"Anyway, we get to the slip, and at first it seems like it's another seamless op for Tommaso. The passwords work, the guy in charge of the unloading takes us into a shed to pick up Tommaso's load. It's one crate, and it weighs a ton. Takes two men to shift it.

"The van is like a mobile dress store. There's a passenger seat in front—that goes to Duda—and Stan and I, we're sitting on the floor in the back because there aren't any seats. The whole thing is filled with clothes racks for hanging clothes on when they're being picked up or dropped off. And that's where the guys at the dock dump Tommaso's one big crate.

"We're heading up Ewing when the most awful thing happens: the crate opens from the inside. And this guy climbs out. And every horror film you've ever seen—we're in that movie. Stan and I, we're kids, we scream. Donny pulls over to see what's going on, and this guy pulls out a gun and points it at Donny and tells him to keep driving and he'll tell him where to go. So Donny drives, and we go way the hell out of the city. To this day, I don't know where. Guy gets out and says to wait. He goes into a house. We wait. And then he comes out of the house, and we drive him back to the Guisar slip, and the guy at the dock loads him onto the freighter."

"It was a hit," I said.

"I'm sure it was a hit," Reggie agreed. "Donny was so freaked he drove off the road and got the van all banged up. We got home about three in the morning. Mom was passed out and Dad was probably with a girl-friend he had down in Cal City.

"When we got back to South Chicago, Donny says to Duda, 'We're telling the Viper we're done. The Lit-vaks, anyway. You can hang on if you want.' Duda says he'll tell Val the Litvaks are two-faced, like all the

Jews, and Donny jumps him. Stan and I, we just stood and watched the two of them pound the shit out of each other. Donny won, of course. If he hadn't, Stan and I would have piled on."

"Donny told me about it." Sonia was speaking in a hoarse, quiet voice. "Not the same day, but about a week later. He said Boom-Boom warned him that Val was setting him up so he'd have leverage over him. How did your cousin know?"

"He never talked to me about it," I said. "Probably the fact that Val wanted you to use your dad's van clued him in. If something went wrong, it would be Donny and Tad holding the bag, but Donny first since it was the Litvak van. Mostly, though, I'm guessing Boom-Boom bailed because he was getting big thrills skating in front of people like the Golden Jet. He didn't need cheap thrills from running a two-bit Mob boss's errands."

Although, was Val really a small player? He had controlled a lot of money flowing through the South Side, from illegal gambling to booze and drugs and probably sex. He could have exacted vengeance from Boom-Boom for stiffing him in the first place, or Donny for turning away from him.

"Val threatened Boom-Boom." The memory suddenly came to me. "I only heard the end of the conversation. We were walking up Exchange, and he pulled over—he drove that big Toronado—and he called to Boom-Boom."

My cousin had told me to stay on the sidewalk, not to come with him. He'd bent over to talk to Tommaso through his open window. Sergeant Hawley had been in the front seat next to him; I remembered being upset that a police officer was riding with a Mob boss.

And then Boom-Boom backed away from the car, shouting, "Yes, you gave me a pair of skates, but that doesn't mean you own me. The Red Wings gave me a jersey, but they don't own me, either."

Boom-Boom refused to tell me why Tommaso was threatening him. I couldn't tell my dad my worry over seeing Sergeant Hawley with Tommaso. My mother had just had her first surgery. My father was gaunt from worry and overwork: he was pulling extra shifts to buy the fresh fruit she longed for. I had forgotten the episode in my fear over my mother.

"So Boom-Boom Warshawski was a hero, and the Litvaks were bastards," Sonia said, bitter. "Now Saint Victoria of the Mills can climb even higher onto her holy mountain."

"Sonny, the Litvaks were fuckin' lucky," Reggie said. "We were accessories in a crime. I have never wanted to dig into what crime. I don't want to know if we dropped a guy off so he could murder someone. I'd like to think he wanted one last kiss from his mother before going on the lam.

"Stan and I, we made a pact never to talk about it, and I'm pretty sure Donny never did, either. I never told Melanie, and I'm sure Donny never told Ashleigh. And I hope to Christ neither of you repeats word one of this."

"Of course not," Sonia said. "You know you shouldn't have to ask— Oh, Warshawski here, the cop's daughter. You going to turn us in?"

I ignored the jab. "Brad heard the guy Donny was talking to say, 'Sonia bailed you out back then, but she can't get your ass out of this sling,'" I said. "Did you bail Donny out, or is there some other episode whoever it was could be talking about?"

Sonia started to snarl that no one had made me God, to sit in judgment on her and her brothers, but Reggie cut her off. "You were always rescuing us, Sonny. That isn't a secret. You'd claim Donny was looking after Gregory while you were at Girl Scout meetings, when he was really hopping on truck tailgates to help himself to cases of cigarettes. Not to mention all the times they picked me up and you said they were confusing me with Stan, or the other way around. I don't remember you being there that night, but I've blocked so much of that memory, maybe you were."

"Not really. I was out, with Gregory, of course. I knew Donny was getting close to something I couldn't help him escape from. But—"

She flashed me a look. Pain, rage, some combination.

"I was alone. I was lonely! You guys and Donny were off together having adventures and I was home with the baby and the drunk. But that night, morning, I guess, Donny came back. He was all in pieces, shaking, throwing up. I don't know if he knew who was in the crate, or what he'd been doing in that suburban house, but I knew he needed me.

"I told Dad I'd gone to a party at Rainbow Beach and that Donny came to find me, only he ran into one of the concrete barriers there. Dad didn't really believe me, but of course Mom was passed out by suppertime, so he didn't have any way of knowing if I'd been home or not. I didn't exactly bail you guys out, as much as make it harder to prove where you'd been or what you'd done."

Reggie rubbed the base of her neck. "You went out on too many limbs for us, Sonny. We should have done more to help you with that rat Geary."

"If Donny picking up and dropping off a career criminal is what Donny's caller was talking about, then it must have been either Duda or Tommaso that Brad overheard on the phone," I said. "Does either of you have any idea what they wanted from Donny?"

Sonia's eyes were unhappy above her mask. "Since all this started, Donny's been hiding from me. I guess he knows I'll make him tell me the truth. Maybe he's protecting me."

"I don't know the Litvak family's other secrets, so I have to suggest the only thing I do know: this invention of Reggie's. It went missing just about the time Donny got that threatening phone call."

"Donny?" Reggie was incredulous. "Donny wouldn't know a piece of software if the bytes rose up and nipped his ass."

"He wouldn't have to know how to use it; he'd just have to know how to get a copy to give to whoever wanted it."

"I can't see him doing even that," Reggie said. "And why would he? He knows how important the Skyrocket is to me. He'd never stab me in the back by stealing it and giving it to someone else."

"He'd never willingly betray you," I agreed. "But how much damage would it do to *you* for the story of your night in the van to come out? It wouldn't be hard for anyone who knew you'd been implicated to look up unexplained mobster activity for that year. Maybe a hit that was never solved, or a boy kissing his mom good-bye. Donny could lose his job; Ashleigh would have a big club to hit him with in a custody battle. And potential investors would give you a wide birth. You were just thirteen, but still—!"

"You know it makes me choke to say it, but she's right," Sonia said.

Reggie nodded. "Sonny, I could use a glass of water."

Sonia disappeared into the back of the shop.

"Boom-Boom really never talked about that night?" Reggie asked.

"Not to me." I felt a stab of unhappiness; I hadn't thought my cousin kept secrets from me. Of course he did, by that point in his life. He was only sixteen but was already being scouted by NHL farm teams. He was probably having sex with the girls he met when he went to scouting events. No way would he have shared those details with me.

40
Heathcliff Arrives

S onia came back with bottles of water—even one for me.

"I need you to tell me more about the Skyrocket," I said. "You said it could revolutionize drone behavior when you worked out the bugs, but I can't imagine people would be after it if you didn't already have a working model."

Reggie grimaced, looked from me to Sonia. "The demo freaked me out. It worked, all right, but with a side effect I wasn't ready for. I've come up with a working solar antenna that can power the drone without needing an external power source. When I launched it for my first full-scale demo, it started relaying me information from every house it flew over.

"I'd thought of it as a device for integrating data sets

and helping map climate change phenomena. When it was in action, I realized I'd been so focused on making it work I hadn't seen what it could really do."

"Oh," I said. "If it sucked up people's data, it would be the ultimate Big Brother in the sky."

"Yep. It would make Stingrays and Dirtboxes look like, I don't know, decoder rings pulled from a cereal box. Donny was watching the demo on my iPad. He was shouting and swearing, and then he roared off, leaving Brad and Ashleigh for me to take care of. I was blind mad at him for that, and we haven't been talking much since the demo. I didn't even tell him I've pulled the prototype until I can work out a way around the data-theft problem. I thought he'd sent Brad to steal it for him."

"Would Brad know how to break into wherever you've stored your material?" I asked. "I like him, but he doesn't seem that savvy."

"The family discounts him the way they do Gregory, because he's got the same slow speech. Actually, I've seen him do some gaming with drones, and he knows what he's doing. He definitely would have known what to look for if he got into my safe."

He stared at the bottle of water he was holding, as if he could see his drone's whereabouts in it. "I've been so sure Donny took it, or got Brad to steal it, that I haven't thought of other possibilities. It could have a big industrial use. If Donny let word out, anyone at a company like Klondike would want it."

"How dare you?" Sonia said. "Donny would never betray you, and for sure not to a stuck-up oinker like Corky Ranaghan."

"I know that, Sis." He put an arm around Sonia. "You know how Donny shoots off his mouth. He could have been bellowing about how much damage my Skyrocket would do to people's privacy. Someone owing favors to Corky could have seen the Skyrocket's industrial potential and thought he could score big points by bringing it to him."

He turned back to me. "A big problem in data mining these days is data integration. Everybody's spewing out a billion or more bytes a day, but data comes in all kinds of formats. You could set up the Skyrocket to integrate data sets that are too big for ordinary drone use. If you owned a—I don't know—a detective agency that specialized in white-collar crime, I'd look at the cases you'd solved over the past five years, see what the crooks and the clients had in common, mine data for more people like them, send my drone out to create a map that would show you the closest location to potential clients."

"Goose Island and the land spit right across from it

are ripe for residential development," I said. "There's an old mansion right there on the water that the owner's son is trying to sell—against the owner's wishes. My sources tell me the preliminary ideas developers are touting run to nine figures, could be more if the bidding war heats up. I can see Corky drooling over it, but he wouldn't need something like your technology. It's all right there where anyone can see it.

Reggie nodded. "You're right. The only reason Corky would want it would be because he's the kind of greedy SOB who wants to suck up anything no one else has. For serious use, you only want the Skyrocket if you're dealing with a complex set of data."

"Klondike could use the Skyrocket to scope out landscapes for development projects," I said.

"They could," Reggie said impatiently, "but they already know the real estate in the six counties. It's what you just said: they don't need something this expensive."

"There's Ashleigh," Sonia said. "She's got that real estate job that she thinks is beneath her."

"So she does," I agreed. "She told me only an hour ago she might have a chance to head up a whole new real estate company, but could she have stolen your rocket?"

"She was at the Skyrocket demo," Reggie said. "If

she was paying attention she heard Donny yelling about it, but I thought she and Melanie were off in a corner bitching about the Litvaks. Stan says the five of us are attached by a force so strong we can't escape its gravitational pull. It's why he sits on that mesa in Sedona saying 'ohm,' or whatever it is he does. He doesn't think it's possible for him to connect to anyone outside the family, but he doesn't want to be tied to the family the way he thinks Donny and I are."

My phone buzzed at me. It was the burner, with Mr. Contreras on the line. I'd forgotten my promise to call him every few hours. I stepped down the aisle away from the Litvaks.

It was Julia, her voice pitched so high from fear that I could barely make out the words. "He's here! He's come for me, I have to get away, but Uncle Sal won't let me go."

"Julia! I need you to take a deep breath, and hold it while you count to ten in your head. Do that before you try to talk again."

"But what if—"

"Just do it. Then we can make a plan."

She sucked in a breath. While she counted, I could hear the dogs whining, and my neighbor exclaiming disjointedly.

"I breathed but he didn't disappear."

"Tell me who 'he' is. I don't know who's shown up or what he's doing."

"The man from the hospital. The one who came into my room the day I ran away. And he's outside the building, ringing all the bells. Someone could buzz him in at any second. Tell Uncle Sal I have to run!"

Phone at my ear, I ran through Old Comiskey's aisles to the exit, ignoring indignant shouts from Sonia—I couldn't come in here, stir the pot, and then leave without a word.

I kept up a stream of calming chatter to Julia until I was in the car. "Julia, let me talk to Uncle Sal."

I had the engine running, phone in one hand, heading along Thirty-Fifth Street.

"Doll, I don't know who that guy is. Brad recognized him. Doesn't know his name, but says he's the man he saw with his ma the other night."

"Can you see if he has someone waiting in the alley? I'm at least twenty minutes away. The kids need to get out of there as fast as possible."

The old man went into the garden, to the patch by the back wall where he has sunflowers tied up. "Yeah, doll, looks like there's someone waiting in the alley. Big SUV with the motor running."

I'd been afraid of that. I'd used the back exit too many times to keep getting away with it. *Brain, go to work!* I merged onto the Ryan, floored the Mustang, passed two cars on the shoulder who'd run into each other, their windows shattered. I slowed down.

"You there, doll? I'm going back inside, in case someone let the creep in."

"There's a cracked window in the basement, opens onto the north side of the building. Get the kids down there, smash the window so they can climb out. If the guy left his SUV in the alley and he's trying to come in through the front, it should be safe for them to sneak out to Racine along the side. I'm going to park on Eddy Street, right around the corner from us. If the kids aren't there when I arrive, I'll come in and deal with whoever this thug is."

Mitch and Peppy had begun a deep-chested volley. As Mr. Contreras moved back inside, their sound drowned out his voice. I put the phone down and concentrated on the road. Get off at Damen, half a mile closer. Keep an eye out for squad cars, pedestrians, idiots making left turns from the right lane. I honked, swerved, swore, got to Eddy in one piece, and pulled over to the curb.

I didn't see the kids, but when I got out of the car, their heads popped up from behind the thick shrubbery on the corner. Julia ran to me, clutched me.

"We got out, and ran up the street, and then we heard

Mr. Contreras yelling and Mitch barking. I wanted to go back, but Brad wouldn't let me."

I looked at Brad.

"I hid behind a car and looked—it wasn't the guy who'd been with Mom. Some other man, he's pretty big, too, he showed up and he was kind of fighting with Uncle Sal. Mitch was barking at him."

Breathe, count to ten. "You did the right thing in staying put. He wants you two. There's a bike station two blocks west." I dug in my bag for a credit card. "Get bikes, go to Lotty Herschel's clinic. I'll meet you there."

I wrote the address on a scrap of paper and handed it to Brad. "I'm going to make sure Mr. Contreras is safe. You two—take off!"

They stared at me, helpless. I took their arms and marched them across the street. "Keep going in this direction. In two short blocks, you'll see the bike rental rack."

As soon as they were moving, I ran down the street to my apartment. It was Scott Coney, leaning over Mr. Contreras, his mouth almost on my neighbor's nose.

"I don't care if you won the whole damned war by yourself. I want those two kids. I have a warrant."

"And I don't care if you got warrants for everyone on Racine Avenue. Those two kids ain't going anywhere with you."

Mitch shoved himself in front of Coney, forcing him back. Coney kicked him in the ribs. The dog yowled in pain. He stood his ground, but Mr. Contreras was outraged. He punched Coney. He couldn't get much force or lift—the blow landed on Coney's shoulder. Coney's face turned brick.

"That's it, you senile bastard. Your dog bit me, you hit me. It's time for you to cool off in a cell."

"Absolutely not." I used my whip-crack voice.

Coney turned. "You! I should have known you were behind this!" He started for me.

"One. The dog did not bite you—he tried to push you aside. Two. You arresting a ninety-two-year-old man who has a Purple Heart because he's too strong for you? Believe me, that's the story they'll stream on every platform in the country. The FOP can get you out of excessive force complaints, but no one will save you from being a laughingstock."

Before he could decide what to do, a big man with dark curly hair came around the side of the building. "Hey, Coney. They're not in Warshawski's apartment. The boy's been in the old man's place. The girl may have been with Warshawski. I just had Ranaghan's PA on the phone. I need to get out to Palatine on the double."

"Tad Duda!" I said. "Are you telling me you broke into my home?"

He spun on his booted heel and stomped over to me. "Warshawski! Why the *fuck* are you messing in my business?"

"Aren't you in cement, Tad? I've got nothing to do with that. But you being in my space, that is definitely messing in *my* business. Why are you?"

He had a good six inches on me, both in height and shoulders. He leaned over me. I made a show of adjusting my mask to make sure I wasn't breathing in his germs.

"Donny's kid can come or go, I don't care. But you need to produce the girl."

Mitch was growling low in his throat. I put a hand on his scruff. "Yeah, he's a horse's patootie, boy, but we can't go biting him. We might catch something worse than Covid, like his personality disorder."

"You always thought you were cuter, smarter than the rest of us, but believe me, Warshawski, you're not. I want that girl."

"Why? The Viper wants you to ship her down to Florida?"

"The Viper? What the fuck are you talking about?"

"Isn't he your godfather, saving you from your gambling losses?"

"You really are the sorriest excuse of a detective I've ever seen," Duda sneered, "and I've seen some pretty big losers. Where's the girl, loser?"

"Fee-fi-fo-fum. I have no idea where she is. If she's not in my apartment, she's run off again. As Gus and Lacey will have told you, she runs faster and more often than a track star."

Coney said, "Come on, Duda. I'll take care of her soon, but I just got a text from Corky's girl wanting to know where we are."

Tad's face bunched up like the inside of a cabbage. He swung a fist at me, missed, and swore again, but he stomped off with Coney.

Mr. Contreras's face was shiny with distress. He wanted to file a complaint against Coney, he wanted me to call Freeman Carter to bring suit against the department.

"That Coney, he kicked Mitch. And then he lied and said Mitch bit him. He belongs in a cell hisself, not out on the street, beating people up."

I put an arm around my neighbor. "You are right, and those are calls that should be made. Here's my dilemma. I've got the kids on bikes on their way to Lotty's clinic and I need to make sure they're safe. It would be an absolute disaster if they got out of here only for Coney and Duda to find them on the street.

Do you want to come with me and call Freeman from the car? He can take care of lodging all the complaints and so on."

Mr. Contreras shook his head. "You go after the kids; that's the best thing. I'll call Mr. Carter. I'm kind of wore out, tell you the truth, doll. But that big guy, you called him Duda? He's the one Julia was scared of. And that Coney—that was his SUV parked in the alley, so Duda must be some super boss in the police, huh?"

"Tad Duda is someone Brad's dad and my cousin Boom-Boom used to hang out with down in South Chicago. Except Boom-Boom realized he was poison and left him alone. He's not a cop, he's a cement maker. And I believe he's having an affair with Brad's mother."

41
Aunt Sonny Comes Through

I settled Mr. Contreras in his apartment. Tad Duda had said he'd searched both my place and my neighbor's. He hadn't broken down the doors, which was a plus, but it frightened me that he'd gotten inside. My door has three locks with keys that supposedly require a signature to order.

I couldn't take time to deal with that now. As soon as my neighbor was in his armchair, feeding Mitch bits of hamburger as a cure for Coney's brutality, I took off. He urged me to take Peppy, which I didn't want to do.

"Julia is pretty jumpy right now, what with Coney and the other guy and worrying about her grandma. Peppy'll keep her calm."

I supposed he was right. Against my better judgment, I jogged back to the car with her and got under way. While I headed west on Belmont, I called Mrs. Coltrain at the clinic. The kids hadn't shown up yet.

"But, Ms. Warshawski, you know we can't keep them here. I'm not even sure we can let them in because of our distancing needs."

"I'll move them on as soon as we all get there," I promised. "I needed a meeting point where they could be safe until I hooked up with them."

I asked her to text me as soon as they arrived, but as the minutes went by without any word from her, I imagined one alarming scene after another. They hadn't been able to get bikes out of the rack, they'd been picked up by cops, Duda and Coney had shot them. I drove up and down the side streets, trying to keep panic at bay.

I finally found them, on bikes, half a mile north and west of Lotty's, pedaling more or less toward O'Hare. I pulled over in front of them, let Peppy out of the car so they'd realize it was me, not a marauder.

"We didn't have phones, we didn't have GPS." Julia, in tears, flung herself onto Peppy, who licked her face ecstatically. "We couldn't find the address. We couldn't ask anyone for help in case they turned us in."

A complication I hadn't imagined. They'd never actually navigated the city's streets the way Boom and I did as children. Their devices spoke to them and told them where to go. I wondered if that was the best use for Reggie's Skyrocket—to give directions from an all-seeing drone. The software would cleverly sort out who was trying to go where and then speak through your earbuds in the accent and timbre of your choice.

"Sorry, Vic," Brad muttered. "I guess I'm one of the useless Litvaks, like Mom is always calling Dad's family."

"Hey, none of that. We are a team here, which means we're relying on each other. You are doing a great job of staying calm in a horrible situation."

"Is Uncle Sal okay?" Julia asked.

"He's fine, just a bit tired—he's ninety-two and doesn't bounce back as fast as he'd like. We need to get out of the road, we need to find a safe place for the two of you until I can get some of this sorted out."

"And my grandmother," Julia said. "You promised to rescue her."

"I promised, and I will." Not that I had a plan of any kind, but surely something would come to me.

Julia wedged herself into the Mustang's narrow backseat with Peppy. Brad sat in the front, long legs pulled up to his chin to keep the seat from crushing Julia.

I wondered if my burner phone had been burned, but I handed it to Brad. "Do you know your Aunt Sonia's number? Can you call her and tell her we're heading to Old Comiskey?"

He didn't know the number by heart. His device usually called people for him, just as it propelled him through the streets. I risked unwrapping my smartphone long enough to look up the number and dictate it to him.

I'd been afraid Sonia wouldn't pick up an unknown number, but she was still at work—it could have been a customer, looking for a jump. Brad told her I was driving him to the shop.

I told him to ask if cops were hovering around.

"She says no," he reported, but she'd told him we were on the news. I was a fugitive, harboring two teens whose parents and guardians were desperate to have them safely home.

Even without the GPS beacon, my Mustang was a bright red invitation to be pulled over. I obeyed all traffic signals, kept pace with the mid-speed cars on the Ryan, pulled in behind the auto shop when we'd managed to get there safely.

There were a couple of SUVs in front of the store, but Brad phoned his aunt again and she opened a back door for us. When she'd finished with her customers, she found us near the piston heads and brought us to her cube of an office.

"So you're a kidnapper and a fugitive, Warshawski. I guess even Holy Victoria has her evil side."

"You have no idea, Sonia," I said. "Trouble is, Tad Duda is playing an active role in hunting Julia and Brad. And he's got one of Chicago's finest running interference for him. I can look after myself, or at least I am prepared to take the risks involved in standing up to Duda and Coney. But the kids aren't."

Sonia listened quietly as I spelled out the events of the last few days, not interrupting with her usual shots at me.

"It's up to Brad whether he wants to return either to Ashleigh or Donny, but Julia absolutely cannot go back to her uncle and aunt. They locked her up, tried to starve her into signing some papers for them. I know this is a big gamble, turning to you for help, but I'm hoping you can put these kids up for a few days. I'm sure it goes against the grain to keep Brad's location a secret from Donny, but everyone knows how much you despise me, so I'm banking that no one would think I'd turn to you for help."

She gave a loud snort of laughter. "You're not so bad

after all, Warshawski. Of course I want to look out for Brad, and if Julia's on the run from the boys in blue, I'd like to help her, too. But I need to think about Donny. If he's in trouble, it's like you just said—I'm the first person he'll go to. Which means if someone's watching him, they're watching me. What I want to suggest— Gregory could put them up."

"Gregory?" I was startled.

"Gregory," she repeated firmly. "No one ever thinks of him, or if they do, they make fun of him, like Ashleigh last week, calling him the most useless person on the planet. He's not. He's smart and sweet, but he likes a low-key life. He lives in Ukrainian Village. He's got an extra bedroom for his vinyl collection, so the girl could sleep in there, Brad on his pullout couch. And if the dog goes with, no one will think it's strange for him to have a dog show up suddenly. It's the advantage of having people think you're weird: nothing you do seems odd because they think everything you do is odd."

I blinked at Sonia's rapid generalship.

"You think we ought to ask him first?" I said.

"On it." She moved away from us to have a private conversation with her brother.

"Is that your uncle?" Julia asked Brad. "Is he safe?"

"Yeah. He's kind of hard to talk to, but he's okay, like Aunt Sonny said. Vic, what's going to happen? You're not going to just leave us there, are you? I mean, there's my mom, my dad, the Skyrocket."

"And my grandmother." Julia stuck her chin out, stubborn.

"Yes. Your mom, Brad. I think I know who she was with in Julia's grandmother's house."

I went to the computer on Sonia's desk and looked up Tad Duda. We found pics of him on Tommaso Cement job sites, mostly in hardhats that concealed his halo of curls, but you could see enough of his ruddy, manly jaw to recognize him.

Brad nodded unhappily. "I guess it could've been him."

When Julia saw him she gave a little whimper. "That's the man at the hospital who came to the apartment today. Who is he?"

"His name is Tad Duda. He owns the cement company across the river from your house. You never saw him in the yard there?"

She shook her head. "But what? He watches our house and thinks because *Nagyi* is old, he can bully her into selling? Does he know Uncle Gus?"

"Yes. When I was at your house yesterday, I saw Gus in the cement works yard talking to him. Tad and

Gus know each other, and they may be working some angle together."

I looked at Brad. "The same people who are after Julia are the ones who attacked you. They're looking for something they think you or your dad has. I'm guessing it's your uncle's rocketship, because I don't know what else it could be."

Brad winced, his whole face contorted in pain. "I don't have it. I don't know where it is. Is that what the man who threatened Dad wanted? Is he a thief, like Mom is always claiming? I hate my family! No wonder no one at school ever wants to be around me. They can smell the Litvak cooties ten miles away."

"Litvaks include your aunt Sonny. I wouldn't have brought you here, looking for her help, if I didn't admire and respect her. I told you this before, but your grandparents were a very difficult, uncaring set of people. Sonia made sure that your dad and your uncles got fed, that they had clothes to wear to school. She sacrificed her own education to take care of your uncle Gregory. You could do worse than be part of her family."

He nodded, almost imperceptibly, and turned to study a poster advertising brake linings.

Sonia came into the room. "Gregory says it's fine if they stay with him, including the dog, as long as she doesn't chew on his records. He should get that collection insured. He has a complete set of Beatles first releases, some vintage Duke Ellington, other stuff. Anyway, getting you there. The less time you're in a car around me or Gregory, Vic, the safer you'll be. So best take the L."

"We can't take Peppy on the L," Julia said.

"And you have to have Peppy?" Sonia's voice was at its harshest, most challenging.

Julia knelt with her arms around Peppy. Before she started a useless fight with Sonia, I interrupted with my worries about the Mustang. "Do you have some nondescript car that I could borrow?"

Her heavy frown shifted from Julia to me. "You're reminding me what a major pain you usually are, Warshawski. It's always push, push, push. As soon as we do you favor one, you need favor two."

She gave the sigh of the long-suffering. "But the boss left his old Nissan here. He took off for New Mexico for a month in his new Lexus. Don't wreck his car or you'll replace it. Take the kids and go before someone else drops in uninvited."

I left the Mustang keys with Sonia. She looked wistfully at my muscle car but agreed it wouldn't be smart for her to use it.

"You get Brad and the girl clear, and I get to drive this pony for a week. Deal, Warshawski?"

"Sure, Sonia. Long as you don't wreck it."

When we were in the Nissan, taking the side streets north and west to Gregory's, Brad said, "What is my mom doing with that creep? He's the guy who threatened Julia in the hospital, right? He told her he'd kill her granny if she didn't give him what he wanted. Is he using my mom? Pretending he's in love so he can get the house on the river? She can't give that to him. I don't understand."

"I don't understand, either," I said. "Even though he's up past his eyeballs in debt, no one's going to give him big money for muscling the title away from Julia. I don't know what he thinks your mother can do for him. All I do know is that I want you two to be safe. I wish I could keep you at my side so I could protect you in person, but if you stay with me, you'll be in quintuple danger. So when you get to Gregory's, stay there. Stay away from—"

"Windows," the two chorused.

"Stay away from OS, too." Brad offered the joke shyly, and I laughed.

"Definitely stay away from your social media accounts. Don't go to the cloud looking for photos. I know that's like asking you not to breathe, but the people Duda owes money to have the resources and the desire to track your online footprint. It would take them five minutes to get Gregory's IP address and find you at his apartment. So—do I have your word?"

"You have my word, Vic," Brad said.

"Mine, too." Julia spoke through Peppy's fur.

42
Feeding the Ducks

We had to stop at a Buy-Smart outlet on our way to Gregory's so the kids could stock up on the basics—change of clothes, toothbrushes, another cup for Julia. Dog food and dishes for Peppy. A new supply of burner phones. I gave one to each teen and kept three for myself. I got Brad to program each phone's number into all five phones so we could reach each other.

Gregory's persona was so awkward that I hadn't expected his home to be attractive, but it was, in a pared-down fashion. There wasn't much furniture, but the pieces were good-quality contemporary. He had an oat-colored sofa on a chrome frame that was big enough for Brad to sleep on. Since it faced a fifty-inch screen, Brad seemed fine with letting Julia use the spare room.

Although he had a daybed in it, Gregory's spare room was more soundstage than bedroom, and he was nervous about letting Julia in there. All the walls were lined with shelves, most holding records, but some with books on the history of recording, or biographies of musicians. He also had a collection of turntables and speakers. He squirmed awkwardly from foot to foot, but finally said he didn't want Julia or Brad touching the records or the turntables.

"And the dog—is she going to chew on my stuff?"

Peppy, realizing she was in the conversation, went over to him and put a paw on his leg.

"Uh, okay, I guess she can stay, but she can't have water in this room. She can only be in here if Julia is in here, too. If she chews on one of my records or pees inside, you have to leave."

Julia nodded solemnly and promised to be super careful. "She's amazing. She sits and stays and comes, she brings Uncle Sal the newspaper in the morning. I wish I could have brought Mitch, he's better at protection, but Uncle Sal needs him more."

I left right after that. I hadn't called Mrs. Coltrain back to let her know I had the kids, because I'd been too worried about being tracked. Even though I had new burner phones, I waited until I was a good three miles from Gregory's place before I phoned the clinic.

"Oh, Ms. Warshawski, thank goodness you phoned. I'm glad the children are safe, but Dr. Herschel needs to speak to you!"

Lotty came on the line and I filled her in on how the afternoon had shaped up. "I was lucky that Duda was in a hurry to be gone—he was ready to break my jaw and Coney was itching to put cuffs on me. Anyway, the kids are safe, I hope."

Lotty interrupted the rest of my narrative with an impatient, "That's good, that you got them away in time. I've had three messages this afternoon from Mrs. Pariente. She needs to see you."

"The synagogue?" I said.

"Something about the synagogue, but she wouldn't say on the phone. Can you go to her? I'm not sure she'll talk on the phone."

My shoulders were sore, my glutes were throbbing, I hadn't eaten for eight hours. I'd have to leave the Nissan and walk half a mile to make sure I wasn't followed.

My "Sure, Lotty," came out as a snarl, but of course I couldn't leave Donna Ilona in the lurch.

Unlike my own apartment, where the alley was no longer safe, I was able to come at the Parientes' building from behind. It was five-thirty; the streets were full enough of commuters and children that I blended in.

Donna Ilona greeted me with relief. She was making an Italian cabbage dish, *involtini di verza*, that I knew from my own mother, and the smell made me drool. Fortunately my mask hid my greed.

"Thank you for coming." Donna Ilona took my hands between both of hers. "I know from Dr. Lotty that you are exhausted, running around the city to help us, but this is something important. You've been on the news, you know, and the reporter talked about Julia Zigler. Istvan Reito, from the synagogue, saw you as well. Emilio says you've met him. I told you that his wife looked after Estella with me. He said he needs to talk to you about Julia's grandmother. It's very urgent."

"Julia's grandmother?" I echoed. "What does he know about her?"

Donna Ilona threw up her hands. "I don't know. It is confidential, law business. He is very nervous now, about being out in public and also about being seen with you. He has a son who is an actor, and the son fixed him up to look like an old woman. His son Gideon is taking him over to—" She held up a scrap of paper and read from it. "Yes, to the north end of Diversey Harbor. They will be on a park bench. Istvan will have bread to feed to the ducks and you can talk to him at the water."

That sounded like reckless endangerment, but Donna Ilona said, "Gideon will be nearby, and one of the other actors is dressed like a homeless man and will be on a park bench to help look after Istvan. They should be safe, at least long enough for you to talk to him."

It still seemed like a horribly risky way to hold a confidential conversation, but I promised to go at once.

"At least—Donna Ilona, before I leave, could I have just a taste of your *involtini* to keep me going? I didn't have time for lunch."

She exclaimed in horror: How could she have been so unthinking? The sauce wasn't quite done, but if I could eat them without the sauce?

She had stuffed the leaves with rice and mushrooms and a small amount of cheese. No meat, she apologized, but it helped stretch their Social Security to save meat for special meals.

That made me feel guilty about taking food from her, but not guilty enough to turn my back on the *involtini*. The rolls, with a swallow of coffee, got me back on my feet with a better attitude than I'd had going in. I was whistling "Three Little Birds" as I walked back to the Nissan.

Chicago is made up of many small worlds that seem

to have nothing to connect them except the roads that run through them. I drove east past Orthodox temples and schools, through South Asian markets, to the remnants of the Appalachian immigrants, and on to the glistening condos for the affluent of all backgrounds that line Lake Shore Drive.

The lake made me long for a quiet afternoon, time to run, read, relax without worrying about a taser in my back. When I got off the Drive, I took an extra few minutes to let Mr. Contreras know that, so far, everyone was safe. He was feeling better, but he missed having Brad and Julia in the apartment. I cut him short as gently as I could and made my way to the harbor.

I walked around the north perimeter, looking for elderly women with homeless men nearby. There were a surprising number who fit that profile, but as I reached the east end of the walkway, a man of about sixty came over to me, his eyes alight with pleasure above a mask decorated with the names of playwrights.

"Nancy! So good of you to come. Mother is eager to see you."

Nancy? I guess that was my stage name. I followed him to a bench where a person was sitting, clutching a pocketbook and a paper bag. The makeup and costume were good enough to stand up to the setting sun. Gideon had given his father a wig of blue-tinged gray hair, curling around his face. Istvan was wearing a beige dress with long sleeves and a calf-length hem, along with thick support stockings that ended in gender-neutral suede shoes.

The next bench over, a man was sprawled with an empty bottle on the ground next to him. He must have poured it over his head, because the smell of cheap brandy was like a cloud around him.

As we spoke, Reito occasionally tossed pieces of bread onto the walk, which kept ducks and pigeons waddling around, and also earned us curses from joggers and cyclists. Gideon had created an entire small drama, complete with stage set.

"I didn't know you were acquainted with Mrs. Zigler until I heard the news reports about her granddaughter," Reito began.

"I'm not. I've never met her." I recounted my history with Julia.

"He wants the title to the house, which I believe is in a lockbox in your firm's offices," I finished. "I know nothing about estates and wills. I wouldn't think a form like that signed by a minor would be binding, but since he's established himself as her guardian maybe the courts would accept it."

"The Zigler story is a hard one," Reito said. "It's a

family story, which means that there are deep wounds
and fissures surrounding all the parties. I don't know
how much you know about Silvia, but she came to this
country as a refugee after the 1956 uprising."

"That's all I know about her. And she became a social worker, married, had two children."

Reito steepled his fingers, then remembered he was
supposed to be a woman interested in feeding ducks.
He scattered more bread on the walk.

"Silvia Elek, her name was. She was a brave, foolhardy girl, who got away from Hungary and the Communist reprisals by the skin of her teeth. In the way
of refugees, when she reached Chicago, she sought out
her landsmen. We met at a concert that the soprano
Vera Rózsa gave to raise money for refugees, and then
our paths crossed frequently over the years. When your
language is one that no one knows or understands, you
seek out occasions to use it."

He was silent for a bit. Gideon murmured something
about time, but I shook my head: Reito had to tell the
story in his own way.

"Everything Silvia did, she did with great panache,"
he finally said. "That house on the river looks run-
down now, but when she married Augustus Zigler, they
turned it into a cross between a salon and an interna-

tional refugee hotel. They had concerts in that garden, and dances in the house. Augustus kept a boat tied up by the garden gate, and he would take parties down the river to Lake Michigan.

"At the same time, anyone who needed a bed for a night or a year could sleep in the spare rooms. You might find a Polish mathematician or a Chinese ballerina in the kitchen when you arrived for a dinner party."

His jaw worked. "Then the children were born. Augustus number three, and Emma. And they were folded into the crowds and causes that Silvia supported."

"Her husband didn't?" I asked.

"Augustus supported her because he adored her, but he wasn't a man who believed much in grand causes. He was in a way Silvia's anchor. She knew she needed someone with a foot on the ground for ballast, to keep her from floating away, since her head was often in the clouds. But all these people coming through the house had a negative effect on the son. He resented the attention his mother gave to strangers, and a child, after all, does need its mother's attention."

He gave a twisted smile. "I practiced estate and trust law, and I have seen every possible unhappy family configuration you can imagine. The child resenting the mother for directing her affection to lovers or émigrés is a common one.

"For Gus, as he likes to be called, extra problems developed. He began stealing from his mother, little bits of change from her purse that she wasn't even sure were missing, and then bigger amounts that she couldn't overlook. When he was in his teens, he started hanging out with the truckers and cement workers on Goose Island. Nothing wrong with that, but he began betting on the craps game they have, or used to have, under the bridge. And then on sports, and so on. He forged Silvia's signature on checks, stole her credit cards. It was a nightmare.

"Augustus, the father, was dead by then. The family had very little money besides what Silvia earned. There were too many sleepless nights. She threw him out of the house, she changed the locks, she had to keep one step ahead of him constantly as he found ways to hack into her bank accounts. And then he did something even more extreme.

"His sister Emma, five years younger, was like a copy of her mother, even to that wild tangle of hair. She fell in love with a boy from Brazil who was in this country studying. Gus persuaded the boyfriend to lend him money to cover some of his debts, and then, instead of trying to repay him, he reported him to Homeland Security as a member of a drug cartel. His sister was five months pregnant at the time. The boyfriend was Black, by the way, so his protestations didn't carry much weight. He was deported.

"Silvia never forgave her son. She spent a lot of money on legal fees overturning the estate plan her husband had set up, to make sure Gus could never inherit as much as a piece of art, and she put everything in trust for Julia. Now that the land the house is on may be valuable, Gus is lusting after it. He's still in debt to bookies and so on, he's been bailed out, I don't know by whom, but if he could get the title to the house and make a deal with a big developer, he'd have enough money that he could gamble for a decade before he was broke again."

Reito was sweating with the effort of telling the story. His son, watching nearby, came over with a cup of water. He patted his father's cheeks, drying out his makeup.

"Artwork reminds me," I said. "When I went to see Gus and Lacey, they had two pieces in their front room that would be valuable if genuine. An oil that might be by Monet and a Nevelson piece. It was small, so maybe it was a study for a big sculpture."

Reito frowned, thinking. His thick eyebrows met above his nose. The one detail his son had neglected, tweezing his brows.

"I don't think they're Silvia's, at least, not a Monet. An Impressionist work would involve so much paperwork for an estate that I am sure I would remember if we'd had to value and insure it. I don't know how Gus could have acquired it, except perhaps by stealing it."

"I see," I said, digesting the information. "If Julia died before Silvia, what would happen?"

Reito gave a small smile. "I don't believe Gus knows that his mother named a successor heir, if Julia dies without a family of her own. That is the Refugee Rights and Resettlement Institute where she was a social worker."

"I knew Gus was in hot water financially, but I had no idea of the scope of the problem," I said.

A duck was nibbling hopefully at my shoes. You could write a junk sociology piece on how we're all nibbling on each other.

"You mentioned Klondike. Corky Ranaghan has been snuffling around the synagogue. I can see he'd bail out Gus for the rights to develop the land around the Zigler mansion, but why is he after the synagogue?"

"He's trying to pressure me into turning over Silvia's documents," Reito said. "Gus's methods with Julia were crude and haven't yet succeeded. I had a phone call from Ranaghan after I got home today, telling me he could make the inspection report disappear in exchange for Silvia's lockbox. I watched my father's business in Hungary disappear under theft from a fascist government. I know these tactics and I will not give in to them."

"Silvia gave Julia the lockbox key before the ambulance took her to the hospital in January," I said. "Gus and Lacey seem to have thought if they could torture Julia into signing over her inheritance, they could also get the key from her."

Reito frowned. "Maybe they would be able to persuade my firm to give them Silvia's lockbox if they had both the form and the key. I hope not, but Corky Ranaghan can be very persuasive."

He got to his feet, slowly, stiff from sitting so long. His son was there immediately to offer an arm.

"I have the key; Julia kept it safe, but she let me take it. Can I give it to you? I'm a moving target right now, and I don't want this falling into Corky's or Gus's hands."

I dug the key from my inside pocket and held it out to Reito. His son objected: I couldn't expose his father to further risk.

Reito smiled. "I won't be exposing myself, Gideon—

you will. You can take this down to the firm in the morning and tell Cleo to put it in the vault with Silvia's box."

Gideon grimaced but took the key from me.

"How did Corky get access to the building?" I asked as the pair walked away. "Raamah Calabro is the first name you see when you do a title search, and Ranaghan assured me the city had Raamah Calabro's permission to go into the synagogue. But Donna Ilona told me he was one of the founders, and that he's been dead for many years."

"Raamah Calabro produced a title for the inspector?" Reito stopped in his tracks. "What does the grandson call himself? Roger?"

"Robert," I said.

"I believe if you looked up Robert Calabro's birth certificate, you wouldn't find it. But if you looked for a man of the same age named Raamah, there it would be. It wasn't so uncommon, for Jews of that generation to give their children a Jewish name but call them by a Gentile name. They wanted to blend in, be accepted. It's different today, when everyone is flaunting their ethnic origins. Even my own granddaughter wants people to know she's Hungarian—as long as she doesn't have to learn to speak it."

He handed me the paper bag with the remains of the bread and stumped up the walk with his son. I went to the water's edge and tossed the bread in. Ducks and geese arrived, as if conjured out of the water, and seagulls began their dive-bombing. Apparently no one likes to share.

43
Run, Rabbit, Run

There's a large hospital half a mile north of the harbor. I went there to unwrap my smartphone and check my messages. Because they're close to the lake, picnickers and joggers crowd the grounds along with staff taking their breaks. A crowd wouldn't block my GPS signal but would make me harder to spot on foot.

I had a list of phone calls, starting with Sergeant Pizzello. Murray, Sonia, Peter. I wrote down their numbers, wrapped my phone back up, moved around the hospital to a side street so narrow that if a car stopped, it would back up traffic. I sat on a curb by a fire hydrant, the only open space on the street.

I called Pizzello first. "Am I still public enemy number one?" I asked.

"People are keeping an eye out for your car. If they

find you, they're to take you directly to Homan Square. If I put a trace on this call, I could score some big points and prove to my watch commander that I really am on the blue team."

"I know it's hard to split yourself between your team and your sense of justice," I said quietly. "I watched my dad walk that tightrope a lot of times. It's why I never wanted to join the force."

"What, you think your sense of justice is so great you'd be standing up to your watch commander like Joan of Arc, making people who compromise feel like heels?" Her tone was bitter.

"No. I'm no more immune than anyone else in my longing to be liked and be part of the team. I'd be tying myself in knots every night, wondering what my breaking point would be. I went through the same turmoil at the PD, giving in to pressure to accept plea deals when I thought the client was innocent, or at least had a viable case."

"And so you became an independent voice, crying in the criminal justice wilderness."

"I'm returning your call, Pizzello. Is that why you wanted to talk? So you could mock the way I work?"

She didn't apologize, but she did come straight to the point. "Coney has you in his sights, but he's responding to pressure from someone higher up, at least that's what Finchley thinks. If you can get whoever that is off your case, Coney will go back to Homan Square and leave you alone."

"This afternoon, he was providing transport for Tad Duda. Coney would have cuffed me then except that he had an urgent message from Corky Ranaghan to go somewhere else. Duda wants Julia Zigler; he broke into my apartment looking for her while Coney stood watch in the alley behind my building."

"Did they find her?"

"I won't lie, Sergeant: she was staying with me. But she ran when she saw Duda, and I don't know where she is right now." Okay. I would lie. It was good to have a cop in my corner—two, counting Finchley—but trust has limits.

"Right before she took off, she phoned me, in terror. Duda was the man who came into her hospital room with Jan Kadar. Probably he murdered Kadar."

Pizzello thought that over, then asked why Duda or Klondike cared about Goose Island.

"I have to believe that Klondike is interested in putting a big development right where the Zigler mansion stands. The only reason they want Julia is to coerce her into giving up her rights to her grandmother's house."

I gave her a thumbnail of what I'd learned from Istvan Reito.

"This is Chicago," Pizzello said. "I can't imagine they'd worry about a piddly detail like getting legal access to the title. Remember when everyone in town was debating how to renovate Soldier Field and in the middle of the night the mayor went in and knocked the top off it? There has to be some other reason they want the kid. They have the grandmother. If they have the kid, they can write whatever history they want about ownership. After they've torn down the mansion, or sold it for fancy condos, whatever it is they want to do."

I thought of Silvia, the Hungarian rebel, lying helpless at Archangel. They could kill her so easily. Why didn't they?

"Yes," I said. "If they can get Julia, they can threaten her life unless Silvia changes the terms of the trust. But now they're saying Silvia has dementia, so her son is applying for power of attorney. If she really has dementia she won't necessarily understand the threat to her granddaughter. I need to get her out of that nursing home before she dies, or before she deteriorates so much she can't find her way back to herself."

"Good luck with that," Pizzello said drily. "But if you think I can back you up if you break into a nursing home, wrong. My team does not condone B & E."

"Unless it's Lieutenant Coney overseeing the operation."

"Cheap shot. Anyway, I thought you said it was the Duda guy who did the breaking in—Coney was off-duty, helping out a member of the public. Later, Joan. Get on your horse, but watch out for burning stakes."

It was close to one A.M. in Malaga, Spain. I unwrapped my smartphone again—no apps on the burner, no way to call Peter on it. He was still up, just getting back to his apartment after another late-night meal with his jolly colleagues.

"Vic! I've tried calling and I've gotten increasingly worried. I tracked you online and saw the cops are after you. What happened?"

"They are after me, so I have to be brief—too easy to track my phone. I miss you, I can hardly imagine you now." His body, sunburned, the arms around me, the arms I loved to touch.

"I miss you, too. And I'm four thousand miles away, so please don't do something reckless. If something happened to you because you were reckless—" He broke off the sentence.

"All I have to do is keep a bent cop and a cement company from capturing a teenage girl. And not get in their gunsights in the process. Shouldn't be too hard."

I was trying for a light tone, but he said, "I can picture you. That's the problem. I've known you to jump out of windows, or camp in the park disguised as a homeless woman, or plunge into the Pigeon River when the ice is breaking up. Don't do any of those things, please, Victoria. At least not until I'm four inches away, not four thousand miles."

"Peter, I want to stay safe, for me as well as you, but the safety of too many people depends on my running risks. Please don't abandon me if I do—I couldn't bear it."

"I won't, Vic, but your recklessness makes me feel as though you want to abandon me," he said, and then the connection was gone. I blinked back tears. Recklessness included indulging in tears while my phone kept signaling my location. I wrapped it back in its Faraday cocoon and then unwrapped it again.

I was close to Lake Shore Drive. A footpath under the drive led to a boat harbor. Homeless people were camped out all along the footpath. It was another set of non-intersecting worlds: the homeless, some with tents, some with nests of blankets, and the joggers and cyclists zipping past them to the lakefront.

Sundown, boats were coming in from a day on the water while other people, getting off work, were getting ready to cast off. I walked along the wooden landing areas and found a big cabin cruiser with its motor running. A half dozen people were on the deck, drinking beer and chatting.

I took a moment to erase my phone. *Was I sure I wanted to do that?* Yes. When I climbed aboard, someone called out, wanting to know who I was.

"I'm Alison. Tim said to be here by six. Am I late?"

I had the wrong boat—no worries, kind of mistake that happens all the time. I knelt to tie my shoes and slipped my phone under the cushions on a bench that ran the width of the stern. I gave a cheery wave, apologized again for the disturbance, and climbed back down to the wooden landing spoke. I jumped across a gap to the next spoke and made a circuitous way back to Lake Shore Drive.

Returned to the underpass, past people trying to create shelter on concrete. The intersection of Belmont Avenue with the drive and Sheridan Road created a small park. I sat cross-legged under a low-hanging tree and called Murray from a burner I hadn't used yet.

I told him about my rescue of Brad and Julia, although not where I'd parked them. I also talked him through Reggie's description of his Skyrocket and what it could do.

"Before that, I had a strange call from Corky. He wants something that Donny or Brad have, and I don't know what that could be except for Reggie's drone. You know someone threatened to reveal Donny's complicity in an old crime unless Donny got them something they wanted. Do you know what crime they're talking about? Was it an old Mob hit?"

"Likely," Murray said. "The feds revealed identities of dozens of hits in the Outfit trial, but there are still some that haven't been solved. One of the Viper's old rivals was shot out in Melrose Park about the time Donny would have been sixteen, but the feds could never get their informants to squeal, and that one is still unsolved."

"It would be awfully risky for Duda to finger Donny for that," I said.

"He'd get immunity, claim he was just a passenger in the Litvak van," Murray said. "With Coney at his side he'd probably skate. I'm with you on that gizmo of Reggie Litvak's, though. You don't need it to do the stuff Klondike takes on."

"One thing is clear," he added. "Any project on Goose Island, or across the river from it, is going to get a lot of scrutiny. And that is why Corky or Suntasch or whoever it is needs the title so badly. If they just wanted to tear down the Zigler mansion and put up a condo, they could go in tonight with a wrecking ball. But if it's part of a big project, the title has to be theirs without any baggage weighing it down. And that's why they're so desperate for the girl. You really don't know where she is?"

"I really don't." She could be in bed with Peppy or out for a walk or in the living room watching TV with Brad. I had no idea.

I switched to another worry. "I know you and Mr. Contreras don't get along easily, but his story needs broadcasting. He's calling on Freeman Carter to help file an excessive force complaint, but putting today's assault out where the whole city can read about it may make Coney's higher-ups put the brakes on him."

"And you want my megaphone? That'll cost you extra."

"Murray, I've given you so many exclusives this week that you should put my byline on your next five stories."

I'd been trying to keep an eye on the traffic going to the harbor while we'd been speaking. I could only see foot traffic, or cars coming from the north, but I saw a flash of blue strobes on the far side of the underpass: cops were arriving at the harbor. I told Murray I needed to run.

44
Wild Tooth Chase

Two squad cars and an unmarked car had arrived, parking so as to block entry and exit from the harbor. I watched from the edge of the underpass, crouching behind the tent of a man who swore violently at me for encroaching on his space.

Coney got out of the unmarked car with Officer Tillman, the henchperson who'd driven me to Homan Square last week. The two went down the central pier toward the *Tooth Ferry,* which I hoped had sailed. Officers from one of the squads split up and started down two of the side branches of the pier. Someone from the other squad began inspecting driver's licenses of everyone lined up trying to leave. They would be busy for a while.

"Thanks for your hospitality," I said to the man with

the tent. I fished in my pocket for a five. "Let me buy you supper."

He took the money but kept up a stream of invective as I moved away from the action. I was so weary by now that my only coherent thought was desperation for a bed. I found the Nissan and drove down near my office. Tessa was packing up for the day. She told me that a cop had shown up midafternoon, asking for me, but hadn't bothered her when she assured him I was out. That was a relief. I was tired of people around me ending up as collateral damage and even tireder of being on the run.

I called Mr. Contreras, to make sure he and Mitch were safe. I called Lotty, to assure her that I was safe and that I'd spoken with Mrs. Pariente. I called Gregory, to check on Brad and Julia.

"Uh, yeah, they're all okay. I guess the dog is pretty well behaved. I'm picking up pizzas for supper."

When we'd hung up, I went into my back room, where I have a daybed, and lay down. Set a timer for forty-five minutes and slept. When the chimes finally woke me, I had that cloth-headed feeling you get from sleeping too heavily at an odd time. I took a shower, in cold water, and jogged a half mile up and down the long hall, forcing myself back to alertness.

Gus and Lacey were behaving badly, no argument.

They were desperate for control of Silvia's house, but Gus was in debt so deeply he couldn't hope to arrange a big development project. He'd have to turn the title over to Corky or one of Corky's surrogates and get whatever slice the big boys were willing to give him.

If Corky was pulling all the strings, he was the person offering Ashleigh a chance to lead a real estate company, which so far existed only in her head. He was offering Gus and Lacey a share of profits he hoped to make from the sale of the mansion. The piece I still couldn't make sense of was what he wanted from Brad or Donny. It had to be the Skyrocket, but the Skyrocket wasn't necessary for him. Maybe he just wanted to own it as something he could sell to someone like Google for a few billion dollars.

I wanted access to everyone's emails and text messages. Failing that, I'd have to rely on old-fashioned legwork. I drove north again, not to Archangel, but to Gus and Lacey's place in neighboring Glenview. Gus's truck wasn't in the drive, but the Kia Soul was there. My lucky evening—Lacey was home alone.

She came to the door and frowned in a way that would deepen her wrinkles before she hit fifty. "Why are you here? Have you found Julia?"

"I found her, Lacey, but she ran away again. I was

hoping she'd come back here? I know you and Gus are eager to resume caring for her."

Lacey bit her lip, trying to decide how to react. While she made up her mind, I moved past her into the house, following the sound of a television into the front room. She'd been watching a costume drama with Scottish accents and serious carnage.

I tried to get on her cultural wavelength. "*Game of Thrones?*"

"*Outlander,*" she replied shortly. "We don't have Julia, so you might as well leave."

"Doesn't it seem like an insult to you, to be offered a share in the profits from selling the Zigler mansion, when you could get the whole bundle if you sold it yourself?"

The room looked different from when I'd been in here before. The artwork was missing, that was it, replaced by an outsize flat screen. Maybe they'd moved it in here after getting rid of the artwork.

She muted the TV. "What business is this of yours?"

"Julia Zigler's well-being. You want her to give you the title—which she can't do because it isn't hers to give—but even without it, someone is talking about making the mansion the centerpiece of a new development across from Goose Island."

"That's private information. How did you—did that little brat—"

"Lacey, there's no such thing as private information anymore, not when your doorbell sends the name and face of your callers straight to Amazon or Apple or whoever. I know you and Gus are in debt, and I know he thinks his mother treated him badly, so that he has a right to the house—"

"Of course he does!" she cut in. "And Silvia treated him like dirt. She adored all those smelly refugees and immigrants. He never knew who'd be in the house when he came home from school at night. The Zigler family has a proud history, and she actually let that Brazilian Marxist live in the house with her and Emma when Emma was pregnant. And he was Black, but she thought he was more important than her own son! Gus reported him to the authorities and Silvia acted like he'd robbed a bank. She changed the locks on the house and made sure he knew he didn't get the house! And now! We're stuck with paying her hospital bills and she won't even consider taking out a mortgage on that barn of a place."

"She got tired of Gus stealing from her to pay off his gambling debts is what I heard."

"You heard wrong. Everything was Emma, Emma,

Emma, and when Emma died it became Julia, Julia! Silvia escaped from a Communist country. You'd think she'd back her own son up when he turned in a Communist who got his sister pregnant, but no, she sided with the Marxist. If you ask me, Silvia was never a refugee. She was a spy who made up a story about fighting Russian tanks when all along she was spying on the United States and selling our secrets to Russia."

"The secrets she heard as a social worker in a small agency would, of course, be of inestimable value to Putin and his pals. Knock it off, Lacey."

"It's easy for you to preach. You never had to deal with the money problems we're facing. And Silvia's medical bills on top of it all! That's why we need—" She cut herself off.

"Need what? To steal Silvia's artwork and sell it for this ludicrous TV?"

"Silvia's artwork?"

"Lacey, I saw the Monet when I was here before. And that piece in the corner. If Gus is in over his head with debts, you sure didn't get those at Sotheby's."

"They're not Silvia's! Although we'd be entitled if they were. They belonged to someone Gus was helping out, and they gave them to him instead of a fee."

"Must have been quite a job he did for them."

I left the room abruptly and started looking through the house. Lacey grabbed my arm, telling me I had no business, no right.

"Of course I don't," I said. "But if Gus has taken up fencing stolen property to make ends meet, I want to see what else he's parked here."

In a back room, maybe Julia's room when she'd been staying here, I found five other pieces of art. I didn't recognize them the way I had the ones in the front room, but they were clearly not objects found at a garage sale. I snapped pictures with my phone, with Lacey dancing around me, trying to punch me and to grab my phone.

"If you must know, we're storing them for Archangel," she finally said. "They belong to some of their rich patients who are worried about their safety. Archangel said if we'd store them in our own house, they'd take something off of Silvia's bill. After all, no one would think of breaking into a crummy house like ours looking for valuable art."

"Have you lost your mind?" Gus stormed into the room. Neither of us had heard him come in.

"This is Warshawski. She is the fucking enemy. Don't go blabbing crap to her. She's hiding Julia, she's hiding from the police, she knows where the photos are. She is fucking poison."

He turned to me. "You're not going to poison me, Warshawski. Scott Coney will be here before you know it."

He put me in a headlock. I dropped my chin as low as I could, turned under his armpit, stomped hard on his right foot and ran to the door while he howled that I'd broken his toes.

45
The Romance of Heathcliff

I was more confused when I left Gus and Lacey than I had been before. Gus was helping himself to high-end artwork and someone was helping him sell it, but what that had to do with his mother's mansion or Reggie's Skyrocket was beyond me.

Maybe he thought the device would help him identify what houses to burgle. That was certainly possible. The data sets Reggie alluded to could include insurance data on high-value private collections. If Gus could access those, he'd know which houses to target. But it still didn't make sense. He'd obviously been helping himself to artwork for some time, before the Skyrocket came on the scene. Maybe he'd heard about the invention and thought it would make his thieving easier.

If Gus knew about the Skyrocket, who told him?

Say that Donny was so proud of his brother that he bragged about Reggie's invention. Maybe Donny tried to leverage some pay out of Klondike by offering Corky Ranaghan access to the Skyrocket. Word would have drifted around, to Duda, maybe, and then to Gus.

That scenario bumped me up against the Litvak family loyalty. But there was another player in the game: Ashleigh, with her expensive tastes. Had Donny gone into debt to try to keep her attached to him? The Lincoln SUV, the wardrobe, the diamond pendants in her ears. I'd thought those were gifts from a lover, but what if they all came from Donny?

Regardless of who showered her with baubles, she was having an affair with Tad Duda. Say after the demo, even though Ashleigh and Melanie were in a corner sneering at their spouses, Ashleigh got enough of the gist of the Skyrocket to tell Tad. During pillow talk, she lets fall word of the rocket, maybe just to keep Tad's attention. Corky holds Tad's markers; Tad tells Corky he can get the drone if Corky wipes out his debt. It could have happened like that.

I drove across town to the Breslau–Litvak house but passed it without slowing. I parked a good distance away, to preserve the anonymity of my borrowed wheels, and walked back. I didn't have any way of knowing how much time Coney had spent at Belmont

Harbor, trying to trace my smartphone, but I'd have to assume that he was back on land now, prowling the streets.

It was close to ten, and the streetlamps didn't show much outside their individual pools of light. I tripped a few times on uneven joins in the sidewalk and slowed my pace. I passed the occasional dog walker, but in this residential quarter of the city, there were few people on the streets at this hour.

I was four doors from Ashleigh's house when an outsize pickup passed me and pulled up in her drive, dwarfing her Navigator. I moved out of the lamplight onto the lawn of a neighboring house. I couldn't see the driver's side of the pickup, but when the driver came out, he didn't check the street, just walked up to the front door. I couldn't see that, either, so I cut across the neighbor's yard, staying well away from the door. In the light from Ashleigh's hallway, I made out Tad Duda, all in black.

"Tad. Hello. Did you find Branwell?" She spoke with her usual coolness. She must have spent years practicing that nonchalance, but at least her first question was about her son.

"Coney took me to Warshawski's place, but your boy and Gus's girl were gone. They're not at her office, or with the doctor. We thought they could have gone to ground with your sister-in-law, but there's no trace of them at Sonia's home or the auto shop where she works. A couple of teens out on the street can't stay hidden for long. At least, not if they don't have street sense, and your boy is definitely one of the most clueless kids I've ever been around. Hard to believe he's Donny Litvak's son."

Ashleigh didn't try to defend her son. Fortunately, she also didn't mention that he might be with Gregory, the most useless of the Litvaks. Tad apparently had forgotten about the baby glued to Sonia's hip. Or, more likely, Gregory had never registered in his consciousness.

"Speaking of not being much like your husband, where the fuck is Donny? He's been avoiding me for days, and I need those rocket pics."

"I don't know, Tad. I haven't seen him since that insane confrontation at Warshawski's place two days ago. And I don't know where the data stick is. Why do you care so much?" She backed away from the door; he followed her into the house.

I watched their progress through the house by the lights that were turned on. They ended up in the back, in the room I guessed to be Ashleigh's office.

I wanted to be James Bond, with an arsenal of props from Q that would let me listen in on the conversation. I wanted to be lucky and have them open a window. Or

I wanted to be foolhardy and try to sneak quietly into the kitchen. Option three, as always.

The back door opened onto the kitchen. I'd left my picks in the Nissan, but the catch was simple. A credit card between the tongue and the groove did the job.

The kitchen was unlit, but the glow from lights in the hallway beyond let me see my way clearly enough to keep from tripping over a stool near the door. I could hear Tad and Ashleigh, but not quite well enough to make out the words. I slid past an eating nook and crept closer. They were in a room across a narrow hallway from the kitchen. The door opened toward me, shielding me from view.

A board creaked when I stepped into the hall, but Tad was speaking, and at a volume that masked the sound. Maybe working around heavy equipment had made him deaf. Or maybe his need to exude power made him bellow.

"Don't lecture me about what we did or didn't do with Warshawski. Without the Skyrocket, I have to scramble for cash, which meant I had to get to Palatine to seal a deal there for Ranaghan. And then the bitch led Coney on a wild chase out onto the lake—she dropped her phone on a boat that he went after. By the time he got back, she was long gone. We went to the old guy, we went to that doctor she hangs out with, even went to those old kikes she's been visiting, but no luck."

My skin turned cold and clammy. Lotty—Mr. Contreras—the Parientes—if they'd been threatened or harmed—I wanted to leap into Ashleigh's room and throttle Tad. I wanted to race out to check on all the people I cared about. I stood still and kept listening.

"Tad, darling, you know I'm a kike, too," Ashleigh said, her voice still cool, unemotional.

He gave a bark of what was supposed to be laughter. "You're a JAP, through and through, Ashleigh. It's what I like about you. Whatever made you think Donny Litvak was the person who could look after you?"

"Probably the same stupid impulse that made me think you could help me. All you South Chicago slum dwellers, you're all boors at heart, despite whatever veneer you paste on yourselves. Sonia may seem cruder than V.I. Warshawski, but Warshawski's just as coarse underneath. And now she has my son."

Duda laughed again. "Coney's ready to kill her, so my guess is, she'll be caught resisting arrest pretty soon. That will get her out of your life, but you're stuck with me, princess."

"I don't care whether Warshawski lives or dies," Ashleigh said. "But I want my son back. I thought you needed the girl Warshawski's been protecting. I hope you can restrain Coney until I know Branwell is safe."

Ah, motherly love. The heart beats warm beneath the ice.

"No one's going to hurt your boy as long as he tells us what he did with the pics. You get that sorted out, you'll get your real estate operation. If you can't do that, you can sit back and watch Lacey Zigler run it."

"Lacey?" Ashleigh said. "Give it to Lacey and watch her run it into the ground. She had one clever idea, but she doesn't know how to work a sale."

"There are plenty of girls with cute tits who can be taught how to work a sale. You were born slick, but it's teachable, Ash, it's teachable."

I just had time to slip back into the kitchen before he strode down the short hall to the front door. When the door had shut behind him, Ashleigh gave a loud, long scream, like a steam engine with too much pressure in the boiler.

Under cover of the noise I made it out of the kitchen into the backyard. I huddled in the shadows at the corner of the house, watching the Ford's headlights come on. Duda backed into the road, gunned the engine, roared up the street loudly enough to rouse the neighborhood dogs. Lights came on in a number of the houses, curtains twitched: Had the ugly crimes of the central city come to disturb the bucolic peace of the northwest side? No one felt bold enough to come outside to check.

I waited five minutes, in case Duda circled back, before ringing Ashleigh's front doorbell. She took her time, but before I rang again, she opened the door, and then tried to shut it.

"You!" Her voice was full of loathing.

"Me!" I agreed enthusiastically, my shoulder between the door and the jamb. "Coney hasn't shot me yet."

She pulled her phone from her sweat pants pocket, but I took it and brushed past her into the small foyer.

"You're correct: I'm just as savage as Sonia under my thin civilized veneer. But before you call Tad Duda or Scott Coney, do remember that you still don't have your son."

She turned pale as my words registered. "You were eavesdropping. How—?"

"The walls are thin and you and Heathcliff aren't subtle. At least, he isn't. What attracted you to someone who calls you a Jewish Princess and thinks your family are kikes?"

"I see why Sonia calls you Saint Victoria of the Mills," Ashleigh said. "You really do believe you sit on top of a mountain high above the rest of us. Why I do what I do is none of your business."

Her comment was spiteful, but at least she sounded angry for a change, instead of like a world-weary diva.

"It's my business if you're conspiring with Tad Duda to have me killed," I said. "Or if you watch like a spectator while he roughs up the people I care about."

"Let's talk about you and your son and Donny and the Skyrocket. You took it, right? Step me through the timeline. At the demo, you and Melanie hung out on the sidelines, making crude comments about the Litvaks. Then something happened that got Donny so furious that he left without you and Brad. What was it?"

Ashleigh shrugged. "Donny is perpetually angry about things that are too boring to contemplate. He saw something when Reggie was showing off his toy that made him shoot off like a rocket himself. Leaving me with Melanie and Reggie and *Branwell.*"

"Your buddy Tad needs to recover some photos, and Gus Zigler wants them, too. What do they show?"

"I don't know why you think I'd tell you anything, when all you do is look down your nose at me. Suffice it to say that the rocket suddenly seems amazing to a lot of people. Including people with a lot of power and money."

"Like Corky Ranaghan, the slab of bacon."

She gave her theatric tinkle of a laugh. "He may

look like an entire meat case, but his brain never stops working. Tad made him see the rocket's potential. If he can get it, he can use it to help pinpoint real estate prospects. He's offering to put me in charge of a brand-new project that would help elderly people sell their homes so they could move into assisted living. But of course we need the rocket, and we can't use it if someone's going to blackmail Tad with a bunch of stupid photos. It's ironic in its way. Tad tried to pressure Donny into stealing the rocket for him."

"Yes, over an old Mob hit where Donny and Tad were at the scene when they were in high school."

"Is that it?" She sounded as indifferent to Mob hits as she did to her husband's anger. "Donny said something about it, about being threatened, I mean, but he said he wouldn't betray Reggie. Those brothers and Sonia—they all mean more to each other than anyone else in the world. Look at Sonia. She couldn't stay married because her husband wouldn't devote himself to Donny and the twins!"

"Donny wouldn't betray Reggie," I repeated, trying to get the narrative back on track. "Then what happened?"

"Donny said, what difference did it make if Tad exposed him? He couldn't be any more unemployed and in debt than he already was. He said no to Tad, so Tad came to me."

She cut herself off, her cheeks flaming.

"You met Tad because you staged some of the houses where Tad was pouring cement," I supplied.

"If you must know, I met him at a Klondike company outing, before the pandemic. Corky invited a lot of his contractors, and Tad was there. I thought that meant he was one of the money men. He has that kind of jungle essence that powerful men exude. It started out innocently enough. And of course I didn't know that Tad was in debt as bad or worse than Donny's."

Adultery always starts out innocently enough, I thought of saying, but I wanted her to keep talking. No Saint Victoria remarks.

"But Corky Ranaghan found out about the Skyrocket," she said. "They couldn't keep it a secret from him, which they should have realized, because Corky always knows about everything that's going on. At first he was angry with Tad and Gus for getting themselves exposed, but when he realized what the rocket could do, he said they were off the hook as long as they could get the pictures back. And bring him the drone and the special device that Reggie designed."

"What do these pictures show?" I asked.

"I don't know. They gave Corky the key on how to make money from old people's houses, but Tad and Gus are in a compromising position in one of the photos."

"Having sex?" I was incredulous. I didn't think sex scandals stopped anyone from anything these days.

"Tad won't tell me, but if it was sex I expect he would. He knows I'd find it thrilling to see him and Gus go at it, if that's what they were doing. Anyway, I know nothing about photos or who has them or what happened to the rocket. All I know is that I'm not giving up my chance to run a major real estate unit, just because someone along the way lost some stupid pix."

"So you stole the rocket?" I asked. "How? Did you offer a cushy deal to Reggie's sons?"

"They're too young. And too arrogant. You couldn't make a deal with them. No, I went to Reggie's house at a time when I knew he had to go into Metargon to work on something in their big machine shop.

"It was so easy—Melanie was on Zoom counseling schoolchildren, the twins were out doing whatever instead of going to class. Reggie leaves a key to the shop in a cupboard over the kitchen sink. He even has the key to his safe in there. I was in and out in five minutes. Not even you could have done it more smoothly."

"Likely not," I agreed. The advantage of a family like the Litvaks—everyone was in each other's business all the time, so you'd know when the key players would be occupied.

"And then everything disappeared. If your son didn't take them, Donny must have them, right?"

She leaned over her knees, head in hands. "I guess so. How could I ask him, though, when—when—"

"Right," I helped her. "When you'd stolen it in the first place. And you were sleeping with Tad. What did you think when Tad picked up your own son and strip-searched him in an alley? What excuses did you make for him?"

"I asked Tad—I wondered—but he assured me that it was connected with that girl you pulled out of the lake. Gus Zigler's niece."

"And it was convenient for you to believe him. Okay. Tonight, Tad said you were tied to him. He bought you the Navigator?"

"God, no. Tad's mind doesn't run to sweetheart gifts. That was Donny. He thought an extravagant present would make me decide to cling to him. When I'm not furious with him, I feel sorry for him. He's as big a loser as his brother Gregory, when you get right down to it."

"Losers?" I said. "You're the one who committed a serious theft. Does that make you a winner?"

"Oh, please, Vic. Sonia's right when she says you

like to lord it over the rest of us. Everyone's out for themselves. I just want a bigger piece of the pie."

"What was Lacey's one clever idea?"

"She had a plan for identifying prospects. Corky saw it could be so much bigger than she thought it was, and now she's huffy because Corky knows I can run real estate and she's just a glorified file clerk."

"But Tad thinks—"

"Tad thinks he's the king of the universe. He's a great fuck, but he doesn't understand that Corky is king. Tad's body, Corky's brain, that would be a good combination. Goodbye, Vic. This had better be the last time you come to my house, unless you bring me my son. I want him back."

"If I see Brad, I'll let him know he's breaking his poor ol' mother's heart."

"His name is Branwell," she snapped.

"And Tad's name is Heathcliff. I know—I read it in a book. Not *The Count of Monte Cristo*. Somewhere else."

46

Thicker Than Water

I hugged the shadows on my way back to the Nissan. Ashleigh was such an unguided missile, I wouldn't put it past her to call Duda or Coney as soon as I'd left. Duda's casual comment that I could be shot for resisting arrest was something that could easily happen in this town.

Coney had already shrugged off forty-odd complaints for excessive force. The Chicago police unions had iron-clad defenses against any challenge to their acts, no matter how heinous. It had taken nineteen years of complaints to shut down a police torture ring, nineteen years of state's attorneys and mayors turning a blind eye on the well-documented proof of what was happening in my old neighborhood.

The end of the ring had not resulted in any sanctions

against the cops involved—they'd all retired with full pensions. It also hadn't ended the maltreatment of suspects in custody, just shifted the location. I could see my body being taken from Homan Square and dumped in the Chicago River, turning into a float fish for some poor angler to hook.

I'd better check on Lotty, the Parientes, and Mr. Contreras while I was still mobile. I was tempted to call Sergeant Pizzello for help, but if Coney was watching either my building or the Parientes, he'd learn that Pizzello had visited them. That could jeopardize Pizzello's position on the force as well as make her unwilling to give me any other help in the future.

I phoned Lotty, who said that the police had come around to question her about me, but no one had tried to be violent with her.

"That's a relief," I said. "But they also went to the Parientes' and to Mr. Contreras. I tried phoning both of them, but the calls went to voicemail. I'm worried that if I go to check on them, Coney or Duda may have the buildings staked out."

Lotty thought it over. "It's eleven o'clock and it's likely everyone is asleep. Let's assume that, because for people who are old, and as frail as the Parientes, a midnight wake-up would be very frightening. I'll send Jewel to check on them in the morning. She's often there, dropping off meds or taking blood pressure. I don't know what to suggest about your neighbor."

In a building as small as mine, of course I knew the names of everyone who lived there, but I didn't think any of them would be willing to try to get into Mr. Contreras's place to check on him—especially not with Mitch guarding the premises. In the end, I phoned Murray.

"Warshawski! Where the heck are you? I tried calling you, and the phone was answered by some guy with a voice like gravel who was trying to locate you."

"That would be Lieutenant Scott Coney, or maybe his sidekick, Officer Tillman, whom you photographed trashing my belongings a few days ago."

I told him how I'd sent Coney out to sea, which made him laugh.

"It is funny, except he has my phone. Listen: I just left Ashleigh Breslau. She's deep in bed with Tad Duda." I gave him the highlights of what I'd learned.

"Incriminating photos?" Murray said. "That's very tantalizing. Not sex, not rock-and-roll, so it must be drugs."

"They're running drugs out of empty houses and Donny saw them in the photos—no! What an idiot I am. They're stealing art objects. I saw some of them at Gus's house. They know what high-end houses are standing empty, and they break in and steal. How they fence it is another category of questions, but that's what Donny must have seen on Reggie's tablet during the rocket. Reggie was worried about the private data that his invention was vacuuming, but the image resolution was also at a high level. Donny was furious that Duda or Gus could be trying to blackmail him when they were committing burglary."

Murray was enthusiastic about my theory. "All we need are these pictures. If they're on a data stick, that's why Duda or whoever strip-searched Brad."

We agreed that it was crucial to find Donny and learn what he'd done with Reggie's device and the peripherals.

"The other piece of the jigsaw is this real estate division Corky's setting up for Ashleigh to run. Lacey Zigler is involved somehow. She had one clever idea, Ashleigh said. It has to be connected to the art theft because that's where everyone made the connections— Corky to the Skyrocket, Ashleigh to house sales, Tad Duda to getting out of debt."

"You going undercover as a home buyer, Warshawski? You get yourself a big house like the Zigler mansion, move in with your ornery neighbor and the dogs, and you'll never have to worry about your condo board again."

"I will be a more zealous investigator if I can figure out a way to get rid of the bull's-eye that Coney's painting on my head. Until I do, I can't go home to check on Mr. Contreras. Duda has a special device for getting past a lot of locks. Mr. Contreras will have bolted his doors from the inside, so you should be able to see from outside whether someone broke down his doors. He's not answering his phone, but he sleeps deeply."

Murray groaned but promised to check on my neighbor. "And I can call you back on what number?"

"If he's fine, call this number." I read off the number of another burner. "Let it ring twice and hang up. I'll answer the next call. If you have an idea for getting Coney off my back, hire a plane to skywrite the message."

I was both exhausted and agitated, bad combo. I needed a good night's sleep but couldn't go home or back to the cot in my office. I had a key to Peter's place. He'd been away for close to a year. I had to gamble that Coney and Duda hadn't dug deeply enough into my life to know about him.

I still was cautious about the car. I parked six blocks from Peter's building and waited in the Nissan, half dozing, until I got the report from Murray. My neighbor's doors were intact, so no one had broken in on him.

I let myself into Peter's apartment. I needed sleep more than I needed anything, but if Coney had picked up my phone and was answering it or, worse, listening to voicemail messages, I had to stop the service. I took one of the burners and spent half an hour navigating through endless menu options (*Press 1 if you are being driven insane by our poor customer service; Press 2 if you've given up hope*). I finally managed to report the phone as stolen and get it disabled.

I showered, and fell instantly into a deep and blissful sleep. When I finally woke, still in the muzziness of sleep, I stretched an arm out for Peter. The empty bed brought me fully awake.

It was past ten. If Lotty or Murray or Gregory wanted to reach me, they couldn't. A panicky adrenaline seized me. I imagined terrible injuries to all the people I hadn't been able to help and began a frantic set of calls. I started my check-in with Gregory.

He spoke with his usual hesitation. No one had bothered him last night. He was at work. Liquor suppliers may not be essential businesses, but there's no way you can work remotely at one of their warehouses. Gregory said he hoped the kids would be okay on their own. Peppy hadn't hurt his vinyl collection overnight.

"Brad seems like a good person. The girl is pretty nervous."

"Yes, she has a lot to be nervous about," I agreed.

I called Brad and Julia, who were feeling lonely and isolated and wanted to return to Mr. Contreras, even if meant risking being picked up by Lieutenant Coney.

"Uncle Gregory's okay," Brad said. "I mean, he's not used to having people in his house, and so it's a little strange, but he's at work and the place is so quiet, it feels like we're in a—an isolation tank. We can't get in touch with anyone, we don't know if anyone's after us. At least when we were with Uncle Sal we felt like we were in a family or something."

"He's right," Julia called out, her voice tinny since she was farther from the mike. "And Peppy isn't happy. She wants to be in the garden with Mitch. We have to walk like five blocks to the park, and then I'm scared someone will recognize me. If we can't go back to Uncle Sal, let me go to my house. Brad can stay there, too. You know we have tons of room."

"Darling—" I started marshaling arguments: her granny's house had no heat, no electricity, her uncle Gus would be prowling around. I shut myself up. Most people aren't persuaded by arguments, and teens are even less persuaded than most people.

"Julia, sweetheart, give me twenty-four hours. If you can hold out until noon tomorrow, I will either make it safe to bring you home, or find a way for you to live with Uncle Sal until it is safe to go to your own house."

There was a pause, and then she gave a reluctant assent.

"What about me?" Brad asked.

"I want to sit down with you in person and talk through what you'd like to do, and what you can do. If you want to go back to your mother, you can do it right now. Julia won't be safe at your house, so you'd go without her. Again, if you can give me one day—I know it's not easy, being unconnected from your devices and unconnected from your friends." Surely even these two lonely kids had friends they wanted to text or chat with.

"It's okay," Brad said gruffly. "I'll stay here with Julia. Do you think my dad's in trouble?"

I took a moment to answer, decided he needed me to be honest. "I learned last night that he decided to stand up to the man who threatened him in that phone conversation that brought you to my office in the first place. Donny is either hiding or he's in trouble."

"You mean you think he's dead!"

"It means I hope he comes either to your aunt Sonny or me before the day is over."

Jewel Kim, Lotty's advanced practice nurse, was my

next call. She'd visited the Parientes on her way to the clinic this morning. They were unharmed but badly rattled by a late-evening visit from the police.

"The police were looking for you, Vic," Jewel said. "Of course, Mrs. Pariente had no idea where you were, but she says she told them you'd asked about Robert Calabro, and she feels ashamed for having said that."

"I'd like to reassure her, but the Parientes are better off if I stay far away for a few days. Lotty is safe, right? Mr. Contreras is, or at least he was safe at midnight last night." Probably safe.

"What about those two kids who came to you?"

"Even if I knew where they were, it would be better for you not to know."

I keep a toothbrush in Peter's bathroom. I found jeans and a long-sleeved tee I'd left behind. Clean clothes, clean teeth, I could tackle anything. I hoped.

If I was going to get Scott Coney off my back, it would help to know as much about him as possible, who his protectors were inside the CPD and out, and any foibles that might give me leverage. I looked longingly at Peter's computer. It would be pleasant to sit at his desk, use his machine, but as soon as I logged on to my subscription databases, I'd be traceable. It was maddening not to know how much surveillance I was under, but I couldn't take a chance on being tracked to Peter's. As I'd been lecturing the kids, having a safe-house means you have to keep it safe.

Peter sunburned easily, a handicap for an archaeologist, but he had a collection of straw hats he wore on digs. I took one, stuffed some tissues into the lining to keep it from falling over my eyes, and made my way to one of the library's big regional branches.

Before I did anything else, I finished the client report I'd been working on when Brad had come into my office two weeks ago. Their job candidate had an active presence in QAnon chat rooms and was said to have been one of those inside the Michigan State Capitol when armed seditionists overran it a year ago last fall. It was up to the client, of course, as to whether that made for a qualified or a dangerous employee. When I sent my report, I attached an invoice and a message that I couldn't do more work if they chose to hire the guy.

I turned from my client to researching Scott Coney's life. He was an exemplar of the Irish South Side, with three generations of family from Bridgeport. Coney himself was living now in the Mount Greenwood neighborhood, a white enclave on the southwest edge of town where police and firefighters clustered. Coney was married, he had two children—the daughter who had posted the video of him on TikTok, and a son who was still in primary school.

His father and grandfather had both been Chicago cops. His mother, Marguerite Ranaghan, had grown up in McKinley Park— Marguerite Ranaghan. I stared at the name, then started a feverish hunt through genealogy websites and old Chicago phone books. Marguerite's oldest brother had five daughters before finally producing the son he craved, Brendan "Corky" Ranaghan Jr.

Corky and Scott Coney were first cousins. No wonder Coney was driving around Chicago threatening private eyes and doing cavity searches on teenage boys. Family sticks to family on the South Side—the loyal Litvaks, the steadfast Ranaghans. Boom-Boom and V.I. Warshawski.

Coney wasn't a stakeholder in the Zigler escapade. He was Corky's muscle. It wouldn't matter if the entire CPD and the Cook County state's attorney lined up to condemn him. He was attacking me for his family.

"Well, back at you, Ranaghans," I said. "My family includes Brad and Julia, the Parientes, and Silvia Zigler. And we will not let you run over us."

A librarian appeared next to me. Could I keep my voice down? Also, there was a limit of one hour on the computers, and I'd been online for almost eighty minutes. Time to log off and leave.

One of my burner phones buzzed as I was walking back to the Nissan. Mr. Contreras.

He cut short my worried questions. "That lady cop was here, the one you sort of get along with."

"Sergeant Pizzello?" I was astonished. "What did she want?"

"She needs to see you, doll. She tried to call you, but your phone was out of order, and you wasn't in your office, so she came here."

Pizzello had left a number. Mr. Contreras read it slowly, twice, to make sure I'd gotten it right.

"Them kids okay? I miss them, and it ain't the same here with just Mitch."

"They miss you, too," I said. "They would be so much less isolated with you than where they are now. I hope things will loosen up soon. In the next day, if I'm lucky."

I hoped the kids could curb their impatience for another twenty-four hours. I wasn't betting the bank on it, which meant I needed to act quickly.

I tossed the phone I'd been using and called Pizzello from a clean one.

"Warshawski! You're still alive."

"Made it to lunchtime in one piece," I agreed. "I hear you've started making house calls."

"At the lieutenant's request. If you had a phone and voicemail like most of the country, I'd be able to do the work the city pays me for."

"I wanted to get out from under Coney's surveillance for a few hours."

She laughed when I told her about putting the phone on board the *Tooth Ferry*. "That explains why Coney was in an even sunnier mood than usual. He was at Area Two this morning, trying to rip a stripe from Lieutenant Finchley, but no one knew why."

"In retrospect, ditching the phone was maybe not my smartest decision. Now I have to get a new one and so on."

"Yeah, in retrospect it would be good if you'd make it easy for people to reach you. Or for the lieutenant to reach you. We found Donny Litvak last night."

My heart seemed to stop beating; my hands turned cold. "Where?" I could barely get the word out.

"He's not dead," she said. "Don't know why, but he isn't."

He'd been found inside the front gate of the Zigler mansion, badly beaten. "Since the news coverage of you and the girl being in that house, it's become a tourist attraction. A jogger found him and called 911."

Donny had been taken to the nearest emergency room, but he hadn't had any identification on him. It wasn't until this morning that he'd recovered sufficiently to answer questions. He wouldn't give his name, but he'd said I was his next of kin. When the hospital couldn't reach me, they'd involved the CPD.

"He has broken ribs and a broken leg, which they set. The squad assigned to the hospital put a message out on the CPD frequency, saying an unknown white male was trying to contact V.I. Warshawski. Your name stirred a lot of people into action. Finchley and Coney arrived at Litvak's room at the same moment. They damned near came to blows. I was the Finch's driver; I can tell you it was an ugly scene.

"Coney said he knew Litvak and knew you weren't related to him. The Finch said that proved Coney didn't know him; he'd vouch for the fact that you were his next of kin."

"How did the Finch recognize Donny? I didn't know their paths had ever crossed."

"He didn't know who it was," Pizzello said. "But he knew Coney was gunning for you. While they were arguing, I got one of the wheelchair attendants to wheel

Donny out to my squad car. He's at Area Two, waiting for you."

"How'd you get his name?"

"He coughed it up when he saw we were protecting him from Coney, but he won't let me notify his wife or his family. How soon can you get here?"

"Now, I guess. If I'm not there in twenty minutes, it's because Coney's shot me."

"He'd like to, Warshawski. You might start wearing Kevlar around town. Come in the back entrance."

47
Holding Cell

Donny was in a holding cell, because it was empty and he could lie on the metal bench. His right leg was in a cast, and both hands were heavily bandaged. His face was swollen and purple, the right eye almost completely shut.

"Hey, Donny. Who'd you piss off that badly?"

He struggled to sit up. "Hey, Warshawski." His lips were puffy and the words came out slurred. "Don't tell Sonny or the boy."

I sat down next to him. "You know Sonia would take care of you better than I can."

"Don't want her in danger. Everyone knows . . . she's my go-to person. They search her place . . . don't find me . . . don't find my number on her phone, they leave her alone."

I hoped he was right.

"Was this Duda? Coney?"

"How you know?"

"Duda and Gus. They are desperately hunting incriminating photos of themselves. My guess is that Reggie's gizmo showed them breaking into someone's house."

"You always were . . . smartest girl at Mirabal High. Couldn't believe . . . when I saw them . . . in action. First, you know, I was . . . fascinated by how clear . . . the images were. Then realized . . . I was looking at Duda. And the other guy, didn't know him. Tracked down Duda, told him off."

"I don't get it," I said. "He threatened to blackmail you into getting Reggie's invention for him before you saw the demo. How did he know about the device?"

"My big mouth," Donny said bitterly. "Even before . . . the demo . . . Reggie talked about it. I thought . . . something Corky could use . . . identify where to build, where to buy, thought he could be . . . Reggie's godfather, invest in production."

Corky turned down Donny's suggestion, for the reasons Murray and I had already been saying. Klondike already has private intel on all the development possibilities in the area, not just Chicagoland, but the adjacent three states. A big data gatherer would be an expensive way of telling him what he already knew.

Donny was panting from the exertion of speaking through his puffy lips. I saw he was missing a front tooth.

"Someone decided it was valuable," I said, "because it's disappeared. And I think Corky is behind it. Otherwise, why would Coney be involved?"

"Yeah," Donny agreed. "Don't know who said what to who anymore. Duda, Corky, Gus, whoever, all pointing fingers. Say I must have Reggie's rocket. Drone, really. He calls it rocket."

His casted leg was stretched out in front of him. He gripped the edges of the steel bench with his bandaged hands, trying to get comfortable. I lifted his legs and helped shift him to a lying position.

"I need a place to crash, Warshawski. Can't go to Sonny. Can't live in Ash's and my house. Bitch would carve me in my sleep. Can't go back to that hole I'm renting—Duda could come around, finish me off. You have extra bed? Need to get strong enough to take on fucking SOB, but leg—six weeks in cast, doc said."

"Coney is keeping an eye on my place," I said. "Duda has already been in my apartment a couple of times. I'm couch-surfing myself to keep ahead of him and Coney." I was running out of ideas on where to park members of the Litvak family.

Pizzello came into the holding cell, with Finchley behind her.

"I don't know why he thought you'd be a soft shoulder to cry on, Warshawski," Finchley said, "but he belongs in a hospital bed. Or at least his own home—I see he's got a wife and kid a couple of miles from here. On the other hand, just as well his family doesn't see him looking like this. They'd run the other way like rabbits."

"Besides which, his wife is, uh, dating the guy who pounded him," I said.

"If this were an ordinary mugging, I'd be thinking ordinary thoughts," Finchley said. "But you're on the scene, Warshawski, which means they weren't fighting over Litvak's old lady."

"Only indirectly," I said. "South Chicago used to be the bailiwick of a guy named Val Tommaso. When they were kids, Duda and Donny ran some questionable errands for Tommaso. Those have come bubbling back to the surface to haunt us all."

"The Viper," Finchley said. "Thought he'd retired to Florida."

"Yes," I agreed. "Tad Duda took over his cement works, but he has a gambling habit that has him in debt way above his eyeballs."

I told him about Reggie and the Skyrocket, and the difficulty in finding a safe place for Donny. Donny struggled upright, trying to stop me talking about the Skyrocket. When he couldn't, he groaned and lay back down.

"He can't camp out at Area Two," Finchley said. "We need the cell for ordinary muggers and buggers. Might be good if Coney and Duda thought Litvak died in the OR."

"It might be good for getting Coney off Donny's neck for a few days, but it would freak out his kid."

"Where is Brad?" Donny demanded.

"He's safe. I hope."

"Goddamn it, Warshawski, that's my boy. You've been keeping him from me!" He gave an involuntary cry of pain and clutched his midriff. I looked indecisively at Finchley and Pizzello.

"Is the kid someplace we can park his old man?" Finchley demanded.

"If I tell you and word leaks out—"

"Yeah. Coney and me are as tight as two peas in pods that are a thousand miles apart," Finchley said.

"He's at Gregory's. Along with Julia Zigler."

"Gregory?" Finchley said.

"My youngest brother," Donny said, eyes still shut. "Whose lightbulb was that?"

"Sonia's," I said. "And their safety depends on everyone forgetting about Gregory."

"Safe with me," Finchley said. "I never heard of the dude."

"Yeah," Donny said. "Everyone writes him off, but not even Tad will forget about him forever. If I was there—"

I cut him off coldly. "If you were there, number one, you'd have to sleep on the floor, and number two, you'd be a total liability if the kids have to bolt in a hurry. Your cast is barely twelve hours old."

"If his family can't take care of him, he belongs in a nursing home," Pizzello said. "They could start doing therapy on the broken leg."

"Yeah, right." Donny's mouth couldn't shape a sneer, but the intention was there. "Me eating mashed-up peas with the old ladies."

I stared down at him. "It's a good idea. In fact, it's a great idea. And I take back my objection to his death. We'll get Murray Ryerson to leak the news, except he'll say the police are seeking the identity of an unknown man who died after they brought him into the hospital."

"Coney was there," Sergeant Pizzello objected. "He knows I wheeled Donny out of the ward."

"That was a mistake, Sergeant," I said solemnly. "His injuries were much more severe than you realized. He was dead before you got him to the station."

48

The Road to Wellness

It was 10:20 P.M. when we pulled up in front of the Road to Wellness Pavilion. Tom Streeter opened the back doors of his van and handed the wheelchair to me. He and his brother, Jim, carefully lifted Donny out and strapped him to the chair. Brad and Julia jumped out of the back of the van and ran to Donny's side.

Donny was still unhappy with being brought here. He wasn't helpless, he insisted, in words so garbled they were almost incomprehensible. And in a hospital bed, Duda or Coney could finish him off with one blow.

"Dad!" Brad protested. "As long as they think you're dead, you'll be safe. Just remember your name is Conway Kelly."

"How can I remember I'm Irish?" Donny complained. "No one ever let me forget I was the only Jew in South Chicago. I had to fight everyone. Irish, Poles, Italians, you name them, they wanted to prove themselves on me. How can I forget I'm Jewish?"

I'd chosen to arrive just before ten-thirty because it was close to a shift change. Everyone would want paperwork done as quickly as possible, which would mean they wouldn't spend too much time challenging the difference in Donny's insured name and the name we were registering him under.

Lotty had been the hard sell. She agreed, based on Donny's injuries, that a stint in a nursing home would help him heal, but the orthopedist who'd set his leg had to be the person to order care. She hadn't treated him, she hadn't seen X-rays, and she didn't have privileges at the hospital where he had been treated, so she didn't have access to his records.

"Lotty, I took on helping out the Parientes as a favor to you. Now it appears that there's a connection between the Parientes' problems and the attack on Donny. I'm hoping to use his admission both to keep him out of harm's way and to get the monkey off the Parientes' back."

"You helped them, so now I need to help you?" she said.

"In a nutshell."

Her eyes narrowed to angry slits. She walked away

from me, conferred with the philodendron on her windowsill. She turned around but stayed on the far side of the room. "Oh, very well. But I'm not happy about it."

"Neither is Donny, if that's any comfort." I took the referral forms to Mrs. Coltrain, who got us a room at the Archangel facility in Northfield.

While Lotty was angry, Murray was enthusiastic. The paragraph he'd put out on his feed had already collected sixty thousand hits.

Police are anxious to identify a man who was found badly beaten on Goose Island. He was treated for head, hand, and leg injuries but died on his way from the hospital to his home.

Murray persuaded Luana Giorgini, a former *Herald-Star* buddy who was still at the paper, to insert the piece in the online edition, along with a photo I'd provided of Donny's badly damaged face. Murray also ran the story on his own *Chicago Roundup* podcast. By the time we left for Northfield, the networks and Global had picked up the item and were putting it on their news feeds.

The other eager participants were Julia and Brad. I hadn't wanted to involve them, but Brad needed to know his father was alive. If he saw his picture in an online story, he'd recognize Donny despite the bruises. It would be horribly cruel to let him think his father was dead. When I was worrying about how to handle the situation, Jewel Kim suggested I bring him along.

"Nursing homes often have teen aides," Jewel said. "They cheer up older people."

"At ten-thirty at night?" I was skeptical.

"I don't think the admitting team will think about that. None of you will be allowed beyond the front desk, anyway—let them think whatever they want."

When I pitched the idea to Brad and Julia, they were ecstatic, mostly at the prospect of being released from isolation. However, when I explained what I was trying to do, and what the risks were, they became solemn.

"Vic, this is so important," Brad said. "I'll do my best not to fuck up."

"Me, too," Julia said. "You're amazing, Vic."

"You will do fine," I assured them. "I wouldn't ask you to take part if I didn't have complete confidence in both of you."

We had to bring Peppy with us. Mr. Contreras reported that our building was under constant police surveillance, so I couldn't drop her at home.

I called Gregory, who was still at work, to say I'd taken the kids to another, safer place. He was greatly relieved. He'd been nervous about being able to protect them, and even more nervous about whether his vinyl collection would survive their visit.

I also called Sonia. I didn't like having too many people know the reality about Donny, but like Brad, Sonia would be beside herself with grief and rage if she saw the stop press. Of course, she wanted me to bring Donny to her.

I put Donny on the phone. "Sonny, I'm radioactive. If Coney or Duda don't believe the story, you'll be the first person they'll check out. Warshawski's got a plan. I'm not saying it's a good plan, but it's the best we got right now."

I had asked Jewel Kim to lend me a thousand dollars when we were at the clinic. "If I don't survive to repay you, get Lotty to make it good," I said. "She'll be angry with me, but she won't want you to suffer."

Just at that moment, Lotty had walked into the back office where Jewel and I had been speaking. "You're right on both subjects, Victoria. I am angry with you. If your recklessness brings you to harm, I will be angrier. And in neither case should Jewel suffer."

She had summoned Mrs. Coltrain to take her ATM card to a nearby machine and get cash for me. We took the money to Roosevelt Road to pick up essential supplies, which included renting a wheelchair for Donny. Sergeant Pizzello had sent Rudy Howard, her young rookie, back to the hospital with the chair she'd used to spirit Donny out of the way.

We had to move Donny, and quickly. Aside from the fact that the station's holding cells were needed for arrestees, word would spread through the city in nanoseconds that Donny was alive, even if not well.

"Cops gossip as much as any other group of people doing the same job," Finchley said. "Difference is, we put it out on our internal bulletin boards, pretending it's all work-related. Coney would get here about five seconds after the first clever person tweeted that we had Donny in a cell. Fact is, someone may already have figured that out."

I needed a place to leave Donny until we were ready to drive him to Archangel, but I was out of ideas for safe spaces. I finally called on the Streeter brothers, a trio of laconic men who have an indecipherable business model. They do some heavy moving, they do some bodyguarding, one of them plays drums with a local band. I've worked with them ever since I was with the Public Defender. Jim, the drumming brother, had been picked up for possession and I got him off. They're not exactly in my debt, but if they can, they do put me to the front of the line when I need help.

Jim and Tom pulled up behind the station with their big van. They'd bolted a cot to the floor, and they carried Donny out as if he were no heavier than an end table. Lotty, brittle with anger and disapproval, had given me script in the name of Conway Kelly for the drugs she imagined Donny needed—he'd left the hospital too quickly for discharge orders. We stopped at a pharmacy to fill the prescriptions. The brothers drove him to a park a mile from Area 2 where he could sleep the afternoon away in the back of the van.

The Streeters let us take Peppy to their workshop. She also wasn't happy—she'd been in too many strange places lately—but she knew Tim and cried only a little when we left. Julia was heartbroken, but too many things had to go right in the next ten hours to include a dog.

Tonight, when we brought Donny to the Archangel facility, Jim and Tom were wearing the white uniforms of orderlies, which I'd acquired at a uniform shop on Roosevelt Road. The gates to the complex were shut. When Jim, who was driving, buzzed for admission, he made sure the gate attendant saw a nondescript logo on his jacket sleeve. He held out a clipboard with Donny's admission forms on it, and we were buzzed in. First hurdle jumped.

At the Road to Wellness Pavilion, Jim and Tom wheeled Donny to the admissions desk. I hung back with the kids, stepping forward only when the admitting clerk asked for next of kin.

Aides and nurses were clocking out as the shift

ended, while graveyard shift arrivals were pushing past us to get to the locker rooms. As I'd hoped, in the general confusion, the desk clerk paid scant attention to Donny's stage name. When the clerk asked about it, Tom leaned over the counter, muscles bulging, and whispered, loudly, "He's connected. They don't want him bothered while the leg heals."

I wasn't sure "connected" would mean anything to the intake clerk, but she nodded as if she understood and summoned a crew to escort Donny to a private room. She told Tom and Jim they had to leave.

Tom surprised me by saying he was Donny's bodyguard. "If I can't stay with him, Mr. Kelly will have to go to a different facility. Didn't they explain all that to you when they booked the room?"

The clerk was flustered, called her superior, who wasn't answering the phone. "I guess you can stay here for tonight, sir."

Brad and Julia surged forward, hugged Donny, and said loudly that they loved Uncle Conway and hoped he would get better quickly. Tom lifted Donny from the chair; Jim folded it and led the kids and me out to the van. I didn't stop to see whether the nursing home staff would bring another chair or leave Tom to carry Donny to a room.

Back in the van, Brad got into the front seat with

Jim. Julia and I sat on the cot and changed into the pink uniforms I'd bought on Roosevelt Road. Julia was giggling—stage fright.

"We have to move quickly, my sister. And when we're inside, we are quiet, our heads are down. We're doing a hard job for very little money. We're not happy to be at work."

"I know," she said in a small voice. "Vic, really, I'm scared. What will happen if—if they catch us?"

"I will create a diversion and you will run like the wind for the back door. You will get in the van with Jim and he will drive you to safety."

"And you'll be okay?"

"I will be fine." I spoke with a conviction that I didn't actually feel.

49
Dirty Work

It was ten to eleven when Julia and I joined the tail of the graveyard shift workers going through the rear entrance into the Memory Care Pavilion. When I'd been here last week, I'd noticed that the attendants wore their IDs on lanyards, and quite a few had the photo sleeve turned around so you couldn't see the ID. I'd bought us lanyards and stuck white paper into the plastic sleeves. No one tried to look at them. The guard holding the door open was impatient with us. *Come on, girls, you're not Beyoncé—no one's waiting on your big entrance.*

"You girls new?" one of the women asked as we followed her up the stairs.

I nodded.

"She's a little young to be working. She your daughter?"

"She eats," I said shortly.

"Don't they all," the woman said, and stomped off down a hallway to our left.

Everyone was heading that way, into a room at the far end. I put a hand on Julia's arm to hold her back, and we ducked into a room labeled CHAPEL. When we couldn't hear any more talk or footsteps, I moved partway up the hall to see what was happening in the meeting. No one was putting out an alarm for intruders—the shift head was handing out work assignments.

"If you don't have a mask, pick one up from the stack by the door," she reminded the crew.

Julia and I were already masked—the one plus of the pandemic, it was easier to avoid close scrutiny. People emerged from the meeting room armed with bags of cleaning supplies. I left Julia in the chapel and worked my way inside to stand in line for supplies. The woman ahead of me dropped her bag; when she stooped to pick it up she glanced at me. The eyes above her mask widened in fear. She got to her feet and said, "Why you follow me? I report you!"

I grabbed two bags of supplies from a cart and darted from the room in her wake. Before she could speak to a supervisor, I touched her arm, jerked my head toward the chapel. She followed me, her whole body vibrating with suspicion. She stood in the chapel doorway, hand on the doorknob.

"Ms. Queriga, I'm not following you. Please don't report me. I'm only here to try to help the old woman who took your phone. This is Ms. Zigler's granddaughter. All we want is to find her grandmother and leave, without anyone trying to arrest us. I didn't know you would be here tonight—I thought you worked the day shift."

I spoke slowly, but I wasn't sure she'd understood. I was sweating, afraid that a supervisor would stop by at any second to see why we were in the chapel. The same thing must have occurred to Queriga; she moved all the way into the chapel and let the door close behind her.

"Spanish," she said.

My Spanish is abysmal, but as I got my tongue tangled on syntax, using Italian vocabulary when I couldn't remember the Spanish, Julia surprised me by jumping in. She said, very simply, that she was looking for her grandmother, that we didn't know Señora Queriga would be working tonight, and we wished her no harm.

Queriga looked from Julia to me, and then spoke a few rapid sentences in Spanish.

"The baby is sick," Julia translated. "She has to work sixteen hours a day to try to pay the bills. And she hopes we can help my *nagyi*."

Even I could understand Julia's request for the *numero* of *Señora Zigler's habitación;* Queriga shook her head and said she didn't know the names of the patients, and now everyone was late, we needed to hurry.

I complimented Julia on her Spanish.

"My dad is Brazilian," she said. "They don't teach Portuguese in Chicago public schools so I chose Spanish. How do you know that lady?"

"You remember I told you your granny tried to phone me? She had taken Ms. Queriga's phone."

"Then why did she say she doesn't know who my granny is?" Julia demanded. "She must remember who took her phone!"

I shook my head. "Ms. Queriga didn't know her phone was missing until later in her shift. She didn't see your granny take it. We'd best get going. The clock is ticking."

We began a hasty inspection of patient rooms. The inmates were in bed, some with TVs still blinking pictures at them. Some were moaning and thrashing, but most were heavily asleep. The beds all had raised guardrails. Even so, many of the patients were also restrained with straps. Many of them were lying in smelly linens. Why did they have a cleaning crew here at all, if they left people lying in filth? I wanted to clean their bodies, change the sheets, but we didn't have supplies for that—we were supposed to do the minimal, run rags along the sinks, make sure toilets were flushed.

Although patient names were on the doors, I wanted Julia to look at their faces, in case Gus had his mother admitted under a pseudonym. I hated asking her to do something so distressing; many of the features were hard to recognize, so slack were the faces from drugs and disease. I kept an arm around Julia's waist, and she clung to me as we moved from bed to bed.

The memory unit was laid out on two floors like a five-armed octopus. The first arm held the administrative offices and the chapel. By the time Julia and I finished touring the second arm, the work shift meeting had ended and we started encountering other workers.

"Are you looking for something?" one of them asked me.

"We were told to clean up a bed—I thought it was in 1–213"—the room we'd just emerged from—"but maybe I misheard."

The woman looked over her shoulder. "Serena is in a foul mood tonight. Don't let her catch you not knowing where you're supposed to be."

Julia and I nodded fervently. In the fourth arm, I found an industrial bucket and mop. Better cover than just walking the halls. We used our clean-up excuse three more times by the time we'd inspected all the ground-floor rooms.

The stairwell doors were locked, as were the elevator doors. My picks and my credit cards were with Peppy at the Streeter brothers' warehouse. I looked around wildly, heard voices approaching. Took off my lanyard and tried to slide the plastic sleeve through the tongue of the lock.

"Vic!" Julia's eyes were enormous in her pinched face. "Someone will see you."

The speakers rounded the corner of the arm where we were standing. A man and a woman. The woman was probably an administrator. The man was Uncle Gus. I dropped my lanyard into the bucket and started mopping like a madwoman.

"Chica!" I said to Julia. "You belong in that room!" I pointed to the one behind me.

"I'm going up to see her now," Uncle Gus said. "If she dies before she signs the power of attorney, Serena, those bills you're charging will go unpaid, and any arrangements we're making for the future won't include you. I hope you're keeping her alive."

"Don't lecture me. Last I heard, you don't have any

authority in this facility." Serena. She turned to me. "What are you doing? Eavesdropping?"

I gestured with the mop.

"And who are you? Where's your ID?"

"Sorry," I sniveled. "Fell in bucket."

I stuck a hand into the fetid water and started to lift the lanyard. Serena backed away in disgust. Gus hadn't paid any attention to me. I was a low-paid worker, beneath notice.

Serena slapped an electronic card against a plate in the wall and the stairwell door hissed open on its hydraulic hinge. She and Gus headed up the stairs. Before the door shut completely, I slipped my lanyard between the lock's tongue and the jamb.

Julia had been watching me furtively from the doorway across the hall. We crept into the stairwell. I ripped a piece from the hem of my uniform tunic to stuff into the lock so we wouldn't be trapped in the stairwell.

We could hear Gus and Serena above us on the second flight. We hugged the wall and followed them. Julia started to sneeze. I pressed her face against my chest, but a small snort still escaped.

The pair above us stopped briefly, then Serena said the wiring in the fluorescent bulbs was always making a popping sound. Julia's nails were digging into my back.

We heard the hydraulics as the second-floor door opened. I spoke into Julia's ear. "Stay here. If I'm spotted and trapped, I'll yell, and you go back to the first floor and make your way out. Got it?"

She nodded against my breast, trembling. I ran up on my toes, soundless on the concrete risers. Gus and Serena were just exiting, turning right down the hall. I stuffed another piece of fabric into the lock and peered down the hall in time to see them disappear into a room at the far end.

I went back into the stairwell, beckoned to Julia, and moved with her into a patient room near the stairwell. This one housed a single bed with a man in it. He was staring at the ceiling, calling loudly for Mary.

I went to his side, put my fingers on his wrist. "I'm here," I said. "Don't worry. I'm here." I squatted next to the bed so that my face was at his ear level, and began singing one of the Italian lullabies of my childhood.

"Vic!" Julia gave an urgent whisper. "They're coming back."

A curtain shielded a toilet and sink. "Get behind there."

Julia moved just in time. Serena stood in the doorway, Gus behind her.

I took a package of wipes from my bag of supplies and began sponging the man's neck and forehead.

"Were you singing to him?" Serena demanded.

"He unhappy." I spoke in my mother's heavily accented English.

"You're not here to make people happy, you're here to clean the bathrooms. If they're crying for water, give them water. End of story."

"Si, señora," I muttered.

She switched on a light and read from the patient chart stuck in a holder next to the door. "He's due for another injection at one A.M. Tell Riva to give it to him now."

"Si, señora," I muttered. I had no idea who Riva was or how to communicate with her, but in desperation, I pressed the nurse call button.

I continued wiping the man's forehead, my own skin prickling as Serena remained in the doorway. Finally she switched off the light and moved down the hall, away from us.

I muttered to Julia to stay put and went into the room next to the man's. Gus and Serena were waiting in the hall, watching me. I stayed for three minutes, crossed the hall to the next patient, the hair rising on my scalp. After I'd gone to the third room, not singing or dancing or anything that might make a scared person feel safer, an elevator bell dinged and a woman in scrubs headed for the old man's room.

"He's very agitated tonight," Serena said. "That

stupid girl"—pointing at me as I moved down the hall—"thought giving him a concert would solve his problems. You should up his sedation."

The woman in scrubs went into the man's room. I followed, despite a sharp reprimand from Serena.

"Maybe she need help."

"I can handle him," the woman in scrubs said.

"I make clean," I said.

She rolled up the man's sleeve, found a vein, gave him a shot. I took the used needle and alcohol swab from her and pushed the shower curtain back so that it folded around Julia. The nurse watched while I disposed of the needle in a sharp's box: I wasn't an undocumented addict, pocketing hospital supplies.

She nodded, went back out and down the hall. "Where do you find them, Serena? You advertise for stupid?" she said to the woman with Gus.

"Singing to him! Archangel's got talent," the nurse said.

The trio went into the elevator together, shaking their heads over the stupidity of the low-paid workforce. The elevator doors shut on their merry laughter.

As soon as the doors closed, I went back for Julia. We ran down the hall together, to the room Gus and his pal had visited. It was occupied by a single woman, her body strapped to the bed, her arms separately restrained in cuffs. Her eyes were shut, her breathing slow, heavy. Julia ran to her side.

"It's her, it's my *nagyi!*" In her joy she forgot to keep her voice low. "*Nagyi! Nagyi!* Wake up. It's me, it's your Yulchia." She hugged her, but the woman remained unresponsive.

"Oh, Vic, what's wrong? Have they killed her?"

"She's heavily drugged. Keep talking to her, but in a soft voice so no one hears us. Even people in comas can hear what is said around them. Keep telling her you love her."

I didn't want to turn on a light, fearing it would rouse a nurse or administrator. There were no curtains on the barred window, and lights from the parking lot outside shone in. I could sort of see what I was doing, unbuckling the straps fixing her to the bed, finding the magnetic buttons on the wrist restraints. Nervousness was slowing me down, but I finally freed her. When I lifted her, the sheet came off the bed, stuck to her body, and a terrible smell rose with her. Bedsores covered her buttocks and thighs.

I couldn't take time to cut the sheet away; I wrapped her in it and slung her over my shoulder. It was like lifting a bag of dried leaves. "We're going to get you safe," I murmured, "and then we'll see that the perverts who did this to you rot in prison."

"What do we do next?" I asked Julia.

"We go out the back way to the van." Julia repeated the instructions I'd drilled into her this afternoon. "Jim is waiting in the delivery bay. He will drive my *nagyi* to the Grete Berman Center for victims of torture. They will let me stay with her."

"Right," I said. "If we get separated, you do not worry about me, you stay with your granny. The people at Grete Berman are expecting you. I explained everything to them this afternoon. They have the medical staff who can nurse her back to health."

Her mind as well as her body, I hoped, but I didn't burden Julia with that worry.

I stuck my head out the door. "Now we make a run for it. Down the stairs, and out the back."

"Don't drop her." Julia trotted anxiously next to me.

"Do my best not to, baby." Her *nagyi* was a featherweight but still a weight. I was panting by the time we reached the stairwell. Julia opened the door just as the nurse arrived at the top of the steps.

"Where are you two going?"

"Laundry," I panted. "Smell? Very dirty."

The nurse backed away from the proffered sheet. "Does it take two of you to change a bed?"

"Training. New girl," I cried, and bolted down the stairs.

Everything went smoothly until we reached the rear exit. When Julia pushed the door open, an alarm blared. Loud swooping honks, as if from a prison tower.

The Streeters' van was parked just inside the open gates leading to the road. When the alarm sounded the gates began to close. Jim gunned the engine, got the van into the gap between the gates and the posts. His brother jumped out to open the van's rear doors but couldn't push the gate away from the sides of the van. Voices were shouting at us from the building.

"Get up on the tailgate," I gasped to Julia. "Pull that handle down."

She managed, somehow, and got one door open.

Hands were grabbing me from behind.

"Get in now!" I screamed at Julia.

"*Nagyi!*"

"Go!" I cried.

I shoved Silvia inside, tried to follow, but I was pulled away. Two sets of arms. I kicked, twisted, kicked some more, saw Tom jump into the passenger seat, saw the van take off, the open door bouncing crazily on its hinges.

"Fuck! It's that Warshawski bitch!"

50
Pedal to the Metal

Inside the van, Julia lay on the floor, arms tight around her grandmother. She was sobbing, trying to keep Silvia's head from banging against the van floor. The door was open, they could both be jolted into the street. Would Uncle Gus murder Vic? She needed to pee, what if she did that right now, peeing her pants like a baby in front of Brad?

The van slowed, eased to a stop. Tom and Brad slid around the front seat into the body of the van. Tom bolted the door from the inside and lifted Silvia onto the cot they'd used to transport Donny. As soon as he'd fastened a strap around her, the van took off again.

"Is she dead?" Julia wept.

Tom pulled the sheet away from Silvia's face and laid two fingers on her neck. "She's still alive." He repeated the same advice Vic had given: sit next to her, talk to her softly, tell her you love her.

"Can you—we have to get *Nagyi* to the torture people, but will you go back and rescue Vic? Uncle Gus is there; he'll tell them to hurt her." Julia's teeth were chattering. "Maybe they'll even kill her. I heard her say Coney wants to kill her and pretend she was resisting arrest."

"I don't think they'll kill her," Tom said. "They need to know where your granny is. And none of us are going to tell them."

"But they photographed your license plate while we were waiting," Brad said. "They can track the van."

"You two are too sharp; you notice too much," Tom said. "This afternoon, while you and Vic were off running errands, we borrowed the tags off Scott Coney's SUV. We'll have those in the North Branch of the river as soon as we get Granny Zigler into the hands of the angels."

"But they can torture Vic," Julia said. "And Duda, he's even scarier than Coney. If we knew where they were—Brad, we need your uncle's rocket. Can you go and beg him for a drone? If we could follow them we'd be able to save Vic!"

Brad muttered something that no one could hear over the van's engine. They bounced their way to the

Grete Berman Center for the victims of torture. At the entrance, Jim conferred with someone through the intercom in the gatepost. An attendant, dressed in casual civilian clothes, came out to escort them into the facility. It was a brick mansion, built in the robber baron era, and expanded in the years since the Berman Center had taken it over.

More attendants appeared to help transfer Silvia Zigler onto a gurney.

"I'm staying with her." Julia's chin jutted out.

"Of course you are," they assured her. "You're vital to her recovery. You can hop on that gurney next to her, if you want, or walk next to it and hold her hand while we get her inside and make her comfortable."

Their escort rode the van back to the outer gate to make sure that they actually left the premises. As Jim drove toward the river, where he planned to dump Coney's license plates, Brad said with studied nonchalance, "Do you think it would be a good idea to do what Julia said? Get a drone to track Coney and Duda?"

"Is that something you can do?" Tom asked.

"The thing is, I have my uncle's Skyrocket software, and the solar antenna he designed."

There was silence in the van, and then Jim said, "Vic told us that you'd been strip-searched by someone looking for photos your uncle's drone captured. I didn't know you had the whole package. What'd you do? Swallow the components?"

"Gross," Brad said. "Besides, I don't think a data stick would survive being in your gut and then your shit. When Uncle Reggie said it was missing, I thought my dad had taken it, because of the man who threatened him. Do you know about that?"

"Vic only gave us a sketch. We don't know the details," Tom said. "How did you hide the data stick when they strip-searched you?"

"I didn't have it then. I didn't even know it existed. But on Tuesday, when everyone was screaming at me—I first thought maybe Finnercon—my cousins—had taken the drone and the data stick. It's the kind of thing they'd do, to get people stirred up. But something about how my mom was acting, I thought, what if she took it and was letting Uncle Reggie blame me. She'd already—well, never mind that.

"Anyway, I took off on my bike. First I just rode as hard as I could to get away from them all, but the more I thought about my mom—well, anyway, I rode home. The antenna and the data stick were where she always hides things, in a shoebox on her side of the closet. She bought these Armani shoes, and they're like, sacred, no one can touch them. I took the Rocket components, and when I went to stay with Uncle Sal—with Mr. Contreras, I still had them in my backpack."

Jim pulled over to the side of the road. "Are you telling me this drone setup could help us keep track of Vic?"

"We'd need a drone, and not one just off the shelf at Buy-Smart. It'd have to be, like NSA quality. I only have the software, and you'd have to program it to access databases, like license plates and stuff. And also, I mean, I'm a gamer, I know drones, but Uncle Reggie's software is pretty complicated." Brad's voice trailed away. "And you need a data set to program into it, and we don't have any data about those guys, about Coney or Duda. I guess that was stupid, like all my ideas."

"Not stupid, but time-consuming. Maybe too time-consuming. However, we have one piece of data. We know Coney's license plate number."

"Yes, because it's on this van. That doesn't help," Brad cried.

"We have *our* license plate number—it's on Coney's SUV. If he's driving, we'll find him. Hey, Jimbo, put the pedal to the metal. Brad, what's your uncle's address?"

Brad couldn't tell him, since he didn't have a phone. Tom looked it up while Jim hit ninety on the expressway. They passed a state trooper, who pinged the license plate, saw it belonged to a brother in law enforcement, and let them go unhindered.

51
Out of the Frying Pan . . .

I was a dervish, whirling, crouching, kicking, slicing. A good uppercut broke Gus's nose. He yelped, backed away. Two guards were circling me from behind.

The memory care unit doors were open. I bolted through them and down the hall, looking frantically for sanctuary.

"Stop her," a guard shouted.

A woman emerged from an office, yelling for backup. I veered right, sprinted down another wing. Someone blew a whistle. One of the guards appeared at the far end of the corridor and headed toward me. He was running full tilt when a woman pushed a laundry cart across his path. He knocked the cart over, lost his balance, and fell heavily into the laundry.

"Señor, sorry, sorry!"

It was Gisela Queriga. I couldn't stop to watch or help, but ran to the end of the hall and out an emergency exit. Down the path to the gate. Couldn't find the panel for unlocking the magnetic switch. Spotted a depression in the ground under the fence, rolled under, started to run, and suddenly felt as though my face had caught fire. I collapsed to the ground, rolling in the grass, couldn't open my eyes. I pulled my mask from my face but couldn't stop a paroxysm of coughing.

"You've been running, Warshawski, but you can't hide, not from me. On your feet, cunt." Coney.

I lay retching, eyes shut, couldn't see the foot as it slammed into my rib cage.

52

The Pit and the Pendulum

"Where are they?"

A hard slap across my head.

A bright light was aimed at my face. Even without the light, my eyes hurt too much to do more than take in the gray metal table in front of me. My hands were chained to it. My lips were swollen. Speech was more painful than the whacks I was getting from someone outside my range of vision. Duda was bellowing, but it was probably Coney who was hitting me. I must be back in Homan Square.

Home, Home on the square. The ludicrous jingle lodged in my head.

"Where's the girl?" Whack.

Where the cops and their acolytes play.

"Where's the old woman?" Whack.

Where all that is heard . . .

Whack.

Are discouraging words . . .

Whack.

And they hit you by night and by day.

"I need to know about the Skyrocket. Someone took it from your girlfriend, Tad. Must've been Warshawski."

A new speaker. The voice faintly familiar.

"You know the drill, Duda, you and Gus both. You behaved like complete assholes, doing your B & E number on the North Shore and in Barrington. The only thing standing between you two cretins and swimming with sharks is you getting that damned drone back."

Corky Ranaghan. The man with the strings in his hands.

"You gave her too much pepper," Corky said. "Hitting her isn't helping."

"You know money, Corky, but I know interrogation," Coney said. "She gets hurt until she talks."

People talk to stop torture, but they don't tell the truth. I thought about trying to reveal that fact, but I couldn't shape the words. Corky was right. They'd overdone the pepper spray.

"Leave her alone for half an hour until the spray wears off," Corky said. "She's not going anywhere."

Home, home on the square. Now I'm going no-where. Except to my grave. They weren't bothering to hide their identities, which meant they knew I wouldn't be around to identify them. Coney would get his wish—shooting me in self-defense while I was resisting arrest.

The door banged shut. The klieg light stayed on. My head and neck throbbed from the beating. Tomorrow I'd have a stiff neck. If I was still alive.

They'd kill me if I told them what they wanted to know. They'd kill me if I didn't. *Act now, V.I., your one and only chance.*

I cracked my eyes open, saw my hands. I'd fought hard; the heels of my hands were swollen and tingling from where I'd gone into someone's chin. I hoped Duda's.

A Styrofoam cup was near me on the tabletop, with about an inch of coffee and a couple of cigarette butts in the bottom. Stains. Coffee, I hoped. A paper clip. Some half-dried viscous substance, maybe soy sauce, or blood. A paper clip. About a yard from me, way beyond my manacled hands.

I leaned onto the table. My forehead just reached the clip. I kept my head on the table, eased the clip toward me. Let anyone looking through the peephole think I was being sick. Not that far from happening. The pepper and the stale coffee and cigarettes made my gorge rise.

Moved my mouth along the top, tried not to imagine the spit and snot embedded in it. Got the clip past my thickened lips. Kept my head on the table, worked the clip sideways between my teeth. Bit down on it, lost it in my mouth, back again, easy does it. Tongue holds clip steady, use teeth to make a dent in the side.

Head still on table. Lift hands, can't quite reach mouth, bend neck down, yes, it hurts but just do it, don't whine. Hardest moment, transfer clip to hands. Drop it on the floor and you're dead. Easy, easy, fingers have just enough sensation in to feel the dent. Pull one end of the clip straight, my handmade Allen wrench. Turn left wrist, find the keyhole, stick the straight piece in. Twist, hands wet with sweat. Ratchets click back, left hand free. Dizzy with relief. Working the right hand, easy peasy. Ratchets click open.

The light went out. I slid from the chair, crouching low, backed up to the wall and worked my way to where I thought the door was. The blackout was complete. The room had no windows, no lights, and I was disoriented by dark and pain. I finally found the door and stood up, flat against the wall next to it. I waited for it to open. Coney would unload his service revolver into me—she was resisting arrest.

I ran through my "Home on the Square" song a few

times, silently, followed by "L'ho perduta" from *Figaro*. That must be five minutes. I pulled on the doorknob, half expecting it not to open, but they must have counted on the handcuffs.

I squatted again, squeezed through the opening, rolled, ready to bounce to my feet and run—but the hall was completely dark.

Coney and Duda were shouting, swearing.

"Don't you assholes have emergency backup?" Duda.

"I'm not the fucking building engineer." Coney, snarling. "I can't get my phone to come on."

"Mine isn't working, either." Corky.

More voices joined them, more panic. No one could get a phone signal. More swearing. Bodies thudding into each other.

I stayed put, back against the wall, trying to sense where people were congregating. Emergency exit signs glowed at either end of the space I was in.

Not much time before the power comes on again, use it, Warshawski. Fifth grade, surrounded on the playground, terrified. *Cop's daughter, get her.* Boom-Boom seeing the mob, fighting his way to me. *Vic, elbows, use your elbows.*

Elbows, Vic, elbows with all the heft of anger, fear,

and practice behind them. I muscled my way past soft guts and hard abs, past outcries of *Watch your fucking arms, moron—jerk—dirtbag.*

Reached the green exit sign. Window beyond covered in fireproof glass blocks, no light beyond, no way to see where I was going. I found a door, cautious footwork, found a stair. If this was Homan, I was on an upper floor. The ground-floor windows were bricked over. So, clutching the rail, one dizzy step down at a time. Twelve steps, a landing, turn, down twelve more, fumble for a door, opened on more blackness, and then a flash of light sweeping the space. Tried to duck back into the stairwell.

Hoarse whisper crying, "Vic? Vic—Jim Streeter here."

53

The Great Escape

The van jolted down Polk Street. The square was thick with blue-and-white strobes. We'd had a tense few minutes getting past them. Tom, who was driving now, said, "Scott Coney's van—check the plates, moron. Got a prisoner in the back we're taking to County for him—he got carried away."

I was strapped onto the cot in the back, a very convincing display of Coney's overexcitement during interrogation. Light still hurt my eyes. I could speak more easily, but my lips were sore, and I had a painful cough.

A patrol officer shone a light on me. "Yeah, that looks like Coney's handiwork." He snickered and shut the doors.

When we turned north on Kedzie, Reggie said, "Look out the windows on the west."

He touched a button on his computer, and the black windows on the Homan Square building began to glow yellow-white.

"Vic, this was so amazing!" Brad was bubbling over with excitement. "The Skyrocket, Uncle Reggie got it to block all the signals going into the building. It was like, *whoosh,* a hand from heaven turning off the lights all at once, along with people's phones, everything. All the doors unlocked. Tom and Jim and I went in, but I don't know how we found you."

"We were damned lucky," Tom said. "We each took a floor, not knowing where you'd be held. We thought we'd have to go room by room in case you were chained somewhere."

"I was, but I used low-grade technology to get free."

Brad asked what I meant.

"I gotta see how to do that," Brad said. "Picking up a paper clip with your teeth and unlocking your cuffs? OMG, I wish I could see that creep Coney's face when he sees you got yourself out of there."

I tried to laugh but ended up coughing. "Yes, that would be worth the price of admission."

Tom turned onto the Eisenhower, but pulled off

again at Ashland, an exit with three major hospitals in spitting distance.

"I don't want a hospital, I want a night in bed. Maybe a day, too."

"Not doing this for you, Warshawski," Tom said. "While Jim and Brad were getting you into the van, I found Coney's SUV and took our plates off. He can track the van via the license plates if he figures out we made the switch—which he easily can—Archangel took our picture when we were waiting for you. Also the patrol guy saw Coney's plates on the van just now. I need to make the switch."

He worked fast. We were back on the road in under two minutes.

"Brad, we're about to go over the Chicago River. You drop these over the edge." He handed Coney's plates to Brad.

"But won't they recognize the van?" Brad worried. "They have you on camera."

"This time tomorrow the van is going to be a bright shiny blue instead of dull dirty brown. We're okay. Warshawski, where are we taking you? Your dog is at our place, remember?"

Peppy. How could I have forgotten her? Between Archangel, Julia and her grandmother, Brad, the

Skyrocket, the Shaamar Hashomayim synagogue, I felt as though I was carrying a giant plastic bag so filled with unwieldy shapes I couldn't see around it.

I wanted to go home, be in my own bed. "Coney and Corky are going to be sorting things out for a while. I'll be safe. Or if I'm not, I'm too beat up to worry about it. Can we swing by your place for Peppy? Brad, I know Mr. Contreras will be delighted to have you back."

"Why don't you come home with me?" Reggie suggested. "Time you learned you can rely on the crazy glue that holds the Litvaks together. At least some of the time. Your choice, Brad."

Brad didn't say anything.

"The twins are off camping," Reggie added casually. "Your aunt is visiting her mother. You'd have to put up with me, but I can fry a mean egg."

It was five in the morning by the time I managed to climb the stairs to my own home. Peppy stayed with me, following me first to the dining room, where my tablet lay. I took selfies of my swollen, battered face, my torn clothes, my bruised wrists. I sent them to Murray with a note that more words would arrive later in the day.

Gus and Duda showed up in the photos Reggie's gizmo was taking. The boys were removing art objects out of someone's house. They need those photos to keep their sorry behinds out of prison. Donny saw them in action when Reggie was doing his demo. He confronted them, so they started gunning for Donny or anyone they thought had the pics. I can't write more. Can't think more. You figure out Lacey Zigler's clever idea.

Peppy went with me to the shower, where I spent twenty minutes, washing the pepper spray from my face and body. She watched anxiously as I took my Smith & Wesson from my closet safe. If Coney or Duda broke in on me I was not going to have any compunction about firing first.

She gave a great sigh of relief when I finally collapsed into bed. We were both asleep within seconds. It was past two in the afternoon before I surfaced again.

54
Recovering

I had a to-do list as long as *War and Peace,* and about as interesting. My arms and legs were still swollen and sore, and it was hard for me to galvanize myself into action.

Still, Peppy needed to be outside, I needed to reset my biological clock. I put on loose-fitting clothes. I don't like to carry a gun inside the building, but Coney had me unnerved enough that I put on a shoulder holster under my sweatshirt.

Sitting in the garden, with the spring sun on my face, I called Peter in Malaga.

"Oh, baby, I'm proud of you and terrified all in the same breath. You seem so—so indomitable that I wonder if you really need me."

I felt a sinking in my diaphragm. "Peter—I'm not

indomitable. I need you, I need love, like everyone else."

"You're not like everyone else," he said slowly. "Most people don't risk their lives for people in need. I guess I'm the lucky guy who gets to be your lover."

"Is that sarcasm?" I asked.

"No. It's the truth. But spare a thought for the people who love you before you leap off the next cliff without a parachute. We need you, too. Okay?"

"Okay," I muttered, but the call left me with some reassurance that I badly needed.

My next port of call had to be Mr. Contreras. He wanted every detail of how we'd managed to get Julia's grandmother out of the nursing home. He also needed to know how I'd acquired my black eyes and the bruise spreading from my jawline into my hair.

He was miffed that he hadn't been part of the team: Hadn't he proved a hundred times that he was a useful man in a fight?

"We could have used you, for sure," I said, internally thankful he hadn't been there for Coney to spray with pepper.

Murray had left a dozen text messages, which I read on my tablet. I needed to get a new smartphone, but in the meantime, I called him on one of my burners.

"Warshawski, this stuff is sizzling hot. How'd you

get out of Homan Square? That place is locked up tighter than a supermax."

"Luck. The power went out, which meant the doors opened automatically."

"Com Ed is baffled," Murray said. "I talked to a buddy in their community relations department. They can't find any problems with power lines or transformers, but service was interrupted in that one square block for about thirty minutes. How'd you do it?"

"I didn't do anything but thank the patron saint of prisoners for giving me a break. Listen: Corky Ranaghan was in the interrogation room, along with Duda and Coney. I don't know if anyone else was there as a witness—I was blinded, partly by kliegs, partly by pepper spray."

"I can't run that based on your recognizing his voice," Murray said. "I need an actual eyewitness."

"I was temporarily blind—"

"Too narrow a line, Vic, and you know it. I love you like a brother, but I'm not defending an eight-figure libel suit on your say-so."

"Like a brother? More like a hungry mosquito at a family picnic," I grumbled. Still, he was going to run the story of my abuse in Homan Square. It would make for good headlines and would also provide fuel for lawyers trying to get access to clients whose whereabouts

diabetic Foot CARE
for nail care + shoes
bleeding issue-prostate
sleeping thru the night
major Depression +
grumpyness
forgetfulness
new meter

the CPD kept secret. But it wouldn't keep me safe from Coney. Or Duda. Or Corky.

I called Freeman Carter. I'd sent him the interview Murray had recorded, along with the selfies I'd taken of my battered body. Freeman said he'd add that to an excessive force complaint, but he wasn't hopeful it would get Coney off the streets.

I called Sergeant Pizzello and filled her in.

"Hot potato, Vic. You know I can't go head to head with Coney. Anyway, he let you go, right?"

"Wrong. There was a power outage at Homan Square. I managed to slip away in the dark, because the outage unlocked all the doors. I do not know when or where the monster will strike again, but I hope you have some nice remarks for my funeral. By the way, Coney may be driving his personal SUV without license plates. That would be kind of funny."

"Did you take them off?" she demanded.

"I was in his custody, Sergeant. And I wouldn't have access to the private police lot out there on Homan, even if I hadn't been peppered and beaten."

"Maybe, Warshawski. I just can't help thinking that when you're locked up and Homan Square loses not only electric power but cell tower access, you were pushing the buttons."

"If I had that capability, Pizzello, I'd be Wonder

Woman. Believe me, with her powers, I'd be enforcing law and order in this sorry town."

I was getting ready to hang up when Pizzello said, "Before I forget, that dry cleaner on Lunt—her stolen clothes turned up in an alley a couple of blocks away. Some of them, anyway. The neighborhood had been helping themselves."

That was good news, sort of, for Rana Jardin at the cleaners. It would cut down on her uninsured losses, if the clothes were still in decent shape.

I told Pizzello I was sending my selfies and my recorded interview with Murray to her and to Finchley. "Maybe that can spark a little departmental review of Homan Square. By the way, it was probably Tad Duda who killed Jan Kadar, the janitor at Beth Israel. And very likely Duda or Coney, or the two of them together, who murdered Ariadne Blanchard—you know, Julia Zigler's roommate at the hospital," I said. "Surely *someone* in the CPD has enough protection to start an investigation?"

"That's low, Warshawski, and you know it."

"It's accurate, Sergeant. If I hand him to you on a platter, with applesauce and dumplings on the side, will you act then?" I ended the call with a snap.

I called the Grete Berman Center. After they'd been appropriately careful about verifying my identity, they told me Silvia Zigler was resting comfortably. They'd treated her bedsores, and they were titrating her meds so that she could gain consciousness without a damaging jolt to her system. It was too early to tell whether her mental functioning had been harmed by her weeks of heavy medication.

"Still, when she opened her eyes, she greeted her granddaughter by name, which is a good sign," the social worker told me.

My last call was to Lotty. All these conversations had filled the afternoon; it was past four. Lotty was through with her day's surgeries and had time to talk. Her anger during our previous conversation had made me reluctant to speak to her. However, when I told her about the conversation between Uncle Gus and the administrator, where he hoped to get his mother so confused she'd sign anything, Lotty gave me a reluctant imprimatur.

"Jewel talked to the people at the Archangel rehab center," she added. "You know I didn't want to cross an ethical line over signing onto Donny Litvak's admission, but so far his alias is holding up, and he seems to be in the right place for the care he needs. The Archangel administrators may have treated Silvia Zigler with appalling cruelty, but their rehab staff seem to know what they're doing."

I told Lotty about the report on Silvia's steps to recovery; she agreed that recognizing her granddaughter as soon as she saw her was an encouraging sign. "But Zigler is a long way from being able to return home. You say that her place on the river is a three-story mansion? Even if she can recover her strength enough to move back, I don't see how she can manage such a big place—especially if the men you've been fighting still want it.

"Max told me that someone on the Beth Israel board, a woman who's in real estate, thinks that the property is already available. The board member says that development proposals are very high, in the two- to three-hundred-million range. The board member said developers are calling the location Treasure Island."

While I digested that news, Lotty added, "You escaped last night, Victoria, but you don't have the resources to keep fighting men like Lieutenant Coney or this Corky financier. You have to stop the battle while you're still alive."

"I'm not going to feed Silvia Zigler and her granddaughter to them," I said.

"Don't bark at me," Lotty said. "I wouldn't want you to. But if Ms. Zigler would sell to another company, she'd have a fortune to support both herself and her granddaughter. And if these men you're fighting no longer had a chance to buy the property, they'd stop harassing the Ziglers, and you."

"Lotty, it's a great idea for Silvia Zigler's welfare, but Coney wants me dead. If this were a Clint Eastwood movie, he'd make my day by letting me shoot him before he plugged me. And that would mean I'd be put away for beaucoup years for being a cop killer."

I needed a better idea. If Corky and Coney and Duda thought the Zigler mansion was Treasure Island, maybe I could figure out a way to exploit that.

55
Preparing for Battle

Mitch and Peppy needed time together, time with my neighbor and time with me. All my phone conversations had depleted me. I hired an Uber to take me up to where I'd left Sonia's boss's Nissan. I picked up a picnic, collected the dogs and Mr. Contreras, and drove to Max's home in Evanston. He lives on a short street with its own beach. He let us lounge out there in peace, my neighbor and me wrapped in blankets against the cool air, the dogs digging in the sand or splashing through the waves.

Max appeared at one point with a glass of Brunello for me, and grappa for my neighbor. He spoke to me then about the Beth Israel board member Lotty had mentioned.

"I don't want to interrupt your rest, Victoria, but

are you sure that Ms. Zigler hasn't already signed away the rights to her home? My board member said the Goose Island location has come up in confidential discussions about where her company is looking to invest."

"I'm not sure of anything, Max, but I'll look into it. Tomorrow. Today I'm taking a brief vacation."

He looked more closely at my bruised face. "Yes, I'd say you'd earned a few hours off. Has Lotty seen you? No? Maybe just as well."

In the morning, I was still sore and headachy, but the swelling had gone down in my lips and hands. It was time to get back to work.

Murray's piece had run. My bruises looked so lurid in the online edition that some comments claimed I'd used makeup to create them. The piece was picked up widely and generated a lot of online chatter about police brutality. People from every jurisdiction, not just in the States but around the world, offered examples. The details about Homan Square made enough of a splash that I thought I might have another day or two before Coney came after me again.

Murray had persuaded one of the tech writers from the *Herald-Star* to contribute a sidebar on the power outage at Homan Square. Com Ed hadn't found any problems in their power lines or substations.

Homan Square has backup generators, which did not kick in, so the best guess is someone was jamming electrical signals in that square block area. The Chicago Department of Aviation is checking for drone activity in the area, and Com Ed has been looking for anyone in the community with that kind of technology in their homes, but so far, neither the city nor Com Ed have any explanations.

There was then a long discussion of vulnerabilities throughout the entire U.S. infrastructure.

I called Murray to thank him. "I'm working on another big story for you, Clark Kent. I'm hoping to mount an expedition to Treasure Island. If I get all my ships lined up and ready to sail, would you want to come along? It'll be short notice. Not tomorrow, probably, but hopefully by the day after."

He was more than eager, pummeling me with questions.

"Patience, Murray. You know what Madame Blavatsky used to say: All will be revealed."

The report from Max's board member was bothering me. If word was out that Silvia Zigler had signed over the title to her house, perhaps her son had forged her signature on a transfer deed.

I called Istvan Reito, Silvia's estate lawyer. He was

also worried. "If Ranaghan is starting that rumor, he may be trying to persuade someone into flattening the Zigler mansion, without realizing it isn't available for development. And once that happens, we could spend years in court, while Julia loses her inheritance to legal fees."

I was getting scared, which meant I had to act even though I was still sore and swollen from my time with Coney.

I bought a new smartphone, got the in-store geniuses to load all my apps and contacts and so on from the cloud, and drove out to the northwest suburbs to see Brad and Reggie.

Reggie's wife and sons had returned, so we met in the shed Reggie used as his home workshop. After the other night's excitement, Brad had reverted to his more usual awkwardness. He was all right. Uncle Reggie had given him a secure phone so he could talk to his parents without the call being traced. He'd had a brief conversation with Ashleigh, who wanted him to come home. He'd talked to his dad; Donny was going to be discharged in a couple of days.

"But then where will he go? He can't go back to Mom, not if she's hanging out with the guy who tried to kill him. And I can't go there, either."

Reggie nodded. "I'd be glad to have you here, Brad.

You've got a knack for electronics that I'd never known, but our dynamic here isn't the best."

That seemed like a euphemistic way to say his sons were pains in the butt, at least as far as their behavior to Brad went.

"I'm wondering if Brad would like to move into the Zigler place for a few days," I said, "assuming we could get power and gas turned on, and a few other adjustments to make it livable. I'd like to get it ready for Julia's grandmother to come home to."

"Vic—that's a very risky place for him. Not a good idea at all." Reggie frowned.

"Would Julia be there?" Brad said. "She, uh, she probably needs—maybe she wants—" The treacherous color flamed up in his face.

"Your help?" I suggested.

"Probably not, she's—she's like you, she doesn't need people—"

"If she's like me, she'd be glad of help. Reggie, before you give a categorical no, let me explain the help I need. Brad, it would mean you talking to your mother."

"Vic, I can't!"

"Before either of you says no, no, no forever, let me explain what I'm imagining."

We spoke for an hour, and Reggie finally developed

some enthusiasm for the idea. Brad even agreed to spend a night or two with Ashleigh.

Before I left, Reggie took my new phone, inspecting it for malware. "You reloaded this from the cloud? You were smart to get rid of the old phone. Someone's tracking you. I've removed that little goober and put in an app that will block an attempt to start following you again."

It was a relief to drive into the city without worrying that an eye in the sky was reporting my whereabouts to Coney or Duda.

My first stop was at the Parientes'. It had been only three days since I'd last seen them, but so much that was dangerous had happened, I was worried for their safety.

For most of us, the fatigue from the pandemic was making all other problems harder to deal with. I hated seeing how drawn and pinched Donna Ilona's face was. She kept interrupting herself, forgetting her place in sentences, apologizing.

"Don't apologize," I said. "I'm wondering if you could help me."

She brightened: I had done so much for her and Emilio, she longed to be able to pay me back.

"It could be risky," I warned her. "And if Lotty

hears about it, she'll carve me up in the OR without an anesthetic."

"You will not ask me to jump into the Chicago River, will you? Or unlock handcuffs with my teeth? Then I will be happy to help."

My final stop was at the Grete Berman Center. Reggie had made my phone safe, but I was still nervous about using it. The staff wouldn't let me see Silvia—her health was far too fragile—but they sent Julia out to the gate to talk to me.

She gave me a convulsive hug. "Oh, Vic, you're safe. I read about you, how you were tortured by that jerk-face cop. And then you got out? Using a paper clip with your teeth? You are so amazing! How is Mitch? How is Uncle Sal? Is Brad okay?"

She'd finally lost the pinched look around the eyes that had been worrying me. She'd needed her *nagyi*, at least as much as she needed food.

"How is your granny?" I asked.

"She's already better. She knows me, and she asked about the house, she remembers stuff, but Chiara—the social worker—she said not to talk too much, not to give her bad news because she can't take in too much right now, and bad news will jar her brain before it's healed." She wrinkled her nose. "She had some technical explanation, but that's all I can remember."

"I want the house to be in good shape and ready for her when she's ready to come home. She may decide it's too much for her, and decide to sell it, but she should have the chance to live there as long as she wants to. And I need you to help me get it ready for her."

Julia nodded solemnly. "Of course, Vic. I'll do anything you want. Even jump into the river after you."

I shuddered. "Let's try not to get to that extreme."

After that conversation, I turned my attention to my own recuperation. In the days since escaping Homan Square, the time that I wasn't resting or playing with the dogs, I spent reconnecting with my clients.

I was amazingly productive, completing long overdue investigations, writing reports—the stuff that lets me pay my bills. Mercifully dull, requiring a certain mental acuity but not physically demanding.

In the midst of this activity, Lieutenant Finchley came to see me. He wanted more details about what happened at Homan Square, and how I had ended up there. I didn't see any point in lying to him about extracting Silvia Zigler from the memory care unit. Finchley in turn forbore to comment on my actions, focusing instead on whether I was sure Coney had been there.

"A CPD lieutenant picking up a perpetrator in a suburban jurisdiction—he should have cleared that with the Northfield force. I'll make a few inquiries. Drop a word in Captain Mallory's ear—in a discreet way."

Captain Bobby Mallory had been my dad's closest friend on the force. He was close to retirement now but still wielded power within the department.

I didn't hear from the Finch, or from Bobby Mallory, but I also didn't see any signs of Coney or his henchman, Ben Tillman, hovering near my home or my office. I remained vigilant but felt easier going about my business.

I carried my gun for one day, but one of my father's sayings came back to me and persuaded me to put it away. *I never rely on a weapon,* he'd told me more than once. *Having a gun primes you to use it. It shuts off your brain from thinking of other options, and your brain will help you out of a rough spot better than a weapon will.*

Knowing that Reggie had made my phone safe was also a help. I took the time to bring Sonia's boss's Nissan back to her and to collect the Mustang. Sonia was gruffly grateful that I'd gotten Donny into a rehab facility.

"Ashleigh came around, looking for Donny and Brad. She even went to Gregory, so good thing you moved the kids on from there. I told her Brad was spending a few days with Reggie, so I expect she went there next."

We talked about whether Donny could stay with her when he left Archangel. He was making good progress with his therapies, and I was nervous about leaving him under the Archangel roof a minute longer than he had to be. Even though Sergeant Pizzello had leaked the news to the media that Donny had died in police custody, there were too many hostile eyes in the Archangel facility. At any moment some friend of Gus or Duda might recognize Donny and out him.

Uncle Gus actually came to see me at my office. He wanted to know where his mother and Julia were.

"I don't know, Mr. Zigler," I said. "I thought you had your mother safely ensconced at Archangel's Memory Care Pavilion. Weren't you waiting for her mind to be deconstructed enough by heavy medication that she'd sign a new estate plan for you?"

He reddened. "How dare you say something like that? My mother's health is a major concern for me. What did you do with her?"

"Nothing, Mr. Zigler. Your pal Tadeusz Duda must have told you he helped the Chicago cops pick me up at the Memory Care Pavilion and take me to Homan Square to torture me. It's only because of a miraculous power failure at Homan Square that I escaped and that I'm here talking to you right now."

He shifted uncomfortably in his seat.

"Corky isn't happy with you and Tad," I said. "He thinks you were a couple of horses' patooties for your methods of acquiring art objects."

"I don't know what you're talking about," he said, but not convincingly.

"Corky wants the Skyrocket, or he'll cut you loose."

"I don't need the damned Skyrocket. Lacey figured out everything without any fancy drones or software. Corky can screw himself for all I care."

"Except for the pictures floating around, showing you and Tad leaving someone's house with their valuables." I stopped short. "Lacey's clever idea. High-value houses belonging to people who've ended up at Archangel. She'd have access to their names if they were sent to Archangel from the hospital where she works. Easy to check if anyone's living there, and if not, you and Tad help yourselves."

"You can't go around calling me a thief. That's how you get sued for slander."

"It's only slander if it's false," I said. "By the way, someone told me they'd seen your niece going into your mother's house. I haven't tried to investigate—I'm still recovering from the damage Duda and Coney inflicted on me in Homan Square. If Julia's using the house, though, perhaps it means your mother is getting ready to come home."

"So you do know where she is?"

"I don't," I lied firmly. "I'm just telling you what I heard—from someone who may not have known what they were talking about. Maybe now is the time to get in touch with your mother's trust lawyer and see if he'll help you persuade your mother to sign a new will and a new trust document. Assuming you can locate Ms. Zigler."

"What, old Istvan Reito? He's another senile old fart who's outlived his usefulness."

He hurried from my office and was on his phone before he reached the street door. I called Corky Ranaghan.

"Ms. Warshawski—that was quite a story your friend Ryerson published about you. A real soap opera, reenforcing the left's whining over police brutality. That plays well with so-called woke street thugs these days, but I don't give it much chance of affecting anyone's business decisions."

"Gosh, Corky, I hope you're not implying that Murray's story wasn't accurate. Maybe your cousin Scott could interview you the same way he did me, and then you could decide whether it was fake news or not. Some talk-show hosts say torture is no worse than fraternity hazing, and they could be right, since people die from both."

His voice sharpened. "I hope you're not wasting my time as well as your own with this call, because I'm too busy for theoretical discussions."

"Pity," I said, "because Gus Zigler was just here. Speaking purely theoretically, he thinks his mother is coming home. He's hoping, still theoretically, to talk her into signing a new deal. I got the feeling his need for money was too great for him to wait on working things out through Klondike. He'll either sell Silvia's house or work on Lacey's clever idea on his own, but those are just theories, of course."

I hung up before he could answer.

56
Treasure Island

The sedan pulled up as close as possible to the front of the Goose Island mansion. When the driver had produced a wheelchair from the trunk, a woman in an old-fashioned nurse's uniform got out and helped a frail, white-haired woman from the sedan and into the chair. As the nurse wheeled her patient up the walk, Julia Zigler burst from the house. She knelt next to the chair, seizing the old woman's hands, holding them against her cheek.

The nurse tapped Julia gently on the shoulder, said something that made the girl get to her feet. The driver lifted the old woman out of her chair and carried her into the house. Julia and the nurse followed with the chair. After a few minutes, the driver emerged from the house, and the sedan retraced its route to the world overhead.

It was late afternoon. Days were getting longer and warmer as April ended, but down by the river it was still cool and the light was uncertain, especially under the bridge. Someone turned on lights on the first two floors, including in Silvia Zigler's bedroom. She had a corner room, with big bay windows overlooking the garden, so that lying in bed she could watch the trees and the birds.

The heavy branches were just starting to come into leaf. The pale green gauze couldn't block the view if someone with binoculars was peering into the room from the far side of the garden. Julia was sitting on the king-size bed, talking animatedly to the woman, who lay with her eyes shut, patting Julia's hand. The woman appeared to be very old. Binoculars magnified the wrinkles crisscrossing the old woman's cheeks and forehead. Her eyes were sunk deep into her face. Time in the Memory Care Pavilion seemed to have added a decade or more to her age.

The nurse appeared with a tray and tried to coax the old woman into eating. She drank a few spoonfuls of soup but made a shooing gesture. The nurse turned out the bedside lights and retreated to a spot not visible from the windows. After a few minutes, the girl left the room.

The house was quiet. The noise from the nearby

traffic thumping over the bridge made it hard to hear sounds from the garden. Geese along the river's edge honked softly as they settled for the night. Owls nesting in the garden hunted for the small animals who burrowed around the tangle of roots. You couldn't hear their frightened cries in Silvia's bedroom. You couldn't hear the splash as a pair of men in wetsuits climbed out of the water and slipped into the garden.

An hour or so after that, an SUV pulled up in the same spot the sedan had used. Five men climbed out. Anyone inside the house could have heard their loud laughter as they swaggered up the walk. The front door was locked, but one of the men had a key. He opened the front door and invited the other four inside with a parody of a courtly bow.

He shone a flashlight around the big front room, found a lamp, and switched it on. "This house could be left standing and anchor a new development," he said. "Ashleigh Breslau worked out a design when she was in here a few weeks ago with you, Duda."

"Last things last, Zigler," another of the men said. "Let's deal with your mother and get this project on the right footing to go ahead. You know the way—lead us to her."

The five pounded their way up a grand staircase that rose from the front hall. The second-floor landing was a square, with a protective railing around three sides. The balusters had been hand-carved, with a pattern of leaves and vines. Wall sconces also in the shape of leaves were lit, although the teardrop bulbs were a bit strong for the fragile glass.

"Fuck, Zigler, this is a fucking mansion. No wonder you're pissed with the old lady for bypassing you. Let's go make wrong things right."

They trooped down the hall to Silvia's bedroom. Zigler gave the door a perfunctory knock and pushed it open.

"Wakey, wakey, Mother. Time to do a little legal work and then we can get you back where you need to be."

"Augustus?" The woman in the bed's voice was quavery and thin, barely audible. "What are you doing here? Who let you in?"

"This is my home, Mother. Julia is a minor. She didn't need her key, so I persuaded her to let me have it. Let's get a light on, let's get you signing a new trust agreement. The Klondike attorneys drew it up. You'll find it's watertight." He bent to switch on the bedside lamp.

"I will have to read it first, but not tonight, Augustus, I'm too tired. Leave it on the table. I'll see it in the morning."

"We're not here to argue with you, old woman.

We're not leaving until you sign, so do it now and get it over with." It was the biggest of the men, standing at the foot of the bed with a gun.

"No weapons, Duda. We don't want to attract an audience."

"No one's going to hear us in this deserted mausoleum."

"The girl is here. She could call the cops."

"Corky, you're turning into an old lady yourself. I am the cops. It's always hard when a citizen doesn't identify themselves and gets shot, but you learn to get over it."

"Mother, do you want Julia to find you here with your blood and brains all over your pillows?" Gus Zigler said. "Sit up and sign the form."

The woman flicked back the cover and swung her legs around to land a hard kick to Augustus's diaphragm. She rolled over as Duda and Coney fired.

Strobe lights flashed in the room, so suddenly they blinded the men. The bouncing lights picked out random images but not the woman in the bed. Coney had started firing; he emptied his clip into the pillows.

"That wasn't your goddam mother, Zigler, it was the fucking Warshawski bitch. You great ape, you were standing right over her and you couldn't tell the difference? I want her dead."

"Coney," I shouted, "you just murdered a bunch of pillows."

I sprinted toward the staircase. Broken field running, crouching low. Strobes came on in the hall. The gang were firing recklessly, round after round. I made it to the stairwell, slid down the bannister to the half landing, swung over the rail, hung for a second, and dropped.

"Safe," I yelled.

Above me, thuds: bodies falling heavily, tumbling down the stairs, screams of pain.

The front door opened. A voice called through a bullhorn, "This is the Chicago police. Drop your weapons. I repeat, this is the Chicago police. We have the house surrounded. Drop your weapons."

"Lieutenant Finchley," I said. "What a welcome surprise."

57

Happy Families

Lotty was furious. "How dare you involve Mrs. Pariente in your insane plan? It's bad enough that you
risked your own life—but you know how frail she is."

"Have you talked to her?" I asked. "She was thrilled
to be part of the mission. It's been years since anyone
expected anything more of her than making *orecchie
di Aman* for Purim."

"And the girl!" Lotty ignored me. "You risked an
old woman and an adolescent. And how you avoided
being shot yourself—!"

"Timing. We had rehearsed it, but of course a hundred things can go wrong."

We were in the living room of the Zigler mansion.
Max had come with Lotty. The Litvaks were well represented: Reggie, Donny and Sonia, along with Brad

and Gregory. Murray had come, with a photographer. He was under oath to report, not to record or exploit. Julia was there, as were the Streeter brothers, and of course Mr. Contreras had come with the dogs. He was as miffed as Lotty, but since that was mostly because I hadn't called on him to play a role, Lotty didn't consider him an ally.

"Oh, Dr. Lotty, don't be mad at Vic. She was wonderful," Julia said. "My *nagyi* is still recovering at the Berman Center, but all Mrs. Pariente had to do was lie in *Nagyi*'s bed for a few hours. Then the Streeter brothers arrived. They climbed out of the river—it was so exciting! I let them in the back door and they carried Mrs. Pariente away. They wanted to take me, too, but of course I couldn't leave our house, not while Uncle Gus was threatening it. It was a little bit dangerous, but I knew Vic would keep me safe. Uncle Reggie, he had these drones programmed, they were taking pictures of everything, they showed that scumbag cop and the man who came to kill me, they showed them shooting at us, and they recorded everything Uncle Gus said. It was *fabulously* exciting."

"Where do you find them?" Lotty said to me. "These teenage girls whose only ambition is to be as insane as you are?"

"Lotty, you escaped a danger bigger than I'll ever

face," I said. "You were nine years old when your grandfather put you on a train with your four-year-old brother so the two of you could escape to England. I don't know how you did it, how you kept from falling apart when German guards searched you at the border. What we did was only a notch more dangerous than driving a car down Lake Shore Drive."

"And *Nagyi* was like that, too," Julia said. "She was my age when she took part in the uprising in Hungary, and then she had to leave Hungary or be put in prison or even killed, so she figured out how to get past the Russian and Hungarian guards. She told me today she's proud of me, standing up to Uncle Gus and helping her keep her house."

Max put a hand on Lotty's shoulder, massaged it gently. "They're right, Lottchen. And you know, they did save Silvia Zigler's life, and they saved her house. If everyone sat at home watching Netflix, we'd never have any justice in this life."

Reggie had made copies of the videos the drones took of Coney, Corky, and Duda as they tried to kill me—aided by Gus Zigler and Coney's regular hench-man, Officer Ben Tillman. One of the highlights was the net Tom and Tim Streeter rigged in the main stair-well. When I'd called out, "Safe!" the Streeters pulled the net tight across the stairs. It trapped the quintet.

Corky broke a leg and Duda an arm, though we learned that only after they'd been treated.

Reggie sent copies of his videos to Freeman Carter, who in turn gave copies to the Cook County state's attorney, along with the federal prosecutor for the Northern District of Illinois.

Corky was so well connected in Illinois that local law enforcement didn't want to touch him. However, my old buddy Jonathan Michaels told me that the federal prosecutor seemed interested.

As for Corky's cousin, Lieutenant Coney, he was beside himself with fury at Finchley for arresting him. He and the other four men were pointing to injuries they'd received the night they broke into the Zigler mansion.

Coney wanted the Streeters and me arrested for assaulting a police officer. The Chicago police union president was backing Coney, of course, but since between him and Coney they'd racked up over a hundred excessive force complaints, the state's attorney was reluctant to accept their uncorroborated testimony, especially after Freeman shared Reggie's videos with her. It was reassuring to know she wouldn't bring charges against me any more than she would against Corky.

"But I don't understand about the videos," Murray said, "or at least, I don't understand about your Skyrocket. I knew it disappeared, and you were moving heaven and earth to get it back, but I thought it never worked properly."

"I didn't use the rocket that night in the mansion," Reggie said. "I programmed a fleet of tiny drones that could record voice and action; they also set off the flashing strobes that disoriented the mob. My Skyrocket, it's much more complex. We found it, and maybe we'll make it operational. I'm working on it—but I'm counting on help from this guy here." He slapped Brad on the shoulder. "Donny, you got yourself a winner here. Take care of him."

Brad turned crimson and stared at his untied shoes.

58

Old Heroics

Cases like this are really situations, not cases. They never get wrapped up tidily, and certainly not speedily. The lawsuits over Archangel's malpractice, not just with Silvia Zigler but with other patients in their memory care unit, were going to drag out for years. Some loose ends were tidied more quickly—Freeman got a restraining order on Corky's use of the title to the Shaamar Hashomayim building. The state's attorney was persuaded to bring charges of fraud against Raamah Calabro for selling the title to Corky.

The city turned a blind eye to the old men continuing to worship, despite the building code violations that arose from Corky's stealth inspection. And between Lotty and the generosity of local tradesmen, the building was repaired.

There were also some happy endings. Donny and Ashleigh's marriage, for instance. He forced Ashleigh to move out of the house in West Ridge. Donny filed for divorce, and he and Brad started family counseling together. Brad was spending a lot of time at Reggie's shop as well. In the middle of the pandemic, and the terrible attempt to destroy the republic in the new year, when everyone's spirits were frayed, Brad's development heartened me.

Peter finally came home, later that spring, and our own reconnection helped the healing of my own body and spirit.

I also took pleasure from seeing Julia Zigler blossom. She lived with me—and Mitch and Peppy—while waiting for her grandmother to recover enough to come home. While she stayed with me, work crews repaired the mansion. We'd go over once or twice a week, let the dogs hunt rats and rabbits in the garden, check to make sure all the damage from Duda and Coney's gunfire was properly taken care of.

Julia and I had a schedule—me catching up with all my clients, trying to assuage their highly justified annoyance with me; Julia catching up with her schoolwork, assuaging her teachers' highly justified annoyance with her. As the muggy Chicago summer heated up, we both felt we had earned gold stars.

When Silvia Zigler finally came home from the Berman Center, I felt a pang at letting Julia go back to her. The dogs and I spent a day at the riverfront mansion, helping Silvia move back in, making sure she had all the food she needed.

She had filled out and was walking with a brisk step. Her eyes were bright. It was hard to believe she was the same person whom I carried out of Archangel two months earlier.

"Vic—if I may call you that. My granddaughter speaks of you so often, it would feel strange to call you Ms. Warshawski. You're welcome here, as long and as often as you'd like, but I don't need to be swaddled. You saved my life, and Julia's as well, and we're grateful, more than grateful, but we don't need caretaking."

"Everyone needs care taken of them," I objected. "Me as much as anyone else."

She smiled. "Of course, we all need love and a sense of being cared for, but having been terrifyingly helpless, I'm eager to be independent, for as long as I possibly can. Lying around and letting someone else wait on me—that's not how I've ever lived and I don't plan to start now."

"Vic knows what a hero you were, Nagyi, fighting off Soviet tanks and Hungarian secret police."

Silvia shook her head. "I was your age then, my darling one, and my friends and I, we thought we could bring justice and liberty to our country. So many of my friends died, I can hardly bear to think of their lost lives, when what came after was as bad as what went before. And then, here in America where I thought I could be free, I became helpless again. What difference did some seventy-year-old heroics make for me when my own son used systems of power to try to kill me? The only thing that kept me going was rage, a fury that he would not succeed."

Julia looked from her grandmother to me in alarm. "Nagyi, please don't talk like that, please!"

I put an arm around Julia's shoulder. "Ms. Zigler, these are harsh times. All of us feel stretched to the edge of endurance. But your courage, your example, gave Julia and me the strength to go past that edge.

"When I was young, and starting out as a public defender, I shared your passion and your belief that I could bring justice to the world around me. I've had to learn the hard way that sometimes the best you can do is save one person, but it's not a waste or a loss to save one person. In rescuing you, we also saved Julia, and I believe she will repay that with amazing feats of valor."

Some of the tension went out of Julia's thin shoulders. "You were a hero, too, Vic. Fighting off those jerkface creeps, that was almost as hard as Nagyi fighting off the tanks."

Silvia pulled her granddaughter close to her. "I'm sorry, darling. My bitterness got the better of me. I forgot the old saying my own grandmother gave me: if you kill one soul, it's as if you destroyed the whole world, but if you save one soul, it's as if you protected an entire world."

She mustered a smile and held out her other hand to me. "You saved me, and you saved my Yulchia, Vic, so in fact you protected two entire worlds."

Thanks

I wrote this book during the first year of the pandemic. Some of my writing friends found the isolation a time that focused their creativity in new ways. Others found themselves unable to summon ideas or creative wit. I unfortunately fell into the second category. I found myself constantly second-guessing my ideas and my narrative arc, writing and discarding multiple drafts. I hope that, in the end, there is something in this book that will entertain you and keep your mind off your troubles for a few hours.

I am grateful to Lorraine Brochu, who read the manuscript many times, keeping track of characters and timelines as the story morphed. Thanks to Margaret Kinsman, who talked through the plot problems with me and helped me think about them in a new way. Above all, thanks to my editors, Emily Krump and Carolyn Mays, who helped turn a rocky draft into a finished novel.

The original idea for this story came from Doug Foster, although I've twisted and stretched the plot in so many ways that he may be hard put to recognize it.

Ella Logue advised me on the language today's fifteen-year-olds use to describe verminous people. Dashiell Goode advised on how this same cohort uses the cloud.

Josh Coles, director of the McCormick Bridgehouse & Chicago River Museum, was helpful with photographs of Chicago's bridge tender houses. Because of restrictions imposed by the pandemic, I wasn't able to explore the museum in person.

The Homan Square police station on Chicago's West Side does exist. It is reportedly a black box where people can be detained without access to attorneys or family members. I first read about Homan Square in the *Guardian* in April 2016. I haven't figured out a way to visit the station in person, so the interior scenes are strictly products of my imagination.

A fair amount of action takes place on and around Goose Island, a human-made island in the Chicago River. True Chicagoans will note that the Zigler mansion is not on Goose Island, but I felt it slowed down the narrative to keep referring to "the thumb of land sticking into the Chicago River facing Goose Island." I hope you will overlook my authorial license.

Vince Baggetto introduced me to the craps game played under the Chicago Avenue bridge.

Since I always get help from many people, forgive me if I overlooked you in this note.

About the Author

Sara Paretsky is the *New York Times* bestselling author of twenty-three novels, including the renowned V.I. Warshawski series. She is one of only four living writers to have received both the Grand Master Award from the Mystery Writers of America and the Cartier Diamond Dagger from the Crime Writers' Association of Great Britain. She lives in Chicago.